BLUE HOUR

Advanced Uncorrected Proofs
On sale: 08.22.2

BLUE HOUR

A LOVE STORY

Laida Lee

Cover Design:
Graphic design by Ron Liew
Oil pastel & cyanotypes by River Kenji Fujimoto

Cover Paintings:
Winter Moon over Toyama Plain (Fuyu no tsuki (Toyamagahara)), Kawase Hasui, 1931
The Declaration of Love, Jean François de Troy, 1724

Draft edits by JiLien Liew
Final edits by Sana Abuleil
Interior formatted by Akadil Belgara

ISBN 9781069669209 (paperback)
ISBN 9781069669216 (ebook)

First edition: August 2025
www.laidalee.com

Sensitivity Note

This book contains themes of sexual violence.
While I have committed my best
efforts to avoid gratuity in my depictions,
I know it may still be triggering for some.

To you

Chapters

Part I: The Moon

Part II: The Sun

PART I

THE MOON

*T*he rank odor of death clings to him, disease and the artificial tang of chemical cleaners lingering in the threads of his clothes.

Drifting out of the morgue, the world around him blurs as if he's peering through a screen, submerged in water. His mind suspended in a numbed silence.

He stumbles upon a quiet beach and sinks into the warm sand. The steady rhythm of the waves soothes him, his breaths syncing with the moon's. His bag rests across his lap. He feels the weight of his sketchbook nagging at him. What a waste to be so untouched in a place like this. He is reminded of the savings he's sacrificed to be here. He should try to make the most of it, try to capture some of the beauty of this place. His father alone hadn't been worth the cost, after all.

He tries sketching a distant lighthouse but loses interest halfway. He attempts to capture the fluid grace of a surfer, but the figure comes out awkward. So, he moves on to the villas dotting a far-off island, but as his eyes trace the horizon, his senses are suddenly swallowed whole by the uncanny magnificence before him. The dusk clouds streak pink and orange across the deepening purple-blue sky; the red sun shimmers on the waves, casting a surreal glow on the water. Around him, families, lovers, friends— all smiling, laughing, *alive*.

A fog descends over him, blurring his perception, dulling his emotions. The vibrant seascape turns flat and lifeless. He gasps for air, lungs working faster than they can fill. He's hyperventilating—and no one sees him. Not even once. Like he's stepped into a movie scene, an extra without a role. He looks down at his hands, unable to gauge their distance from his eyes, can't feel where they attach to his body.

He blinks—his father's grey face, eyes closed, lips blue.

A cold panic grips him when he realizes he has to strain to hear the sound of the waves. Frantically, he gathers his things, moving in no particular direction, urged on by an overwhelming need to escape this sense of unreality.

His feet are almost out of the sand when he sees her. Sitting near the water in a hoodie, jeans, and sneakers, immune to the blazing Sicilian sun. He looks down at his own sweater and takes in the crowd around him, bronzed bodies in swim trunks and bikinis, a tableau of effortless vacation bliss. The two single anomalies in this beach vacation catalog. It reassures him somehow, this sense that he's not the only one out of place.

Settling back down, he pulls out his sketchbook to draw her. Her head, hidden beneath the shadow of her hood, rests on her knees as she gazes out at the Mediterranean Sea. Her arms are wrapped tightly around her legs, a small figure, easy to miss. The visual juxtaposition of this dark, hooded figure against the vivid sunny backdrop pulls him further back from the edges of his unmoored mind, grounding him in the reality of her presence.

He looks at his finished drawing and sees dejection in it. He wonders if he's projected it onto his sketch or captured some verisimilitude of her aura. He studies her, adding details to her hair, strands escaping from her hood, blowing gently in the salty breeze.

When he looks back up, her eyes are on him. The eye contact sends a jolt through him.

They stare at each other for a wordless moment before he offers what he hopes is a friendly wave, suddenly self-conscious.

She raises her hand, cautiously returning his wave before standing up and walking toward him, not exactly looking friendly.

She can see her pencil-self reflected in his book. He's a talented artist, she admits. There is a notable resemblance even from a distance. She wonders if this is a tourist trap.

"I don't have any money," she says when she reaches him.

"I don't want your money," he replies with an American accent.

"So, you're not selling this?"

"No."

"Then, why are you drawing me?"

"You're the most interesting thing on this beach," he says, looking up at her. The sunset behind wraps her in a golden halo, like the sun is bowing out just to crown her in its light.

A distant part of her recognizes this could be a compliment, but she's not feeling charitable towards him, given that he already ruined the last twenty minutes of her beach time. She spent it doubting the potent sense of surveillance she felt, questioning if the feeling was a paranoiac side-effect of her trauma, or if someone truly was watching her. There is no relief in finding truth in the latter. She is rarely able to shake the sense of being watched these days.

"Don't you think you should ask before drawing someone?" She can't hide the sharp accusation in her tone.

A puzzled look crosses his face. "I'm sorry. You're right. I should have asked you first."

She holds out her hand for the sketchbook.

In the past year, she has been exposed to more unsolicited pictures of herself than anyone should have to endure in a lifetime. Yet, looking down at her pencilled likeness, she does not feel the wonted churn of fear and shame. She can't remember the last time seeing a picture of herself didn't stir those feelings. A faint, almost unfamiliar sense of relief washes over her, like maybe, just maybe, she's not destined to forever dread seeing her own image.

"To be honest," he continues. "People usually find it flattering when I draw them. It never really crossed my mind that it could be unwelcome until now."

"What are you going to do with it?" she asks.

"Just keep it. It's kind of the only decent thing I've drawn this trip. It's yours if you want. For free, of course," he adds.

She studies the drawing. Even in pencil, she looks sad. At least, no one knows why Pencil Her is sad. There's something comforting in this version of her existing, sitting on a beach, pensive, yet untouched by everything that's happened. She shoves the book back at him, suddenly paranoid her touch might stain the paper, scarred from proximity, her melancholy contagious.

"You keep it."

"You sure?"

She nods.

"Okay, thanks. Sorry again."

She stands around for a while, feeling awkward and unsure of what to do now. She starts to walk away when he asks, "Is it about your soul?"

"What?"

"Like, how some cultures believe that pictures steal pieces of your soul? Are you worried that I've trapped a piece of your soul in here?" He taps the sketchbook as he speaks.

"I've never heard that before."

"Some indigenous traditions say that pictures capture parts of your soul, and when you die, those pieces are trapped, can't follow you to the afterlife."

She thinks of the photos on her father's computer. The thought of her soul being trapped in those hard drives makes her skin crawl. Thousands of her images, body and soul bared. How much of her soul had been stolen from her? How much is left?

Seeing the horror in her eyes, he immediately backpedals. "I'm sorry, that wasn't... I'm not myself today. That was fucking weird to say to a stranger. I'll just—sorry." He starts packing his things, his movements rushed as he tries to escape his own awkwardness.

"Wait," she says. "Tell me more."

"Well..." He settles back down, hesitant. "They believed that capturing someone's likeness made their soul vulnerable, that the image could be used in rituals to manipulate the person's spirit."

This sends a chill down her spine. She imagines the men who have seen those pictures, what they did with them, performing their own cursed ritual in a way, forever tainting her spirit.

Noticing her growing discomfort, he tells her, "This isn't real, by the way. I shouldn't have even brought it up."

"So, you don't believe it?"

"Not at all. It's just a myth. I was just curious why you had that reaction. And, I guess," he pauses. "I was also trying to find something to say, to keep talking to you."

She squints down at him for a moment, then asks bluntly, "Are you a human trafficker?"

"What? No! I'm scaring you. You should just go. No, *I* should go, since I'm the one being weird right now."

A human trafficker would probably not insist on leaving, she thinks. "Can I see your other drawings?" she asks, taking a seat next to him, a couple of feet away.

The book is filled with sketches, everyday scenes: trees, birds, a quiet alleyway, the endless ocean. Most of all, people. So many different faces, captured in fleeting moments—smiles, frowns, laughter, solitude. The fact that he doesn't only draw young women comforts her, if only a little.

As she flips through the pages, she looks up. "I understand why people believe that myth." His drawings of people seem to capture something beyond appearances, a quiet intensity. It is as if with each illustration, she can feel their emotions below the surface, almost hear the hum of the world around them. Each face feels alive, every scene holding someone's quiet story.

"I don't think I'm storing anybody's soul in here." He sort of laughs, but it lands offbeat—more like the shape of a laugh than the real thing. "I'm just keeping a visual record of what I see. As much as I try to copy their likeness, replicating their image isn't as valuable to me as capturing what *I* see in them. People don't usually stay still long enough for me to finish drawing them—except you today. Their faces move. Their poses change. Ultimately, I choose which expressions to give them, what emotions I want the drawing to convey."

She flips to a page of an old man reading a book on a train, and he asks her what she thinks of the man, "From how I drew him."

She studies the picture for a moment before saying, "He looks upset."

He nods. "He only looked like that for a second, but in my picture, he's stuck like that. I guess, if part of his spirit is in this picture, maybe I trapped some of his unhappiness away. I'm okay with that."

She flips back to her picture. Maybe some of her sadness is now locked away here, forever out of her body. Her next breath comes easier.

"When I look at these, I remember what I thought about these people, where I was, how I felt drawing them. If anything, part of *my soul* is being captured in here. Or, maybe, I'm capturing the spiritual essence of the time we shared together."

She wonders how old he is. Guys her age don't talk like this, unless they're being pretentious. She takes a bet on his sincerity when she asks, "What will you remember about drawing me?"

He looks at her, then down at the drawing for a long moment before answering, "The numbness, the distinct absence of feeling. How that scared me, made me feel alone. And when I saw you, that hollowness sort of went away."

"Because I came to talk to you?" she asks.

"No, even before that. Like, I was looking at the world through a pane of glass, locked out from it somehow. And when I saw you, I thought, at least someone else is on this side of the glass with me."

"So, are you here on vacation?" he asks after a long pause.

She nods. "With my mom and sister."

"Girls' trip. Cute." He glances around, scanning the beach. But no one nearby looks like they're with her—no one watching out for her, waiting for her to come back.

She returns his question.

"Not vacation," he answers.

"Do you live here?"

"No."

"Visiting someone?"

"Sort of. I came to see my dad," he says, a little inside joke with himself. His mind replays the moment the coroner's assistant pulled back the sheet, revealing that cold, lifeless body. He wonders how this stranger might react if he told her the real reason for his trip: to identify the corpse of his father, found washed ashore two days ago, discovered by vacationing families and horrified beachgoers.

"Does he live here?" she asks, drawing him out of his bitter reverie.

He doesn't live anywhere, he wants to say. "He moved here last year." Not a lie.

"This is a beautiful place to live."

He just nods along.

"Is this your first time visiting him?"

He feels compelled to be honest with her. Like if he tells the truth, she might reciprocate, something that feels strangely important to him right now. This is the first real conversation he's had since his arrival. So far, he's only really spoken to taxi drivers, hotel staff, cops, and people at the morgue. Talking to them felt like wading through a swamp; talking to her feels real in a way he hasn't felt in a while.

"Actually, he's dead."

Her eyes widen slightly at that. She doesn't say anything, just waits, listens.

"That's why I'm here. To deal with the body. I just came from the morgue, believe it or not."

After a spell of silence, all she says is, "That sucks."

A small snort escapes him. It does fucking suck, but, "It's okay. He was an asshole." He lets out a half-laugh.

He's not expecting it when she starts laughing with him. "Mine too," she says, which makes him laugh more. And there they are, two miserable people with asshole dads laughing together on the beach.

He can't even tell what's funny. Maybe he's laughing at her laughing, and she's laughing at him laughing. The kind of laugh that feels a bit delirious, like maybe you should be crying instead, which just makes it all the funnier.

As their laughter dies down, he looks at her, caught off guard by another jolt. She's still smiling from laughing, her hood fallen back, dark hair spilling loose. In that moment, he knows the exact combination of paints he'd use to recreate the precise shade of auburn that catches in her hair when the light hits just right.

"I'm Sam," he says, unable to stop smiling himself.

"I'm Lacy."

"Lacy," he repeats, thinking, *is really beautiful.*

The sound of her name on his lips makes her forget herself for a second. Makes her realize she hasn't heard her name spoken without pity or accusation in a long time.

Sam writes her name down in the bottom corner of the drawing, where artists usually sign their own names.

"So, you were saying that your dad's an asshole too?" he asks.

She nods, nothing more to add.

"Sorry about that."

"It's alright. He's in prison."

She doesn't volunteer any more information, and he doesn't ask any follow-up questions. They sit in silence for a spell, both wanting to know more, both wanting to share, neither knowing how to start, where the line is.

Lacy ventures, "Can I say something that might be callous?"

"Go for it," he replies, unable to imagine this girl ever being callous.

She takes a deep breath. "Sometimes I think it'd be easier if he were dead."

"I've thought that too," he admits quietly, "when he was alive."

"And?"

He shrugs. "I guess it doesn't feel that different. He wasn't around much." Tilting his head, he asks, "Yours?"

Lacy thinks of her father's digital eyes, always watching. "He was around too much."

"Do you miss him?"

"Never," Lacy says, shaking her head.

"Never?"

She nods. "Never."

"You must hate him."

"He's not worth the energy," she says, the words almost a scoff.

"I hated my dad when he was alive, too," Sam nods. "The hate hasn't gone away. I just don't have anywhere to put it now. I think if he were alive, at least I could tell him. Isn't that fucked up? That part of me wishes my father were alive just so I could tell him I hate him."

"What would he say?"

"No idea. Maybe he wouldn't even care."

Silence stretches between them as she seems to retreat to her own thoughts, her gaze lost in the shifting waves.

"Sorry, if that got too…" He tries to find the right words.

"No. I'm sorry," she says, snapping back to the moment. "Your dad just died, and I'm talking about wanting mine dead." *Definitely callous.* "I think I forgot how to talk to people normally."

He doesn't want her to apologize. In fact, he never wants to talk normally with her—not if it's not like this. Her candor is refreshing.

He's spent a lifetime grappling with complicated feelings toward his abusive father. Feelings that have only become more tangled now that he's gone. He used to picture his emotions as boxes on a shelf, stacked neatly, waiting to be picked up and analyzed when needed. Now they're scattered across the floor, contents spilling out. Ignoring the mess has always been easier than cleaning it up, and in this moment, he doesn't feel the need to fix it for her to understand the feeling behind his words.

"Good. I think this is how you should always talk to people," he tells her, his voice soft but certain.

She shakes her head, a smile tugging at the corners of her mouth.

"Or just save it all for me."

They watch as the sun sinks below the indigo horizon, until they cannot tell where the sky meets the ocean. Still seated in the sand, they are amongst the last souls on this beach. The air is crisp, the waves whisper soothing hymns, and for the first time in ages, Lacy's mind feels less clouded.

"You can't be serious. Your biggest fear is school?" Sam asks her, bemused. "You're going to have to face that fear soon."

Maybe the plane will crash on my way back, she almost says, but it feels too morbid to voice. Besides, she doesn't want to die. She simply wants to stop existing. Maybe come back another time when the world feels less painful to live in. But the thought of leaving her sister to deal with their mother alone is unbearable, almost as unbearable as their mother herself. Finally, she settles on saying, "Maybe the world will end in four months like the Mayans predicted."

"You would rather the world end than go back to school?"

"Yes. Is that selfish?"

Sam shrugs. "I don't know you well enough to say. I think killing yourself is a selfish thing to do. Killing the whole world? Probably a little selfish. I wouldn't mind, but I'm the company your misery loves. Don't you think facing the hordes of angry people in the afterlife might be worse than going back to school? You hate it that bad?"

Lacy nods.

"Why? You're bad at it?"

"No, I'm actually quite good at it," she says, her smile flat, not reaching her eyes.

"Then?"

"I'm just not looking forward to it."

"Do people ever actually look forward to going back to school?"

"I did."

"What changed?" Sam waits for her to elaborate.

"I lost all my friends. Became a loser." She tries to say this matter-of-factly, but the tinny quality of her voice betrays her. Her sister will be starting high school this year. They had been looking forward to attending the same school again since Lacy graduated from elementary school. Now, Lacy dreads the thought of Sophie walking into her freshman year, friendless, more than she dreads her own lonely senior year. She takes a deep breath, the thought weighing on her chest.

Sam scoffs. "There's no way you have no friends."

"How would you know?"

You're too pretty, he thinks, but it feels too flirty. More forward than he wants to come off right now. "You just don't seem like that kind of person. I was popular. I'm good at discerning these things."

She doesn't doubt he was popular. A thoughtful artist who actually pays attention to the things you say. Asks you questions. Definitely a popular kid. Not to mention his looks.

"Trust me, I am a loser," she affirms.

Lacy's father had also secretly filmed some of her friends when they came over. No one could ever want to stay friends after a betrayal like that. No parents would let their children near her, not after everything that had happened.

"Well," he frowns. "I was only cool in high school, and I just graduated, so maybe I'm a loser now, too."

"I don't think *you* need high school to be cool."

"True. Then, I'm still cool, and you have at least one cool friend. That raises your social capital, I'm pretty sure."

It's her first time hearing someone use the term "social capital" in real life, a phrase she's only seen online. She asks him what it means, and he explains.

"Do you like to read?" she asks.

They talk about books for a bit, sharing their favourites. He writes her recommendations in another corner of her drawing, then flips to a blank page, writes his own list, and tears it off for her. Her young adult fiction picks feel a bit amateur against his list of classics and non-fictions. She feels inspired to be more well-read. It's been a while since she has felt inspired by anything.

"The moon is missing," Lacy says, looking up at the cloudless night.

"She's hiding from us," Sam says, unable to tear his gaze away from her. The moonless sky gives the stars a night to shine, and he sees them sparkling in her eyes, dark as the horizon, deep and dreamy in a way that makes you think the best of the night is yet to come.

"I feel you," Lacy says to the moon, wherever she is. "I was such a moody kid. Happy some days, sad others. Loud one second, quiet the next. I was so sensitive, anything could make me cry. My parents hated it. After my sister was born, I tried to be stronger. We couldn't both be crybabies. I stopped crying, but I became so much more miserable. One time, my sister heard my mom call me bipolar, and they got into a huge fight about it. My dad got mad at both of them for fighting, which only made things worse. And I just hid in my room, feeling so anxious that I was the cause of the whole mess.

"After, she came into my room and I remember thinking to myself, *don't cry, don't cry, don't cry. Not when she just fought for you.* She just pulled me into her arms and let me cry. She told me it is okay that my moods changed a lot, that I am like the moon, going through different phases—some days I am loud and shiny, glowing brighter than ever, other days I am quiet and sad, hiding away, not wanting to be seen."

On nights like this, Lacy wonders if the moon is okay, what she could be hiding from.

"Your sister sounds smart."

"She is probably the smartest person I know."

"What phase of the moon are you today?" Sam asks.

Lacy is pensive and sincere when she answers, "Same as this." She nods to the moon. For a while now, Lacy has felt this way: "Dark and hidden away."

"Me too," he sighs, understanding.

They sit in comfortable silence, letting the sounds of the night fill the space between them, neither caring about the time.

After a while, he speaks again, his tone lighter. "Don't think I'm as hidden away tonight, though. Can't be, since I'd like to talk with you all night."

She feels the same, something warm stirring inside her. "Yes. Maybe I'm more like a crescent moon tonight. Just a sliver peeking out."

"Well, the sliver shines brightly enough for me."

*L*ooking out at the sunset, Sam feels a sense of déjà vu as he returns to the same spot on the beach. He's only been awake for a few hours, last night stretching into the early morning, talking with Lacy until the sun was almost up. On his way back to his hostel in those hazy pre-dawn hours, he debated whether he should have asked for her number. What if she doesn't come back?

Like an answer to a prayer, he sees her sitting in their meeting place. This time, she's brought a blanket. A pang of regret hits him as he wishes he'd thought to bring something too. Well, he has brought something. He feels for it in his back pocket, still wrestling with himself on whether he should give it to her.

"Cool blanket," he says as he approaches. He notices the spread. "You brought food too?"

She shifts to the edge of the blanket to make room for him. "My mom went overboard at the market today. We've been eating out for every meal and are leaving the day after tomorrow. I don't know when she expects us to eat all this." She gestures towards the food. "We need help getting rid of it."

Sam, having not eaten much today, looks hungrily at this generous spread of fruits, cheeses, breads, and "Mussels?"

"Yeah, I definitely don't want to pack that in my suitcase," Lacy says, handing him one.

Sam tries to pace himself with the food, matching Lacy's slow, deliberate bites, but it's too good. He can't help it. Lacy doesn't seem to notice, seeming a little distant today.

"Not hungry?" he asks.

"Just tired," she says, stifling a yawn. "I didn't get much sleep."

"Sorry for keeping you up so late last night."

"You didn't. I wanted to stay up."

"Did you have to wake up early today?"

She nods. "Yes. My mom hired a private tour guide for us. He has been taking us to see everything. Our schedules are full."

"It's nice that you have your evenings free," he says, thankful for the time he gets to spend with her. "She's okay with you being out alone at night?"

Lacy shrugs. "She doesn't care enough to argue about it. All I'm missing is dinner at *another* fancy restaurant." They were starting to blend together for her. "Besides, she invited Marco to join, giving him my spot is easier than changing the reservation."

"Who's Marco?"

"Our tour guide." Lacy struggles not to roll her eyes.

"You don't like him?"

She shrugs again. "He spends more time flirting with my mom than he does actually guiding the tour. It's like he's paid to flirt with her."

"Is your mom single?"

She nods, surprised by the question. No one's asked that before. No one's had to.

"Do you usually like the guys she dates?"

She pauses, considering. The idea of her mom dating is still so new. The separation from her father is so recent. Lacy had grown up watching her mom flirt with men for attention, but actual dating? That's different. Now, she seems to give attention to any man who gives it back to her. "The bar seems low."

"I know the feeling," Sam laments.

She waits to see if he wants to say more, and when he doesn't, she asks, "Do you want to talk about your dad?"

"Not really." He shrugs, his posture indifferent.

"I'm here if you do."

"I know." He believes her, trusts that she would listen, perhaps even offer the right words instead of the useless condolences he's received so far. Even if he wanted to talk about it, he wouldn't know how, barely aware of what he's feeling most of the time. With each passing day, more of his emotions drip from the boxes, mixing across the floor, indistinguishable.

"Do you want to talk about *your* dad?" he asks.

"Not at all," she responds too quickly. "I don't even want to think about him."

"Do you?"

"What? Think about him?"

He nods.

"Yes. And no. It's hard not to." She struggles to explain. "Do you?"

He pauses, the question sinking in. "I never believed in ghosts, and I still don't, not in the traditional sense, at least. But it's like... he's haunting me. I don't consciously think about him, but his presence is always there, lingering, pressing in on my mind from all sides, never allowing me a moment's peace. I get what you were saying before, about not wanting to waste energy on him, but he never leaves."

Lacy thinks of her own ghost, lingering in the dim hallways of her past. She knows exactly what he means. With Sam, she feels her meaning would be understood by him without needing to find the perfect phrasing, a natural ease in conversation. It is rare to meet someone who speaks in the way you like to. Like a strum on her violin heart, plucking the strings of a song she loves. The only other people she's felt this with are her sister and her best friend, Wilhelmina.

She imagines returning home, eager to tell Mina about meeting a cute boy on vacation, how excited and giddy her best friend would have been for her. Now, that's a fantasy long passed. Mina and her, no longer friends.

By the time they finish eating, the sun is halfway tucked beneath the blanket of the horizon, slowly drifting to sleep. The moon graces the dusky blue sky, delicate and thin, like the edge of a silver petal.

"Yesterday, you said you weren't cool anymore because you graduated. Do you really think that?" Lacy asks.

He leans back and runs a hand through his hair, like he's trying to push away the thoughts clouding his mind. "Yeah, I peaked. All my friends are off to college and I'm not going. People who don't go, sort of just get lost somewhere... No one remembers them."

"That's bleak. Why aren't you going to college?"

"Don't know what I'd do besides art," he exhales, looking out at the horizon, "which seems like a quicksand of debt to me. And I'm already broke."

Lacy has never had to think about money. She wouldn't call her family rich, but Police Chiefs make a decent salary. Well enough for them to live in a four-bedroom house. Enough that her mom never had to work. She never really knows how to respond when people talk about not having money. Mostly, she just feels bad, like she does now for Sam. It seems absurd that something so arbitrary could shut so many doors.

"What're you going to do then?" she asks.

He shrugs, the movement casual, but a little resigned. "I'm not really good at anything else besides this," he says, patting the sketchbook peeking out from his bag. "Guess I'll get a job somewhere and then..." He lifts a shoulder, half-hearted.

"You could make a living from your art without school."

"Just yesterday, I was accused of being a charlatan for drawing you."

She rolls her eyes, the corners of her mouth curving up despite herself. "You could post your work online, be discovered that way. Artists are always posting their art online. They gain lots of followers, and..." She falters, realizing she doesn't actually know how they make money. "Well, they must make money somehow to do it full time."

"Promising," he teases, smirking.

"At the very least, you could post videos of yourself drawing and make money from the views."

"You think I'd get enough views to make money?"

"Obviously."

"Why obviously?"

She pulls her knees to her chest, looking away from him. "You know why."

"Enlighten me." He grins, head tilted in playful amusement.

She gestures vaguely in the direction of his face, refusing to meet his eyes, cheeks flushing slightly.

His smile widens, and she interjects before he can say anything more. "Anyway," she says firmly, "Art always finds a way. You don't have to go to school to learn something you already have in here." She pushes a quick finger to his chest, and his skin buzzes at the touch. "People who like art are always called to the siren song of creation. And if you sing your song loud enough, the right people will hear it. They will find you."

Generally, Sam avoids thinking too much about his future, not wanting to be dragged into a spiral of hopelessness. Listening to Lacy, it's as if the fog begins to lift. For the first time, he can see the horizon—not clear, but there.

Maybe the rest of his life doesn't have to feel so gloomy. Maybe he can carve something meaningful out of it.

"Your advice is better than my guidance counselor's, but office hours are over, and we have better things to do."

"Like what?" Lacy asks, raising an eyebrow.

Lacy feels completely out of her depth as she stands before the towering wall of wines in the supermarket.

"Any preference?" Sam asks, glancing over at her.

Her experience with wine is limited to sneaking sips from her mom's glass at Christmas, only to discover she doesn't like it. At parties, her friends always handed her the fruitiest, most juice-like drinks, knowing she wouldn't touch anything stronger. For a moment, she considers lying, wanting to seem cooler and more cultured in front of Sam, but she remembers she doesn't want to pretend with him.

"No. I don't really like wine."

"Me neither, but when in Rome." They are not in Rome.

Sam picks up a bottle, studying the label as if he understands Italian. He does not. "Do you want anything else?"

Lacy grabs a bar of chocolate at the checkout and offers to pay, but Sam shakes his head. She had already brought so much food for them, he wanted to contribute. When the cashier rattles off the price in rapid Italian, Sam doesn't catch a word. He hands over all the bills in his wallet. It isn't much. The cashier counts them, then raises three fingers to him. He'd fought the urge to grab the cheapest bottle, not wanting to seem cheap, but coming up short is decidedly more embarrassing. Without hesitation, Lacy digs into her bag and hands over some coins.

As they step outside, Sam feels the sting of humiliation and starts to apologize, but pauses when he notices Lacy smiling. "That was my first time buying alcohol. She didn't even check my ID!"

They find a fountain show at a marina. This area is much louder than the beach. Laughter and music spill from nearby boats, the air thick with conversation and the clinking of glasses.

They watch the water dance in rhythmic spurts, sipping the wine straight from the bottle. Lacy can't help the fleeting, almost juvenile thought of their lips touching as they share the bottle.

A drunken middle-aged man stumbles over, slurring an invitation for Lacy to join him on his boat. She declines politely, feeling a knot of fear settle in her chest. Sam notices her unease, a surge of protectiveness flooding his veins. He steps in front of her, blocking the man's view, and tells him to fuck off. The man sizes him up, then stumbles away, muttering expletives under his breath.

Sam turns to her. "Let's go back to our beach."

Lacy smiles, relieved. She likes the way he says *our beach*.

Despite not drinking much, the wine hits Lacy harder than she expects, and she has to hold onto Sam's arm to walk.

"Should I take you home?"

She shakes her head and points toward the shore.

As they approach, she feels a wavy of nausea rush over her. She dashes toward a nearby trashcan, but her hand misses the lip and plunges straight into the bin, getting cut on a shard of broken glass.

Sam is there in a flash, his hand steadying her shoulder. "Are you okay?" he asks, his voice full of concern.

She waits for the nausea to pass before nodding. "Do you have water?"

He hands her his bottle. As she takes a drink, the thought of their lips touching flashes through her mind again. She giggles.

They sit on the sidewalk, and Sam takes her hand tenderly, inspecting the small cut. He pours water over it, then blows on the wound gently. The coolness of his breath against her skin eases some of the sting. He rummages through his bag, pulling out a small pouch. Inside are bandages and a small tube of ointment. Lacy can't help but be impressed by his preparedness.

Taking her hand again, he applies the ointment with a delicate finger. She squeezes her eyes shut at the smarting sensation. He whispers an apology, his voice so gentle it almost makes her forget the pain. He blows on the cut once more, and the chill of his breath lingers on her hand. As he places the bandage on, he catches her gaze in his peripheral. The tender warmth in her eyes makes his heartbeat quicken.

They eventually make their way to the beach, where Sam lays out the blanket for her. Without hesitation, Lacy lies down fully, stretching her body and feeling the sand envelop her. Her eyes close as she wills away the headache slowly creeping up. Sam props his bag under her head like a pillow, urging her to drink more water as he offers her bread.

"I'm sorry."

"For what?" she asks, still under the haze of the wine.

"Getting the wine."

"You didn't force me to drink it."

They lie in silence for a long moment as she nibbles on the leftover bread. When her headache starts to subside, she mumbles, "Can I have the chocolates?"

Sam watches as she breaks off a small piece and raises it to her lips, his gaze drifting over her face. She stares up at the sky, her cheeks flushed from the wine, her eyes soft and dreamy.

"You look really pretty right now." He didn't mean to say it out loud, but the magic of the grapes have loosened his tongue.

"I do?" She smiles, and the way she looks at him sends a flutter through his chest.

He nods, feeling slightly shy now.

"Will you draw me?"

"Really?" His eyes widen in surprise, but he doesn't say anything else, not wanting to question the opportunity presented to him.

"Um, how should I...?" She fidgets, unsure how to pose.

"Just be. Whatever is most comfortable for you."

She doesn't move, lies still as she looks up at him, smiling softly. She tries not to laugh at how ridiculous she feels, how tipsy she is.

At the sight of this, Sam takes a deep breath, feeling his own blush creep up on his cheeks. He's thankful to be looking down at his sketchbook, glancing at her too often.

Seeing the way she's looking at him flips his stomach inside out.

"What are you thinking about right now?" she asks, trying to distract herself from her own nerves. She finds him so endearing—this boy who carries a tiny first aid kit and sketchbook everywhere, always ready to help, always ready to capture a moment. Her heart melts at the look of concentration on his face, her stomach fluttering every time their eyes meet.

He shakes his head, a small smile playing at his lips.

"What?" she asks.

"You don't want to know."

"Tell me," she insists.

He shakes his head again and takes a swig from the bottle.

"Please," she begs.

"I'm thinking about how I want to draw a nice picture of you."

"Liar."

He puts down his sketchbook, leveling a gaze at her. "You really want to know?"

She nods.

"I'm thinking I really want to kiss you right now."

The flutter in her belly turns into an accelerated pulse. A blush spreads across her cheeks, and it only makes him want to kiss her more.

"See? Told you you didn't want to know."

She doesn't know how to respond, so she just eats more chocolate, trying to ignore the warmth spreading through her.

Sam digs through his bag and pulls out a small rectangular box. Without a word, he runs to the shoreline, then hurries back to her, holding a shell filled with water. He opens the box, revealing a palette of paints. He dips a finger into the shell water, then into the paint, rubbing it on the back of his hand before dabbing it onto the page.

When he turns the sketchbook to show her, her breath is stolen away.

There she is, lying on the blanket with her fingers at her lips, the faint pink of her cheeks captured by pink sea water, so subtle it almost looks natural, emanating straight from the page. Just like his drawing yesterday, this one captures her perfectly, but here, she looks so serene. So safe.

At the entrance of Lacy's hotel, Sam asks, "Can I see you again tomorrow?"

"It's already tomorrow." Lacy laughs, still a little giddy from the wine.

"Can I see you later, then?"

"See you at sunset," she says with a nod.

"See you at our beach."

"There's an antique store near the beach I want to check out. Will you come with me?"

He nods. Of course, he would. He would go anywhere with her. His fingers twirl the metal chain in his back pocket. Earlier today, he had stumbled upon an antique market near his hostel and bought something. "You like antiques?" he asks.

She nods. "I like old things. Things people keep for a long time. Pass down. Analog ways of holding onto memories." She thinks of his drawings. Noticing the unreadable way he's looking at her, she asks, her voice a little quieter, "Is that lame?"

"No, not at all. I love that about you."

She blushes, either from his choice of words or the wine still buzzing in her bloodstream.

"I was at an antique market this afternoon." Sam draws from the last dregs of his liquid courage, ignoring the voice telling him how ridiculous it is to give someone he's only known a day a gift. He takes her hand, "I got you something." He opens her palm and places the chain inside.

Lacy's breath catches as she gazes down at the delicate silver necklace, a crescent moon pendant carved from an opalescent pearl, framed by thin silver filigree.

She's received plenty of jewelry in her life. Her mother, with her luxurious tastes, has gifted her many pieces, always minimal, always expensive. She appreciated them, of course, though they were never quite her. But this? She could never have designed something so perfect for herself. Strange how someone she just met could give her something that feels like it was waiting for her all along.

"I..." she tries. "I don't even know what to say."

"Say you like it," he teases, his voice light, carrying a hint of vulnerability.

The necklace had been the first thing that caught his eye at the market. Finding it felt like fate as he'd been

45

thinking about her, about the way she described herself as the moon, then, there it was, silver glinting in the sun.

He hesitated at first. The price would cost him a few meals, and he knew buying something as personal as jewelry for someone he'd just met was impulsive—weird even. But walking away from it felt wrong, something he knew he'd regret, like it had already belonged to her.

"I love it, Sam." Lacy's voice is reverent as she cradles the pendant in her hands, as if it's the most precious thing she owns. Her eyes, full of wonder, gratitude, and something else he can't place, meet his. His stomach does another flip.

"Thank you," she whispers. "You have no idea how much I love this."

"Do you want me to put it on for you?"

Lacy nods, and Sam steps behind her. He moves her hair over her shoulder, his knuckles brushing her skin as he fastens the clasp. When she turns to face him, the sight takes his breath away. She looks so beautiful. The glow of the lamplight against her skin, the sparkle of the necklace between her collarbones. He feels an almost ridiculous urge to draw her in this moment, try to capture this feeling forever. Remember this moment, remember how badly he wants to kiss her. How new this feels. How long it's been since he's felt anything new.

Then, Lacy rises on her tiptoes to kiss him below his cheek. "Goodnight, Sam."

Back at the hostel, Sam lies in bed, scrolling through his phone on the weak hostel Wi-Fi. He's looking up how artists make money online. As he reads, a small flame of hope grows in his chest.

It's been a long time since Sam has dared to dream. Tonight, he sleeps and dreams of Lacy. His heart is full, knowing tomorrow will come, and with it, the promise of seeing her again.

Lacy returns to the hotel room and finds her sister, freshly showered, sprawled out on their mom's bed, mindlessly scrolling on her phone. Sophie informs her that their mother is spending the night at Marco's, barely looking up at her.

Lacy's eyebrows knit together in disbelief. "What? Why? Where?"

Sophie shrugs, her fingers still scrolling absently, her expression distant.

Lacy sighs, rolling her eyes. She's barely had time to process her night with Sam, waves of attraction, self-consciousness, and fear swirling through her. Now, she's added worry to the mix as she thinks about her mother spending the night at some strange man's house.

"Did she leave a number? An address?"

"I have Marco's number," Sophie says, her voice unbothered.

Sophie waits impatiently for her phone to be returned as Lacy adds Marco's number to her own—a flip phone, the first cellphone she ever owned. She had replaced her smartphone with it, not wanting to be tempted by the internet, a realm that now scares her. This phone is just for emergencies. Not like anyone is contacting her these days anyway.

She digs through the shopping bags from today, swiping an expensive candle her mother purchased. She lights it, setting it on the edge of the bathtub. Lacy hates showers, hates being naked. She had purchased a hidden camera sensor for their trip, meticulously combing every corner of every room they had stayed in. She's found nothing. Still, the feeling of exposure clings to her. Even at home, she undressed only in the shower with the curtains pulled tightly shut. After washing, she'd put on her robe behind the curtain, then crawl into bed to change beneath the safety of the sheets. Never wanting to be seen. Never wanting her nudity exposed.

Sharing rooms with her mother and sister this whole trip, she hadn't wanted them to witness her strange dressing ritual. Unwilling to expose her body, she'd been showering and changing in the dark. Her visibility relied upon the light seeping in from beneath the door or the faint glow of her phone screen. Lighting a candle feels like a luxury.

In bed, Lacy tosses and turns, the sheets twisting around her legs, trapping her in the chaos of her own thoughts. She rubs her thumb over the pendant at her neck, pressing its cool surface to her bottom lip. The memory of his jaw beneath her mouth sends a nervous flutter through her stomach.

For so long now, the very idea of men, romance, or even thinking about her own sexuality, had stirred nothing but fear and disgust. Now, something foreign courses through her. A spark, as exhilarating as it is terrifying. She had felt an irresistible pull looking into Sam's eyes—the urge to kiss him. Worse yet, she saw the same desire mirrored in him, a deep current threatening to wash her away.

Her chest tightens, heat blooming low and steady, even as icy fear prickles along her spine. The quiet rebellion of her body, its longing uninvited, its hunger inconvenient. An aching war between what feels safe and what feels possible.

The blaze of the ceiling lights overhead jolts Lacy awake. The TV in the corner blaring Italian news. Her mother frantically shuffles around the room. Noticing her daughters stirring, Dawna exclaims, "Pack your bags! He's waiting in the lobby for us!"

Lacy blinks, her mind swimming with questions. Too groggy to form a coherent sentence, she stays silent.

"Get moving! I don't want to leave him waiting!" Her mother calls from the bathroom.

"Who?" She hears her sister ask. Her own thoughts blurry puzzle pieces that don't fit together.

"Marco!"

Lacy squints at the clock: six a.m. She barely got any sleep. Across the room, her mother folds and packs her clothes in that frenetically neat way, so signature to Dawna—almost aggressive in its precision. Her eyes are ringed with dark circles. Looks like she hasn't slept either.

"Why is Marco picking us up at six in the morning?" Sophie asks.

"He's taking us out on his catamaran!"

"Was this in the itinerary?" Lacy rubs her eyes, trying to recall the schedule. She distinctly remembers no wake-up calls before nine.

"No! Marco owns an island, and he's taking us there. Your mom is being spontaneous! Start packing!"

Lacy stares at her mother, then her sister, dumbfounded. A bitter taste of resentment spreads across her tongue at the realization that her mother has made this decision without so much as a heads-up.

"You're seriously bringing us to some random man's island?" she asks dryly.

"He's not a random man, Lacy. We've spent every day here with him."

"Because he's our tour guide."

"A tour guide I happen to like. How auspicious!"

Lacy rolls her eyes. What could be auspicious about forming a bond with someone you've paid to be with you every day? "He's taking us to an island? Surrounded by water?" she asks, her hands crossed tightly across her chest.

"And we're going in his catamaran! How stylish!" Her mother says, completely oblivious to Lacy's growing unease.

"He's taking us on his boat. To his private island. Surrounded by water. And this doesn't scream danger to you? A trap, maybe?"

"A trap for what?" Dawna asks, dismissing her daughter's concerns with a wave of her hand. "I spent the night with him. We can trust him."

Lacy scoffs, her voice hardening. "Because you're such a good judge of trustworthy men."

Dawna's head snaps toward her, eyes wide with shock and hurt, immediately twisting guilt in Lacy's chest. She thinks of how haunted she is by her father's betrayal and reminds herself to be compassionate towards her mother, betrayed by her husband.

Lacy sighs and tries again, softer this time. "How do you know we can trust him? That this isn't some human trafficking setup?"

Dawna looks at Sophie. "You've spent time with him. He's a good guy, right?"

Sophie looks between her mother and sister, both staring at her, expectant. "I mean... He seems fine." When she sees Lacy roll her eyes at this, she quickly adds, "That doesn't mean we can trust him, though."

Dawna shakes her head and continues to pack. "We can't live our lives thinking every man is going to hurt us, girls. It's no way to live."

Lacy thinks of her own trepidation about Sam.

"We got burned by one, doesn't mean we have to let what happened take over our lives. We can't change what happened, but we can choose whether we let it hurt us."

Lacy did not inherit her mother's penchant for optimism. Dawna never lingers in negative emotions, never lets them sink their claws into her. Lacy, on the other hand, feels entirely pliant to her suffering, yielding under its weight. Her mother's steadfast resistance to anguish—that refusal to fall apart—set against Lacy's own inability to rise above the pain, often makes her feel like a failure. Dawna had spent the night with a man she had only known for a few days, yet the thought of kissing a boy sends Lacy into a panic. Was she to be forever beholden to her shadows? Their claw marks digging deeper into her soul.

At the thought of Sam, her mind snaps into focus, and she's out of bed in an instant. She's supposed to see him today, was supposed to have one last day with him.

"We're going to the island right now?" she asks, her voice sharp with urgency.

"Yes, we want to avoid the busy marina. Start packing. Marco's waiting!"

Lacy is frantically putting on her shoes.

"Where are you going?" Sophie asks.

"To the gift shop," she says as she dashes out of the room.

The shop is closed. She goes to the concierge, "Can I buy something from the gift shop?"

"It opens at ten," the concierge replies.

Lacy had noticed a beautiful ring in the shop yesterday and, upon receiving Sam's gift, had made up her mind to buy it for him. A silver rhodium ring with an intricate cameo sun, carved against black agate. A sun to go with her moon.

She describes the ring to the concierge and asks if she can pay for it now, and that "A boy will come and ask for me later." She hopes anyway. "Can you give it to him?"

54

The concierge doesn't agree at first, stating the ring is an antique and too valuable to be handed to some stranger, but seeing Lacy's desperate eyes start to well up, he finally concedes. In her haste, Lacy had forgotten her wallet in the room. She dashes back to the elevators as the doors open to her sleepy sister, holding out her wallet. Lacy snatches it from her and runs back to the concierge.

$\mathcal{S}$ am finds himself restlessly wandering through the antique market again. No treasures jump out at him today. His wallet thanks him. He examines ceramic dishes, vintage watches, old home decor, all without any real interest. His eyes are glued to the time on his phone, willing it to move faster.

He buys a tray of arancini from a stall. They taste incredible. He saves a few for Lacy.

Eventually, like a needle magnetized North, he is pulled towards the beach, towards *her*. He knows she won't be there yet. He's a few hours early. But with each step, the restlessness in him eases.

He waits in the sand, sketching the beach, trying to capture it under a new light, *their beach*.

As the sun begins to set, he looks around for her, spinning his pencil between his fingers, anticipation thrumming in his chest.

When the sky finally darkens, Sam is left sitting alone. He tries to ignore the tight, gnawing sensation that spreads in his chest, something like fear or sadness. Was he too much last night? Had he come on too strong when he told her he wanted to kiss her? Was the necklace too much, too soon? It wasn't like he hadn't noticed her apprehension around him, around men in general, the way she had shrank back, paling, when that drunk guy had gotten too close.

He looks down at the sand, digs around for some shells, needing something to keep his hands and mind busy. His body feels stiff with worry, disappointment. He places the shells on his sketchbook and draws them, hyper-realistic studies done in a state of dissociation. His mind blank, too anxious to house the thoughts pressing in.

Night falls like a heavy cloak. She's not coming. He writes *Going to your hotel. Will come back here if I don't find you. Don't leave,* next to the drawing of shells and tears off the page. He rolls it up and sticks it into the sand, feeling foolish with each step. *She's not coming.*

At the hotel, Sam feels like an even bigger fool as he tells the woman at the front desk that he's looking for someone named Lacy. No, he doesn't know her room number. No, he doesn't know her last name. No, he doesn't have her number. The lobby is far too fancy. He feels out of place.

"You are looking for a girl called Lacy?" the concierge beside the one helping him asks.

Sam nods.

She tells him to wait while she finishes up with another guest. Then, she plucks a Post-it from under the monitor, calling him over. She pulls out a small box from a drawer behind her, opens it, and looks back at Sam, her eyes narrowing slightly.

"Aspetta un attimo," she says before making a phone call.

Sam waits, the soft murmur of rapid Italian filling the air between them. He wonders, for a brief second, if she's speaking to Lacy. The thought makes the flame in his chest burn brighter, improbable as it is.

"Sei sicuro?" she says into the receiver, her eyes flickering back to Sam.

She hangs up and hands the small box to Sam. "Miss Lacy checked out this morning, but she requested we give this to you."

Sam blinks, unsure he's heard correctly. "Wait, what do you mean she checked out? Of the hotel? Did she check into another one?"

"I do not know."

"She's not leaving until tomorrow. Why would she check out today?"

The concierge just shakes her head.

"What time did she check out?"

Shaking her head again, the concierge replies, "I cannot share this information with you."

"Do you have a phone number I can call?"

Another curt shake of her head.

"Do you have her last name?" he asks, the desperation in his voice rising.

"I cannot share guest information," she says, her eyes now suspicious as they flick to the box in Sam's hand.

Sam hasn't even registered what he's holding as he tries to make sense of Lacy being gone, completely out of his reach. He was planning to ask for her contact information when he saw her today. He finds a nearby chair, sinks onto it dejectedly as he opens the box. His breath stalls when he sees the ring. A silver band and a circular black plate bearing a sun carved from white stone. Something in the memory of yesterday's sky tugs at him, the moon and sun lingering in that azure dream, if only for a breath.

Marco is clearly infatuated with Lacy's mother, barely sparing her and Sophie a second glance, which Lacy is more than content with. She watches, a flicker of annoyance in her chest as Marco tops up her mother's wine. It's barely nine in the morning. Sophie complains of motion sickness, looking slightly green around the edges. Dawna nods in exaggerated sympathy, though Lacy is certain her mother's queasiness is from the wine, not the boat. The boat that Lacy is beginning to suspect doesn't actually belong to Marco after watching him argue with the dockhand, then slip him extra cash just to get it started. He listens to her mother's ramblings with rapt attention, delighting in her intoxicated chatter. Lacy isn't sure how this will end, silently prays her mother will survive the fallout.

"What did you buy at the gift shop?" Sophie asks, her voice strained, trying to distract herself from the growing nausea.

"Uh..." Lacy stalls, trying to think of a response. "This," she says, showing her the necklace hanging on her neck.

Her mother leans in close to examine it, then reaches for the pendant. After a moment, she pulls back slightly. "I hope you didn't spend too much on it."

Lacy stands, huffing in irritation as she moves to the other side of the boat.

Sophie follows behind her. "You wore that to sleep," she says, pointing at her necklace before retching over the side of the boat.

To Lacy's relief, the island is inhabited by others. Marco doesn't own the whole thing. His uncle owns a villa here, just like he owns the catamaran. Lacy isn't sure whether her mother misheard or if Marco was embellishing, trying to impress her. She's also relieved to discover there's a water taxi service. They're not stuck on the island, land-locked. Dawna rescheduled their flights to extend their stay. Lacy is anxious about living in a stranger's home, but she admits there's a sense of relief in not going home yet.

With Marco keeping her mother busy, Lacy and Sophie are left to their own devices. They get their own rooms. Their first taste of privacy since the trip began. Lacy explores the ancient villa, and despite the strangeness of it all, she finds herself drawn to it. The villa feels alive with history, each object infused with memories. A museum in itself. There is a library, and the few books in English are classics. She spots a title Sam had recommended, and wonders what he's doing now, if he's received her gift, what he thinks of it, and whether it suits his style. A part of her wonders if the concierge actually went through with her request. She didn't have a receipt or any proof of payment since the shop was closed. She could call the hotel but wonders if the confirmation would only make her more anxious.

Lacy reads by the beach, in her room, in the courtyard. Her mother spends all her time with Marco, mostly drinking. Unlike Lacy, her mother despises solitude. Lacy grew up witnessing it. Whenever her father wasn't around, Dawna would fill the silence—hosting guests, chatting on the phone, or going out with friends. If no one was free, she'd take her daughters to the mall. Lacy, on the other hand, had always liked being alone. But now that she has no one, it feels different. She's not so sure she's good at it anymore.

There are days when she still yearns for her mother, a mother. But lately, talking to Dawna just made her feel worse. It's in these moments that she seeks out her sister, who could usually be found in the theatre room, working her way through the DVDs.

Lacy lies on the couch across from Sophie, trying to focus on her book, trying to focus on the movie, unable to do either. She can't stop thinking about Sam. Did he think she stood him up? She briefly regrets not leaving him a note, some way for him to contact her. But then, she imagines him calling her at home and wonders whether they would keep up the calls, or whether the distance would slowly erode their connection, conversations shrinking until there's nothing left to say. She'll never know, and the uncertainty consumes her waking thoughts. In a strange way, she feels grateful for it, a less dreadful worry stone her mind can endlessly turn over. There's something comforting in the proof that someone who saw her so clearly exists in the world somewhere. The thought also terrifies her, feeling seen by him. How intense his attraction to her felt. As romantic as it is to imagine moments with him, her feelings for him unsettled her. How he understood the shape of her pain without knowing her scars. She's okay with Sam remaining a fantasy, the mystery of it more romantic anyway. It's safer this way.

They stay at the villa for two more days before her *spontaneous* mother books a cruise to Greece. Once again, Dawna doesn't check with her daughters before inviting Marco to join them. Lacy pilfers a few books for herself and some DVDs for Sophie.

In Greece, Marco arranges private tours, chauffeurs, and books Lacy and Sophie their own room at every hotel. They don't ask who's paying for all of this. At their last stop, however, there's only a one-bedroom suite available, and the sisters end up sharing the sofa bed in the living room.

That night, Dawna goes out to dinner with Marco alone. Lacy orders room service for her and Sophie. She's reading in bed while Sophie watches an old Greek movie with no subtitles, when their mother and Marco stumble in.

"Is she okay?" Lacy asks, noticing how drunk her mother looks.

"She is okay. We had a little too much fun tonight," Marco tells her.

Dawna waves, blows them a kiss, and mutters something barely intelligible about showering.

Marco sits on the sofa bed beside Lacy, and she can smell the alcohol on him. He tries to make conversation with her about the book she's reading, but it's obvious he doesn't care. He leans his head against her arm, and Lacy shifts away, feeling the walls close in. Sophie shuffles to the edge of the sofa bed, pulling her sister away from drunken Marco. Thankfully, he doesn't move any closer, as he stares at the movie with glassy eyes.

Her mother emerges from the bathroom and crawls into bed. Smelly Marco follows quickly behind, shutting the door behind them.

Lacy's eyelids are heavy, losing focus of the words on the page when she hears Marco's muffled voice from behind the wall, asking her mother for sex. It makes her skin crawl.

"I'm tired," her mother says.

"You are not tired. We did not do much today."

"Marco, tomorrow, okay?" her mother responds.

"Cara mia, don't be so ungrateful. I've been so good to you, no? And Lacy and Sophie."

Lacy feels bile rise in her throat at the thought of her and her sister's names swimming in his putrid mouth. She sits up, unsure of what to do. She wants to leave but doesn't want to leave her mom or sleeping Sophie.

"Marco, just go to sleep," Dawna yawns.

Marco is persistent in his begging. Lacy hears him whine and grumble while her mother maintains her refusal.

After a moment, there's silence. Then she hears the bed creak, sheets rustling. Marco's voice lowers and becomes more muffled. She can't make out what he's saying. The bed creaks again. She hears him moan, and her body goes cold. She covers her mouth, trying not to gag or scream.

The creaking of the bed grows faster, steadier. She can't hear her mom at all. She wants to run into the room, but her legs are frozen. Would her mother even want her to intervene? There's no screaming, no sounds of struggle, no "no". She lies back down, burying herself under the duvet, hoping it is thick enough to block out the sound of Marco. She presses her arms against her ears. She hears heavy breathing and realizes Sophie isn't sleeping, she is hyperventilating into her pillow. Lacy touches her own face, realizes she's crying, a steady stream of tears soaking into her own pillow. She tries to control her breathing, stop the tears. They can still hear him.

Lacy's mind keeps returning to how drunk her mother got tonight. Was she even awake right now? The thought snaps her out of her fear, and she snatches the hotel phone, brings it under the covers with her. Sophie watches with wet eyelashes, trying to steady her breathing as Lacy whispers to the concierge about bed bugs in the room. A few minutes later, room service knocks. They both face away from the front door, pretending to be asleep, Lacy's arms wrapped tightly around her sister. The knocks continue until Marco finally storms out, grumbling as he stalks towards the door.

He argues with the room service staff, but eventually, he relents and lets them in. Her mother stumbles out of the bedroom, still groggy, standing next to her daughters while the hotel staff checks the beds. Marco glares at Lacy, somehow knowing she was the one who called. The staff members leave after finding no evidence of bed bugs. Dawna climbs into the sofa bed beside Sophie and falls asleep immediately.

Lacy falls asleep, head on her sister's shoulders. The warmth of her sister beside her is a comforting weight as she falls into a fitful slumber.

She wakes to the sound of her mother and Marco arguing on the balcony. His bags sit neatly by the door— clothes folded too perfectly, zippers aligned, a sweater draped just so. She tries to make out the words as Marco's voice shifts from sharp to desperate. At the sound of the balcony door sliding open, she shuts her eyes fast. Marco mutters under his breath as he stomps through the room, grabs his bags, and slams the door behind him.

Lacy stays still, pretending to sleep, listening to the familiar sounds of her mother's morning routine—water running, electric toothbrush humming, the soft clink of lids unscrewing from jars and tubes. The careful rustle of methodical packing. Then her mother's hushed voice as she calls the concierge to book their flights home. Polite, almost cheerful. You'd never guess a man had just raised his voice at her.

On the plane ride home, Lacy tries to read in the middle seat, but her mind can't focus. Sophie sleeps by the window, her head tilted against the glass.

"I was fine last night, you know," her mother says, not looking away from the flight path tracker on the screen. "I am never in a situation I don't want to be in."

Lacy is caught off guard. Dawna rarely spoke on serious matters. Even after finding out her husband had been selling photos of her daughters online, she didn't say much to them, feeling like they had talked about it enough to the detectives and lawyers. It had happened, and they had come out on the other side. What more was there to say about the matter? Lacy understood this. Even if she wanted to talk about it more with her mother, what would she say? Everything seemed obvious. She could have had the entire conversation in her head and come to the same conclusions. Lacy had expected the same treatment from her mother regarding Marco.

"Did you actually like him?" Lacy asks.

"That doesn't matter."

"How can it not?"

Her mother sighs. "You're young. When you're older, you'll realize how little liking the guy matters compared to what he can do for you."

"What did he do for you?" *Force you to have sex with him?*

Dawna sighs again, as if this is the most tedious conversation of her life, like Lacy should already know all this. "All the money we have now is from selling our house, the savings I have access to, and child support from your dad in jail. How do you expect me to pay for your uni next year?"

Lacy doesn't answer. She doesn't know, and has never had to think about this.

"Do you think that will last forever?" Dawna continues. "I looked him up, you know. Marco's family owns the touring company he works for. His family comes from money. Money he liked to spend, and he was easy to please. I could have gotten him to move to Canada. Or maybe we could have left town and lived in that villa together. Do you know how lucky we were to find him?"

"Lucky? He forced you to have sex with him!" Lacy whisper-yells.

"No one forces me to do anything!" her mother whisper-yells back.

"So, you wanted it?"

"Yes."

"You wanted to have sex with him?"

"I did."

Lacy doesn't reply. Just rolls her eyes and scoffs.

"As surprising as it might be to you, I didn't let your father traumatize me into hating sex and hating men."

"You don't need to tell me that," Lacy retorts, scoffing again.

"What's that supposed to mean?"

"Mom, as if you could ever hate men. How would you survive without their attention? You even married a pedophile."

Her mother's eyes grow wide. For a moment, it looks like she's about to say something, but then she just exhales and spends the rest of the flight pretending her oldest daughter doesn't exist.

At the Edmonton Airport, Lacy loads almost all their bags into the trunk of the taxi by herself. Sophie tries to help.

Their mother is waiting in the front seat of the car. Sophie doesn't know why their mom is upset, but she is used to being iced out along with Lacy and doesn't care to ask.

When they arrive home, Sophie rushes to her room, dragging her bags with her. Lacy follows, carrying both her and her mother's bags.

Halfway up the stairs, her mother finally speaks, her voice quiet but heavy. "I know you hate your father. I hate what he did." A pause, then the words spill out, raw and unsteady. "But the truth is, I miss him. Especially right now, when it feels like I have no one to lean on."

The words are a cold knife to Lacy's heart. She would have rather continued their silent cold war than hear her mother utter such traitorous words.

"He did a terrible thing, and I will never forgive him or trust him again. But women need men. I'm not stupid. As women, we see more than men how this world has been made for them. Yes, they can be beasts sometimes, but they also take care of us. Feminine power is gained by proxy. It's something you need to learn sooner rather than later."

Lacy is speechless.

"You might not think so, but I've done my best to raise you," her mother continues. "I want us to keep living in this nice house. I want to send you girls to a good school. I don't want to see my kids struggle with debt. I want us to live a comfortable life, Lacy. And we can't do that without a man."

"Then find a *good* man."

"Your options shrink as you get older, Lacy. I don't look like you anymore. You think I had worries like this when I was your age?" Her mother scoffs. "Your life will become so much easier when you start being realistic about what's important in life. Having money to pay your bills. Having a roof over your head. Going to a good school and getting a good job."

Dawna's voice trails off, tired and worn.

Lacy exhales loudly—not on purpose, just all the emotions building inside her needing some release. She has no answer that won't start another war, so she simply nods—too slight to be agreement, too drained to be defiance.

At the airport, Sam twists the ring on his finger, his thoughts circling Lacy, wondering if he's truly exhausted every option to find her. It's almost absurd how little he knows about her—not her full name, where she lives, nor anything about her life outside the two days they shared. And yet, it felt like they had talked about everything under the sun. Their hopes, fears, favorite books, comfort movies, the validity of astrology, what if the Mayans are right about the world ending. As if by some unspoken agreement, they'd avoided talking about their actual lives. To step into such quotidian territory seemed like it would dispel whatever stardust held them together.

He glances around as he boards the plane, hoping their improbable magic could extend this far, that he might see her waiting in line or already seated, bound for the same place. Maybe she's lived in his town all along, their paths never crossing until the universe chose the right moment. He considers the odds of running into someone you know on a plane, the serendipity it would take. No such luck today. America is massive. She could be from anywhere. Settling into his seat, he scans the faces around him, all bound for the same place, recognizing none.

He adjusts the ring so the pendant faces inward, running his thumb across the smooth shell. Maybe everyone gets a finite amount of luck. Maybe he'd already spent his allotment meeting Lacy this one perfect time. If that's true, it was worth it. His lips curve into a soft smile. Whatever luck he'd been given, he is grateful for it.

As the plane hits the tarmac at Cleveland Airport, Sam switches off airplane mode on his phone. The screen freezes for a few seconds before a waterfall of notifications pour in.

Just heard about your mom. So sorry for you.
Sending my condolences.
Sharing in your sadness in this moment.
Remember, I'm only a phone call away.
No words. Sorry man.
Please know that I am with you at this time. Call me back.

He stares at the torrent of messages flooding his screen. He presses the lock button, but the screen refuses to go dark, stuck on this endless stream of condolences. Friends, classmates, coworkers—he watches with quiet resentment. They couldn't even bother to get the dead parent right.

Lost in his phone, he's vaguely aware of his seatmates shifting beside him as they ask to get by. He mumbles an apology and helps them pull their bags from the overhead bin. Inching down the aisle with the slow-moving crowd, his phone vibrates in his hand. For a split second, irrational hope flares in his chest—Lacy? It vanishes just as quickly. Of course, it can't be her.

"Hello?"

"Sammy?" a woman's voice says on the other end.

"Aunt Sam?" His mother and his aunt are the only ones who ever call him Sammy.

"Oh, Sammy." She sounds like she has a cold. "I've been calling you nonstop."

"I was in Italy."

"Where are you now?"

"Back in Cleveland. Getting off the plane."

"Oh, Sam," she sighs, voice hoarse. "You gotta come home."

"I'm on my way. Is everything okay? Are you at our house right now?"

"Yes, I'm here, honey. Come home." Aunt Sam is crying now.

"What's wrong?"

"Sammy, don't you know?"

"Know what?" Panic creeps into his voice.

"Your mom, Sam. My sister..." Her voice trails off as she starts to cry.

Sam stops in the middle of the aisle. He feels the press of people against his back as they come to a halt behind him. "Aunt Sam, what are you talking about? What about Mom?"

The rumbling behind him grows, groans and shouts, but Sam is frozen still.

As the gulf before him expands and the crowd begins to push forward, a flight attendant notices Sam's distress and guides him into a seat, allowing the flow of traffic to continue.

Once the plane is empty, she takes a seat across the aisle from him and asks if he's okay.

He can still hear his aunt sobbing through the phone as he scrolls through his notifications.

I'm at a loss for words. Your mother was an angel.

ur parents are in my thoughts and prayers.

Just remember she's in a better place now. Sending healing prayers.

my deepest sympathy for your losses.

I cannot imagine the heartache and pain your feeling. Be kind to yourself.

Why is everyone getting this wrong? His grip on his phone tightens.

"Aunt Sam, it was my dad," he asserts. "My dad is the one who died. His body's being shipped from Italy. That's why I went."

He hears his aunt's shaky breaths as she composes herself. "Look, Sammy, I don't know what the right thing to do is right now. Just...come home. Come home and we can talk about it."

"Talk about what? Just ask my mom. She'll explain what happened with my dad. Please, can you just put her on the phone?" He feels a burning sensation behind his eyes.

"Sam, I can't. I'm sorry."

"Please just put my mom on the phone." His voice rises, coated with desperation. "Just pass her the phone."

"Sammy..." his aunt's voice breaks.

"Please," he begs, desperate. "Please, please, please. Please just pass the phone to my mom. Please!" His vision starts to blur as his throat constricts.

"It happened yesterday. Or the day before. We don't know yet. I just flew in this morning. We've been trying to get a hold of you."

"It was three days ago. Not yesterday. My dad died three days ago." He inhales sharply and tries to steady his voice. "Can you please just find my mom? She's probably sleeping in her room. Wake her up and tell her I'm calling. I need to talk to her."

"Sam... She's dead. She killed herself yesterday."

When the news about Dominic broke, Dawna's friends flooded her with calls, offering their sympathies, words of comfort, even meals for her family. For a brief moment, they were the talk of the town. Everyone felt bad for them. But as more details emerged, like how her husband had photos of other girls, her daughters' friends, sympathy curdled into distrust. Suddenly, being friends with her daughters took on a sinister implication. Especially Lacy, her popularity seen as a weapon instead, a wider web for victims. It didn't matter that they, too, were caught in the web.

The calls stopped. The caretaking gestures faded. Whispers and suspicion grew in their stead, thrusting them into an unfamiliar kind of exile. She's lived in this town for decades, raised her family here, and is a part of the fabric of this place. None of that seems to matter anymore.

How could she let that happen? How could she not have known? Questions whispered behind closed doors, in hushed conversations she was no longer privy to. Dominic was her husband. Wasn't she always renovating the house? How did he install all those cameras without her noticing? If she really didn't know, then she's a bad mother. What kind of mother can't sense the danger her daughters are in? What kind of woman marries a predator?

Never mind that all she did was pick paint colours and furniture while Dominic oversaw every project in their home, never ceding control to her in any household matters. Never mind that their contractors were complicit, turned a blind eye to the cameras. Never mind that other cops were part of this sick ring of monsters. Never mind that this town had idolized her husband, that her own friends had defended him whenever she dared to complain about her perfect domestic life.

Naively, Dawna had assumed this would all blow over eventually, the way small-town scandals always do. After all, she herself had played this game before, sat in the villain's seat. How many times had she gone to those town-mom get-togethers where the name of someone who wasn't present would inevitably come up? It always started with something small, something so benign it was never worth bringing up to the person directly. Just harmless venting, a chance to process feelings with the girls. The others would nod and encourage, insisting this was a space free of judgment. As expected, someone else would chime in with their own relatable tale of grievance, then another, and another, until suddenly, the subject's flaws become too glaring, their behavior unforgivable. The conversation shifts. This wasn't just gossip anymore; they all had a moral duty to stop this behaviour. Something had to be done. But how could they confront her? Someone who never self-reflects. Someone so defensive. No, no, better to protect their own peace. It's too emotionally draining to be around such an emotionally immature person. Slowly, silently, invitations would stop. A quiet expulsion.

Dawna remembers when they did this to Abby. Kim had been the one to bring it up—how Abby showed up empty-handed to her Canada Day barbecue but took home the most leftovers. "She was the only one who didn't bring anything to my Christmas party," someone adds. "She *forgot* to pay me back for dinner for like two weeks! I had to remind her!" "We went for brunch last week and she didn't even try to offer to pay, even though I covered the bill last time. I offered again just to test her. Do you think she declined? No." "She was the only one who didn't offer to help with my baby shower." The others piled on with their own stories of Abby's cheapness, her selfishness, turning her inconsiderate nature into a prism to be studied, every angle examined under new light. Eventually, the group decided to take a break from her. She was incompatible with their dynamic anyway. If she really cared, they figured, she'd ask. Proof of her self-awareness. She should be the one to initiate the conversation, give them the opening to finally confront her.

But Abby never asked. And just like that, she was ousted.

Months later, Dawna ran into her at the supermarket. It was awkward at first, but as they caught up, carefully skirting her exclusion, the flow shifted, became more nat-ural. On the drive home, Dawna remembers all the things she had liked about Abby, and the little annoyances faded with time. A sense of moral superiority swelled in her chest. How cruel her friends had been to Abby. She wasn't like them.

So, she invited Abby over for dinner and posted a picture on Facebook, knowing her friends would see and wonder, how had they reconnected? What did they talk about? Did Dawna tell her everything they had said? Had Dawna and Abby talked about them the way they had once talked about Abby? Of course, they would never ask. Not directly. Too gauche.

And, predictably, someone else eventually reached out to Abby. A casual invitation. An attempt to pry under the guise of catching up. And just like that, Abby was back in the fold.

Dawna had assumed the same would happen to her. Let them have their fun gossiping. She would leave for a while, go to Europe, have the time of her life, take obscure pictures teasing a new man. When she came back, they would all be dying to know everything.

Except now she's back, and no one has reached out. No comments on her posts. No quiet overtures. Not even from her daughters' friends.

Someone would eventually, she tells herself. Her friendships had felt shallow at times, sure, but don't all relationships feel that way on some level?

Summer is slipping away, just a few weeks until the start of school, and Dawna knows her daughters are dreading it. She had watched their friendships evolve since kindergarten, seeing them have a much easier time than she had—differences inconsequential when making friends at this age. She had eavesdropped through their bedroom walls. Sophie, her youngest, as quiet as she is clever, with her small circle of loyal quirky friends. Lacy, happy and kind. Not afraid to feel things deeply, believing every one of her heartaches and joys to be the most important thing in the world. A pretty girl who attracted people effortlessly. She had always envied her daughter's ease in making friends, being a good friend.

Where were her good friends now?

Their home felt isolating. The girls spend all their time in their rooms, the once lively shared spaces a reminder of the emptiness of her life.

This had to change.

The grand house that had once been her pride now felt suffocating, its open spaces pressing in from all sides. The walls have eyes. This is no longer a safe place.

They have to leave.

She would never be accused of not protecting her daughters again.

*L*acy grew up with the same classmates from junior kindergarten to high school. The town was so small that a new family moving in was always an event. The whole school would be in a frenzy whenever a new student joined, everyone eager to meet them, be the first to claim them as a friend.

Now, she is the new kid. And no one even notices.

In this big city high school, her presence barely registers. There are more people in this hallway than in the entirety of her old school. Back home, a new student was assigned a "first-day buddy" to show them around the school—it would take less than ten minutes to walk through it. The buddy stuck with them from class to class, ate lunch with them, and introduced them to people. This is evidently not the practice here.

She is comforted by her sister's presence by her side, but at the same time, overwhelmed by the sense of protectiveness she feels for Sophie. They had picked up their schedules from the attendance office and were now meandering the halls alone.

Until recently, Lacy hasn't thought much about her social skills. Making friends was always a matter of time and proximity, not something that required effort. But now, she realizes for the first time that making friends is a skill—one she hasn't honed.

She ducks around loitering students, scanning for classroom numbers as they walk down each hall, helping her sister find her class. Slowly, she starts noticing the curious, assessing eyes on them. The confusion on their new faces standing out. She doesn't know what to do. Is she supposed to introduce herself? Wait for people to come up to her? She tries to recall how she had approached new kids back home, but the memories blur. Maybe how you meet someone doesn't actually matter. Still, she can't shake her shyness, nor shed the awkward way she stands, like she knows she doesn't belong.

She starts making mental plans to look up online schooling options tonight when a boy in flannel walks up to her.

"Are you lost?" he asks.

She nods, unable to find her voice.

He takes the schedule from her hands. "A18," he reads, then bows dramatically, one arm pointing out in the correct direction.

"I'm actually trying to find my sister's class, C17."

He leads them up two flights of wide stairs that face a wall of windows framing the cityscape outside. This place looks like a movie set compared to her old school. Everything is so different now.

"The school is a big H with three floors," he explains. "Each floor is labelled A, B, or C. We're on C right now," he says as they reach the top landing. "The '1' in C17 means it's in the first column of the H." He draws an invisible vertical line downward with his finger. "We're at C3 right now," he adds, drawing another line beside it. "We have to cross the bridge, C2," he draws a horizontal line between them, "to get to C1. Make sense?"

It is a genuinely helpful explanation.

"Totally! Thanks!" her sister chimes in, voice chipper. Even Sophie is different here. Lacy's the quiet one now. Role reversal.

They find Sophie's class, and Lacy watches as her sister asks complete strangers if any of the seats are taken. *Who is this girl?*

"Damn, all your classes are on A and B. No maths or sciences?" the guy says, studying her schedule, still in his hands. "I'm never going to see you. All my classes are on C."

"Are subjects divided by floor?"

"A is for arts, drama, sports. B's for English and humanities. C is for the nerds."

She glances at him. Only people who look like him call themselves nerds with pride. As if being good-looking and self-assured isn't interesting enough, you have to be self-deprecating too.

"What's your name, nerd?" she asks, not intending for her tone to come out as deadpan as it does.

Fortunately, he laughs. "Jacob."

Jacob walks her to her class, entering as if he owns the place. He daps up his friends, greets the teacher like they're long-lost buddies.

The bell rings, followed by the national anthem. Jacob stays for it, placing a hand over his heart dramatically.

"We have a new student in our class," Jacob declares at the front of the classroom after morning announcements end. "Come introduce yourself!"

Heat rushes to her cheeks. She knows she's bright red. Cursing Jacob with every step, she walks to the front, musters all her courage, and gives the class a small wave. She introduces herself quickly and hurries back to her seat.

The boy beside her raises his hand. "I'm new too, actually." He stands. "I'm Edward." Unlike her, his voice rings with confidence.

The teacher shoos Jacob out of the classroom, but the smile on his lips undermines his attempt at discipline.

Her homeroom is History, and their teacher delivers his lesson like he's done it a hundred times, anticipating the questions before they're asked. Lacy and Edward are paired with the students sitting behind them for a group discussion, a chance for the teacher to go on his laptop. Edward is good at initiating conversation. He keeps everyone engaged, pulling them into the topic, making them feel included.

Turns out, she and Edward have all the same morning classes. Same lunch period too. She wonders if that's by design. Either way, she's thankful. It's like she ended up with a first-day buddy after all.

She learns that Edward is also from a small town. Not as small, nor as far north as hers, but enough to make her feel a little less alone.

At lunch, Yasmin from English invites them to sit with her and her friends. Edward introduces himself and Lacy to everyone. When Yasmin asks why they moved to the city, Edward explains matter-of-factly that he was bullied for being gay at his old school. He says it like it's nothing. It's the first time Lacy has met someone who is publicly out.

"My mom sold our house and bought a condo here," is all Lacy says.

Sophie has a different lunch period. Hers is right before Lacy's. She had texted her, asking how it was going, but got no reply. Hopefully, it just means she's too busy making friends.

Halfway through lunch, as Edward and Yasmin are making plans to go to the mall after school, Jacob bursts into the cafeteria, surrounded by a loud entourage. Lacy catches Yasmin watching him, her gaze trailing after him.

"New girl!" Jacob shouts across the room.

He jogs over, grinning. And in that moment, Lacy gets it. Why Yasmin is staring. Why other girls are staring. Jacob has that fluid, boyish charm, the kind that farms crushes without even trying.

"New girl," he repeats, sliding into the seat beside her. "How's your first day going?"

"Good."

"Nice. I see you made some friends." He glances around the table, his gaze landing on Edward. Reaching across her back, he claps a hand on Edward's shoulder. "Edward, right? I'm Jacob."

Jacob chats with them for a bit before moving on to another table.

Yasmin watches him go, then turns to Lacy. "How do you know him?"

She watches Yasmin's eyes harden as she relays her interaction with Jacob this morning. Yasmin then proceeds to info-dump about him. How she and Jacob have lived on the same street since middle school, waited at the same bus stop, played at the same parks. She spills about his home life being rough, about him failing two classes last year and not graduating, about how he had skipped fifth grade so he's still the same age as everyone else.

Lacy wonders if Jacob knows his lore is being recited like this.

Then she wonders if people back home are doing the same to her.

They definitely are.

They recycle old gossip faster than the local processing plant churns through cardboard. And hers isn't even that old yet. It's only been a week since they moved.

"So, what do they serve in the cafeteria around here?" Lacy asks without caring for the answer. She doesn't want to learn anything more about Jacob from Yasmin.

Weeks pass, and they're absorbed into Yasmin's friend group. Edward more so than Lacy. She increasingly feels like his shadow, tagging along only because he never forgets to include her.

As the semester unfolds, the adrenaline that once fueled her mask wears off. The novelty of a new city, a new school—it all wears thin. And from every corner, the shadows of her real life begin to creep back in. Conversations are hard to get through. Arranging the muscles in her face into the appropriate expression for other people feels like a full-body workout most days. Finding the right words feels pointless when everything she says comes out flat and boring.

People try to include her, probably out of kindness, but she wishes they'd just let her sit in silence. Let their voices and the cafeteria chatter become brown noise while she gets through each meal. Her "lunch" is usually a single cookie and a chicken tender, which she sometimes struggles to finish.

Unlike Lacy, Dawna and Sophie seem to be thriving in this new life. Their mother joined Pilates classes, a book club, even the condo's event planning committee. She's rarely home now, which leaves groceries and cooking to Lacy, who mainly visits the frozen meals section of the grocery store. Sophie never complains. Sometimes Dawna does, but on those nights, she orders takeout. Most nights, Lacy eats alone—if she eats at all.

Sophie throws herself into school. She's joined the film club, horror club, and anime club. Within a few weeks, she's surrounded by friends.

It's as though her family has shed their old identities, leaving their pasts behind like old coats. No one in their new lives seems to know anything about where they came from. Meanwhile, Lacy feels stuck in her old skin—tight, tired, impossible to peel off. She longs to be someone else, but the weight of her being is suffocating.

Edward never leaves her behind. He makes new friends steadily, but never replaces her. He checks in about homework, waits as she packs her things after class, even when other friends are clearly waiting for him. It all means more to her than she can functionally reciprocate. He tried talking to her about boys once. Her disinterest so obvious, he never brought it up again. Boys had shown their interest in her, at first. But her apathy, occasional sullenness, and refusal to ever flirt back eventually wore them down. Most lost interest. Others negged her.

Eventually, Yasmin and the other girls stopped trying, too. And the other girls in her grade already had their friend groups. Few wanted a pity project. Some weren't kind to her, especially because she got attention from boys they liked. The fact that she didn't seem to care only made it worse.

Halfway through the semester, Edward gravitates towards a group of queer kids. Lacy hangs around them at lunch but is friendless otherwise. She has no one to blame but herself. No one is bullying her. No one is excluding her. She just can't seem to summon the will to maintain any connections past initial introductions. Still, she's grateful for this group. There's no pressure to perform, no need to be louder or more likable. Her quietness is accepted here, mirrored even.

Jacob continues to periodically drop in on them at lunch, becoming friends with the art and drama kids, people he hadn't really associated with before. He fits in here, like he fits in everywhere. One of the drama kids convinces him to join the drama club, and he does. Ends up starring in the year-end school play.

Winter break rolls around and talk of a seniors' ski trip dominates the conversation. Going doesn't even cross Lacy's mind. A week's worth of lunch periods are dedicated to discussing the trip—who wants to go, whether it'll be worth it, rooming situations. Edward asks if she's sure she's not going, and when she confirms, he immediately announces he won't be either. The group groans in unison. Lacy feels responsible for eliciting that sound, like he's only staying back because of her.

After hearing that Lacy and Edward aren't going, Jacob decides not to go either. Then Skylar, Alex, and Val opt out, too. Someone suggests throwing a party, and word spreads fast. Suddenly, more people who aren't going to Blue Mountain are interested in the idea.

After school, Edward finds Lacy at her locker.

"Hey, I'm sorry."

"For what?" she asks, puzzled.

"For making it seem like I'm not going because of you."

"Oh. That's okay. So...it's not because of me, right?"

"I mean, it is a little. I wouldn't have as much fun without you there."

Lacy wonders if that's true. What value does her company bring to someone like Edward? Everyone always wants Edward around. He isn't loud and boisterous like Jacob, but he flows with everyone effortlessly. Never talking too much or too little, never interrupting, never mean, assertive when necessary. If someone is interrupted midsentence, he always makes sure to bring the conversation back to them. Lacy and he often sit together in silence, her reading, him drawing, never feeling the need to fill the space with words. Being around him is like sinking into a cloudy sofa. If people were sofas, Edwards would sell out. She doubts her absence would even be noticed.

"It's also because I can't afford to go," Edward adds. "My dad's already letting me stay in his one-bedroom apartment rent-free. I can't ask him for money for a ski resort," he says, rolling his eyes at *ski resort*.

Lacy is reminded of how she felt talking to Sam about money, how much it limits someone's options. Her mother had been able to move their entire lives across the country to an unaffordable city in under three weeks, all because of the money she made selling their big old house. The house that had become a prison cell to her had ultimately been her way out.

Not everyone has houses they can sell in a pinch.

Edward sighs. "And now everyone thinks I'm hosting some party. My apartment barely fits the two of us."

As if on cue, Yasmin and her friends, Preeti and Sara, saunter over.

"Heard you're having a party, Eddie. When is it?"

"I'm not having a party," Edward replies flatly.

93

"What? I've heard from so many people that you're throwing one for the Blue Mountain leftovers."

"I would love to, but I can't host it at my place."

"Why not?"

"I can't fit that many people."

"Then invite fewer people. Just us, your art kids, and Jacob?"

Edward's silence feels awkward.

Yasmin's entitlement rubs Lacy the wrong way, prompting her to ask, "Why don't *you* host it?"

Yasmin turns to her, as if noticing Lacy for the first time. "I'm not allowed to have people over."

A valid reason, just like Edward's. The difference is, she accepts it instead of pressing.

"Why don't we have it at *your* house?" Yasmin suggests.

Lacy lets out a soundless laugh before realizing Yasmin is serious. "You're serious?"

"Yeah? Why not?"

"Oh, can we?" Edward perks up.

"I barely talk to anyone at this school. Why would I want them in my house?"

Edward and Yasmin both look disappointed, and guilt presses down on her shoulders. She exhales. "Okay... I don't know. Let me ask my mom. Maybe. If no one else can do it."

Edward and Yasmin immediately grab onto her, already celebrating.

"Ask other people first!"

Predictably, word gets around. The next day, Sophie excitedly asks her, "We're having a party?"

Dawna is surprised and excited when her daughters ask to throw a party.

She's been worried about them since the move. Surprisingly, Sophie seems to be adjusting well, but she can see Lacy shrinking further and further into herself. She lost contact with all her old friends and doesn't seem to be making new ones here. All her free time is spent alone in her room.

"Of course! Do you want me out of the house?" Dawna offers.

"If you don't mind," Sophie says. "It's not like we're going to kick you out of your own house, though."

"No! I'll gladly make myself scarce. I want you to have fun with your friends. The space is small enough; no one wants an old lady around."

"Thanks, Mom," Lacy says, watching her mother's smile falter. She quickly adds, "You're not an old lady."

Edward and Val come over early to help set up. Lacy can tell they are not what her mom expected her new friends to look like. Edward, wearing mascara, ripped jeans, and a mesh jersey. Val, towering four inches taller in her Demonia boots, her blood-red pixie cut and industrial piercings making a statement.

Then Yasmin, Preeti, and Sara arrive, and her mom seems much more impressed. Placated by the knowledge that her daughter is also friends with these polite, pretty princesses—Yasmin in a white tube top and matching skinny jeans, her wavy black hair rolling down her back like island waves. Preeti's balayage bob accentuates her scalloped Peter Pan collar and pinafore dress. Sara is pulling off a flowy Florence Welch aesthetic.

More people she doesn't even know arrive.

Jacob enters, immediately pulling Lacy into a hug, prompting her mom to excitedly ask if he's her boyfriend. Lacy rolls her eyes. Her mother was supposed to be out of the house two hours ago.

Lacy had explicitly said no more than ten people. The party has barely started, and there are already sixteen people in her home.

By the time the last guest arrives, the count is over twenty-five. The two-plus-den condo fits everyone, but barely. Lacy watches as people she's never spoken to laugh, drink, and make themselves at home in her space. Did none of them find it weird to show up at a stranger's house? Then again, in her small town, this would never happen. Big parties are held in the woods or fields, trucks carrying kegs, and bonfires crackling into the night. No one ever showed up uninvited because the whole town was always invited.

Dawna reemerges in a red velvet dress, hair and makeup done. "Bye, girls! Have fun, everyone!" she calls, making a show of kissing her daughters' foreheads. She has a date tonight, and she looks good for it.

"Dude," Jacob leans into Lacy, "your mom is, like, really hot. I see where you get it from."

From the corner of her eye, Lacy notices Yasmin whispering to some girls, their gazes snapping toward her as they listen. Every girl knows this feeling.

She backs away from Jacob, searching for Edward. "I'm going to my room. Make sure no one trashes the place," she tells him when she finds him.

"Nooo," Edward whines. "Your mom just left. Stay!"

Sara appears from behind him, noticeably tipsy. "Wait," she says in her fairy-like voice, her oversized bell sleeves brushing Lacy's wrist as she takes her hands. "I came just for you."

The eye contact feels too intense. Sara reaches out, tucking a strand of Lacy's hair behind her ear. Something in Lacy's stomach flips.

"Um..." Lacy hesitates, heat rising in her cheeks. "I can stay for a little bit."

Sara beams, lacing their fingers as she drags her to the couch.

Sophie and her friends migrate from the living room to Sophie's room, their voices muffled behind the door as they settle in to watch YouTube videos on her computer. Meanwhile, Skyler, Alex, Val, Yasmin, Preeti, Jacob, and a girl Lacy doesn't know occupy the couch.

"Let's play Spin the Bottle!" Sara exclaims as she pulls Lacy down beside her.

Lacy feels Edward's gaze on her as he finds a seat beside her. She glances over at him, catching the curious flick of his eyes from her intertwined hands with Sara to her face. He raises a brow, giving her a *what's going on* look. She returns an *I don't know* shrug. She really doesn't know.

Sara chugs the last of her pink grapefruit cooler and places the empty bottle on the marble coffee table with a soft clink.

"If we're gonna do this, we should do it right!" Jacob grins, leaping up and swiftly moving the heavy coffee table to the side. Everyone shuffles down to the rug, and Lacy feels the shift in the room, the energy tightening for whatever happens next.

Jacob settles down directly across from her, eyes twinkling. "Alright. Who wants to go first?"

More people notice the game being played and decide to join. The arrival of Gillian, the beautiful captain of the girls' soccer team, and Connor, the quiet but undeniably hot, tall guy, sends a ripple of excitement through the group. Not everyone hides their discomfort well when the super-wasted loud guy, who's already broken two glasses, stumbles into his spot on the rug.

The drunk guy is about to volunteer to go first when Jacob steps in, using eenie-meenie-minie-moe to decide who spins first. His finger lands on Edward. A hopeful wave of smiles roll through the circle. Edward spins the bottle, and it lands on the drunk guy. An audible "ick" is heard from some in the group. Others can't hide crinkles of distaste on their faces.

Edward, unfazed, smiles at him and raises his eyebrow. "What do you say, Maurice?"

Lacy has never seen Edward interact with Maurice and is bemused, impressed even, that Edward knows his name. Edward knows everyone.

Maurice blushes, draining the rest of his beer. "Fuck it. Let's do it, bro," he says as beer drips down the sides of his mouth.

Maurice crawls across the rug toward Edward and his quick peck on Edward's cheek is met with cheers. The kiss somehow endears the group to Maurice, who has switched gears, now nursing a bag of chips and a bottle of water instead.

On Jacob's turn, the bottle lands between Yasmin and Val. A pinch of panicked lines appears between Yasmin's eyebrows before she turns toward Jacob with an expectant smile.

"Val, you said you don't want to kiss any boys, right?" Jacob asks.

"You can kiss the top of my head if you want," Val replies.

"Cute." Jacob moves closer and plants a kiss on both Yasmin's and Val's heads. Yasmin looks down at the ground, deliberately ignoring Preeti, who's trying to catch her eye.

Sara goes next and kisses an uncontrollably giggling Preeti.

Lacy wants to skip her turn, explaining that she only wants to watch, not play. Boos sound from the circle and those gathered around to watch.

"If you don't want to kiss the person you land on, you don't have to," Jacob says. "You can re-spin."

"No, that's mean!" Yasmin shouts to a ripple of agreement.

"It's not mean. It's consent," Edward asserts.

"I'm fine with that," Alex pipes up. "I won't get offended if anyone doesn't want to kiss me."

"If she doesn't want to play, let's just skip her," Yasmin whines, taking a sip of her spiked lemonade.

"You sure you don't want to go?" Edward asks her.

"Spin it for me," she says to Edward. A kiss didn't mean much to her anymore, not when she really thinks about it. She'd developed a clinical attitude toward sex, especially after the photos. It had lost its significance, and she'd learned to compartmentalize it whenever necessary.

Edward spins the bottle, and the spout points firmly at Jacob. Yasmin's eyes flare, glued on Jacob.

Jacob's eyes soften as he moves towards Lacy, a waggish smile on his lips. Lacy's stomach flips at the sight of this, her brain not so clinical right now. He kneels in front of her, settling back onto his calves as he leans in. Her eyes flutter shut as his lips meet hers. After a few moments, she feels his hands threading through her hair, and for a brief instant, she loses track of time.

She has to catch her breath when she finally pulls away from the kiss.

"I'll take one of those," Edward exclaims, noticing her fluster, lightening the tension. He takes his turn, and everyone moves on from the kiss—everyone except Yasmin, whose heated gaze she can feel boring a hole into her side.

The bottle lands on Lacy, and the crowd laughs as Edward says, "I don't know if I can follow that. But I think we could share a cute kiss."

Lacy laughs too and nods, surprised to find that she does really want to kiss Edward. He gently cups her face with both hands, and she places hers on his shoulders. He presses a soft kiss to her lips, and they both smile into it, the warmth of the moment lingering. In this instant, Lacy discovers a new type of kiss—filled with tenderness and affection, not just lust and desire.

Looking into Edward's eyes as they pull apart, Lacy can't help the smile that forms on her face, the warmth spreading through her chest, or maybe it's just because she's finished another one of the vodka coolers Edward's been handing her.

Gillian lands on Connor, and Lacy is introduced to the simple pleasure of watching pretty people kiss. She giggles as she watches them, the alcohol loosening her mind.

It's Jacob's turn next, and he throws Edward a roguish smile. "You said you wanted one of my kisses?" He spins the bottle with deliberate control, and it lands squarely on Edward. Jacob winks, his eyes locking with Edward's, and the crowd bursts into fevered cheers.

Jacob's personality could easily be grating if it weren't for his undeniable swagger. Some people are just effortlessly cool, and they know it. Lacy thinks of Sam.

She settles back, watching the lightning thread of excitement between their eyes as they move toward each other. Jacob is a master at kissing, so much so that just watching is enough. As their kiss deepens, Edward moves his hand, hooking his fingers in Jacob's belt loop and pulling him closer. Lacy feels a pulse between her legs as the scene unfolds before her.

There is a brief moment of reverent silence as they pull apart, returning to their seats in the circle. The game is heating up, and the air feels thick with unspoken tension.

Preeti kisses Skyler. Maurice kisses Yasmin, though it's clear she doesn't enjoy it. Connor and Gillian share another kiss, and now Connor can't keep his eyes off her. Preeti and Skylar kiss. On Yasmin's spin, the bottle stops briefly on Jacob before rolling on Maurice.

"No way. I literally just kissed you," she whines.

Maurice shrugs, unbothered.

Sara spins next, and the bottle lands on Lacy.

Lacy's heartbeat picks up as Sara wraps her arms around her neck, her own hands finding their way to Sara's waist. Their lips meet, moving together as their heads tilt to deepen the kiss. Sara teases Lacy's lips open, slipping her tongue in. A guy yells, "Yoooooo!" from the background. No one else has used tongue yet, and the cheers and whoops are deafening. The sensation of Sara beneath her hands is intoxicating, almost as thrilling as the feel of Sara's hands in her hair, as amazing as the taste and warmth of her lips. Lacy doesn't understand how she'd never noticed Sara before. She can't get enough of this moment. When they finally break apart, they share a soft laugh, their plump, reddened lips still smiling at each other.

Lacy skips her turn, needing to recover from her kiss—a kiss that's left her feeling more drunk than she wants to be.

Edward's spin lands on Alex. Connor's lands back on Edward, and he gives him a quick peck on the lips.

"Fuck yes," Gia, the girl Lacy doesn't know, exclaims as the bottle lands on Sara. Gia's eyes briefly flicker toward Lacy before she beckons Sara over. Gia steals glances at Lacy as she kisses Sara, and Lacy isn't sure how to feel about it, nor the distaste curling in her gut, jealousy burning in her chest.

Gillian excuses herself to get a drink, and Connor offers to go with her. They leave, and Gia gets up to make another drink, promising to return soon. Four new guys join the game, and everyone shifts to make room. Gia returns and sits beside Sara. Jacob spins the bottle, and no one objects to him starting. The order had gotten messed up, anyway. It lands on Preeti, and he pulls her into a quick but deep kiss. Preeti avoids Yasmin's gaze after this, her eyes cast downward.

Maurice spins next, and the bottle lands on one of the new guys. "Fuck that shit," the guy curses. "I'm not a fag." At his words, the energy in the room shifts.

"Chill out, dude," Jacob sighs, shaking his head exasperated.

Preeti and Yasmin quickly skip their turn, perhaps in fear of landing on that guy.

Gia's spin lands on Lacy, and she expects her to re-spin, on account of the weird competitive energy Gia is sending to her. To Lacy's surprise, Gia leans over Sara and almost pulls Lacy toward her. She climbs over Sara, positioning herself nearly on top of Lacy. Gia's kiss is rough, one hand gripping the back of Lacy's neck tightly, almost squeezing, the other trailing down to rest on Lacy's left breast, giving it a squeeze. Lacy gasps, and the boys' shouts and hollers only heighten her discomfort. She pulls back from the kiss, scooting away from Gia.

Sara rolls her eyes at Gia as she takes her turn. The bottle lands on one of the new guys—not the homophobic one—and they share a quick kiss before it's Lacy's turn again.

Lacy asks to skip her turn again, but is met with protests.

"One last turn!"

"You can re-spin."

Sara nudges her with a flirty grin. "What if you get me?"

Just then, the homophobic guy snatches the bottle. "Just go," he mutters impatiently, spinning the bottle with force.

The bottle lands on Sara, and she beams. "See? I told you."

"I spun it, actually," the homophobic guy says. "You're supposed to kiss me."

"It's her turn," Sara retorts.

Sara climbs on top of Lacy, straddling her.

"Woohoo!" she hears from the crowd watching.

Sara leans in seductively, her lips coaxing Lacy's, her thighs squeezing Lacy's waist. Sara takes Lacy's hand, guiding it briefly to her breast. At this point, Lacy is three and a half drinks in, and that last half has her teetering on the edge of her comfort zone. Sara's underwear, under her flowy white dress, is pressed against Lacy's jeans, right over her crotch, sending an electric pulse through her body. The feel of Sara's lips moving from her lips to her jaw, kissing down her neck, has Lacy gasping softly, a moan escaping her before she can stop it.

"Fuck," she hears the homophobic guy whisper under his breath, and the moment shatters, plunging Lacy into cold sobriety. A sudden wave of awareness slams into her. She is too aware of the eyes watching, of the growing crowd forming around the game. Heat spreads from her face down to her chest. She can't catch her breath as she notices the boys hiding their crotches behind sweaters and couch pillows. Suddenly, she feels the oppressive eyes of all the men who saw her photos online invading her mind. A wave of dread, disgust, and shame crashes over her.

She gets up abruptly, leaving the game behind. She locks herself in her room.

An hour or so later, she hears Edward knocking on her door.

"You okay?"

"Yeah," she tries to call back, but her voice feels small.

"Can I come in? Everyone's gone. Just Jacob, Yasmin, Sara, Preeti, and Gia are in the living room, waiting to get picked up. It's just me here."

Lacy unlocks the door. Edward steps inside, his eyes flicking over the bare furniture. Her room is purely utilitarian, no decorations, nothing personal.

"Are my sister's friends still here?" she asks.

"I think they left, too, or they all fell asleep in her room. It's pretty quiet in there."

"The party's officially over?"

Edward nods. "Edgar got too drunk and angry. The vibes got bad, so people started leaving. It was a really fun party otherwise."

"Who's Edgar?"

"The guy who said 'fag.'"

"Oh."

A strange guilt twists in her chest. Maybe because it happened in her house? But it's not like she invited him. Maybe just from witnessing it, from staying silent. She thinks about apologizing, though she isn't sure for what, or how. The words sit heavy on her tongue, awkward and unformed.

Edward studies her. "Are you really okay?"

"Yeah. I just drank too much. Got carried away in the game. Got embarrassed."

"About what?"

Moaning out loud? The words refuse to leave her throat. She can't say them, can't acknowledge it even happened.

"I got too drunk," she reiterates.

Edward nods. "Okay. We'll all be gone soon. Get some rest. And seriously, you didn't do anything embarrassing. We were all just playing a game."

Gia appears in the doorway. "You weren't embarrassing. You were hot."

Edward shoots her a look, like, *What are you doing here?*

"The girls are leaving. They want to say bye. Do you want to say bye to them?" Gia asks Lacy.

Lacy just wants them to leave. But instead, she says, "Sure," noncommittally.

Yasmin, Preeti, and Sara come into her room to hug her goodbye, thanking her for hosting.

Sara gives her a quick peck on the lips.

"How did none of us know Sara's a fucking lesbian?" Yasmin is heard saying by the door as they put on their shoes.

"I'm not a lesbian," Sara replies.

"How are you getting home?" Lacy asks Edward.

"Jacob and I are taking the bus together."

She nods and glances at Gia.

"I rode my bike here," Gia says. "Just need to sober up a little before I make that journey."

Lacy checks her phone. 1:26 a.m. A girl shouldn't be biking home alone at this hour. "You can sleep over if you need."

"Really? I'll leave early in the morning."

Around two, she says goodbye to Jacob and Edward. Her mother still isn't home. She sets up the couch for Gia, leaving out some clothes for her.

Gia hesitates. "I don't have a toothbrush."

Lacy sighs. "I don't have a new one."

"Can I use yours?"

"You don't mind sharing a toothbrush?"

"No. Do you?"

"Sort of."

"I'll use it after you, then buy you a new one tomorrow?"

The thought of Gia using her toothbrush makes Lacy's stomach turn, but she's too drained to argue. She washes up, leaves a fresh towel and her toothbrush for Gia, then climbs into bed.

Lying in the dark, she hears the faint sound of Gia brushing her teeth. A few minutes later, Gia enters her room without knocking and sits on her bed.

"How are you feeling now?" Gia asks.

"Tired."

"Do you still feel embarrassed?"

"I don't know. A little."

"You shouldn't." Gia moves closer. "Why do you feel embarrassed?"

Lacy doesn't want to talk about it anymore, especially not with Gia. "I don't know? I got too carried away. I don't want people to see me that way."

"Why?" Gia lowers her face toward Lacy's. "You were being sexy." Then, she kisses her.

Lacy freezes. Her head is still swimming from the vodka, her stomach unsettled.

Gia climbs onto the bed and straddles her. Her kisses are fast, urgent, uncoordinated. Her lips move to Lacy's neck, her hands roaming over her body.

Keys jingle at the front door. The sound of it opening.

Gia jumps off her, diving under the covers just as Dawna steps into Lacy's room. Lacy squeezes her eyes shut, feigning sleep, hoping her mother won't notice the extra body beside her. Dawna lingers for a moment before quietly shutting the door.

Gia reemerges, stifling a laugh, alcohol still on her breath.

She pulls the blanket over them both and starts to kiss Lacy again, her hand grazing over Lacy's chest.

Lacy doesn't even know if she likes Gia, isn't sure she even wants her in her bed right now. Her mind still feels foggy, disoriented from the alcohol, caught in the war between her head, her heart, and her body. Gia's touch confuses her, but the sensation of lips on her skin, the slow circling of fingers over her nipple, ignites something deep in her, a traitorous physical response she doesn't quite understand.

She finds herself kissing back, trying to reclaim some control as Gia's hand slips beneath her waistband.

In the morning, Gia is gone, true to her word.

Lacy wakes up alone, her stomach twisting, not just from the drinking, but from the uneasy weight that settles deep within her when she tries to think about what happened with Gia last night.

Something best ignored, she decides.

Lacy doesn't talk to anyone for the rest of winter break. She locks herself in her room, ignoring the world outside. Not even obliging Sophie's invitations to watch movies in the living room. The days bleed into each other, silent and cold, and she lets them.

Back at school, she cannot face people, not even Edward. She steers clear of everyone. It's easier that way. Edward and Lacy no longer share any of the same classes this semester, making it effortless to avoid him.

Sara and Preeti are in her Philosophy class, but after being blatantly ignored for the first few days, they've stopped acknowledging her entirely.

Gia is in her Law class, but for some reason, she can't seem to meet Lacy's eyes either.

At lunch, Lacy avoids the cafeteria. Sometimes Edward finds her, tracking her down in whatever empty hallway or stairwell she's chosen that day. He doesn't ask why she's pulling away. He doesn't push. He just sits with her, offering quiet companionship she isn't sure she deserves.

Sometimes Alex, Skylar, or Val join them. Lacy doesn't engage. She cannot look them in the eye, cannot face the people who have seen her so vulnerable.

As the days grow warmer, she stops lingering in hallways. Instead, she leaves school entirely during lunch, walking home just to crawl back into bed. Distance and silence stretch between her and everyone else. Even Edward eventually stops trying.

Her senior year slips by in a blur of avoidance and indifference. She doesn't go to prom, which devastates her mother. Dawna pleads, but Lacy doesn't budge. When graduation approaches, she tries to skip that too, but isn't strong enough to fight her mother's will this time.

"I'm not missing seeing my daughter's high school graduation," Dawna scolds, and that's the end of it.

Walking across the stage in front of her entire grade is worse than she imagined. The weight of a thousand eyes on her makes her stomach twist, her skin itch. But like everything else, it passes. A brief moment of suffering, then it's over.

In the parking lot of the hockey arena where they've just graduated, Edward calls out to her, jogging to catch up.

"Hey, Lace. There's a graduation party tonight at Connor's house," he says, breathless but hopeful. "You should come."

She shakes her head. "No, thanks."

He studies her, but doesn't push further, knowing there's no point.

"Did you get into UofT?" he asks instead, following up on their conversation from months ago, unfinished.

"Yeah."

"So, is that where you're going?"

"Probably."

"Did you get into all the schools you applied to?"

She nods. She had applied to three different History programs, the maximum the base application fee allowed. She was accepted into every one of them. Despite every other aspect of her life slipping this semester, she'd managed to keep her grades up. She didn't have much else going for her, after all.

"What about you?" she asks.

"Humber," he says. "Architectural Technology."

She nods, remembering the moments they shared, sitting together in companionable silence. Reading beside him as he sketched, always absorbed in his drawings, some corner of the school, or a building just across the street. She tries to picture him now, in a bright classroom full of windows, surrounded by plans and designs for things that don't yet exist.

"I hope it goes well for you," she tells him. And she means it, quietly sure she won't see him again. She will miss him, she realizes, though she doesn't say it out loud. And, as if he knew what she was thinking, he steps forward to pull her into a hug.

"You too," he says softly.

Standing in his embrace, she says, "Thank you," without thinking.

Edward tilts his head to look at her. "For what?" he asks with a small laugh.

She doesn't answer. Doesn't know how to convey the gratitude she feels for him and this moment, that someone like him exists, even if his honey gold heart feels too big, wasted on someone as undeserving as her. Better, she thinks, to let him pour that love into people worthy of it.

There's no guidebook on what to do after your parents die. No one explains how to plan a funeral, what to do with their accounts, or what to do if there's no will. No one to show you how to keep up with bills when everything feels like it's crumbling around you.

Sam's aunt, a professor at Ohio State, stays with him for the rest of the summer to help with everything. Her wife, Jackie, also a professor, drives in a few days a week. She wants to stay longer, but can't. She's teaching a couple of summer courses. Together, they take care of him. They make food for him, clean up after him, and help make decisions that feel too heavy for a child to bear. *Are you still a child if you don't have any parents?*

They talk to lawyers for him, explain all the steps he needs to take, and reassure him that his opinions matter, even when it feels like he has none to offer.

Sam got a job as soon as he turned sixteen and started handing over money from his first paycheck, contributing to the bills without ever really knowing how they got paid. So much of his money went to his mother, but he was never sure how much of it actually went towards paying the bills. His relationship with his mother had been strained, and he hadn't realized how strained until now. He wishes he had talked to her about what would happen after she was gone. What she would have wanted. But teenagers never think about having those kinds of conversations with their parents. Why would they?

Mia's threats of suicide were nothing new. They surfaced whenever arguments boiled over or any time his father threatened to leave her. But when Leo did actually leave two years ago, Mia never followed through on her threats. She was devastated for a while, but then she started to improve. She picked up more shifts at the store, spent more time with her friends, bought new clothes, and even started going to yoga. She was trying.

His father's return to Italy seemed to mark a turning point—things were finally improving for both of his parents. Leo had found steady work and appeared committed to it. He'd settled into a nice place. But when he started dating someone and began posting photo after photo with his new girlfriend, Mia spiraled. He'd never posted pictures with her, never taken her on the kinds of dates he now seemed to be enjoying. And the setting didn't help. He was living in a small town on the Sicilian coast, each photo looking like a perfect vacation snapshot.

Sam's parents had broken up countless times over his lifetime, and each time had been brief. His father always returned to his mother. But this time was different. His father was in a new country with someone new, and Mia couldn't handle it. His parents were still technically married, a fact Mia reminded her husband of every time she called, which was often. She didn't care about the international call charges racking up on her phone bill. She left hundreds of voicemails, begging him to come back, threatening to kill herself once again. But Leo had grown numb to it, knowing her threats were empty. He didn't care anymore.

That's when his mother slipped back into her depression, sinking so deep into the void that Sam couldn't reach her. She struggled for a while, and Sam had to skip a lot of school to work so he could cover the bills. Eventually, his mother seemed to emerge from the depths of her despair. At least, that's what Sam thought. This cycle had been long, and he believed she had made it through unscathed. He hadn't realized until now how deep she'd been in it.

In the last few months, Mia seemed lighter. She was chattier whenever they were home together, even asked to see his drawings sometimes. She'd started doing yoga again. She had also started to reach out to her estranged sister, talking on the phone a few nights a week. Their relationship was healing, they were becoming close again, like they used to be—so close Mia had even named her son after her sister.

When he was in middle school, his aunt, whom he had known as his uncle, began wearing her hair down, dressing in more feminine clothes. He was too young to grasp the weight of it—not her transition, because that was simple. A person telling you who they are and accepting it as truth—that's how children understand the world. What confused him was everything around it.

The fights. The way his mother's voice would sharpen on the phone with her. The late-night arguments between his parents, behind doors that did little to muffle his father's disgust. The way his father spat out his vitriol, how, without realizing it, Sam absorbed that reaction before he even understood what it was for. Before he understood what terrible thing his aunt had supposedly done.

And then, one day, she was just gone.

Still, every year, without fail, she sent him birthday cards, crisp bills tucked inside, even as silence stretched between them.

A few years ago, he found her on Facebook and sent her a message. By then, he had unlearned so much on his own, had seen the world far beyond the narrow walls his father had been trapped behind—a prison of his own making, the keys in his hand. And he needed to know if that was really all it had taken to lose her. If it had truly been that simple. That disappointing.

She explained to him that his father didn't agree with her lifestyle, felt like she was a bad influence on him, and his mother had agreed, worried her presence would confuse him. She said all this without any resentment or accusation, just explained that she didn't want to interfere with their parenting and was happy that Sam had reached out. They continued to talk here and there, but it wasn't until last year when his mother invited her over that he saw her for the first time in over a decade, and met her wife.

Now was the second time.

Sam is overwhelmed by the immense gratitude he feels for his aunts, but it's buried beneath layers of grief, confusion, and guilt. Guilt because he knows this situation is unfair to them, taking on all this responsibility and labor when his parents had essentially abandoned her, excommunicated his aunt from their lives. When he was younger, he didn't understand why, but now he sees it for what it was: pure bigotry and betrayal. On top of the guilt, he feels a deep current of sadness for his aunt. And for his mother who had just got her sister back, just begun to understand and respect his aunt for who she is. Now that connection is lost, left fractured forever. All of it feels too complex to unravel. Not right now, at least. He doesn't have the words. He doesn't have the energy.

So, here Sam and Jackie are, stepping in as his guardians. They had done everything for him, handled the funeral, the cremation, closed his parents' accounts, and even offered for him to move in with them in Columbus. He agrees. There's nothing left for him here. His friends are all going off to college. His parents are gone. Staying doesn't make sense—not in a place where he feels like a stranger in his own life.

By the end of the summer, Auntie Jackie heads back home to get the house ready for his arrival. Aunt Sam helps him pack up everything worth taking and sells what might earn him a bit of money. She stays up late into the night, preparing her courses for the upcoming school year after he's already asleep, quietly taking care of final details, like forwarding his mail and booking the moving van. In the final week of summer, a new family moves into his house, and Sam drives away, toward a new chapter of his life.

*I*t takes Sam less than a year to be promoted to dairy manager at the grocery store where he now works. Not a recognition of his service, more a matter of convenience, as the previous manager had been caught doing cocaine in his car, and no one else wanted the position.

That's not to say that Sam isn't a good worker—the opposite, in fact. He's so good that management tends to take advantage of him. The world taught Sam early that the reward for good work is always more work. Like now, as he works a double shift, stacking bags of rice to cover someone from a different department who texted last minute that he wasn't coming in.

After three years in grocery stores, he's worked in every department imaginable. Once the other managers realized how cross-trained he is, he became the go-to guy for covering no-shows. Sam doesn't mind. He needs the money.

Despite his aunts' objections, he contributes to their mortgage and saves the rest of his pay, not having many expenses himself. Money was never secure growing up, aside from the paychecks he and his mother brought home from working at the same supermarket. She'd gotten him a job there, worked as the cashier for most of her life. She'd seen store managers come and go, watched problems pile up, all while she kept her department running smoothly. Despite over a decade of dedication, she was never offered a promotion, though management always came to her for help. She never complained.

Sam inherited her work ethic. Maybe out of fear of turning out like Leo. His father never held a job for more than six months, always complaining, quitting, or getting fired, his failings always blamed on others. Sam never wants to be like that. So, if it means managers taking advantage of him, so be it. It's not like he has anywhere else to be.

It's been a year since his move to Columbus.

His aunts' house is old, charming, and more spacious than anywhere he's ever lived. Auntie Jackie converted her office into his room, and she and Aunt Sam now share an office space. He has a big window overlooking the backyard and his own bathroom, something he's never had before.

Both of them, being academics, pushed for him to apply for college, not realizing just how bad his grades were. He barely scraped through high school, convinced the school only let him graduate so they wouldn't have to deal with him another year. And the thought of incurring a student loan terrifies him. His parents had spent their whole lives in debt, owing everything to banks and money lenders, renting their house, leasing their cars, financing their couch, their TV, hell, most of their furniture. His father had taken out loans for his endless cycle of hobbies. A gaming computer. A motorcycle. A fucking outdoor pizza oven. He refuses to live like that, owing everything to corporations and predatory lenders, unable to call anything his own.

He doesn't know how long this living arrangement will last. He imagines his aunts probably don't want him living with them forever. He's saving so that when the time comes, he can leave without causing any more trouble.

His life here has settled into a steady rhythm. He works, does the grocery shopping, and makes dinner for his aunts, who are usually too busy or too tired to cook. Their fridge and pantry were practically empty when he first moved in, which surprised him considering the dozens of cookbooks that decorated their shelves. He started making recipes from them, partly to keep busy, partly to repay their kindness. He is getting quite good at it.

In the evenings, they sit in the living room, reading or watching movies. It's a peaceful life. The most comfort and security he's ever known. He has a hard time enjoying it, though. Every moment of peace soured by the empty pit that's taken up permanent residency in his stomach.

He thinks about how much time he wasted with his mom, ignoring her, fighting with her, choosing to spend time with friends he already saw at school for eight hours a day instead of staying home with her.

On nights when he sits with his aunts, not even talking, just existing in the same space, he thinks about how easy it is to feel close to someone. How he could have had this with his mom. He thinks of the nights she sat alone, watching telenovelas, and how effortless it would have been to just be with her. But he never did. Never learned her language. He wonders how isolated she must have felt in that small town, how her own son never cared to learn about her culture. And now, with her gone, he's lost his only tie to it.

It's not just that they rarely spent time together. It's also that most of his memories are of helping her through mental breakdowns, talking her off the ledge. Rarely did they share moments of peace. He never just talked with her. Never asked her questions. There's so much he doesn't know about her. And now it's too late, like a key to a treasure box sinking to the bottom of the ocean.

✦

Lacy's second year of university is significantly easier than her first. She's gotten the hang of the readings, and her classes are simply more interesting. There are fewer students and more engaging professors.

She also finally upgrades her phone. Her old flip phone has become a real inconvenience. Last year, she had to open up her laptop every time she needed to check her class schedule, emails, the weather, and transit routes.

She didn't make any friends in her first semester, always rushing home after class. Living close to campus was convenient but isolating. The loneliness became overwhelming, and over summer break, she decided it was time to come out of her shell. She was once an affable, agreeable girl. She could be that person again.

So, she starts to make an effort to make friends in her lectures and tutorials, joins group study sessions, and says yes to invitations for coffee or meals between classes. To her surprise, talking to people is easy. All she has to do is ask them questions. It's an almost foolproof way to avoid revealing anything about herself while getting people to like her. They are flattered by her interest in them, feel connected to her, project themselves onto her.

Occasionally, she passes old high school classmates on campus. She smiles at them, trying to overwrite their memory of the sullen girl she used to be.

Her depressive, self-isolating habits subside as her social world begins to open again—a relief to her mother and sister. She starts spending more time with Sophie, too. That is, when she's not busy with her own expanding social life.

In her Women and Gender Studies class, she grows close to a girl named Josie. Josie is from a small town in British Columbia, and Lacy feels a quiet kinship with her. Josie is smart, funny, charismatic, and always surrounded by people, mostly queer art and humanities majors. They remind Lacy of Edward and his friends. She wonders why these confident, popular people always seem to take her under their wing. Nevertheless, she's grateful for it.

One night, at a dorm party, Lacy drinks too much, and Josie takes her to her room to rest.

Josie reaches for her film camera. She joined the campus camera club, her commitment to the art of photography becoming more than a hobby. "I've been getting requests for shoots around campus. It's turning into a whole thing," Josie tells her.

Being photographed by Josie is socially stylish. People want to be seen through her lens. But when Josie points the camera at Lacy, she hides her flushed face behind a pillow.

"Come on," Josie begs. "You look so cute right now. And the redness of your face won't even show. It's black-and-white."

Lacy shakes her head.

Josie lowers the camera. "What's your deal with pictures anyway?"

Lacy never allows her photo to be taken. Not even casual selfies.

"I just don't like them."

"Why?"

"I don't like looking at pictures of myself. And I don't like the idea of other people having pictures of me."

Josie sighs. "I can never understand pretty girls with image issues. It's so boring. People hit on you all the time, tell you you're gorgeous, but you're somehow convinced you're ugly? If that's really how you feel, it's pathetic."

Lacy has always admired Josie's sharpness. She rarely minces words. It impresses people as much as it unsettles them.

"And if you don't actually believe you're ugly," Josie continues, "then you're just fishing for compliments. And I'm not going to fall for your bait."

Lacy sits in silence. She doesn't know how to dispel Josie's assumptions without revealing the trauma she's been trying to leave behind. Not when she finally seems to be building a life untouched by the shadow of her family's scandal.

Josie softens, just a little. "Look, I know I'm being harsh, but it's because I actually like you. Just not *this* part of you. I'd rather you be authentic so I can like you completely."

Authentic. Lacy rarely is. She's so used to the mask, she's not sure there's even a face beneath it.

She looks at Josie, the most self-assured person she's ever met, someone whose opinion of herself is never shaped by anyone else's. She envies that.

So, she tries.

"I don't think I'm ugly," she says carefully. "My whole life, I was kind of groomed to take pride in my looks."

Josie tilts her head. "What do you mean?"

"When I was a kid, I did some modelling. I was too young to understand what was going on. All I knew was that I had to listen to the adults in the room. Now, there are all these pictures of me posing, wearing clothes, not wearing clothes. I was a naked baby in a diaper ad. None of it was my choice." She shrugs. "I just don't want to add to that."

Josie nods slowly. "Okay. I get that. But you have agency now. You get to choose how you act, what you wear, where you go, how you pose. You're not a naked baby anymore. So, what are you worried about?"

Lacy feels something catch in her throat.

It's been almost four years since her father's crimes, and she still can't move past it. She wonders if she ever will. Is she just never going to have any pictures of herself again? She thinks about Sam's drawings. About her dad. The thoughts tangle together in her sangria-clouded mind, and her eyes begin to burn.

Josie notices. "Hey now," she says gently. "Oh my god, I'm sorry. I wasn't trying to pressure you. I just wanted to understand."

Lacy feels Josie's arms wrap around her as tears begin to fall.

"Girl," Josie sighs, "I wouldn't have invited you here if I knew you'd be a sad drunk."

Lacy lets out a flat laugh. The kind of laugh that happens when sadness runs so deep it circles around to absurdity.

For a fleeting moment, she's reminded of laughing with Sam on the beach.

✦

Sam is stocking ice cream when a customer taps his shoulder. She is smiling at him, expectantly.

"Can I help you?" he asks.

"Sam! It's me! Don't you recognize me?"

He doesn't.

"I was your babysitter! I can't believe you're here."

Sam blinks. "Babysitter?"

She laughs. "Maybe when you were like five or six?"

A vague memory resurfaces. A girl, maybe a teenager, watching TV on his couch. His parents had started leaving him home alone far earlier than they should have. It wasn't a sudden decision but a gradual neglect—quick trips to the store that turned into hours, late-night parties that bled into morning, fights that ended with one or both of them storming out, leaving him behind in a silent house. He'd learned how to fend for himself early on, barely remembers needing a sitter.

"Oh. Hi."

"Wow, you're all grown up now." She beams.

He wonders how she can even recognize him.

"You grew up nicely," she says, giving him a once-over. "How's your family doing?"

"My parents died last year."

Her face crumples into an exaggerated look of horror. "Oh my god, Sam. I'm so sorry."

He shrugs and quickly returns to stocking the ice cream, not wanting the cartons on the skid to start melting.

"So, do you live here now?"

He nods.

"When did you move here? Are you going to Ohio State?"

"Last year. Nope."

"Are you living alone?"

"No. I live with my aunts. They teach there."

Her face lights up. "No way! I just graduated from Ohio State! I wonder if they ever taught me." She pauses, like she's expecting him to say more. "I didn't even know you had family here."

Another nod.

Women tend to talk *at* him, and it usually works out fine. It worked with Vivian, the cashier he's been casually seeing. By seeing, he mostly means fucking in her car.

Anna—he learns her name only when she scribbles it onto the back of a receipt, along with her number—talks at him a little longer before finally heading off.

✦

As the fall semester comes to a close, Lacy and Josie become inseparable. They make plans to see each other over winter break and even choose to take some of the same classes next semester.

On the last day of school, Josie invites Lacy to a Cherry Bomb event with her friends and asks if they can have an after-party at her place. Her house is empty, her sophomore sister somehow invited to the senior ski trip, and her mother is on a trip with her book club.

Unsurprisingly, more people than expected show up at her house, everyone inviting their friends and hookups from the club. Somehow, the party devolves into a game of spin the bottle, an uncanny déjà vu that Lacy isn't quite sure how to feel about.

This time, however, she's less self-conscious. She's overheard and sometimes even seen some of these people have sex. Dorm life rarely offers privacy. Hell, people were practically having sex in the club they just left. She refuses to let herself be embarrassed. Actually tries to enjoy the kisses she shares with no shame.

"Now we're talking," Josie giggles as her bottle spins toward Lacy. There's a coy glint in her eye that Lacy's never seen before. "Come here, baby girl."

Josie kisses her like she's been waiting for this moment for a while. Her hand finds Lacy's waist, fingertips slipping slightly beneath her top. Heat spreads between Lacy's legs at the sound of Josie's sighs. It's been a while since she's kissed someone she's genuinely attracted to. She doesn't even realize until now that she's attracted to Josie at all.

A flash goes off. Someone snaps a picture of them with Josie's camera.

Josie immediately pulls away, scolding the culprit. Then, she leans in close and whispers, "Don't worry, babe. I won't let anyone see the picture."

As the party winds down, Josie stays behind. They lounge on the couch, Lacy's head resting on Josie's shoulder. She can't stop thinking about the picture.

Her father had captured photos of her kissing Mina. They were having a sleepover, talking about boys, about kissing, deciding to share their first kiss to avoid the risk of it being with some stinky boy with bad breath. Even after all her other friends had drifted away, Mina had stuck around, defying her parents' wishes. It wasn't until the authorities uncovered pictures of them kissing circulating online that things truly fell apart. No one can forgive a violation like that.

"The film developers will see it."

"Huh?" Josie murmurs, half-asleep.

"You said you wouldn't let anyone see the picture. But the people developing the film will."

"Babe, I develop the film."

That soothes Lacy, only momentarily.

"How?" she asks.

"I'm taking a workshop. Do you really want me to go through the process?"

Lacy nods.

Josie sighs, sitting up and shaking off her drowsiness.

"So, the pictures just hang there in the darkroom for days?" Lacy asks when Josie finishes her impromptu lecture.

Josie nods, groggily settling back onto the couch and pulling Lacy into her arms, snuggling against her neck.

"So... won't the people using the darkroom see it?"

Josie sighs, exasperated. "Yeah, I guess. Lace, there are way worse pictures being developed in there. Some people are straight-up doing boudoir shoots. A picture of us kissing at a party isn't even going to be noticed. Can you stop harping on this? Let's just go to bed."

Lacy hands Josie a new toothbrush, but Josie is too tired to wash up. They crawl into bed, and as Josie wraps her arms around her, Lacy whispers, "Can you...not develop that photo?"

"If it really means that much to you, I won't," Josie reassures her. And as they drift off to sleep, Lacy feels safe in her embrace.

Lacy wakes to the smell of bacon. Wandering into the kitchen, she finds Josie making an extravagant breakfast with whatever was left in the fridge. They spend the day lazing around, watching TV, and venturing out for snacks and weed.

It's Lacy's first time getting high, and it's nothing like being drunk—everything feels expansive, light, and unexpectedly hilarious. The weed blurs the edges of her usual self-consciousness. Or maybe it's just that Josie, usually so brutally honest and direct, is more subdued, too. Her sharp remarks dulled. The world feels softer, more manageable.

One weed-hazy night, they're making out on the couch, and Lacy, emboldened, slips her hand under Josie's shirt, cupping her breast. Josie's moan sends heat pooling between Lacy's legs. Josie takes off her top, and Lacy's mouth finds her nipple. The sounds she elicits from Josie spur her onwards. Josie strips off her bottoms, and Lacy clumsily rubs between her legs, unsure of her movements. Josie takes her hand, steering her motions, until she comes once. Then, she guides Lacy's head down, tells her what to do, how to taste her.

They stumble to the bedroom, where Josie coaxes Lacy's pants off. She spreads Lacy's legs, kneeling between them, and Lacy doesn't need to give her instructions, wouldn't even know how. Josie knows better than her what will make her feel good. Lacy comes undone beneath her. She wonders if this is the night she loses her virginity. Not sure what that night with Gia counts as.

Josie ends up staying the rest of winter break. They spend their nights tangled in each other, Lacy learning new ways to touch and be touched. One evening, they're smoking on the balcony, watching the city flicker to life beneath them. The sound of people talking and laughing begins to fill the air, streetlights buzz, cars blur into long streaks of red and white lights. The high settles over them like a blanket, slowing time, stretching each moment out. They sit together in easy silence until a shiver slips through Lacy, the December night's chill sneaking into her bones.

"I'm gonna take a bath," she tells Josie. The thought of sinking into a pool of heat feels like the exact kind of comfort she needs in this moment.

"Can I come?"

"What?" Lacy blinks, caught off guard.

"Can I take a bath with you?"

She's not sure how to answer. "The tub won't fit us both," is what she settles on.

"That's fine. I didn't really want a bath anyway. I just want to hang out with you in there."

There's something unexpectedly sweet about Josie not wanting to be away from her—not even for something as mundane as a bath. Lacy says yes before she can think better of it, and dread follows right behind her agreement.

Josie helps start the bath while Lacy moves to her room, pretending to gather clothes but really trying to catch her breath. The bathroom feels too bright, too small. She realizes, head heavy from the weed, that she can't do her usual undressing-behind-the-shower-curtain routine since the tub is already filling with water.

"Where are you going?" Josie asks, noticing Lacy beginning to retreat.

"To change in my room."

"Change for your bath? What are you gonna do—put a bathing suit on?"

Hmm, not a bad idea.

Josie catches her considering and gives her a look. "Are you serious?"

"No. I'm just getting a candle," Lacy says quickly, darting back out, shimmying out of her clothes and throwing on her robe.

When she comes back with a candle in hand, Josie is crouched by the tub, trailing her fingers through the water. Lacy shuts off the lights and places the candle on the vanity.

"Spooky," Josie laughs. "Is this how you always take baths?"

Lacy nods. Since her trip to Europe, she'd taken to using the bathroom in the dark, lit only by a candle or the soft glow of her phone screen. The darkness becoming a kind of comfort blanket.

"You getting in?" Josie asks, swishing the water. "I made it nice and warm for you."

Lacy stands there in her robe, frozen. Her chest tightens, breath too shallow. She feels a little light-headed.

"What?" Josie laughs. "Do you want me to close my eyes or something?"

Lacy nods. That would help.

"Oh. You're serious." Josie's smile falters. "I've literally eaten you out," she says, her tone only half-joking. "I think you can take your robe off in front of me. I can barely see you anyway." Josie makes a show of squinting at her in the dim glow of the candle.

She's right, of course. They've done more intimate things. But somehow, standing there naked feels like a different kind of exposure.

Josie rolls her eyes, dramatic now. "Fine." She covers her eyes with her hand, and Lacy dashes across the floor, stepping quickly into the tub, holding her robe out of the water as she slides it off and drapes it over the curtain rod.

When Josie hears the splash of Lacy's body sinking into the water, she peeks, eyes flickering briefly to the dark water, then settling back, staring at the shadows dancing on the wall in front of her.

"Wanna listen to music?" Josie asks.

"Sure," Lacy says.

Josie pulls down Lacy's robe, balls it up behind her head like a pillow, and starts tapping around on her phone. A song begins to play, soft and slow. They sit like that for a while, both high and quiet, letting the music weave between them. When Lacy likes a song, she says so, and Josie tells her the name and artist without looking at her phone, her eyes closed as she leans back against the wall. It's peaceful. Easy. The kind of quiet that asks for nothing. Wrapped in warm water and dim candlelight, Lacy forgets she's naked, her body no longer something to brace against, just another part of the aphotic calm.

When the water cools and Lacy's fingers are pruned, she shuts the curtain and pulls the plug. Reaching for the empty space where her robe was, she remembers Josie still using it as a pillow. Standing in the tub, the water draining around her legs, she asks softly, "Can I have my robe?"

"Come get it," Josie says, not moving from the floor.

Lacy hesitates. She knows Josie isn't being mean. Knows she's just teasing, but still. Her body stiffens. Her heart starts pounding again. She can't open the curtain.

Josie senses it. "Are you going to stay in there all night?"

Lacy doesn't respond.

"Can *I* open the curtain?" Josie asks gently.

Still, Lacy says nothing. Some part of her just wants this to be over, even if that means Josie forcing the curtains open.

Josie peeks through, slowly drawing the curtain back.

Lacy stands there, wet and cold, unsure of how to hold her arms, where to look. Her jaw clenches to stop her teeth from chattering.

Josie doesn't stare. She doesn't look away. She just looks at Lacy. And then wraps the robe around her, tying it gently at the waist. She pats her dry through the fabric and helps her step out of the tub.

She finds Lacy's clean underwear and kneels, holding it open so Lacy can step in. Her movements are slow, careful. Then sweatpants. Then the robe comes undone, and Josie pauses. Her eyes linger for a breath on Lacy's chest before she helps her into a shirt.

"Let's go to bed," Josie says softly.

They wash their faces and brush their teeth together in the lambent glow of the candle.

The next day, when Lacy showers, she steps out onto the bathmat naked. No robe. No rush. No panic. Just water trailing down her skin, steam curling around her like fog. She gets dressed outside the tub.

After a week, Dawna and Sophie are back home and don't seem to mind Josie being around, despite Lacy never actually asking for permission to have her over.

Josie and her sister get along well, bonding over niche films. Sophie is ecstatic to learn Josie is taking a course on horror films, cannot hide her excitement when Josie invites her to sit in on the lectures next semester.

Dawna is relieved to see Lacy have a close friend again. The nagging suspicion that they might be more than friends lingers in the back of her mind, but she pushes it aside. Lacy had only ever dated boys in middle school and high school. Why should she assume any different now?

By the start of the new semester, Lacy and Josie are, for all intents and purposes, a couple, though they've never actually defined it. They spend nearly every free moment together—waiting outside each other's classes, holding hands in public, trading hoodies like borrowed pieces of comfort. No announcement, no conversation, just a soft understanding that this is how things are now.

As summer break approaches, Lacy helps Josie pack her things at the camera club. In a stack of photographs, she finds the picture of them kissing at the party. Multiple copies.

Upon noticing the look of shock on Lacy's face, Josie snatches them away.

"You said you wouldn't."

"Lace, it's not a big deal."

"It is to me."

"Do you know how controlling you're being? Telling me I can't develop my own film? My own photos? I'm in this picture too, you know."

Lacy starts to tear up, and Josie doesn't try to comfort her. Just rolls her eyes, sighing as she leaves the room, leaving Lacy alone in the dim orange glow of the darkroom.

When Lacy finally calms herself, grounding her racing thoughts with a few steady breaths, she steps outside and finds Josie laughing with some friends. Her laughter rings out carefree and effortless. When she spots Lacy, her face lights up. "Hey, come meet my friends from Camera Club," she says, like everything is back to normal, as if the tension between them never existed.

David, a club member, asks if Lacy is into photography too.

"Not really."

"She hates my photography, actually," Josie quips, a sharp edge to her voice.

"That's not true," Lacy murmurs.

"She never lets me take her photo."

"What a shame," David says, his gaze skimming over Lacy, quick but deliberate.

"Tell me about it," Josie says, side-eyeing David. "I have one single photo of her, and she won't even let me show it to anyone."

"You didn't even take that picture," Lacy argues, annoyed.

Josie rolls her eyes. "It's a picture of the two of us, and I'm not even allowed to share it."

"Wait," another guy chimes in. "Is it the one of you two kissing?"

Josie shrugs and nods at the same time.

"I saw it."

"Me too," someone else says.

More people confess to seeing it.

"No fair," David pouts. "I'm the only one who didn't get to see it."

Josie shrugs and puts her hands up, like she has no choice in the matter.

"Aw, come on," David teases. "Let me see."

Everyone stares at Lacy expectantly. It doesn't feel like a choice.

"Whatever," she mutters as she leaves the room.

Even though she hasn't said a word about it, Lacy knows Josie can feel her frustration. It hangs heavy between them, thickening the silence as days pass without a word. Both of them trapped in a miserable stalemate.

Eventually, Josie caves and shows up outside Lacy's building.

"Babe, I know I was being an asshole." Josie's voice is pleading as they sit across from each other in the stiff lobby chairs. "Please stop punishing me."

"I'm not punishing you," Lacy replies, her voice cool, even as her chest aches.

"I know I messed up. I apologized. You can't still be mad at me."

But Josie hasn't apologized. Not really. Hasn't said the words *I'm sorry*—as if the discomfort of her guilt is absolution itself. As if showing up sad earns her forgiveness. And maybe it does. Lacy misses her so much it physically hurts. The pleading in Josie's eyes pulls at something tender. She wants the fight to be over. She's tired. Tired of the ache, the silence, the way everything feels slightly off without Josie in her day.

"Okay..." Lacy sighs, her voice softer now. "Just don't do it again."

And she believes it—or needs to. She tells herself there's no way Josie would do something like this again. Not after this. What harm is there in letting it go? The fight was hurting them both, and she couldn't see the point in holding onto it anymore.

She invites Josie to stay over. Josie offers her an edible, but it hits Lacy too hard, leaving her body sluggish and mind detached.

That night, they have sex, muffling their moans with hands on mouths, the tension of their fight melting away with each touch.

Josie tells Lacy she loves her as she comes on her hand, then says it again after, as if she needs Lacy to know it wasn't just said in the heat of the moment. She *really* means it.

Lacy doesn't say it back. But she feels it, she thinks. And for some reason, she starts to cry after the sex. Maybe from their fight. Maybe from the *I love you*. Maybe from the weed. Maybe all of the above.

Josie holds her, stroking her hair, whispering soft comforts as if she can will Lacy's tears away. The words rest on Lacy's tongue, aching to be spoken. But how can she tell Josie she loves her when she feels such an immense sense of disconnect? How can she expect trust from Josie when she has never fully given herself over?

Maybe it's the edible unwinding her mind, but she takes a deep breath. "I have to tell you something."

She relays the story of her father's crimes, not with many details, just enough for her to understand what transpired. Saying the words aloud is hard enough. Josie's face shifts, stricken with horror as she listens. Josie says sorry, this time with real weight behind it, finally grasping the depth of Lacy's disdain for pictures.

Josie kisses her, then makes love to her again.

As Lacy comes, she almost says it back. Almost.

The school year ends. Lacy assumes Josie will stay over with her again over summer break and is surprised when Josie books a flight home.

At first, they text and call each other every day. But as the weeks drag on, Josie's messages start to dwindle. The three-hour time difference apparently too inconvenient for her. Lacy doesn't fight with her about it.

She spends the summer in a fog of loneliness. In the beginning, she tries to meet up with friends, but as the weeks pass, she slips back into her depressive routine— falling asleep and waking up in front of her laptop, her eyes glazed over whatever's playing. Nothing catches her interest, except the occasional joint on the terrace when no one's home.

In the final weeks of summer, Sophie enlists her older sister's help with a project, a short horror film. Lacy spends her evenings tagging along with her sister and her friends, carrying equipment, props, and costumes while Sophie brings her vision to life.

Sophie is usually behind the camera, but she's confident and unbothered when she has to step in front of it, guiding her actors on where to stand, how to move, giving direction without hesitation. She doesn't flinch when the lens is on her. Lacy can't help but compare herself to her little sister, how strong and brave Sophie is—everything Lacy feels she's not.

When the film is finished, Sophie hosts a small watch party at their place. Lacy is genuinely impressed by what her sister has created. She's proud of Sophie, her voice, her dreams, her creative future luminous. Lacy's own feels dim and uncertain.

$\mathcal{A}$ week later, Anna stops by the store after not hearing back from Sam. She invites him to dinner once his shift is over and waits in her car until he's done.

They end up at a nearby sports bar, and to Sam's surprise, he finds himself enjoying her company. Anna has a way of keeping the conversation flowing, always asking the right questions. When she asks about his parents, Sam is surprised at the quiet gratitude he feels for the opportunity to talk about his mom. It's brief, but it makes her feel a little less gone.

He learns that Anna has a degree in Communications. When he asks what that even means, they share a laugh at her inability to *communicate* a good explanation. He also finds out she once took one of Aunt Sam's Intro to Philosophy classes.

She asks about his schooling, and though she tries to mask it, there's a flicker of surprise when he tells her he isn't in college. When she asks about his plans for the future, she's caught off guard again by his only answer: working at the grocery store. When she asks about his hobbies and he struggles to answer, it dawns on him how pathetic his life has become.

"I used to draw," he says, trying to salvage his response. "And I like to cook," though he isn't sure it counts as a hobby, more of a necessity living with his aunts.

"So, you don't draw anymore?" Anna asks.

"Not really." Just little doodles on shipping invoices when he's bored.

"Why not?"

He shrugs. "Haven't been in the mood."

"What do you like to draw?"

"People, things. Whatever catches my eye."

"Would you draw me?" she asks, beaming.

The words pull him into a memory—warm sand, ocean waves, starry eyes.

As they spend more time together, Sam begins to appreciate Anna's presence in his life. He has no real friends in this city. His coworkers barely count, their interactions confined to working hours. Before Anna, no one had truly made an effort to get to know him. Or maybe he had never really let them.

Vivian had tried, but she lacked Anna's persistence. He's a tough oyster to crack, and honestly, he doubts there's even a pearl worth finding.

One night, Anna invites him to go to a trivia night at the sports bar. Sam waits outside the store, chatting with

Vivian on her smoke break. Anna pulls up, and Sam doesn't notice the flicker of disappointment in Vivian's eyes when she sees Anna. Vivian stubs out her cigarette and gives him a lingering hug before heading back into the store.

"Who was that?" Anna asks, voice curt as he gets into the passenger seat, her gaze fixed ahead.

"Vivian."

"You guys seem close."

"She works cash."

Anna nods. "Are you guys close?"

Sam shrugs. "I don't know." They don't talk often, just here and there at work. He slept with her a few times. Did that make them close? "Why are you asking?"

Anna shrugs, saying nothing.

Her energy is off all night. She's quieter than usual, distant, distracted.

"Is everything okay?" he asks after trivia. They lost.

She nods, avoiding his eyes.

"Okay."

She drives him back home, and just as he reaches for the door handle, she blurts, "I didn't realize you were talking to other girls."

What? Is she jealous? Sam had always taken her flirty jabs as playful banter. She is nine years older than him, currently interviewing for corporate jobs, and looking for an apartment. Their lives are in totally different places. Had he been misinterpreting their time together all along?

Seeing the confusion on his face, Anna lets out a nervous laugh. "Sorry! Just kidding. Ignore what I said."

"Do you *like* me?" he asks, genuinely surprised.

Anna is quiet for a long moment before finally nodding. "Do you?"

She's cute, but he never considered her in a romantic light. Sort of saw her as an older sister figure since she used to be his babysitter. He feels put on the spot, unsure how to answer.

"Oh my god," she groans, covering her face. "I misread this whole thing. This is so embarrassing."

"Hey. No. It's fine," he reassures her. "I just... didn't realize you felt that way. We could give it a try, I guess. Go on a date or something."

"So, these haven't even been dates to you?" she whimpers.

He stays in the car with her for a while, comforting her, his words practiced from the hours spent helping his mother work through her low points. Slowly, Anna begins to calm down. By the time they part ways, they've set up a proper date for the weekend.

As he steps out of the car, Sam feels a little uncertain. A little confused.

✦

Lacy is eager to be reunited with Josie at the start of their third year. She meets her at her new place in Chinatown, just a short distance from campus. This year, Josie had found a room up for rent in an apartment above a bakery, sharing the space with two other students, Lauren and Becca.

One of her roommates is leaving the house when Lacy arrives at the door. Lauren is in her senior year, athletic looking, with a confident ease about her. She leads Lacy up a narrow staircase to Josie's room.

After so many months apart, Josie's face lights up with a wide grin the moment she sees Lacy. She leaps from the floor, where she had been unpacking her suitcase, and practically tackles her, tumbling them onto the bed. With a swift kick, the door clicks shut behind them, and they're wrapped in each other's arms, laughing, kissing, their hands like roaming explorers reacquainting themselves with familiar landscapes, falling into the rhythm of their desires, longing and relief colliding.

Josie, undeclared for the past two years, has finally settled on Psychology as her major. Lacy is focusing on English and History this semester. Much to their disappointment, they don't share many classes this year.

With both of them buried in coursework, they don't see each other as often. Still, Lacy devotes most of her free time to Josie. The few friendships she once had faded into casual acquaintances, reduced to passing smiles and brief nods.

They spend most of their time at Josie's place, hanging out with her roommates. Lacy likes them. They're easy to be around, low maintenance in a way that makes socializing feel facile. She watches as Josie grows closer to them, their inside jokes bubbling into laughter and shared glances. Lacy is glad to see Josie settle into this little makeshift family. She's heard enough horror stories about roommate drama to know how rare this is.

They'd made plans to escape to Blue Mountain for their anniversary over winter break, but Josie falls sick and has to call off the trip.

That night, Lacy decides to surprise her, showing up at her house with Buckley's, orange juice, and a tub of phở.

She texts Josie to let her know she's outside. No reply. She calls. No answer.

Lacy glances up at the apartment. Josie has to be home. She's sick, after all.

The apartment sits on the upper floor, its entrance a small, unmarked door tucked next to the bakery. There's no doorbell, no knocker. Guests have to call or text to be let in. Josie still isn't answering, and Lacy doesn't have her roommates' numbers.

Her eyes drift to the fire escape in the alley, its metal stairs leading up to the second floor. She hesitates for a moment, weighing how creepy letting herself in through a window would be. She decides she cares more about seeing her girlfriend than about how she's perceived.

She's halfway up the stairs when she sees them.

The curtains in Lauren's room are drawn, but they're too short, leaving a gap at the bottom of the window. It's just enough for Lacy to see inside, to catch a perfect, gut-wrenching view of her bed.

Josie—naked, sprawled on the mattress. Her head thrown back in a vision of pure ecstasy. Her legs are bent at the knees, spread open. Lauren's face buried between her thighs, one hand reaching up, playing with her breasts.

Lacy watches, her heart plunging into her stomach, a pit sinking deep and twisting. There's also something else, more disturbing, low beneath her stomach, a disturbing pulse of arousal at the sight of them together.

As if sensing her, Josie's head snaps toward the window. Their eyes lock. Panic briefly floods into Josie's face.

Lauren, noticing Josie's sudden stiffness, lifts her head and says something to her.

Josie's attention flickers back to Lauren, her expression smoothing over as if nothing happened. She strokes Lauren's hair, offers a reassuring nod, then tilts her head back against the pillow, pushing Lauren's head further into her for more pressure.

Like she never saw Lacy at all.

Lacy stands frozen on the steps, gripping the takeout bag so tightly her knuckles turn white. She watches a little longer, sees the familiar way Josie touches Lauren, the way she strokes her hair, weaving her fingers into it, rubs her ear, the same things she does to Lacy.

A sickening wave rolls through her, and she's not sure if she wants to scream or cry. Should she bang on the glass? Storm in? Demand an explanation?

But Josie saw her. Met her eyes.

Didn't care.

Lacy can't breathe. Her chest tightens, her vision blurring as she stumbles down the fire escape, bolting out of the alley and onto the sidewalk, the cold night air crisp against her skin. The image burns behind her eyes, and she squeezes them shut, as if she could erase what she's just seen.

That night, she lies in bed, replaying the scene over and over, her stomach twisting in on itself. The pain, a sharp churning thing that makes her curl into herself and sob into her pillow.

She hears a soft knock on her door.

She doesn't answer.

Another.

"Are you okay?" her sister whispers from the other side.

Lacy wipes her face and opens the door.

Sophie takes in her swollen eyes, puffy face, and tear-streaked cheeks, barely holding it together. "What happened?"

Lacy tells her everything. She had never talked about her relationship with Josie with anyone before, but now she unspools their story to Sophie. From spin the bottle to what just happened tonight.

When she's finished, Sophie's expression hardens. "What a fucking bitch," Sophie spits, teasing a sad chuckle from her sister. Lacy had never heard her little sister swear before.

Sophie stays with her that night, listening as Lacy unpacks the night from different angles, her emotions shifting with each retelling. She falls asleep to Sophie's gentle hand rubbing her back.

In the morning, Lacy wakes up to a text from Josie: Sorry didn't see this! Was sleeping.

Lacy stares at the message, astounded that she's pretending nothing happened.

She leaves Josie on read.

Josie calls an hour later. Lacy doesn't pick up. Josie keeps calling. Lacy continues to ignore her.

The next morning, Josie shows up at her door. Sophie answers, unimpressed, and shuts it in her face before telling Lacy.

The heat of Sophie's disapproving glare burns into her as she accepts the bag of buns Josie has brought—her favourite. Josie stands at the door, smiling like nothing's wrong, ready to walk her to school. Her calm smile and casual disposition leave Lacy speechless. She should be yelling. Screaming in her face. But her voice stays lodged in her throat. Had she hallucinated what she saw last night? She can't find the words she wants to say to Josie—the shape of her hurt amorphous on her tongue. Her mouth moves on autopilot, answering Josie's casual questions like a well-trained muscle, fluent in the language of appeasement.

Unable to withstand the weight of Sophie's silent judgment, that fact she's even entertaining this, she rushes out the door with Josie, heart pounding, guilt nipping at her heels.

Josie is extra affectionate, rubbing circles into Lacy's palm as they walk. She stops at their favorite café, orders Lacy's favourite drink.

Lacy doesn't know how to process Josie's preposterous behaviour. She's still reeling from what Josie did, drowning in grief, but she also craves her affection, covets her attention. None of it makes sense.

Josie waits for her outside each of her classes, bringing small treats, walking her to and from lectures. By the end of the day, when Josie suggests dinner, Lacy doesn't refuse.

She tells herself she'll bring it up. She'll confront her.

But she doesn't.

As she sits across from Josie over a bowl of phở, Lacy can't quite find the irony. Josie slurps her soup between effortless chatter, not letting a single stretch of silence settle between them. Lacy replies only when she has to, when a direct question is asked and silence feels too awkward to bear.

While Josie launches into a detailed retelling of a debate she had with some boy in her tutorial, Lacy studies her face, trying to reconcile it with the look she'd seen last night—blank and detached. Had she imagined it? Had she invented that flicker of recognition, followed by the complete absence of it? If Josie hadn't seen her, doesn't know that Lacy knows, then she's hiding a secret. If she *had* seen her, maybe she didn't think she was doing anything wrong. They never formally defined their relationship. Maybe they aren't even exclusive. Maybe this whole time, sleeping with other people has been fine with Josie. But she tells Lacy everything. That much is clear in the precision with which she recounts her arguments, her lectures, even the throwaway details of her day. How could she not say a word about *Lauren*? Holding the shape of that name in her mind sends a pang through her.

By the time Josie finishes her bowl, Lacy's is practically untouched. She's lost her appetite, stomach full from the pit of misery she swallowed last night.

On the way home, Lacy watches Josie on the subway, chatting easily with a stranger. So charismatic. So effortlessly sociable. Lacy could never do that—strike up a conversation like it's nothing. She thinks about all the things she admires in Josie: her boldness, her brutal honesty, the way she fully embodies herself. Josie is everything Lacy wants, and everything she wants to be.

The closer she gets to her stop, the easier it feels to pretend nothing happened. If Josie did see her and didn't think twice about it, then she wouldn't either. If Josie *didn't* see her and is keeping a secret, Lacy would keep it too. It's easier this way. She doesn't want to lose her. She can just tuck this thought away. She's had plenty of practice.

Being apart at home, it eats at her—the image of Josie and L****n looping relentlessly in her mind. Unanswered questions circling—had this been their first time? When did they first kiss? How long has this been going on? She imagines each moment that must have led to it, the flirting, lingering touches, the decision to finally cross the line. Her stomach churns. What if they're doing it right now? They could be. They live together.

She paces her room, pulse hammering. Finally, she calls.

Josie answers, and relief floods her so intensely she almost cries out. She asks Josie to come over. Josie agrees with no hesitation.

That night, they have sex. And the entire time, Lacy sees *them* in her head. She is distracted by self-conscious thoughts, wonders if she's doing a bad job, if L****n is better at this than she is, if she has a better body—more toned, nimble, graceful. She notices Josie trying new things. Knowing where she must have learned these moves from makes her stomach turn.

A sudden horror claws its way into her mind. What if Josie is sleeping with more people? How many people is she sharing a bed with?

Josie's fingers trail along her spine like they always do—slow, familiar, seeking. Instead of comfort, the touch unsettles her. She thinks of Gia's hands on her, how soft they'd been, how sure. How her body had betrayed her, falling quiet and still, compliant. Her mind hovering somewhere above it all, watching as her boundaries blurred beneath the weight of arousal, fear, and disgust. The same sensation rises in her now, that scrambled, choking confusion. She can't tell what she's feeling, can't sort through it fast enough. She squeezes her eyes shut. Just lets it happen.

As Josie falls asleep beside her, Lacy lies staring at the ceiling, gut twisting with a guilt-stained shame. Through the wall they share, she can almost feel Sophie's disapproval pulsing like a low frequency.

It's uncomfortable being here, but the thought of running into L****n at Josie's place makes her skin cold. She hasn't set foot in that house since the night it happened. And over the next few weeks, Josie doesn't invite her over, and Lacy doesn't ask why. The unspoken truth, an immovable weight between them.

They spend most of their time at school or in Lacy's room, where Josie's presence feels at once too much and not enough. Sophie says nothing, but her rancour is palpable. Every time Josie and Lacy pass her, Sophie's eyes flick to her sister's face, scanning for some shred of self-respect. When Lacy grabs her coat to head out, no doubt with Josie, since she has no one else, Sophie watches. No questions. No arguments.

They're not needed.

Lacy already knows what this looks like. She had cried in her sister's arms over Josie's betrayal. And yet, here she is. Still reaching for someone who hasn't chosen her, not fully, not honestly. No apology. No accountability.

She is painfully aware of how pathetic she is.

*A*nna's resolve in spending time with him is unavoidable. Sam finds himself drawn to her easy dependability. Without much effort on his part, he somehow ends up in a relationship. He likes spending time with her, never feels the need to turn down her invitations. She doesn't seem to mind his lack of initiative, always the one planning their dates and steering their relationship forward.

At her request—a reasonable one, he thinks—he stops spending time with Vivian. He and Anna have yet to have a serious conversation about their relationship status, but when Anna ran into some friends at the movies last week, she introduced him as her boyfriend, and it was settled.

A few weeks into their courtship, Anna asks if she can meet his aunts. He can't think of a reason to say no, so he invites her to join them for dinner one evening.

Aunt Sam and Jackie greet her warmly. They trade school stories, laughing over shared experiences from opposite sides of the classroom. The conversation flows easily until they find out she's nearly a decade older than him. Sam feels a subtle shift in the room's energy, a knot of anxiety tightening in his chest. He notices how their smiles no longer reach their eyes, how they avoid meeting hers, how their questions turn more measured, more cautious.

At breakfast the next morning, after a stretch of silence, they bring Anna up, casually, as if in passing. They frame their concern as curiosity, but the judgment in their tone is unmistakable.

"Isn't she too old for you?" Aunt Sam says, her tone more like a statement than a question.

"I don't know," he shrugs. "It doesn't feel like she is."

"Do you feel good around her?" Auntie Jackie asks.

He shrugs again. They've only just started dating. He hasn't had a girlfriend since sophomore year of high school. He's not even sure what "feeling good" is supposed to feel like. A flash of memory surfaces, an Italian summer, the last time he was certain he felt good around someone new. Being with Anna feels nice most of the time. Isn't that enough? "It doesn't feel bad," he offers.

"Do you really like her? Or is it more of a physical connection you share?" Auntie Jackie presses.

He groans at the implication. "We haven't even done anything yet."

"But you plan to?" Aunt Sam asks.

"Probably?" he mutters, discomfort growing. He never had these kinds of conversations with his parents. Having them with his aunts feels infinitely more awkward. "Can we stop talking about this?"

His aunts exchange a look, some unspoken communication passing through the thread of their connection.

"Okay," Aunt Sam relents. "But you have to promise to keep us in the loop."

He agrees, though he's not entirely sure what "keeping them in the loop" means. Is he supposed to update them after their first kiss? Their first fuck? No way. He will not be doing that.

For Christmas, his aunts gift him a laptop. It feels extravagant, too expensive, leaving him with an awkward sense of indebtedness. To balance the scales, he surprises them with a new TV on Boxing Day.

A few months later, for his birthday, they give him a drawing tablet, encouraging him to rediscover his love of making art.

It works.

It's been a long time since he's drawn. The learning curve of digital art provides a welcome challenge in his otherwise uneventful life. He scans illustrations from his old sketchbooks, learns how to enhance and color them digitally. His passion for art reignites, and he begins sharing his creations on ArtStation.

To his surprise, his drawings start to gain traction online, slowly building him a small but dedicated following.

Anna isn't thrilled by this development. She grows dismayed as he spends more time at home, absorbed in his creative pursuits. Determined to connect with his newfound passion, she scours the web for interesting artwork to share with him, positioning herself as an expert. She's a surprisingly good curator, always finding ways to inspire him, introducing him to new artists and innovative techniques.

One day, she shows him an animated YouTube series that blends watercolor paintings, stop motion, and 3D modeling. He's instantly captivated by the mixed-media art style and begins experimenting with it in his work.

His profile explodes when he starts creating fan art for the show, carving out a niche that quickly draws attention. At first, it feels surreal—watching his follower count tick upward, strangers talking about and sharing his work. They talk about his unconventional use of color, his interpretations of character moments, the tiny details he thought only he noticed. He stays up late scrolling through comments, stunned that people care this much about something he made.

As his audience grows, so does his sense of purpose. For the first time in years, he wakes up with something to look forward to—an idea he wants to sketch, a color palette he wants to play with. The creative apathy that once hung over him like a low fog begins to lift, replaced by a drive he didn't know he had in him.

His inbox fills with requests: people want to buy art prints, download his custom brushes, commission pieces in his style. He sets up an online store, not believing people would actually buy anything, but the orders come in faster than he can keep up.

The ripples become waves. His page rises to the top of the platform, drawing attention from companies—big and small—who want to collaborate with him, pay him.

Then the message arrives—from the creator of the animated series, Paul. He's seen his work. Loves his take on the characters. Would he be interested in guest-drawing a segment for an upcoming episode?

Sam stares at the email for a long time, barely breathing. It's something deeper than validation. Like he's been seen. like the things he's been shouting into the void had been echoing back the whole time.

He quits his job at the supermarket to focus entirely on his art career.

Art career. He laughs at the thought, marveling at how real it's become. He remembers Lacy urging him to do this, share his art online, make a living from it. He wishes he could tell her now that he's figured out how.

For a month, Sam collaborates virtually with Paul and a few members of his studio in Canada. It's his first real experience collaborating with other artists, and he loves it. The energy of tossing around an idea, watching it catch fire, everyone building on it with their own skills. It's electric and deeply satisfying, clicking in a way that makes him crave more.

The success of his guest episode brings even more exposure, along with steady passive income. He and Paul keep in touch after the project wraps. The texts grow more frequent, the conversations more personal. What started as a shared creative spark slowly turns into a genuine friendship.

A few weeks later, Paul calls out of the blue. He confides in Sam about a secret project he's spearheading—an animated movie adaptation of a cult-classic science fantasy series from the eighties. Curious, Sam dives into the novels, and just as Paul predicted, he becomes completely obsessed. It's a clever lure, Paul's way of roping him in for the project.

"I really loved working with you," Paul says on a video call. "It was just one episode, but it was epic seeing you in your element. You're talented, hardworking, and you've got a hell of a creative eye. I want us to work together again. Please sign on."

Sam wants to say yes. It's his dream job, handed to him on a silver platter. But joining the project means moving to Montreal. The idea of leaving everything behind and starting fresh in a new country is equal parts thrilling and terrifying. His life already feels small, with so few people who truly matter to him. Why leave them behind only to be completely alone in a new city?

He asks his aunts for advice, and their reaction is pure delight, brimming with ecstatic pride for their nephew. It doesn't even occur to them as an option to weigh. They talk about it as if it's a foregone conclusion, like he's already accepted the job, chattering excitedly about his move, mapping out the details, planning their visits as they reminisce on their fond memories of Montreal, a city they adore.

Talking to Anna about it, however, is a different story.

When he shares the opportunity with her, he's met with neither pride nor excitement. Instead, she sulks, unable to see past the unbearable distance that would stretch between them. She reminds him of the stability he has in Columbus, emphasizing what he'd be risking by leaving her, his aunts, and the life they've built here. The conversation only serves to exacerbate his anxieties.

He has a meeting with Paul to discuss the details. They'd cover his moving expenses, help him find a place, and support him as he settles into the role. The salary they negotiate is higher than anything he's ever earned before. It all feels too good to be true. Sam asks for a few days to decide, needing time to sit with the weight of his decision.

Anna, meanwhile, gives him the cold shoulder, offended that he's even considering it so seriously, that he's so willing to entertain the idea of abandoning her.

Strangely, it's Lacy who surfaces in his thoughts as he meditates on his decision. He remembers her words about singing his song, about how, if he sang loud enough, the right people would hear it. And now, they have.

He signs the contract.

Dreading Anna's reaction, he cowardly avoids telling her for a few days, knowing she'll make it about herself and taint what should be a proud achievement. When she finally finds out, she ices him out completely. But as the days pass, she thaws, not wanting to waste the little time they have left together.

She spends every day with him, staying over at his aunts' house, much to their chagrin. Her presence makes his packing and preparations more stressful, his excitement for his adventure ahead tinged with guilt. He tries to reassure her, selling her on the perks of long distance: She could visit anytime. They'd have a new city to explore together.

All the while, he can feel his aunts' disapproval of Anna's behavior and the distinct lack of support she provides him. They want to talk with him about it, but Anna is a constant shadow, leaving few chances for private talks.

✦

As the school year draws to a close, Josie plans to host a party at her place. Lacy is faced with the choice of seeing Lauren or forgoing the party altogether. Neither option appealing.

When Josie asks her to come early to help with setting up, Lacy agrees, dreading the prospect of spending intimate time with both Josie and Lauren. To her relief, Lauren isn't home when she arrives, and Lacy can't help but wonder if Josie would have extended the same invitation had Lauren been home.

The party is lively. Brimming with students eager to squeeze in one last bout of post-secondary degeneracy before summer break. Lacy mingles with some of Josie's friends she's never met before. When they ask how she knows Josie, she feels a quiet sting of disappointment. Clearly, her name does not come up in conversations. She knows she can't fault Josie entirely. She's never spoken much about her either. It's hard to define what they are, especially in front of strangers. They've never called each other girlfriends, and the idea of introducing herself that way now feels embarrassing, given how little these people seem to know about her existence.

Josie is doting and attentive throughout the party, their connection clear and comforting. It offers some solace, even if the questions linger.

Midway through the evening, Lauren returns home with a boy in tow. Lacy doesn't miss the way Josie's gaze follows them as they weave through the crowd. For the most part, Lacy and Lauren avoid each other, tension lingering, a faint unspoken current.

Later, they join a group playing a lewd party game in the living room. Lacy and Josie sit together, watching the game unfold, Josie's head resting on Lacy's shoulder, her arm draped around her waist. When Lauren asks to join the game with her date, Josie's posture subtly shifts, her head lifting from Lacy's shoulder, grip on her waist slackening. Lacy catches the fleeting glance exchanged between Josie and Lauren.

Without asking, Josie inserts herself in the game on someone else's turn, her voice growing louder, her laughter more pronounced. Lacy can't ignore the way Josie seems to be putting on a show, vying for Lauren's attention. What irks her more is Lauren's apparent indifference, her focus seemingly fixed on the boy at her side, which Lacy knows only further fuels Josie's desperate peacocking, each exaggerated laugh and animated remark a silent bid for Lauren's attention.

Josie launches into a story about an accident she witnessed the previous night, and Lacy notices something she hadn't before, the way Josie always specifies the ethnicities of the people in her stories, unless they're white. Lacy listens intently, trying to discern the relevance of these details, and finds none.

"The driver was this Asian lady, and she hit this Black guy delivering food on his bike," Josie recounts, her tone animated. "She gets out of the car and starts arguing with him, as if he's the one at fault, even though she's the one who doesn't know how to drive. It caused this huge traffic jam, and then the driver behind her had to step in to mediate, and she just unleashes on this guy..."

Lacy studies Josie under this new, less flattering light, unable to overlook her obnoxious, attention-seeking behaviour. A wave of discomfort washes over her, a quiet revulsion she can't quite shake.

When Lauren laughs at some part of Josie's story, Lacy notices the quirk of satisfaction in Josie's smile. Their eyes meet again, this time holding a moment too long, some silent communication that leaves her unsettled.

Unable to conceal her jealousy and unwilling to give either of them the satisfaction of seeing her rattled, *if they even care*, Lacy retreats to the kitchen for a glass of water. She lingers there, striking up conversations with strangers in a manic, overly friendly manner. Her anger propels her into a dissociative state, her laughter too quick, her words too eager. The man she's speaking to seems flattered by her attention, oblivious to her perfervid state. In her periphery, she catches Josie watching her. Someone turns up the music, the man leans in close to say something to her, his face inches from hers. Lacy doesn't register his words but pulls him closer, her gaze fixed on Josie, who is still watching. The flicker of jealousy on Josie's face offers Lacy a fleeting sense of vindication.

At that moment, Lauren rises and takes a seat beside Josie, reclaiming her attention.

Trapped in the kitchen, Lacy feels too self-conscious to return to Josie now that Lauren is by her side, doesn't want to intrude, force herself into their dynamic.

Then, David from Camera Club walks in, his face lighting up at the sight of her. He greets her with a warm hug, as if they're old friends. Josie's eyes are on her again, and Lacy feels herself slipping into that familiar state of dissociation, her laughter too loud, her demeanor frenetic.

As David prattles on about his plans to backpack through Asia, Lacy's gaze drifts back to Josie and Lauren. They've moved closer, their heads bent together in quiet conspiracy, their laughter soft and private. Josie places a hand on Lauren's thigh, and Lauren covers it with her own. The sight sends a surge of anger coursing through Lacy. How can they be so brazen?

Eventually, Josie and Lauren rise and head toward the hallway. Desperate to keep them in her sights, Lacy repositions herself behind David, her eyes fixed on their retreating figures. David, heedless of her disregard, continues his monologue.

Josie and Lauren linger in the hallway, their casual ease betraying a deeper intimacy. The quiet familiarity in the way they are standing together, a closeness born from living together, shared routines, and private moments, only deepens Lacy's anguish. When someone exits the bathroom, the two slip inside, to no one's notice but hers.

Something inside Lacy finally snaps. The drive to hold onto Josie evaporates, as though she needed one final act of disrespect to break free from the spell she'd been under. She stares at the closed bathroom door, torn between confronting them and simply walking away. A part of her wants to make a scene, to finally demand answers, retribution even. But the quieter, more familiar part of her just wants to disappear, fade from Josie's life without a word. Just as Lacy had never been granted an apology, Josie did not deserve an explanation.

"Hey, are you okay?" David asks, finally noticing her distracted state.

Lacy nods, her voice steady. "Want to get out of here?"

*I*t had somehow slipped Sam's mind that Montreal is a francophone city. He should have started learning French earlier, but he spends his free time now studying it, fumbling through language apps and scribbling down words in a notebook. It's a quiet effort, but one that makes him feel like he's expanding—becoming someone new, someone who belongs in this city, like he's stepping into a wider version of himself.

Working with Paul and his team in person feels like a dream. Paul has curated a crew that thrives under his leadership—clear communication, honest expectations, and a steady stream of enthusiasm, especially for ideas that seem impossible to execute. The team is small, the budget tight, which makes Sam feel even more indebted to Paul. HR had gone out of their way to make Sam's transition smooth. They covered his flight, moving expenses, and even the first few months of rent for a furnished apartment near the studio. For the first time in his life, Sam doesn't have to worry about money. He'd built up savings while living with his aunts, and he is okay. More than okay. Still, he can't shake the feeling that he owes Paul something. Some part of him keeps waiting for the other shoe to drop.

He makes up for it with his commitment to the project. He and the team always willing to work overtime because they believe in the vision. There's a kind of intimacy that forms in that shared dedication, and Sam finds himself drawing strength from it.

He commits almost all his days at the studio, often returning home exhausted, but it's the good kind of tired. The kind that comes from pouring all of yourself into something you care about with all your heart.

His first two months in Montreal are more fun than he expected. He becomes fast friends with his coworkers—everyone is passionate about art and animation, so there's always something to connect on beyond the project itself. His friendship with Paul deepens in proximity. Their once-digital rapport translates seamlessly in person. Sam gets along with most people, but it's rare that he really *clicks* with someone, rare he feels that pull to be around them constantly. That's how it is with Paul. He finds himself energized by their conversations, by how seen and challenged he feels in Paul's presence.

They work together all day, and most nights, they hang out after. Sometimes other coworkers join for drinks. Other times, Paul invites Sam over for dinner with his wife, Celeste—a kindergarten teacher with the calming energy of someone who's spent years learning how to soothe small storms. Her presence is grounding.

Paul, a true cinephile, introduces Sam to films he's never heard of before, broadening his understanding of storytelling, character design, and cinematography. These new perspectives are already enhancing his skills at work, refining his eye for detail in ways he hadn't expected. The line between work and life blurs, and for once, that doesn't feel like a bad thing.

For the first time in a long time, Sam feels his life stretching outward, growing in unexpected directions. The boundaries of who he believed himself to be begin to blur, not in a disorienting way, but in a way that feels liberating. His social confidence unfolds naturally, like something dormant waking up. His artistic voice sharpens, influenced by the people around him and the energy they all share. His connection to Paul and Celeste grows, finding a closeness he hasn't had in a while, an easy comfort he didn't realize he'd been missing. There's a lightness to him now, a widening inside his chest, like he's making space for a new version of himself.

And in all of this—new job, new friends, a new city, a sense of belonging—he knows he's been neglecting his relationship with Anna. He still calls her every night before bed, but he hasn't kept up with the level of texting she asked for. She'd been honest with him about her needs, asked that he message her every couple of hours, something that had seemed reasonable at the time, but now keeps slipping his mind. His guilt is like a slow leak, quietly eroding his peace.

Their calls turn tense. The nightly check-ins often end in arguments. Anna accuses him of not caring, of forgetting her too easily. When he tries to talk about his new life—his excitement, his friends, his job—she grows quiet or defensive. Every new name he mentions sounds to her like a threat, a potential replacement. He wants to reassure her but finds himself resenting how small her doubts make his world feel.

Sam is at a flea market, looking for pieces that might make his apartment feel more like home—a reflection of who he's becoming. He's inspecting a large grandfather clock when his phone buzzes.

"What do you mean, you're here?"

"I'm outside your apartment!"

He drives home with the clock awkwardly shoved in the back seat. His heart pounds the entire way back, torn between surprise and unease. When he pulls up, he sees Anna waiting by the entrance with three bags in tow, waving excitedly.

He can't quite explain the mixture of comfort and dread that floods him at the sight of her. He's missed her, missed home, missed his aunts, and seeing her now feels like a gift, a piece of familiarity. But judging by her luggage, she isn't here for a quick visit.

He's happy to have time with her, to hold her again, to share his world in person. But beneath that is the awareness that his rhythm will be disrupted. He's had the freedom to work late, to follow his creative whims, to lose himself in flow. Anna won't be okay with that, not when she's come all this way.

He wishes she had told him she was coming. But then again, he had told her she could visit anytime.

And now, here she is.

And he doesn't know what to do with the way that makes him feel.

As expected, his performance at work begins to slip. He contributes less in meetings, no longer stays as late as his colleagues, always rushing home to be with Anna, a candle burning at both ends.

Three months pass, and Anna is still staying with him. Her vacation days hadn't been approved before she left, and she was fired unceremoniously via email a week into her visit. With no job to return to, she's extended her stay indefinitely.

Sam's salary is enough to cover both of their expenses, but her lack of urgency to find a new job unsettles him. She's taken on most of the domestic chores at home and often surprises him with his favorite treats from the market. He convinces himself that it balances out. That things aren't so bad.

His aunts visit for a week, but the trip is slightly soured by Anna's insistence on joining every plan. Aunt Sam, tired of accommodating her, snaps one night before dinner, pleading for a moment alone with her nephew. Sam is different when Anna is around, quieter, his mind preoccupied with tending to her, ensuring she's okay, rarely able to fully be present. Anna doesn't join them that night, but the atmosphere of the dinner is spoiled by the awkward tension. His aunts try to broach the subject of his relationship, voicing their concerns about her unemployment and their fear that she might overstay her visa. They bring up the age difference again, pointing out the discomfort they feel seeing an older woman rely so heavily on him, both emotionally and financially.

"How long are you planning to stay?" Sam asks Anna one night in bed, after she's given him a hand job.

She's offended by the question and its timing. "What? You want me gone?"

The night ends in argument, though Sam eventually placates her with apologies and make-up sex.

As Anna begins to fill more of his time, Sam starts turning down after-work drinks with coworkers. His budding friendships begin to fray—especially his bond with Paul, who grows increasingly frustrated. It's not just Sam's fading energy at work; it's the growing space between them. Sam feels the guilt of it but knows he'd feel worse if Anna thought he was choosing others over her. With her visa nearing its end, he resolves to retreat into their cocoon for the rest of her stay.

The house feels empty when Anna finally leaves.

But in her absence, something returns. His drive to work. His social life. He reconnects with friends. He, Paul, and Celeste start a standing Friday movie night, gradually forming their own little movie club.

Four months later, Anna announces she's coming back to Montreal. She'd applied to a college in the city without telling him, secured a student visa, and made the move official.

It's no question that she'll move in. And while Sam is excited to have his girlfriend close again, there's a sense of trepidation about living together he can't quite ignore. He confides in Paul, whose long-term relationship with Celeste remains the most solid one he's ever witnessed— aside from his aunts'. Paul listens as Sam voices his concerns, encouraging him to have a serious conversation with Anna, warning that unresolved issues only fester under the same roof. Paul also gently reminds Sam of how much he'd pulled away the last time Anna stayed, urging him not to let that happen again, how hard that was to watch, how much their friendship means to him.

"Anna," he repeats, voice solemn, her back turned to him on the couch. She doesn't respond. Just stares out the window, eyes hard and distant.

Sam always dreads this part. The silence, the withdrawal, the creeping anxiety in his chest. He can never name the feeling exactly. Humiliation? Fear? Resentment? A muddy combination of all three?

"Please just look at me."

Anna doesn't. "Did you even think about how I'd feel when you brought this up?"

"Of course I did."

She scoffs.

"I'm always thinking about how you feel. I didn't mean to hurt you. I just wanted to take a moment to tell you about how *I'm* feeling about all this."

"Do you have any idea what I went through to get my visa?" she snaps, finally turning to face him, disbelief like venom in her throat. "The hoops I had to jump through? I did that for you. *For us.* The only thing that kept me going was thinking about *your* feelings."

This is how their fights always go. First the silence. Then the flood.

"I thought maybe, on our first night back together, you'd be happy to see me. That maybe we'd go out, celebrate or something. Instead, I'm hit with all your concerns about how I'm getting in the way of your work. Like I'm some distraction. A burden. An annoying child who needs scolding."

"That's not what I said," he says, trying to keep calm.

"I know your work matters," she continues, words overlapping his. "I was reminded every time we were apart when I barely heard from you. And now I'm here and I still can't get one night where work doesn't come first. How do you think that feels?"

Sam breathes in slowly. "This is why I brought this up. I don't want you to feel like I'm choosing work over you. I'm doing my best to balance both."

"Well, your best doesn't cut it."

"Anna," he huffs. "This is my dream job. I never even thought I could dream of anything before. I'm proud of what I'm doing. I won't apologize for that."

"Oh, I see," she says, rolling her eyes. "I'm just the poison in your perfect dream life. Sorry I came."

"Anna, please," Sam says, voice thinning with exhaustion. "All I wanted was to talk about how important work is to me. And my friendships. Not more than you—just... alongside you. I need you to understand that."

"Obviously, I understand that. I'm not a child."

"I didn't say you were," he sighs. "Forget it. I'm sorry I brought it up."

Something in his voice softens her. The defeat in it. The way his shoulders slump.

"No, go on," she says, quieter now.

"I just... I don't want to feel guilty for caring about my work and my friends."

"I don't make you feel guilty."

"You do, Anna. You twist my priorities into proof that I don't love you enough. I get anxious every time I stay late at the office or make plans with people, because I know you'll take it personally. So, I don't. I end up sacrificing so many things just to avoid *this*." He gestures towards the charged space between them. "It's taking a toll on me."

Silence settles between them. Anna stares down at her lap. Her mind fixates on one thing: he prioritizes work and his friends over her. She doesn't say it. Bites her tongue. Knows this is exactly what he's talking about. She's doing it again.

"Something has to change." There's no anger in it, just a quiet finality. "I can't keep doing this."

Panic coils in her chest. The fear she tries to bury roars to the surface.

She knows this pattern too well. The slow unraveling. She doesn't want to lose him. She wants to change. Really. Her fear of being left behind is often louder than reason. It gnaws at her, convinces her that any distance, any delay, is proof she's unlovable. But for the first time, his words break through the fog. She sees how much he's been carrying. And she hates it. Hates that her presence feels like pressure instead of peace. That she brings strain instead of solace.

She wants to be better. For him.

✦

Over the summer, Lacy begins to spend more time with David. His attention serves as a balm to her heartache, steady and affirming. He cancels his Asia trip to be with her, and his genuine interest is a comforting distraction, even if she isn't entirely sure what to make of their connection.

Though she can't pinpoint when or how it happened, she somehow finds herself in a relationship with him by the start of her final year of university. David invites her to his family home in The Bridle Path for Christmas dinner, introduces her to his family as his girlfriend, and she doesn't correct him. That acknowledgment is the closest they come to having a formal discussion about labels.

David's world quickly becomes her own. He integrates her into his circle of friends, many of whom he's known since childhood, having attended the same private school from kindergarten onward. The girls in the group have formed a tight-knit squad, and Lacy is swept into the fold with open arms. It feels like a good sign that they all seem to adore David, charmed by his boisterous personality and effortless charisma. Even the coupled-up ones compare him favourably to their own boyfriends, his presence somehow magnifying their partners' shortcomings. Lacy can't deny the way David's bon vivance radiates through the group, his good looks, gregario, and the undeniable privilege of his family's wealth, making him the centre of attention.

Though she doesn't fully buy into his allure, she can't deny the pull he has on her. His flamboyant personality tends to soften her own social reservations, making her feel more at ease in spaces where she might otherwise retreat. His effortless confidence in the world helps her feel less out of place, as if his presence alone grants her permission to belong. The stability and comfort he and his family offer feel almost too easy, like a safety net she can rely on to map out a future that, for once, doesn't seem so uncertain.

Predictably, Dawna adores him. David is the archetypal boyfriend you bring home to impress your mom, and he plays the part well—going out of his way to charm her, showering her with designer gifts for every birthday, holiday, and milestone. He even offers to pay off Sophie's film school tuition after Dawna complains it's a waste of money.

PART II

THE SUN

*I*t takes the studio five years to complete the project, with their film receiving critical acclaim and eventually expanding into a series after being picked up by a major distribution company. Production slowed considerably in the middle stages due to COVID, forcing the team to pivot quickly to remote workflows and adapt to a new, uncertain landscape. Over the course of the project, their staff grows threefold, despite the challenges brought on by the pandemic. Virtual collaboration becomes the norm, with late-night Zoom calls, home-recorded voice-overs, and clunky remote file-sharing systems becoming part of their daily reality. As Sam's involvement with the project winds down, a mixture of relief and melancholy washes over him. The reins are handed off to the post-production teams, and the feeling of completion is both satisfying and bittersweet.

By this point, he and Anna have secured permanent residency in Canada and are working toward citizenship. Anna, having joined the company on his recommendation, now works in the distribution department and remains deeply involved with the project. He can't help but envy her continued connection to it, while he feels somewhat untethered from the work that once consumed him.

As he approaches his late twenties, his life begins to feel steady and grounded. His relationship with Anna settles into a comfortable rhythm, shaped in part by the long months of living together in their isolation bubble and working together every day. Her insecurities are soothed by their constant proximity, and the tension that once characterized their relationship begins to fade.

When Aunt Sam is diagnosed with prostate cancer, Sam makes plans to move back to Ohio to take care of her. This decision causes a rift in his relationship with Anna, who doesn't want to leave Montreal, especially since his aunts make little effort to hide their disdain for her. She accuses him of forcing her to choose between their relationship and her career.

Eventually, the dust settles. He reassures her that the distance won't be as difficult this time since he's taking a sabbatical and won't be caught up with work like last time. He promises to make time for her. She yields, seeing that there's no question about him going. He has to be there for his aunts. He won't let his girlfriend stop him from supporting his family.

Sam's days are spent with his aunts, keeping busy with purposeful tasks. He drives Aunt Sam to her radiation appointments, staying with her in the sterile, quiet waiting rooms, the hum of medical machines a constant backdrop. Sometimes, the wait stretches longer than expected, but Sam never minds. He knows his presence is a small comfort amid her long days, and he's grateful he can be there for her.

After each appointment, Sam helps his aunt settle at home, the comforting rhythm of their time together becoming routine. They lie side-by-side in bed, the soft glow of his laptop casting a gentle light across the room as they watch movies together. Despite the fatigue that follows her treatments, this slow, peaceful companionship lifts her spirit, and even in her exhaustion, her laughter is easy and unforced. These quiet moments offer a closeness that asks for nothing, yet means everything.

Auntie Jackie, the only one still working full-time, is often too busy to assist with the caregiving, leaving Sam to manage Aunt Sam's treatments and take care of the household chores. One evening, noticing the exhaustion weighing on both his aunts, Sam gently suggests to Auntie Jackie, "Why don't you retire? I can pay your bills, whatever you need, so you can take care of yourself and rest."

But Auntie Jackie resists. She's not ready to rely on him for her income, especially when Sam's already taken on so much in managing the household.

Fortunately, the cancer was caught early, and the radiation was able to shrink the tumor enough for Aunt Sam to undergo a successful surgery. Within six months, she's in remission, and slowly, their lives settle back into a more familiar, predictable rhythm.

It's only now, with his aunt's health stabilized, that Sam realizes just how much he's needed this break. The slow, quiet days spent with family are a reprieve from the relentless crunch of animation work that had consumed him for years. Auntie Jackie, with her wife's health scare in the rearview, decides to shift to part-time work, prioritizing time with her family. Together, they read, watch movies, go for walks, and explore new restaurants when Sam isn't cooking for them.

Sam cherishes these moments, finding comfort in the routine they've established. It reminds him of when he first moved in as a kid. How their home had become a steady anchor, offering a kind of grounding he hadn't known he needed until now.

True to his word, he texts Anna regularly and calls her every night before bed, providing the reassurance he knows she depends on. Yet, beneath the routine, there's a subtle sense of relief— like coming up for air.

Just as Sam settles into this slower, more deliberate pace of life, Paul calls. Their friendship, solidified over the years, feels like the closest thing Sam has ever had to a brother. As he picks up, a familiar warmth settles in his chest. They fall into easy conversation, trading stories and updates in their first real catch-up since his return to Ohio.

"I have to talk to you about something important," Paul says, his tone turning serious.

"Okay..."

"I've really enjoyed working with you these past six years, Sam."

Sam nods in agreement, though the gesture is lost over the phone.

"Our baby's been fully birthed into the world," Paul says, his voice laced with a mix of pride and something deeper, something Sam can't quite place. "We've got some smaller projects coming up, but realistically, we won't need as many people at the studio anymore."

A flicker of unease moves through Sam. *Am I about to be fired?*

Paul's silence stretches, and when he speaks again, there's an eager edge to his voice, as if he's been holding his breath. "I want to give you half the company."

Sam's breath catches. "What?"

"I want you to be my partner." The words land between them, heavy and unmistakable.

Sam stares at the ceiling, trying to absorb what he's just heard.

"You were a huge part of our studio's success," Paul continues. "We work so well together. I never want to make art without you."

Sam's chest tightens at the raw sincerity in Paul's voice. He feels the same, more than he could put into words.

"So, what do you say?"

Sam returns to Montreal to finalize the deal with Paul. The vision Paul has for their future is clear: expand the studio and open a new office in Toronto—with Sam at the helm. Sam knows the city well, having visited often, but the level of responsibility involved in running a new studio feels daunting.

"I'll be with you the first few months," Paul reassures him.

Anna is fully on board with the move. Grateful to be included in his plans this time. She assumes transferring her role to the new studio will be seamless, given her boyfriend's new position as co-owner. More than anything, she's eager to live with him again, almost on the verge of breaking from holding back the anxieties she didn't want to burden him with while he cared for his aunt. She's ready to reclaim the closeness they lost during those long months apart.

Their move to Toronto, however, begins on an unstable note. A heavy snowstorm hits, delaying their schedules and making the process of hauling boxes and furniture more precarious and exhausting. It's their first time moving somewhere as a couple. The unavoidable stress creates an atmosphere of tension, not the fresh start they'd hoped for in this new chapter of their lives.

After graduation, Lacy is offered a position as a copywriter at one of the media companies owned by David's family, where she crafts content for one of their radio stations. Lacy is acutely aware of how fortunate she is, how little she's had to work for this role, how much has been handed to her simply by virtue of being David's girlfriend. The ease of it all feels as unsettling as it is comforting, like being swept along by a current she can't bring herself to resist.

David, meanwhile, is completing his master's degree, poised to step into a high-powered role within the family business, groomed to eventually take the reins.

Her life with David is one of opulence: a penthouse apartment, designer clothes, even a luxury car gifted to her by his parents on her twenty-fifth birthday. From the outside looking in, she has it all—a picture-perfect life shared with a successful man, a vibrant social circle, an enriching relationship with her in-laws, and an accelerating career. Life is effortless, full of comfort and excess; she wants for nothing. The only thing she ever catches herself missing—barely even a complaint—is her sister, now in Vancouver chasing her film dreams.

Even her phobia of photographs has been forcefully pushed aside. Being with David means living in the spotlight. Posing for pictures at formal events, caught by professional photographers at every celebration, birthday, and holiday gathering. Her image: curated, polished, made consumable. Crafted for the public gaze. There was no warning, no gentle easing in. No time to brace. The photos just happened, too many, too quickly. His family too powerful, too intimidating to refuse. Eventually, the constant exposure wore her down, dulling the fear. And strangely, she's grateful for that. Still, sometimes, looking at the photos, she barely recognizes herself. The girl in the frame is polished, composed, perfectly lit. She doesn't look real.

David's parents, only having two sons, have embraced Lacy as the daughter they never had. Her mother-in-law, especially, treating her like a living doll, dragging her to shopping sprees, salon appointments, and weekly facials. Lacy looks perfect, her life looks perfect. Yet, she feels so lost to herself, so untethered, that authenticity has lost all meaning to her. But it's what she's chosen. Maybe it's simpler to slip into this role, memorize a script, play the part. After all, who would complain about a life like this?

David graduates with his Master of Finance degree, earned entirely online due to the lockdown. He hardly paid attention to his online lectures, spending most of his time distracted by the ease of virtual classes. Lacy, working next to him every day, probably absorbed more than him by osmosis.

His family throws a celebration more lavish than most people's weddings. The guest list includes everyone they know, and Lacy's family is, of course, invited.

There's a strange energy in the air. Some mix of celebration and cautious reentry into public life after so long apart. People greet each other with hesitant hugs and elbow bumps, unsure whether it's too soon to fully let their guards down. Some are too eager to pretend the pandemic is over, while others still keep their masks on. David is firmly in the first camp. His family and friends never fully respected isolation bubbles—quietly hiring nurses to perform PCR tests at their gatherings, arranging private celebrations and vacations during lockdown, and paying spas and golf courses to open exclusively for them. When vaccines were first announced, his family somehow managed to get vaccinated earlier than the general public, and their social plans quickly doubled.

Lacy is relieved to see Sophie chatting with Oliver, David's younger brother, who has always been something of an outcast in the family. Lacy feels sorry for him, thrust into the shadow of his older brother's golden aura. Her adjacency to David helps her understand, at least in part, the pressure of living up to his family's expectations, though she can't imagine what it must be like to be born into it, to have this older brother as a benchmark.

The evening is filled with speeches praising David, so many guests vying for a chance to ingratiate themselves with him. Lacy knows David is disappointed that she isn't giving one, but he also understands how uncomfortable it would make her. When it's David's turn to speak, he delivers the speech Lacy helped him write the night before, full of gratitude and platitudes. But near the end, he veers off script, dedicating a heartfelt tribute to her, his flowery words dripping with love and admiration. Her stomach drops when he calls her up to join him on stage, and she freezes, blood running cold when he drops to one knee, a velvet box in hand. The room erupts in thunderous applause. Lacy feels like she's outside her body, watching the scene unfold through a pane of frosted glass. Her stiff expression is rooted in shock, her mind unable to process what is happening. She doesn't remember what she says, how the ring ends up on her finger, or how she manages to smile through the congratulations. *This is good*, she tells herself, looking out at the sea of joyful faces. This is what she's supposed to want. Where else could their relationship have led? She should have seen this coming. It was inevitable.

In the car ride home, David apologizes for the timing, explaining that his transition into his new role as vice president of the company will delay their wedding plans. Lacy doesn't mind, not one bit. The thought of planning a wedding, of walking down an aisle under the gaze of hundreds of eyes and cameras, fills her with dread. She remembers the magazine spread of David's cousin's wedding and can only imagine the spectacle theirs will become.

One evening, she comes home from work to find David sitting at the dining table, his expression grim. A manila folder open on the table in front of him.

"We need to talk," he says, his tone uncharacteristically sombre.

He slides the folder toward her as she takes a seat across from him. She opens it, leafing through the pages. Her stomach tightens as she scans the results of a background check conducted by his family's lawyers. Her father's incarceration—a chapter of her life she had tried to bury—lies bare where she eats breakfast every morning. Of course, they would look into her past. She was naive to think she could hide it from David. She had learned from Josie that vulnerability led to heartache, and she couldn't bear to risk that again.

David is hurt, his trust shaken. He questions what else she might be hiding. She assures him there's nothing, no more secrets. The only thing she's kept for herself is the memory of a boy by the ocean, a moment untouched and untarnished by the sands of time. It's not a secret, not really. More like a comfort blanket, a relic of warm salty air, tucked away in the back of her closet.

But David's disappointment lingers, his words sharp as he lectures her about how she's fractured his family's trust. He monologues about the importance of transparency, about how he cannot believe he didn't know anything about his own father-in-law. Dominic's past reflects poorly on her family, and by extension, his. Lacy doesn't argue. She sits quietly, absorbing his anger. What else can she do?

The silence between them is heavy, taut with resent-ment. David, who usually waits for Lacy to join him in bed, goes upstairs without her tonight. When she finally crawls under the covers, she can tell he's pretending to sleep. For-going his usual need for physical closeness, he's distant, his body turned away from her, the space between them cold and unyielding. But as she teeters on the edge of sleep, she feels his hands reach for her, petting and pawing at her body with a restless urgency.

The sex is rough, almost punishing, as though he's driving his anger into her body with each thrust. Lacy takes it, as she always does, her mind drifting elsewhere.

*O*ver lunch one afternoon, Paul asks Sam why progress at the studio is so far behind schedule, disappointment visibly etched on his face, a mix of frustration and concern in his voice. Sam hates seeing that look in Paul's eyes, especially because he knows Paul is right. A good number of Montreal staff members had followed Sam to the Toronto office, and while there were more transfer requests than he expected, Sam was stretched thin covering other departments—administration, legal, HR, and overseeing the design team all at once. They desperately needed more hands on deck, but the hiring process had stalled, bogged down by Anna's overbearing insistence on controlling the entire process. She had somehow manipulated her way into having the final say on all new hires, systematically rejecting every young woman who applied, narrowing the pool, leaving so many applicants who had the exact experience they needed.

Paul carefully broaches the subject of Sam's relationship with Anna, his voice softer but no less direct. "Sam... do you realize how toxic it's gotten?" His eyes search Sam's for any sign of understanding. Sam tries to reassure him, but Paul remains unconvinced. The years of accumulating evidence against Anna too damning, Paul's tolerance for her worn too thin.

Sam shifts uncomfortably in his seat. "I'll take care of the hiring process," he promises.

Hoping to smooth things over, Sam sets up a double date with Paul and Celeste. During the outing, Anna is bubbly and engaging, and Sam feels a surge of genuine relief and joy at seeing her get along with friends who mean so much to him. He leans back in his chair, a warm smile tugging at his lips as Anna laughs, the sound echoing in his chest.

But on the drive home, Anna's tone shifts, the lightness of the evening replaced with something sharp and biting. She complains about Celeste being "too fake" and calls her pretentious. Sam's jaw tightens at Anna's accusations.

"She spent so much time talking about the local election, like who even cares? She obviously just wanted to brag about being friends with one of the people running," Anna whines, her voice laced with irritation.

"Celeste isn't like that," Sam replies flatly as he tries to keep his emotions in check. "And I care about the election, for the record."

Anna rolls her eyes, impatience dripping with every word. "And you know she isn't like that because you know her so well?"

Sam sighs, trying to rein in the frustration that threatens to spill over. "You kept asking her questions about it. Of course, she talked about it for a long time. Why did you even ask her about it if you didn't care?"

"Why do you keep defending her?" Anna huffs, her voice tinged with bitterness.

"I'm not defending her. I'm just telling you the truth," Sam says, his hands tightening on the wheel.

"*Your* truth. What? Celeste is allowed to share all her opinions about the mayor, but I'm not even allowed to have a single opinion about her?" Anna snaps, her tone rising in indignation.

Sam's jaw clenches, irritation bubbling beneath the surface. "That's talking politics. It's different from tearing someone down."

Anna rolls her eyes, her exasperation palpable. "You've got an answer no matter what I say. It's like you want me to be wrong all the time."

Sam exhales a sharp breath, feeling the tension between them thickening.

By the time they reach home, Anna is still sulking, her posture rigid, her eyes fixed ahead, and Sam feels the distance between them stretching. Silence hangs in the air like a heavy curtain. Sam tries to change the subject. "What did you think of the restaurant?"

Anna shrugs, annoyance rolling off her shoulders as she mutters, "I didn't get to order the chicken because you all decided we should share dishes instead of ordering for our own things."

"You didn't want to do that? You said you were happy to."

"It's what everyone else wanted. Like I even had a choice," Anna mutters.

"You could've said something. We wouldn't have forced you to eat with us if you wanted your own entrée," Sam says, exasperated, though his voice remains controlled.

"And feel more left out than I already did?" she mutters, words laced with bitterness.

"It seemed like you were having a good time. I would've never suspected you were feeling excluded," he says, his impression of the night in stark contrast to hers.

"Guess you're bad at reading me," she retorts, the sharpness in her voice cutting through him.

"You could've said something to me. I would've tried to make it better for you."

"You could've said something *for* me," Anna pushes, her eyes narrowing as she continues, "It's my first time meeting your friends, and I feel like you cared more about them liking me than the other way around."

They continue arguing for another half hour, the car ride stretching on with each jab, until finally, they reach the parking garage. Anna is strides ahead of him, her posture rigid with anger, the distance between them unmistakable.

"And Paul," Anna scoffs in the elevator ride up, "bringing up how I shouldn't be in the interviews with you? Telling me I shouldn't be assessing the candidates? Like, does it look like we're at work right now? He just wanted to swing his big dick around you. You own the company, too. You don't have to listen to him."

Sam laughs bitterly to himself. His naivete hits him hard then, the way he believed Anna was sincerely getting along with them, like they would somehow all start hanging out together now. A weight of disappointment settles heavily in his chest.

Paul and Celeste, appreciating Anna's effort, invite them over for dinner. Though the double date was pleasant enough, their concern for Sam still lingers. They hope that by spending more time with them and witnessing his relationship with Anna firsthand, they can better understand his situation and keep an eye on him, make sure he's safe.

But Sam politely declines the invitation. Anna has taken to insinuating that he has feelings for Celeste. He knows that spending more time at their house, no matter how innocent, would only fuel her suspicions and make things even more tense at home and at work. It's just not worth the inevitable drama.

After finding out about Lacy's father, David's parents grow distant, their cloying warmth replaced with polite but icy formality. Though as time passes, the drama fades into the background, either forgotten or intentionally ignored. David's mother, ever the socialite, offers to plan an extravagant engagement party for them. When she correctly assumes Lacy has no strong opinions about the event, she eagerly takes full control, treating the party as much hers as it is theirs.

As if the party weren't enough, David's parents buy them a house as an engagement present. When David's mother takes them to see it, Lacy is at a loss for words, overwhelmed by the grandeur of the gift. Nestled in the Forest Hill neighborhood is a stately house that reminds Lacy of her childhood, with four bedrooms, a well-kept front yard, and an enchanting garden in the back, a hidden oasis in the city. David, however, isn't wowed. "It's a bit outdated," he remarks casually, as if critiquing a hotel room.

Lacy can't believe his churlishness. "It's not outdated. It's classic," she asserts, admiring the traditional millwork and ornate craftsmanship that give the house its character. David's mother, unfazed by her son's comment, offers to renovate it, a sparkle in her eye as she envisions the project.

Renovation plans quickly draw out Lacy and David's differing tastes. Lacy loves the traditional charm of the house, while David pushes for a sleek mid-century modern aesthetic. Their compromise, a mid-century modern home that keeps some of the wainscoting.

David's mother tries to involve Lacy in the process, calling her to the house several times a week to pick out paint colors and tiles. The gesture only makes Lacy feel more like a guest in her future home. Her choices only implemented when they align with her mother-in-law's preferences. It's as if she's being paraded for show, groomed to play the role of David's homemaking wife, opinions valued only when they match the vision others have for her.

During construction, Lacy is taken aback to discover that instead of renovations, the house is being completely demolished, wainscoting and all. David and his mother, without any consultation with her, had decided to design a custom house from scratch.

One morning, as she drives to the house to meet with her mother-in-law, Lacy is shocked to find Edward on site. He's been hired as the designer for the house. Their reunion is astonishing, both of them marveling that fate has brought them back together. Edward has only grown more handsome and charismatic, effortlessly leading the contractors with his easy charm. Lacy, too, has changed, he notices. Her salon-perfect hair, glass skin, and designer clothes are a stark contrast to the unassuming girl he once knew. She's polite, almost too polished, like she's studied a manual on etiquette. *Makes sense,* he thinks, *she's marrying into this family, after all.*

Reconnecting with Edward feels like a gift, as though the universe is offering her a second chance at their friendship, a warmth that had been missing from her life for so long. As their designer, he mindfully incorporates her tastes into the design of the house. She invites him to the engagement party and looks forward to seeing him more than any other guest, especially since Sophie can't make it.

The engagement party is held on a yacht, a lavish affair full of guests Lacy barely knows. The glittering lights of the city shimmer in the distance, but the atmosphere feels suffocating.

It's here that she first experiences the deep, unsettling embarrassment of witnessing your partner be blackout drunk, swearing incoherently and excessively as he monopolizes conversations with garrulous stories, not noticing that no one is paying attention. His voice grows louder and more slurred when he finds a microphone and delivers a verbose speech about his vision for their marriage: two kids, a boy and a girl, an English Bulldog, and a Siberian Husky with heterochromia...

Lacy's stomach churns as she listens to him ramble on, her cheeks burning with a mixture of shame and disbelief.

The stench of alcohol seems to cling to his every word. Abandoning the unspoken expectation to stay by her fiancé's side, she quietly slips away, needing space to breathe. She seeks out Edward, leaving David to his drunken monologue about not wanting cats because they're mean and boring, the words barely making sense at this point.

She runs into her "girl squad", who drunkenly congratulate her with backhanded compliments.

"This party is so nice. I wish my mother-in-law could buy me good taste."

"You look so great! Who's your injector?"

"Your makeup is so pretty tonight. Did David's mom hire a makeup artist for you?"

Trapped in their circle, Lacy can only smile and nod. She is wondering if anyone on this ship has weed when Dawna stumbles over, clearly wasted.

"Are you having fun?" her mother slurs.

Lacy hates getting asked this at parties. A forced mood scan that feels more like a trap than genuine care. "Yeah. It's nice," she lies, desperate to escape this conversation. As if the bride-to-be is allowed to answer truthfully without ruining the guests' enjoyment.

Edward suddenly materializes at Lacy's side as if summoned by some divine whim, effortlessly charming the girls before whisking her away to a quieter spot on the top deck. With a thaumaturgical flourish, he produces a joint from his chest pocket, lights it, and offers it to her. Looking out at the glowing cityscape, he asks her a question no one else has: "What do you like about him?"

Lacy hesitates. "He's good with people."

Edward raises an eyebrow. "No way, sister. *I'm* good with people."

She laughs. "He's just really drunk tonight. He's not usually like this."

Edward inhales another drag. "What else?"

"He takes good care of me."

Edward tilts his head. "Like, *he* does? Or his money?"

What's the difference? she thinks for an uncharitable second. Lacy can't deny the value of financial security, not just for herself but for her family. Her mother has never worked a day in her life. What would she do if Lacy's relationship with David fell apart? Work at a grocery store?

"What's wrong with working at the grocery store?" Edward asks, catching her off guard.

Lacy realizes she'd spoken aloud. "Nothing. It's not the job, it's my mom."

Edward inhales the last of the joint. "Well, if you're happy, I'm happy."

They stroll along the edge of the deck, heads tilted close. Their voices are low and unhurried, words flowing with ease. The sound of their laughter floats between them, like the warm buzz of the joint. Below, the distant hum of the party feels far away, swallowed by the open lake air, as if unfolding in a different world entirely.

Without warning, David slips between them. His arms drape heavily around their shoulders, the weight of him unsteady, and Lacy can smell the sharp, hot tang of cognac clinging to his breath.

"What the hell are you girls whispering about up here?" he drawls, his words slow and muddy, teetering on the edge of playful and threatening, like he's just far enough gone to forget where the line is.

Edward stiffens and Lacy can feel the shift in his posture. He doesn't answer, just tries to pull away, but David's grip tightens, fingers digging into his shoulders hard enough to make Edward flinch. The pressure sends a ripple of unease through Lacy.

"You're not talking about me, are you?" David presses, his voice lilting like a joke that's gone on too long.

Edward jerks free, prying David's hand off his shoulder with a tug, the tension in his body giving way to a flash of anger.

"No, no," Lacy says quickly, her words coming out a little more breathless than she expects, the fog of the high clouding her thoughts. Her gaze flicks from Edward's stiff posture to David's face. "We're just catching up."

David exhales a slow, heavy sigh, his breath warm against her ear. "Well, you can catch up another time. Tonight is our night. Don't run off," he says, voice dropping to an impatient murmur. "Sorry, bro, I need my wife," he calls back to Edward, words tossed carelessly over his shoulder as he pulls her away by the waist, the command clear in his grip.

They spend the night in the master suite of the yacht. David is sprawled on the bed, still drunk and belligerent. "Did you have fun?"

"Yeah. It was nice," Lacy replies, brushing her hair in the bathroom.

"I had a fucking blast!"

"I can tell."

David trains his unfocused gaze on her. "What's that tone? You mad?"

"No."

"Tell me." He gets up to stand beside her. "Did I do something stupid?"

"No," she repeats, turning away from his whiskey breath. "But maybe you should take it easy next time."

"Take what easy?"

"The drinking."

"Why? It's a party! That's the whole point. Merriness! Merriness? More like marry us!" He laughs at his joke.

When Lacy doesn't respond, he grows defensive. "That's why people invite me to things. They need me to be the life of the party."

"You were swearing a lot," she says quietly.

"Oh, fuck off. That's just how I talk. I guarantee you nobody had a problem with it."

"You were monopolizing the conversation."

"Because no one else would talk!"

"You didn't give them a chance to."

David's anger flares. "Better than being fucking mute all the time. Don't take it out on me just because you're not interesting like me."

Lacy tries to pull away, but he's not done.

"You know what my friends say about you? That you're boring. That you're quiet because you have no opinions of your own."

She leaves the bathroom, doesn't want to engage when he's like this, knows he'll say whatever it takes to hurt her.

"That you always think you're better than us," he spits, following her. "How does someone like me end up with someone so cold and antisocial? They think you're a fucking gold digger."

David's word hit their mark. She is hurt.

In the weeks that follow, the stench of David's outburst lingers, leaving their relationship strained. Lacy's disillusionment grows, haunted by the question of whether she's truly happy, and how much that even matters to her. Her life is so intertwined with his—her job, her house, her car—all financially tied to David, as are her mother's expenses and her sister's tuition. The thought of leaving feels impossible. Her entire existence feels owed to him.

David, for his part, is apologetic. He dotes on her at home, showering her with gifts, desperate to make amends. He knows he'd never say those things sober, aware of how much effort Lacy puts into navigating his world and his family. He regrets weaponizing her insecurities against her in the heat of the moment.

In a grand gesture of repentance, he buys her a store as a wedding gift. A space for her to pursue her own passions. It's symbolic. A gift his father had given his mother after their wedding, and David hopes it will give Lacy some sense of financial independence in the wake of his gold digger comment, a chance to step out of his shadow.

She accepts. And just like that, life goes on as planned.

*P*aul asks Anna to take a step back from the company after he sees that Sam isn't able to stand up to her. She starts working part-time.

Bored and feeling rejected, she decides to try flipping furniture as a side hustle. An idea sparked when her algorithm started pushing videos of a guy who buys old furniture, repaints it, swaps out the knobs or legs, and sells it for a profit.

After a long week, Sam is dragged to an antique store Anna found through another video serendipitously fed to her. It's his first day off in a while. He just wrapped up three grueling, back-to-back weeks trying to hit a tough deadline for a big new project. Truthfully, he wishes he could've stayed at home today, sleeping. Between the burnout and Anna's sour mood of late, Sam is completely drained. But he knows a day out might lift her spirits. And judging by the look on her face, it seems to be working.

He knocks the snow from his boots before stepping inside, greeted by a cozy, stylish space that's part antique shop, part used bookstore, part VHS rental store, its air thick with the scent of old paper and sea salt.

A woman balances atop a ladder, changing the light bulbs on an ornate crystal chandelier in the center of the store. At the sound of the door, she calls out, "Be with you in a sec!" Her back is turned to them.

Anna is immediately drawn to an old dresser in the corner, while Sam browses the books. Suddenly, there's a crash of breaking glass behind him.

He turns, and his mind shatters, like the iridescent light bulbs scattered across the floor.

Lacy.

Lacy stares at him, mouth agape. She looks exactly like he remembers, yet so different. In his daze, he can't pinpoint what's changed, thoughts flickering out like broken light.

"Oh my god, babe, be careful! There's glass everywhere." Anna's voice snaps him out of his trance. He didn't realize he was walking toward Lacy.

Shaking herself out of her own bewilderment, Lacy starts climbing down the ladder. "I'm so sorry. Please stay where you are. Let me get a broom."

Sam feels Anna's hands pull him backward, but his eyes stay locked on Lacy as she shuffles to a back room. She reappears with a broom and dustpan, sweeping up the broken glass. He can't look away, afraid she'll vanish if he does.

Lacy bends down, picking up the larger shards, a small cut slicing her hand, and he feels the memory of her small hand in his palm all those years ago.

"Careful," he says, instinctively moving to help.

"Babe. Leave it."

What is she doing here, cleaning the floors of some store?

He doesn't realize he's said it out loud until Lacy responds.

She gives him a quick smile, and a warm sensation spreads across his chest.

"This is *my* store. Not *some* store."

He takes it in now—the old books, vintage treasures lining the shelves, and a green couch tucked into the corner, its velvet fabric woven with the breath of countless conversations.

"This place suits you," he says.

Lacy is still looking down, clearing up the last of the glass. He can see the knowing smile tugging at her lips.

And then it hits him. Did she think he wouldn't recognize her? How could he ever forget? He stares at her, stunned, caught between now and a memory, between this quiet shop and the warmth of a summer long past.

He feels Anna's hand on his shoulder. "Do you guys know each other?" she asks. There's an accusatory edge in her voice, subtle, but sharp. He's learned to hear the shift, trained by years of walking that careful line. But right now, he barely cares. As if time had conspired to bring Lacy back to him. A decade later.

"Babe?" Anna tugs on his arm when neither of them responds.

"Yeah. We're old friends," Lacy says, rising to her feet.

He can't help the incredulous smile tugging at his lips as he watches her. His heart stumbles when he sees the moon necklace resting at her collarbone. He's not wearing his ring. Keeps it tucked away in a drawer at home. He wishes it were on his finger now.

Anna steps in front of him, blocking his view, pulling his attention. Her eyes say what her mouth doesn't: *Who is she?* But his gaze drifts, pulled like gravity, back to Lacy— and the giant diamond glinting on her finger.

"Sam's never mentioned you," says the woman Lacy assumes is his girlfriend, her tone polite.

"It was a long time ago," Lacy replies, her voice calm, though her heart kicks in her chest at the sight of Sam. She keeps her eyes on the woman, focusing hard, too hard, while Sam lingers in her periphery, blurry and magnetic. She doesn't dare to look at him for more than a second. Her nerves humming in his presence.

"Did you go to school together?" the girlfriend asks, tilting her head.

"No."

"Where did you meet, then?"

"Italy," Sam cuts in.

His girlfriend turns to him, eyebrows raised. "I never knew you went to Italy."

Sam looks momentarily dumbfounded, or maybe just somewhere else entirely. He doesn't respond to his girlfriend, doesn't offer a name, doesn't explain. He just keeps staring at Lacy, like he's still not convinced she's real.

Lacy, for her part, is just as frozen. She can't quite process it either. Sam, standing here, in her store, with a girlfriend at his side. It feels impossible. Like an old dream, now twisted into something unfamiliar.

"Do you live here?" Sam asks her.

"I live here," Lacy nods.

"You live here," he echoes, voice soft, almost disbelieving.

"I live here," she repeats, laughing.

"Me too," he says, smiling at the improbability of it all.

"We moved here a few months ago," his girlfriend offers, her gaze flitting between the two of them.

"Six months ago," Sam adds.

Six months. They've lived in the same city for six months without knowing.

"From where?" Lacy asks, finally resolving a question that had hovered unanswered for years.

"Montreal," the girlfriend says.

"Montreal?" Lacy gasps. "We've lived in the same country this whole time? I thought you were American."

"Same here," Sam laughs, shaking his head. "And I am..."

He tells her about his journey becoming an animator, the move from Ohio to Montreal to work at the studio. Lacy listens, eyes glittering with pride, drinking in every word.

"Wow," she breathes, the word falling from her lips like a prayer.

Sam can't describe the look in her eyes or the feeling it stirs in him.

"You did it," she says softly. "I'm so happy for you."

That night at dinner, David asks about the bandage on her hand, just as Lacy finds herself replaying the moment—Sam walking into her store like an apparition, stepping out of the dreamy haze of her memories, materializing before her in the flesh.

"I cut my hand."

"Oh no," David replies, eyes fixed on his phone as a notification lights up the screen.

"Someone I knew came into the store today," Lacy offers, tentative. It's all she's been thinking about. She can't help but bring it up.

"Okay? Our friends go to the store all the time," David says, distracted, not even glancing up.

"No. It was this guy I knew a long time ago."

At the mention of a *guy,* David looks up, brow creasing. "Who?"

Lacy hesitates, not wanting to say Sam's name aloud, as if it's a secret incantation, too precious to cast in this moment. "Someone I met when I was in high school. I haven't seen him in like a decade."

"He looked you up online or something? How did he find you?" David's tone is sharp, a flicker of suspicion beneath the curiosity.

"No. It was pure coincidence. He came in with his girlfriend."

At the mention of a girlfriend, David relaxes, his jealousy dissipating.

Lacy doesn't offer anything more about the man from her past, and David doesn't ask. As far as he cares, he's the first man Lacy's ever been with. The only one. The last one. He reaches under the table, slides his hand up her thigh.

On the car ride home, Anna faces away from Sam in the passenger seat, staring out the window, her knees pointed toward the door. Usually, he has to coax the reasons for her brooding, but this time, he can't focus on Anna. Lacy consumes his thoughts, front and center in his mind. The impossible serendipity of their meeting.

He can already guess why Anna's upset. It's always the same thing. And this time, he doesn't feel like talking about it. Not unless she brings it up herself. Besides, how could he explain Lacy to her? To anyone? Telling Anna who Lacy was to him would only make things worse. Anna would never understand.

As he pulls into their parking spot, she breaks the cold silence. "Why did you go back inside after?"

"To give her a Band-Aid."

Anna, predictably, does not like his answer.

"Sorry," he says instinctively.

"Don't apologize if you don't mean it."

He can sense the fight coming before it even starts. The familiar tension between them weighs heavier than usual. He's too tired for this.

"Okay," is all he says.

"You want to see her again," Anna continues.

His mind is too full, unable to shake the gnawing feeling in his chest from the events of the day. He can't process a response, let alone the one she wants.

"Why aren't you saying anything?" Anna demands.

"I don't know what you want me to say."

"Oh my god, so I'm right. You *want* to see her again."

"I didn't say that."

"You didn't *not* say it."

"So what?" The wrong words slip out before he can stop them.

"I'm not fucking doing this." Anna rolls her eyes and gets out of the car, slamming the door behind her with a sharp finality.

He sighs, a groan escaping him as he sinks into the driver's seat. He can't fault Anna for her irritation. Of course, he wants to see Lacy again. The thought of it stirs something in him he can't quite put into words. Anna is always hypervigilant, always picking up on the smallest shifts in his mood. Usually, she's wrong. But this time, she's got him. He groans again, slamming his head against the steering wheel, trying to ignore the overwhelming impulse to drive back to the store. Guilt and confusion course through him, drowning him in the weight of it all.

As if some unseen force has cast a spell on Lacy's life, another face from her past steps into the store, within the same week. At first, Lacy isn't sure it's her. Her face is familiar yet altered by time, her hair a style Lacy has never seen before, thick and coily waves cascading down her shoulders.

"Mina?" Lacy asks, her voice tentative.

"Lacy?" Recognition sparks in Wilhelmina's eyes.

They smile-laugh as they look at each other, eyes taking the other in, unsure how else to react. There's something in the way Wilhelmina carries herself that feels achingly familiar, like the scent of rain on dry earth, something foreign and utterly known. Their conversation flows effortlessly, as if the years between them had been a mere pause. Two old friends catching up, not two people whose bond was severed by the same tragedy.

Lacy learns that Mina recently moved to the city, works at a bank, and still has that same shy warmth she remembers from childhood. They exchange phone numbers, though Lacy doesn't expect anything to come of it.

But when a text from Mina pops up later that evening, suggesting they meet for dinner, Lacy's heart stalls, caught between curiosity and doubt. Part of her wonders if Mina is simply lonely, friendless in a new city, and will soon move on once she settles in, finds her own crowd and no longer needs the crutch of someone from home. And there's a quieter, heavier part of Lacy that questions whether she even deserves someone like Mina in her life.

When Lacy tells David she's meeting with Mina, he insists on joining. He's never met any of her old friends except Edward, and he sees this as an opportunity to connect with someone from a part of her life he knows little about. Lacy agrees, unsure whether his presence will comfort her or make the meeting more awkward.

At dinner, David is his usual lively self, effortlessly steering the conversation and easing the verbal tension that hangs in the air. Mina is quieter, her silence a contrast to David's boisterous energy, and Lacy is grateful for him. She's almost certain that without him there, the dinner would have been drowned in awkward silences. David makes a big show of how incredible it is to meet Mina, treating it like a revelation, like Lacy's past has always been a blur, her life only starting when he entered it.

He insists on paying for dinner to mark the occasion, a gesture full of ceremony. He's pleased to have witnessed this reconnection, eager to celebrate it, as if it somehow solidifies his place in Lacy's world. When he offers Mina a ride home, she politely declines, opting to walk instead.

Lacy offers to join her, but Mina gently insists she's fine on her own. They don't make any plans to see each other again, and as they part ways, Lacy wonders if this will be the last time their paths cross.

A few days later, Mina drops by the store on her lunch break. Lacy closes the shop so they can grab food. She's nervous at first, unsure how it'll feel to be alone with Mina, so much has shifted between them. But as they sit together, the mood is surprisingly easy, lighter than it had been at dinner. Mina's grown and changed, but beneath it all, she's still familiar in so many ways, radiating that same calm and caring energy Lacy remembers, the kind that makes everything feel more anchored. It's the kind of presence that allows Lacy to speak her mind without fear of judgment or misinterpretation. If her words falter, Mina would help her find their true meaning, together. And in the same way, Lacy's openness draws something out of Mina too. It makes space for her to be messier, looser, a little more herself. Like some old rhythm they'd forgotten, but never really lost.

"Like, it was medicine for horses?"

Mina nods. "There was a horse on the box."

"You're lying," Lacy says, already laughing, the kind of laugh that takes over your whole face.

"I wish I was lying! I ingested that godforsaken paste for like five days straight."

"It was a *paste*?" Lacy slaps a hand over her mouth, but it's no use, she's wheezing now.

"From a tube!" Mina swats her with a napkin. "I thought this was a *safe space*! I'm being very brave and vulnerable sharing this with you."

"Of course," Lacy says, trying to pull it together.

"You should've seen the studies my mom sent me! They had *graphs*, Lacy. I thought it would cure me!"

Lacy nods solemnly. "I'm just glad to see you never grew out of being a horse girl."

Mina gasps. "At least I don't have worms!" She throws her napkin at Lacy's chest.

When their laughter finally dies down, Lacy grins. "Okay, but seriously, what did it taste like?"

Mina's face crumples in horror. "So bad. *So* bad. I had to mix it with peanut butter!"

That sets them off again. Another round of full-bodied, breathless laughter. When Mina snorts, it sounds a little too much like a horse, and that completely wrecks them. Lacy folds over the table, her stomach aching, breath ragged, something old and tender tugging loose inside her.

By the time lunch is over, Lacy feels it creeping in, that ache of nostalgia. The way they could always talk and laugh like this for hours. The ease. The warmth. And in this moment, she remembers all the things she loved about Mina. She invites her to her wedding.

Mina's expression flickers with something unreadable at the mention of David. When Lacy asks what she thought of him, Mina says diplomatically, "It was nice of him to pay for dinner."

Lacy nods, sensing Mina isn't as enamoured by David's charm as others tend to be.

"I sort of wish he didn't come. Sorry," Mina admits, wincing slightly.

"You didn't like him?" Lacy asks.

"It's not that. We're just different types of people, I think," Mina replies, choosing her words carefully. "It would've been nice to catch up just the two of us. There are a lot of things we haven't talked about." The weight of their unspoken history lingers between them.

They meet again for dinner the next evening, just the two of them. The conversation begins casually, catching up more on the last few years, but as the evening wears on, the atmosphere shifts. The unvoiced thoughts of their shared past palpable, heavier than either had expected.

Mina is the first to bring it up. "I can't imagine what it was like for you," she says softly. "Everyone leaving you. I should've been braver."

Lacy shakes her head, her chest tight as tears start to well in her eyes. Mina has nothing to apologize for. She was deeply violated by their friendship.

"It wasn't your fault," Mina insists, her voice full of conviction. "That's what I'm trying to say. You had to bear the punishment for your dad, even though you were a victim too. It must have been so confusing and lonely. I should've been there for you."

At her words, Lacy breaks down. Tears spill down her face, in the middle of the restaurant, the years of unacknowledged pain pouring out of her. Her family had chosen to sweep it under the rug, burying it under layers of silence. The validation in Mina's words is overwhelming, like balm on a wound that's never fully healed. Mina moves to her side, wrapping her in a tight hug, holding her together as she breaks apart. It feels profound to have someone from her past, someone who knew her before everything fell apart, truly see her, truly understand the pain she's carried alone for so long.

"I let my mom get into my head. Let her scare me. After you left, I had so much regret. I couldn't believe that was how I lost you, that I was the one who left."

Lacy laughs, her voice thick with emotion. "I didn't even think you thought about me at all. Except bad things."

"I thought about you all the time," Mina tells her, the words tumbling out. "I looked for you in everyone, always thinking, Lacy would get it, Lacy would've laughed, Lacy would've liked this... I tried to find you on every social media platform. Of course, you're not on any."

As they walk to the subway station, the city noise fades into the background as Mina opens up to Lacy. "I'm not sure I've processed everything that happened with your dad. All I know is that I missed you. Missed the person I am when I'm with you. And losing you..."

Lacy's heart aches at the rawness in Mina's words, a part of her still not sure how to fully let go of the pain of their past.

Mina takes a breath, her eyes soft with regret. "I'm sorry. I couldn't see past my own feelings until it was too late. I couldn't forgive someone who had done nothing wrong. But I promise you, I will never make that mistake again. Not now. Not after the universe brought us back together." There's a weight to her words, a sense of finality.

Healing their friendship won't be easy, Lacy knows that. It will take time. Patience. But as she listens to Mina, accepts and returns her apologies, something shifts inside her, a spark of faith flickers. Not just in their friendship, but in herself.

Anna had made Sam promise not to go back to Lacy's store. They'd argued for hours, with him calling her possessive and controlling, and her accusing him of being inconsiderate and disloyal, convinced he would be unfaithful if he ever set foot in that place again.

Eventually, he conceded. He seriously considered what could come from seeing Lacy again. It wasn't like they could be casual friends, evident from the way his heart pounds at the thought of her, the way his gaze betrayed him when he first saw her. It is too much, too intense. He had to admit it wouldn't be fair to Anna.

One day after work, Paul asks Sam to accompany him to rent some VCRs. Celeste wants to play some old movies for her class. Sam watches as Paul pulls up outside Lacy's store, can't shake the rush of emotions that flood him.

The bell above the door jingles, and Lacy's eyes lift from the book she's reading. A bright, almost uncontainable grin spread across her face as soon as her eyes land on him.

"Hi."

"Hi," he responds, his voice cracking slightly, carrying the undercurrent of unspoken words.

Paul glances between them, raising an eyebrow, trying to make sense of what he's witnessing. He's never seen Sam act or smile like this before.

"What brings you here today?" Lacy asks.

You, Sam thinks, his brain short-circuiting for a moment.

"Do you rent VCR tapes and players here?" Paul asks, breaking the moment.

Lacy nods, moves toward the back room, and returns moments later, placing an old player in immaculate condition on the counter with practiced ease. She leads them to a whole new section of VHS tapes that Sam didn't notice during his last visit.

As she disappears to tend to another customer, Paul can't help but tease, his voice low and amused. "Dude, who is this girl, and why are you acting so weird?"

Sam pauses for a second before answering, his voice distant, trying to make sense of what he's feeling. "We met in Italy when we were kids. Saw each other for the first time like two weeks ago."

Paul gives him a pointed look, clearly about to push for more, when he notices Sam's attention elsewhere. His eyes have drifted to Lacy, catching the sound of her laughter.

As they finish paying, Paul slips a business card from his wallet and hands it to Lacy.

"Oh. Thank you," Lacy says, accepting the card with both hands, taken aback by the gesture.

"Bye, Lacy," Sam says, his voice thick with gratitude for this brief chance of seeing her again.

Once they're outside, Paul elbows him, a grin on his face as he mocks his tongue-tied expression.

Sam rolls his eyes. "Why did you give her a business card?"

Paul smirks. "Because your number's on it."

*L*acy stares down at the business card, both Paul's and Sam's contact information printed in neat black letters. Their job titles sit just below their names. She knew Sam worked at a studio. He'd mentioned it last time, but she didn't realize he owned it.

Curious, she looks up the company, and the results stun her. Project after project, bold, intricate, unmistakably successful. He made these? Pride stirs in her chest, full and bright.

He even has a Wikipedia page. She reads, slowly. Collaborations. Exhibitions. Awards. A list of notable works. All these things she never knew about him. Things he never had the chance to tell her. She finds his website, scrolls through the gallery. Image after image, and then— she sees it.

Pink, orange, indigo. Dusk clouds. A stretch of beach so familiar it steals the air from her lungs.

Her gaze lingers on it.

She buys it.

David unboxes the painting when it arrives.

"What's this?" he asks, holding it up. Lacy has never shown an interest in collecting art, nor in decorating their soon-to-be home. His mother had taken over that task entirely, discarding the pretense of including Lacy's input for the sake of efficiency.

"Who's the artist?"

"A friend."

David gives her a teasing look. He knows all her friends. None of them are artists.

"Who?"

"Remember the guy I told you about? The one I knew ten years ago, who came by the store?"

David's face hardens, the shift instant, jealous rage simmering just beneath the surface. He takes the painting and shoves it into the storage closet.

"We are *not* hanging that in our house. Looks like something you'd find at a liquidation store."

He spends the rest of the night sulking, sharp exhales marking his movements as he paces around the house, his mood poisoning the air. Lacy ignores the tension. She's grown used to it. The engagement party, his new job, the constant delays in their home's construction, and the mounting pressure of their wedding have pulled at the threads of their relationship, leaving their conversations hollow, their connection frayed. She's become quieter, distant, avoids his touch now, without even thinking.

That night, Lacy is reading in bed when David walks in, shirt damp with sweat from a late workout. He climbs in beside her, wraps an arm around her waist, and starts pressing kisses into her neck. His hand slips under her shirt, squeezing her breasts.

She shifts away. "Not tonight."

He pulls her back against him, an iron grasp around her waist. "Come on..."

"David, I'm serious. I'm tired."

"You're reading," he laughs, his lascivious voice low. He grinds his erection against her, breath hot against her ear. One hand slinks below her waistband, the other tugging at her shirt.

She doesn't react. Doesn't move.

He keeps going.

While he tugs his shirt over his head, Lacy lets her mind drift, the way she always does when she's not in the mood. An automatic response by now, her quiet slipping away. But tonight, something won't let her go. She's here. Viscerally present. Every touch lands. Every movement sharp and inescapable.

David climbs back on top of her, his sticky weight flattening her into the mattress. The smell of his breath, still laced with remnants of dinner caught between his teeth, makes her stomach turn. She tries to shift, get out from under him, when suddenly, a thought crashes into her: *What if I tell him no, and he doesn't stop?* It's a train of thought she's never allowed to linger, never let travel far enough for fear to seep into her veins. But now, it barrels forward, full steam ahead.

The fear roots her in place, sharp and cold as his fingers hook into her underwear.

"Stop." Her voice is so soft, barely audible. She clamps her thighs together.

His hands pause, but only for a moment. Then he keeps going.

"I said stop." This time, louder.

He pulls his hand away, stroking her hair instead, his tumescence pressed hard against her crotch. "Why are you toying with me?"

"Please get off me."

"So bratty tonight," he jeers. "Who knew you could be such a tease?"

She manages to wedge her hands between them, pushing at his chest. She can feel the limit of her strength in her arms, knows she won't be able to force him off. "I'm not teasing you. I just don't want to do this tonight. Please get off me."

He lifts himself slightly, staring down at her. "Babe, you're kidding, right? I'm so hard it hurts. Do you really expect me to just stop? That's so mean." He smiles as he kisses her lips, voice coaxing, pleading.

She wants to believe that if she screams, he'll stop. Right?

"Babe, I'm sorry to do this to you," she says gently, trying to mollify him. "I just don't feel well."

"Lacy," he groans, exasperated, his patience fraying. "I'm literally in pain. I won't even last that long."

"Get off me." Her tone is firm this time.

Cold anger seeps into his eyes, sending a chill down her spine.

"I can make you feel good too," he coos, sliding a hand between her legs again, rubbing hard, too frantic, too forceful. She clamps her thighs shut, twisting away. He mistakes her motion for pleasure, thinking she's close, not knowing that he's never made her come. Every orgasm she's had with him has been by her own doing.

He moves to put a finger inside her, and she tries to push him off again, her legs kicking.

She feels the warm dribble of his arousal smear against her clothes. Revulsion floods her. Hatred. For him. For herself. For letting it get to this. Repulsion at his ability to stay erect while she struggles under him in obvious discomfort.

"Are you punishing me for something?" he snaps.

"David, I'm not punishing you. I just don't want to tonight."

"You haven't let me touch you in weeks. My mom says you're weaponizing sex."

Lacy stares at him, eyes widening. "What the fuck is wrong with you?" Why was he talking to his mother about their sex life at all?

"What the fuck is wrong with *you*?" he fires back, voice rising.

"I said no. If you don't get off me, it's rape."

His eyes widen in outrage at her choice of words. "*Rape?!* Are you fucking kidding me? I'm your *fiancé*!"

"I want you to get off me. I don't want to have sex with you."

"You'd accuse me of being a fucking rapist?"

Fear surges through her at the venomous rage clouding his eyes. He isn't moving. His legs tighten around her, trapping her under him. His grip on her breast, punishing enough to hurt. The tip of his erection hovers over her.

She slams her forehead into his face.

"Fuck!" He reels back, clutching his nose. "You fucking bitch!"

She shoves him off, scrambles away, and accidentally knees him in the groin in her frantic desperation. He collapses onto the bed, curled in agony.

"You psycho bitch!" he yells.

Lacy grabs her phone from the nightstand and bolts to the bathroom, locking the door. Darkness engulfs her.

David pounds on the door, still groaning in pain. "You're fucking insane. You probably broke my nose."

Her phone screen glows in the dark. She scrolls through her contacts, mind blank, fingers moving almost on their own. Then she sees Edward's name.

Hi. Are you up? She texts him.

The time reads 12:38 AM. Three dots appear.

Edward:
barely. what's up?

Her hands shake, not sure what to type.

David yanks at the door handle. "This lock is a joke. A fucking paper clip can open this door."

"Don't!" she yells. "Please don't come in. Please."

He shakes the door again. "What? Are you scared of me?"

She doesn't reply.

Edward:
everything okay?

"Why are you acting like you're scared of me?" David demands.

"I told you I didn't want to have sex with you, and you didn't listen."

"I fucking stopped. Do you see us having sex right now?"

"You stopped because I kicked you."

Edward is calling her now, she picks up, but doesn't speak.

"You fucking psycho bitch," David is yelling. "You assaulted me and want to make me the villain? You kicked my fucking dick while it was hard." His voice is shrill and manic. "Open the fucking door, Lacy!"

Edward:
share your location. now.

David rattles the handle again.

Lacy stays silent.

He scoffs. "Fine. Lock yourself in there. See if I care."

His footsteps fade. Lacy lets out a breath. And then, finally, she sobs.

*W*hen Sam enters his apartment, Anna is sitting at the dining table, a blade held over her wrist.

What the fuck. What the fuck. What the fuck.

He lunges forward to her, ripping the blade from her hand. It slices into his palm, but he barely feels it.

"What the actual fuck, Anna?"

Anna's eyes brim with tears. "You lied to me."

Sam kneels beside her, his voice panicked. "What are you talking about?"

"What do you think?"

He stares at her, slack-jawed, blood dripping from his fingertips.

"You lied," Anna repeats. "You went to see her."

How the hell does she know that?

"Don't even try to deny it. I have a tracker in the car."

"You have a *what*?"

"Don't you dare turn this on me."

Sam shakes his head, trying to ground himself in this conversation. "You should've told me."

"Why? So you could've covered your tracks better? You fucking liar."

"Paul asked me to go with him. I didn't even know we were going there."

Anna rolls her eyes, scolding him for not telling her. She laments that she's been spiraling at home for the past hour, convinced he was cheating. One text—one—would've been enough. But hiding it? That just makes it look worse. Makes it look intentional. How is she supposed to trust him now?

Sam honestly understands her side. He knew he shouldn't have been there. He was being selfish. He apologizes, his voice shaky. When she finally calms down, he tucks her into bed.

Unable to take the discomfort of the tension hanging between them, Anna instinctively reaches out, desperate to restore some sense of closeness with Sam. She moves toward him with a quiet urgency, her touch sharp with intent, as if claiming him will erase the distance between them.

But Sam is on edge, the image of her almost slitting her wrist replays in his mind. His heart races with the terror of what might've happened if he hadn't come home in time. He's not in the mood for sex, not now, hasn't been for a while, and probably won't be for a long time. That night, sleep evades him. Anxiety and his past consume him as memories of his mother's suicide, his father's death, and his own dark thoughts flood his mind.

It feels like drowning. Every day, Sam struggles just to keep his head above the current, too weak to tread water anymore. His despondency becomes so obvious that someone at work reaches out to Paul, worried. Paul flies in immediately.

When Paul pries, Sam is too drained to keep up the façade. No longer motivated to protect Anna out of love, he tells Paul everything. His fear that she'll end her life. The thought holds him in place like a rip current he can't escape.

Horrified, Paul urges him to leave. Anna needs help beyond what Sam can give. But Paul doesn't understand what it's like to lose someone to suicide. Sam can't risk reliving his parents' story. He can't be the one who walks away. Can't be the reason she kills herself.

Paul and Celeste move to Toronto to keep an eye on him, but the decision strains their company. With both bosses in one city, decisions stall, deadlines slip. Another weight on Sam's already buckling shoulders.

"*I* won't be here long," she says as Edward and Jacob set up the pullout couch for her.

Jacob—from high school. Edward had never mentioned they were together now. She doesn't ask questions. Can barely process what's happened in her life, much less this new twist in the story.

"Don't worry about that now," Edward says at the same time Jacob tells her, "Rest up. We can figure things out later."

"Thank you so much. And I'm sorry," Lacy murmurs, her voice trembling.

"If you say sorry one more time, I swear to god..." Jacob sighs, still wound tight from his confrontation with David.

"Okay, sorry."

Jacob and Edward almost laugh, rolling their eyes, before Edward asks, "Need anything else?"

Lacy shakes her head. Edward helped her pack earlier, his mind clear and efficient, while she was paralyzed by shock, sadness, fear. She can't seem to regulate the storm of emotions swirling inside her.

She recalls David's confusion when he opened the door to Edward and Jacob, her shock at seeing Jacob barely registering amid the chaos of the night. She had finally stepped out of the bathroom at the sound of the doorbell, and without even acknowledging David, Edward and Jacob swept in to find her.

Jacob and David argued in the foyer, David's voice loud and minacious while Jacob tried to remain steady and calm. With Edward's help, they packed quickly, and he guided her out of the apartment without so much as a glance at David. She can't remember what David said to her as she was whisked out of the apartment, her mind a blur of fear and relief.

"Do you want to sleep, or do you want to talk about it?" Edward asks gently.

She glances at the clock: 2:37 a.m. "You should go to bed. You've done enough for me."

Edward sits down beside her. "Look, there's something you need to know about me. I hope it helps. What I did tonight? I would've done that for anyone. Not that you don't matter to me—you do. I care about you. A lot. But what I'm saying is, helping you isn't a burden to us. So, stop feeling like one."

His words break something open in her, and she starts sobbing again.

Jacob sits on her other side. "Is it okay if I hug you?"

She nods, and Jacob's arms wrap around her shoulders. "What you did today was hard. I'm proud that you reached out for help and that we could get you out of there. You're stronger and braver than you know."

In the days that follow, Edward and Jacob return to David's apartment while he's at work to help her pack up the rest of her things. There isn't much. David had bought nearly everything in there.

David is relentless in his attempts to reach her, his voicemails alternating between begging and crying. But Lacy remains resolute. As weeks pass, David finally grasps that it's truly over between them. His messages turn hostile. He calls her a gold digger, accuses her of wasting his family's money on a half-finished house and half-planned wedding. Edward, of course, is fired by David's mother.

Despite David's earlier claim that the store was fully hers, it isn't. She's evicted, forced to pack up everything, sell what she can, and scramble for a storage unit to house the rest of her inventory. Then the papers come—a formal notice of the debt she now owes David for months of unpaid rent, backdated and itemized. She's annoyed, but considering how much of her life had been funded by David, she counts herself lucky he doesn't expect repayment it all.

Now, she's unemployed, homeless, and severely in debt. Sophie, who recently moved back to the city, is endlessly worried about her sister. She begs Lacy to move back home with her and their mom, but the thought of facing Dawna, panicked and furious with Lacy for pulling their financial security out from under them, feels unbearable.

Instead, Sophie starts visiting her at Edward's house. She stops pushing Lacy to move back home. She shows up regularly, bringing takeout, books, movies, or just her company. They don't talk much about the situation, but Sophie's presence is a quiet anchor. She knows Lacy needs time to sort through everything, but her visits are a steady source of comfort, a reminder she can rely on her, even if there are no solutions.

As Lacy continues to heal, her connection with Edward deepens. She begins to rely on him, not just as a friend, but like family. While applying for jobs, she searches for ways to repay him for his kindness. She takes care of his house, finding solace in the routine.

She learns that Edward and Jacob stayed in touch after high school—not super close, just the occasional comment or like. A few years ago, they ran into each other at a bar and ended up drunkenly making out on the dance floor. Things evolved from there. They've been seeing each other ever since and practice non-monogamy. Edward tells her about it slowly, carefully, like he's still figuring it out himself. It's uncharted ground for Lacy, but she listens, feeling the shape of their connection unfold in his words. Over time, she becomes a confidant. And the more she sees them together, how freely they love, how much room they make for each other to grow, the more she finds herself not just understanding it, but admiring it. There's something beautiful in the way they've built this thing that doesn't try to fit into anyone else's mould.

Sophie and Lacy's bond with Edward and Jacob grows as they all start hanging out together. They buy an air mattress, turning their nights into sleepovers filled with laughter and ease.

She starts spending more time with Mina, too. Lacy opens up about her relationship with David, and Mina tells her about her own abusive ex, who had been the catalyst for her moving so far from home. There's a healing in their shared vulnerability.

Disenchanted by the job search, Lacy begins offering her copywriting services online, slowly finding her footing. She starts contributing to rent while continuing to search for a space of her own. But Edward doesn't want her to leave. He's grown to love living with her and suggests they find a new place together. The small one-bedroom has become too cramped, and he talks about getting an apartment with a balcony, a space where he can garden. When Jacob hears about their plans, he wants in, too. A big milestone in their relationship, one Lacy is happy to be a part of.

Lacy introduces Mina to Edward and Jacob on a slow Sunday afternoon. There's no performance, no forced small talk. They just click. Mina's quiet, steady warmth folds easily into the rhythm of the group. She actually gets Jacob's smart-dumb jokes, matches Edward's curiosity with her own. Sophie shows up later, and she and Mina fall into an easy conversation about their hometown, Mina catching Sophie up on half-remembered gossip about half-remembered people. Watching it unfold, Lacy feels something loosen in her chest.

*S*am has a lunch meeting at a restaurant near Lacy's store. He finds a parking spot right in front of it and is taken aback when he sees the shop shuttered, a "For Lease" sign in the window. He snaps a photo of the vacant storefront, just in case Anna checks his location later, some small bit of protection for himself.

After lunch, curiosity gnaws at him, and he can't resist the urge to investigate. Cursing himself for never learning her full name, he realizes he still can't look her up directly. Instead, he searches for the store's name and stumbles upon a post on a local forum discussing its closure. The comments overflow with praise and regret, lamenting the loss of a place known for its rare VHS tapes, curated selection of classic books, and unique vintage finds. One comment speculates the closure was linked to Lacy's fiancé, which sends Sam down another rabbit hole.

He searches David's name, quickly finding their engagement announcement, along with pictures of Lacy splashed across socialite blogs. Finally, with her full name in hand, he digs deeper into her past and uncovers what happened to her in high school. He matches the timeline and realizes it all happened just before they met in Italy. His heart sinks for her, the story of her father's incarceration and the sorrow she carried with her in Sicily now painfully clear to him.

He wants to reach out, say something, but there's no way to contact her. She doesn't seem to have any social media presence, and there's no trace of where her store might have relocated, if it even exists anymore. Once again, she's lost to him.

That night, Sam comes home to find Anna has gone through his things. His office is a mess of rummaged drawers and opened boxes, pages from his sketchbooks torn out, scattered across the floor. Anna sits in the middle of the chaos, a lighter in hand. Sam's stomach turns when he sees the drawings of Lacy burning in a pot. She's checked his location.

A heavy sense of defeat washes over him, but it also brings a sense of clarity. One he's lacked most of his adult life.

"We're done, Anna," is all he says as he walks out of the room, not caring that his office is a mess, his memories scorched. There's nothing left to fight for. He knows, without a doubt, that he can't be with her anymore.

*L*acy and Sophie spend more time together. As kids, they mostly hung out because they shared a roof. They were good to each other, just moving in separate orbits. But now, things feel different. The time they share is more intentional. Being friends and sharing friends gives their relationship space to unfold in new ways. Helps them see each other more clearly, more gently. A quiet recognition of everything they've been through, together and apart.

Their sisterly bond deepens further as they step into something new together—opening a business. Sophie had always been the one scouring thrift stores, browsing auction sites, and hunting for rare VHS tapes. It was her idea to add the VHS rental service to Lacy's store in the first place. Now, unwilling to let the tapes and machines gather dust in the storage unit, Sophie revives the rental service. She sets up an online directory and offers delivery. It becomes a modest way to bring in a little extra money while keeping Sophie's passion for preserving these relics alive, and Lacy's love for the vintage medium thriving alongside it. Jacob and Edward help with deliveries in their free time. Mina helps them navigate the financial side of things, advising them on taxes and budgeting.

Lacy can't recall the last time she felt this way. Surrounded by people with whom she can connect on almost every level. The feeling pulls her in. All she looks forward to is spending time with them, never getting weary of each other's company. For the first time since her father's betrayal, Lacy feels like she has a real friend group again. People who have her back as she does theirs. People who understand her in ways she didn't realize she needed.

The apartment hunt evolves into a house hunt as everyone begins to talk about how convenient, restorative, and fun it would be to live together. They find a house in Chinatown, on the same street where Josie used to live. Slightly outdated but full of charm. They rent the entire house, each person getting their own room. They decorate the shared areas together, creating spaces that feel cozy and safe. They even have a backyard, their collective sanctuary, flowers for the bees and butterflies, raised garden beds growing vegetables for their meals, and a bird feeder that feeds squirrels more than birds. Wind chimes blowing in the breeze, their soft tinkling filling the night air as they gather around the fire pit on chilly evenings.

As they settle into their new home, Lacy feels something she hasn't felt in a long time—a sense of belonging, a fragile but growing hope for the future.

S am lies in Paul's tub, feeling hollow, yet his mind is unbearably heavy. He flicks the faucet with his foot, letting cold water rush over him. His wet clothes cling to his skin, discomfort sinking into his bones. He welcomes it, hopes it will drown out the disgust and shame writhing through him as his mind ceaselessly replays the night's events.

Anna saw it in his eyes, his resolve. She had finally pushed him to the edge. A desperate remorse gripped her, regret and embarrassment for what she had done to his office, his drawings. She wished she could take it all back. In that moment, she saw herself clearly, how far over the line she had let her emotions take her, how much she had hurt him.

She fell to her knees, clawing at him, tears and snot streaming down her face as she begged him for forgiveness.

"Anna, what are you even fighting for?" Sam's voice was solemn. "I don't even make you happy."

"You do! I am so happy with you. I can't live without you, Sam."

"You're perpetually upset with me. You always think I'm doing something to hurt you."

In that moment of post-mania clarity, she recognized how patient Sam had been to her throughout their entire relationship, how much she had made him endure. "I know I am crazy and controlling and insecure, but I can change. I get it now. I see it."

"Anna..." Sam sighed, stepping back. "I've heard this a thousand times. I think it's time to admit that we aren't a good fit for each other."

Her sobs came harder, and the sight of her shattered him. He crouched down, pulling her into his arms, rocking her as she cried. He knew she wanted to change, but somewhere along the way, he had stopped believing she could. He had loved her enough to stick it out, to hope. But now, he sees this is where his hope had led him.

He never had the strength or courage to stand up to her, to get her help, to leave. He acknowledged that he had enabled her in many ways, out of his own selfishness, because being with her had brought him comfort, because he hadn't wanted to be alone. And in the end, his weakness had stolen ten years from both of them.

He texted Paul, letting him know he had broken up with Anna, knowing there was no taking it back once he had told his friend. There was no trace of gratification or vindication in Paul's response, only concern as he helped

Sam navigate the next steps. Paul offered him a place to stay while he and Anna sorted out their living situation, and asked if he wanted to be picked up right away. But Anna was unraveling, and Sam, despite everything, couldn't bring himself to walk out on her in that state.

One more night. Just to make sure she'd be okay.

He and Anna had talked late into the night, Anna still pleading for him to take her back, her demeanor shifting between calm, logical suggestions for how they could fix their relationship moving forward, and manic, tearful desperation at the thought of losing him. He had done his best to comfort her, but never wavered in his decision to end things.

Finally, exhausted, they had gone to sleep. Knowing that sharing a bed would be a mistake, he had offered it to her and taken the couch instead.

In the middle of the night, a wet dream that felt like a nightmare had ripped him from his restless sleep. He'd woken to find his pants down, Anna's mouth around his cock. He shoved her off him, rough, his strength unchecked in his moment of distress. He looked down at himself, horror twisting through the corrupted pleasure still pulsing in his body, carnally drawn against his will.

Crumpled on the floor, she sobbed that she just wanted to remind him that she could make him feel good. Wanted to bring him some satisfaction. He barely heard her. He'd screamed, his first time yelling at her, confused, scared, furious. At her. At his own body's betrayal. At the sight of blood.

Sam sinks into the tub, the water swallowing his ears and, eventually, his head. He pulls his heavy, wet sweater over his face, momentarily suffocating under its weight, holding his breath until his ears start to ring, and he recognizes this pull all too well—the pitch-black molasses calling him to drown in its sweet escape.

An image of his dad's bloated, waterlogged face flashes through his mind, and he wonders what had pushed his dad past the point of no return, what had pushed his mom. He wonders if this is what will push him, if he's inherited their dark fantasies of oblivion—a blood prophecy. *It's only a matter of time,* he thinks. It brings him a kind of peace.

*A*fter months of avoidance, Lacy must finally face her mother. Dawna has met a man, is moving in with him, and wants her to meet him. Sophie has already met him, her only assessment being, "He seems nice enough."

They meet for lunch at a restaurant. Gerald is a stocky man, much older than Dawna, a wealthy property developer. Loud and gregarious, he reminds Lacy of the type of man David would eventually become.

The conversation between Lacy and her mother is strained. They sidestep their long silence, the weight of their unspoken issues thick in the air. As the meal goes on, the tension eases somewhat. Gerald dominates the conversation. Sophie chimes in occasionally, overcompensating for the icy distance between her mother and sister.

When Sophie asks how the condo sale is going, Gerald interrupts. "Your mother's not selling that place," he declares, almost scolding. "What a stupid idea that would be. A unit that size, in that location? She'd be throwing away free money."

Sophie pushes back, frustrated. She's developed a particular disdain for landlords, having spent years exploited by Vancouver's ruthless rental market. Even their current landlord is terrible, their bathroom sink had been broken for weeks, leaving them with only one functioning bathroom until Jacob finally replaced it himself.

Lacy, however, feels too distant from her mother to form a clear opinion. She cannot deny the small relief she feels, a slight easing of her lingering guilt over Dawna's lost financial stability. She's grateful that she'll have an income, that she won't be entirely dependent on Gerald.

Over the next few days, as they help Dawna pack, Lacy notices a shift in her mother. Her disappointment about David faded, replaced by a genuine curiosity about what happened in the end.

Lacy tells her. She talks about the pressure of being the wife to someone larger than life, of fitting into a role that eroded her sense of self. How she had no life of her own. How he would often pressure her into sex, leaving out the violence of the night that ended things for good.

As Dawna listens, she shares her own stories. Her relationship with Dominic echoing Lacy's experiences. She describes the weight of being married to the town's beloved police chief, the pressure to play the perfect wife. How the envy of other women left her feeling isolated, unable to voice any unhappiness, the loneliness of having no space to process the doubts that unsettled her.

Tears well in her eyes as she speaks. It's the first time they've talked about her father since the incident, and something inside Lacy shifts. For the first time, she feels real empathy for her mother, too young, naive, and hurt to offer it before. Something between them softens.

Gerald's home is a charming townhouse along the lake. When Dawna moves in, he surprises her with a puppy. At first, she's unimpressed, complaining about the work a dog requires, but it takes less than a day for her to fall completely in love with the tiny blonde dachshund.

Lacy watches her mother settle into her life of domestic ease. With their relationship on the mend, evolving even, Lacy feels her own life settling into something unfamiliar—contentment, the kind she once believed would forever elude her.

With streaming platforms and distributors constantly shifting their priorities, and the so-called "not-a-recession" looming, the studio buckles under the strain. In response, Paul and Sam make the difficult decision to close the Montreal office, especially since they're both already based in Toronto. Some staff relocate while others choose to work remotely.

Under Paul and Celeste's advice, Sam lets go of his old apartment. The memories there too suffocating. He's still unpacking everything—the weight of the last decade, the chaos of his relationship, the slow erosion of his sense of self. But moving in with Paul and Celeste feels like coming up for air. He finds comfort in witnessing the small acts of love that build their relationship—a mosaic of affection. Paul waking up early to make her breakfast while she gets ready for school. The way he always knows, just by her outfit, which shoes she'll want that day, pulling them from the closet and setting them by the door. How she always finds his phone and plugs it in before bed, usually lost and lifeless somewhere in the couch cushions. His monthly drives to the Chinese restaurant a town away to pick up chili oil and dumplings she loves. Celeste always stopping at the same odd gas station because it's the only place that sells the strange marshmallow candies Paul likes. Their random drives to random houses to pick up some treasure she found secondhand.

Sam's life starts to fold into their rhythm. The never-ending supply of instant noodles he mentioned liking once, now always stocked in the pantry. His toothbrush, once lying listlessly on the counter, now stands proud in its own cup. Bananas on the counter, even though he's the only one who eats them. Their routines become his and his theirs—nightly dinners, chili oil car rides, marshmallow candies, reading in the living room after dinner.

How easy it is to love and be loved here. It's infinite—the love that pours out of them like water over the falls, like noodles in the cabinet.

Living together also rekindles his creative spark with Paul. They shift their focus away from client projects and return to what first brought them together, telling stories on their terms. They begin brainstorming original anima-tions for their website, rediscovering the joy of making things just because they want to.

His aunts visit after hearing about the breakup, and he speaks honestly with them in a way he never has before. Their warmth and wisdom help steady him, but the scars linger. After years of walking on eggshells, second-guess-ing every word and decision, Sam feels unmoored—drifting through the dark undertow of a life that nearly swallowed him whole.

One evening, Sam stays late at the office, the only soul left in the dimly lit space. As he works, he hears a faint whimper. A small, pitiful sound. At first, he wonders if it's his sleep deprivation playing tricks on him. But the sound persists, pulling him from his desk. He follows it, late past midnight, through the empty halls, until it leads him to the IT closet in the basement. There, tangled in a mess of wires within the network rack, he finds a little kitten. Its orange and black fur patchy, scabs and dried blood crusted on its tiny body. The kitten hisses and scratches as Sam carefully untangles it from the wires, pulls it out as it bites his hand, wrapping the trembling creature in his sweater.

Unsure what else to do, Sam looks up local animal shelters. They're all closed. Panicked, he rushes the kitten to an emergency vet, where he spends hours in the waiting room while the staff clean and tend to its wounds. When they finally bring it back out, patches of its fur have been shaved, revealing a frail, skinny frame. A vet tech tells him gently that if she makes it through the night, she'll be transferred to a shelter in the morning.

Sam stays until dawn, dozing in his car outside the clinic, too wired to fully sleep. As the sky begins to lighten, he checks in with the vet tech, who tells him that the kitten made it through the night. She's going to be okay.

He returns to the office in the same clothes from the day before. No sweater. He'd left it with her in the crate, stained with her blood and his. As he works, he can't stop thinking about the kitten. The way she'd felt in his arms, impossibly light, skin and bones, fragile but fighting.

During his lunch break, he goes back to the clinic. The kitten is still there. No shelter has come for her, all of them at capacity. There's nowhere for her to go. Without thinking much more about it, Sam pays the vet bill and takes her home. He doesn't dwell on what might've happened if he hadn't.

Celeste, despite her severe allergy, is immediately smitten. Her eyes itch, her nose runs, a rash blooms on her hands as she tries to pet the scrappy little thing. The kitten, still feral, is afraid of everyone.

After weeks of Celeste downplaying her allergies, her puffy eyes, stuffy nose, and constant sneezing betraying her, Sam finally accepts it's time to move out. He rents a condo near the studio. There are two bedrooms, one for him, one for his family: his aunts, Paul, and Celeste. He converts the den into an office.

Moving out is bittersweet. His year with them has been more restorative than he thought possible. He'll miss the warmth of living with them, the ease of their shared patterns. But caring for the kitten gives him a new routine, a sense of purpose. The cycle of medications, feedings, and gentle coaxing helps both the cat and Sam heal. Slowly, she starts to trust him, trailing him from room to room. One night, she hops into his lap and curls up as he works—the start of a quiet ritual. Her steady presence mends something broken in him. A small but steady raft in the relentless tide that had nearly pulled him under.

Their landlord repaves the cracking driveway "for free" and doubles their rent in the same week.

Lacy, who's built up a steady roster of clients writing ad copy, ends up covering her sister's share. Sophie's freelance video editing work hasn't been as reliable. Pressed by guilt and her growing reliance on her older sister, Sophie had been quietly pursuing a position at a film studio, guarding the details of her interview like a delicate flame, afraid that speaking about it too soon might snuff it out. She doesn't want to carry the weight of her friends' expectations or excitement—or worse, disappointment.

When Lacy spots her sister in a full business casual outfit pulled from her own closet, she can't help but grill her. Sophie stays tight-lipped, and all day, Lacy fights the urge to barrage her with texts. She knows this is exactly why Sophie kept it to herself. So, when the group chat pings with Sophie's message inviting them out for drinks to celebrate her new job, her heart swells with joy.

It's been almost two years since Sam's breakup. Their studio is thriving, creating and publishing their own content. Sam's life has settled into a steady rhythm. He cares for his cat, works every day, and visits his aunts every few months. He has reconnected with his friends, all of them also his coworkers, and sees them almost every day. Weekly movie nights with Paul and their group have resumed, filling his evenings with laughter and camaraderie. Yet, an undercurrent of melancholy lingers, a quiet ache he's had to learn to live with.

One evening, Sam finds himself at their usual haunt, a bar near the studio, tucked into a familiar booth with Paul, Celeste, and a couple of friends from work. He's nursing a beer, half-listening to the conversation, when something shifts in the air, a subtle tug at his consciousness. He looks up—and there she is.

Lacy steps through the door, snowflakes glittering in her hair like tiny stars. She looks radiant. Healthy. Happy. She smiles as the host greets her and leads her toward the bar.

To Sam's left, Ben straightens in his seat, clearly noticing her too. "Damn," he mutters, and the rest of the table turns to look.

Lacy shrugs off her coat, shakes her hair free from her scarf, and drapes it over the back of her barstool. As if sensing his gaze, she glances up, her eyes locking with his immediately. A slow, wide smile spreads across her face, and Sam's stomach flips, a soft flutter of something deep inside him.

"Do you know her?" Casey asks.

Before he can think, his legs are already moving, carrying him out of the booth toward her. She steps down from the barstool, her eyes never leaving his.

"Lacy." His voice is warm, a familiar knot tightening in his chest at the sight of her.

"Hi, Sam," she says, and the sound of his name on her lips casts a spell, some buried spark inside him flickering back to life.

"Hi," he laughs softly, unable to stop smiling down at her.

She stretches to wrap her arms around his shoulders. He pulls her close, burying his face in her hair, breathing her in, a familiar scent from a lifetime ago.

"I can't believe you're here."

"Me neither."

They both chuckle softly, the sound carrying a quiet familiarity. She gestures for him to sit.

"Are you here by yourself?" he asks.

"No, I'm meeting my friends."

He asks about her store, and she doesn't mention why it closed, only telling him that she works as a copywriter now. She, in turn, asks about his studio, playfully scolding him for not telling her he owns it.

The conversation flows effortlessly, comfortable and easy, as if no time has passed.

Lacy glances over his shoulder, smirking at something behind him. He turns to find his friends staring at them, Paul and Celeste wearing amused smiles. They wave at Lacy, and she waves back.

"They're just entertained because I never talk to women," Sam explains.

She takes a sip of her water. "I don't think I believe you."

"Well, believe it."

"You talked to me on the beach. And you're talking to me right now."

"With you, I don't have a choice." His voice is tender with honesty. "More like gravity."

Lacy blushes, and Sam fights the urge to brush his thumb over the pink blossoms on her cheeks.

"I bet women talk *to you*, though," she teases.

"I'm bad at talking back."

She chuckles. "It probably makes you more endearing."

His heart does a little squeeze at her words.

Her gaze flicks behind him again, and she chuckles at the sight of his friends, who are doing a poor job of pretending not to watch.

"Yeah, they're probably going to act like this the whole time," Sam says.

"Should we go say hi?" she offers.

He's not sure what to make of it, someone so eager to step into his world. "Sure."

They make their way to the booth; his friends squeeze together to make room for her. Introductions are made, and Sam can see the curiosity in everyone's eyes. Something *more* in Ben's gaze, but he chooses to ignore it. Who could blame the guy?

"We met when we were younger," Lacy says when someone asks how she knows Sam, her eyes finding his and holding there. The intensity of her gaze knocks the air right out of his lungs.

"When?" Casey asks.

"When we were seventeen? Eighteen?"

"Oh my god, you've known each other for ten years? How have we not met?" Celeste exclaims.

"No, we haven't seen each other since then." She smiles. "Well, we ran into each other last year, or the year before? Paul was there," she says, gesturing to Paul.

Lacy asks how everyone knows each other, and Celeste introduces herself as Paul's wife, Paul and Sam met online, and Ben and Casey work at the studio.

Just then, a familiar woman walks into the bar and approaches the table, her eyes bouncing between Lacy, Sam, and Paul.

"What?" she gasps.

"Sophie?" Sam blurts, recognizing the new editor he and Paul had hired just that afternoon.

Sophie's wide-eyed gaze lands on her sister. "Lacy— what are you doing with my bosses?"

"What?" Lacy exclaims, her head whipping toward Sam. "*Your* studio hired my sister?"

The table erupts into surprised exclamations and laughter. Lacy and Sophie share with the group the delightful coincidence that they're actually out celebrating Sophie's new job. Paul invites them to join the table, wanting to share in the celebration. The group shifts to make more room.

Lacy's body presses against Sam's side, and he feels a warmth spread through him, a quiet thrill at her nearness.

When Mina and Edward arrive, the booth can no longer accommodate everyone, so they move to a larger table. Jacob is the last to arrive, his lively energy filling the room as he introduces himself to everyone, shaking hands with each person. He hugs Sophie tightly, lifting her off the ground in his excitement for her, tousling her hair like an older brother. As he takes a seat next to Lacy, he plants a kiss on her cheek, and Sam can't help but feel a sharp pang. He looks away before the feeling can settle—it does anyway.

The night unfolds with drinks and laughter as the two groups get to know each other. Sam is struck by how close Lacy's friends seem, like a family. Jacob and Casey realize they had matched on a dating app before, and Ben recognizes Mina from the bank. Small threads of fate had been weaving through their lives all along, brushing past each other until they finally wove together.

At this, Lacy looks up at him, and he wonders if she can somehow hear his thoughts, drawn to the quiet truth vibrating within him. She smiles, and he feels a wave of joy and pride at introducing her to his friends. He can tell they're captivated by her, and he finds himself equally charmed by her friends, charismatic, sincere, and full of life.

Paul and Celeste have to leave to host their weekly movie night and invite Lacy and her friends to join. Mina and Edward opt to head home. Jacob kisses Edward goodbye, and the relief flooding Sam nearly knocks him off balance.

Sam, Lacy, Sophie, and Jacob share a cab. Sophie takes the front seat to mitigate her car sickness. Lacy sits between Jacob and Sam in the back. He wonders if she can feel the electric buzz where their hands almost touch. Jacob's hand rests casually on Lacy's knee, and Sam can't quite figure out their dynamic. Jacob seems like the type who has chemistry with everyone he meets, like he's dating half the group.

At Paul and Celeste's house, Sophie fits right in. Her passion for movies is magnetic, effortlessly drawing them toward her. Lacy watches her with quiet pride, captivated by how easily Sophie connects with everyone in the room.

Sam sits beside Lacy on the couch, their knuckles touching. She steals glances at the moon ring on his finger, her heart fluttering each time she sees it.

Finally, she gives in, reaching out to brush her fingers against it.

"I never got to thank you," Sam says softly.

"You know I was going to meet you that day, right?" she replies, her finger smoothing over the ring's surface. "It was my mom. I had to leave. I had no choice. I'm sorry."

The words wash over him like the warm glow of summer sun, and somewhere deep inside, the lid of an ancient puzzle box snaps shut.

"I believe you," he says.

They sit without words for a moment, the hum of chatter around them the only sound, until she breaks the silence. "Did you wait for me at the beach?"

"Well past sunset," he confirms, a faint smile tugging at his lips. He flexes his finger, admiring the ring as if he's still trying to process it all.

She smiles, but there's sadness in it. "I'm sorry."

"Don't be. I found you again in the end, didn't I?"

Lacy's heart flutters uncontrollably at his words.

"Where's your girlfriend?" she asks.

Sam looks away. "We're not together anymore." His gaze falls to her ring finger, now bare. "I see you're not wearing your engagement ring."

"Nope," she confirms, holding her hand out as if to prove it. "He asked for the ring back. Can you believe it?"

"What a cheapskate," Sam scoffs.

She laughs. "It's okay. I didn't want to keep it, to be honest."

She feels the weight of Sam's gaze on her, and when their eyes meet, everything around them seems to still. The years have changed him, but he's still the boy from the beach. There's something unmistakably familiar in his eyes. She wants to keep looking, drawn to the quiet sadness she sees hidden behind the mesmerizing shades of autumn, but the intensity of his gaze makes her shy.

Her eyes flutter back to the ring. She can hardly believe she's seeing it here. She hadn't even had the chance to look at it the day she bought it. The fact that he's wearing it now, here, in this city they both unexpectedly ended up in, surrounded by their friends... It all feels too big, too surreal to take in. All she can manage is, "It looks really good on you."

He reaches for the pendant around her neck, his fingers grazing the skin at her décolletage, sending a shiver through her.

"I can't believe you kept it. That you wear it. You were wearing it the last time I saw you, too."

"Of course." She reaches for it, her fingers brushing his. "It's my favorite thing ever."

When it's time to leave, Sam walks her out.

"Can I have your number?" he asks. "Just in case you disappear again." His tone is flirty, his eyes earnest.

"*D*ude," Paul deadpans in the middle of their team meeting.

Sam barely hears him, eyes glued to his phone. His fingers fly across the screen, his lips twitching into a grin before he quickly schools his expression, pretending to focus. It doesn't fool anyone. Sam has been texting with Lacy, their conversations pulling him into his phone every time it buzzes.

Paul rolls his eyes but can't quite hide his small smile. He's never seen Sam like this before, so easily distracted, so completely lost in someone. "Hopeless," he mutters, shaking his head, but the amusement in his voice betrays him.

One evening, Lacy and Sophie are lying on the couch together, Sophie watching as her sister smiles into her phone, thumbs tapping on the screen.

"I can't believe you never told me about him," Sophie says, kicking Lacy's foot lightly.

"There was nothing to tell," Lacy replies, a smile growing on her face.

Sophie scoffs. "You ditched me and Mom with that nasty tour guide for days. For him," she retorts, throwing a pillow at her. "Nothing to tell, my ass."

Spring arrives, bringing warmth and sunnier days, and with it, Sophie's birthday. The house overflows with laughter and music, the party spilling into the backyard, glowing under a canopy of fairy lights.

Lacy notices when Sam and his friends arrive, his presence shifting something in her atmosphere. His searching gaze sweeps the crowd, lighting up when he sees her.

"You look really beautiful," he says when he reaches her.

She's wearing a long white dress scattered with tiny blue flowers, the kind he's seen blooming in patches on grassy sidewalks. His words send warmth to her cheeks, and she can't look at him as she thanks him, tucking a loose strand of hair behind her ear.

They find themselves in a circle of conversation, nodding along as the chatter fills the air. But their attention keeps drifting, stolen glances exchanged in the spaces between words. After every laugh, their eyes find each other, both of them silently searching for the right moment to be alone, neither quite sure when it will come.

"I love your backyard," he tells her when the conversation lulls, taking in the lush green sanctuary.

Before she can respond, Jacob whisks her further into the yard, pulling her into a dance as their favourite song plays over the speakers. Edward follows, nudges Sam to join. Soon, they're part of a loose circle, bodies moving in a drunken rhythm, hands reaching for hands.

Jacob pulls Lacy close, his hands on her waist as they twirl, then reaches for Edward, spinning him into an embrace. Lacy finds herself in Sam's orbit, their movements naturally syncing. His hands settle on her waist, hers loop around his neck. The music and the heat of the night seem to pull them into a rhythm all their own.

She spins, her back against his chest, reaches up behind her, fingertips grazing his neck as she dances against him, and he feels warmth bloom through him. Her fingers thread into his hair as his hands tighten around her waist, steadying her, grounding himself. She spins in his arms, their eyes locking, her gaze darting to his lips, his to hers, and for a moment, the world narrows to the shock of want mirrored in both their eyes.

The sudden sound of glass breaking shatters the spell. Lacy pulls away to help clean up, and Sam follows close behind, knowing her track record with broken glass.

As the night winds down, Sam is sitting on the couch with Paul, Celeste, and Ben, only half-listening as Edward's work friend talks about some new outdoor mall their company is building. His attention keeps drifting to Lacy, perched on the kitchen counter, laughing with Jacob.

Jacob's arm rests on the counter by her thigh, their heads close together.

A pang of possessiveness flares in Sam, a feeling he hates but can't shake.

Ben nudges him, eyes on Lacy. "Yo, you think they're together? I thought that guy was with the other guy, but I can't tell with these people."

Paul elbows Ben. "Dude," he mutters, shaking his head.

Lacy catches Sam's eye then. She gives him a warm smile and waves him over.

When he joins them, Jacob slings an arm around his shoulders, and he struggles not to shrug it off. "My guy, enjoying the party?"

"Yeah, it's great," Sam says, and he means it. The house is alive with energy, a vibrant mix of people, all of whom exude an energy of openness.

Jacob is asking him questions about his art when the sound of something else shattering cuts through their conversation.

"Again?" Lacy whines, jumping off the counter to investigate.

"I'll deal with it, sister," Jacob says, downing the last of his beer. "Stay and chat with *your man*." He nods to Sam.

Lacy's cheeks go pink, already flushed from the drinks, and just like that, Jacob becomes Sam's favorite person at the party—well, second favorite.

LAIDA LEE

As the crowd thins, Lacy gives Sam a proper tour of the house. When she shows him her room, he pauses—his painting hangs on the wall, like a window to their beach. She leads him downstairs, and he sees that they've transformed the basement into a cozy movie den, with a giant couch, almost like a bed, facing a projector screen. Scanning the shelves, Sam finds a time capsule of VHS tapes, DVDs, and Blu-rays. He spots a VHS of his favorite childhood movie.

"Want to watch it?" Lacy asks, seeing the tape in his hands.

She wheels in a CRT TV, the nostalgic sight making him laugh. They settle on the couch bed, the glow of the screen casting soft light across the room. The familiar opening scenes play, and for a moment, it feels like they've stepped back in time.

Sophie bursts in with a delighted squeal when she sees the movie, hopping onto the couch bed before hesitating. "Wait, am I interrupting?"

Lacy chuckles. "No, it's okay. Come watch with us," she says, patting the space beside her. Sophie flops down, resting her head on her sister's shoulder, her eyes glassy from the drinks.

The other housemates trickle in to join them on the couch. Edward tosses blankets to everyone before curling into Jacob's embrace. Mina and Sophie snuggle under a blanket, while Lacy and Sam share another.

The party above fades as more people migrate downstairs, turning the basement into a cozy nest of blankets and quiet laughter. Casey and Ben squeeze in beside Sam,

Casey leaning into him and resting her head on his arm. Sam shifts uncomfortably, his body stiff. The press of skin around him makes him uneasy.

Lacy, noticing his discomfort, mouths, *Are you okay?*

He nods, but she's not convinced. Under the blanket, her knuckles brush his, her pinky lightly hooking around his, a timid invitation. He opens his hand, and she slips hers into his, their fingers lacing together. The warmth of her touch steadies him, quiets his unease.

As the movie continues, the party gradually thins out. Ben prepares to leave and, since he lives near Casey, asks if she wants to split a ride home.

Casey turns to Sam. "When are you leaving?"

Sam tries to pull out his phone to check the time, but his movements are awkward since he won't let go of Lacy's hand. He struggles with his left hand, trying to get the phone out of his right pocket. Noticing, Lacy unclasps their hands.

"I'll probably stay a little longer," he says to Casey. "Unless you want me gone sooner?" he asks Lacy, unable to help the smile that spreads across his face whenever their eyes meet.

"You can stay as late as you want," she replies, returning his smile.

"Why?" he asks, turning back to Casey, who seems too distracted watching Sam reach for Lacy's hand under the blanket.

"Oh, um... Nothing. Just wondering," Casey says. She decides to leave with Ben, who insists on hugging Lacy before departing, breaking their handhold again. Sam shifts over to make more room on the couch, and Lacy follows, her hand finding his as her head settles against his shoulder. He leans back, too, resting his cheek on her hair.

By the time the credits roll, Sophie and Edward are asleep on the couch. Jacob lifts Edward effortlessly, and Sam catches the soft, affectionate glance between them as Edward stirs, a look he's seen Paul and Celeste share.

Sophie is out cold, her body heavy with sleep. Sam offers to carry her to her room. Lacy leads the way, watching as he gently tucks her sister in. When they step back into the hallway, the air between them feels charged, the energy of the night sinking into something quiet and unspoken.

At the front door, they linger.

Lacy hugs him, the swirl of emotions from the evening: excitement, trepidation, longing, settling something within her, a key turning with certainty.

Sam pulls back slightly to look at her. "Can I see you again tomorrow?"

Lacy laughs softly. "It's already tomorrow."

"Can I see you later, then?" Sam grins, recognizing their old rhythm.

She bites her lip, her smile too wide to hide. "See you at sunset?"

His heart skips a beat. "Sunset," he repeats, like a prayer.

Sam is supposed to come over the next evening but cancels because his cat isn't feeling well. He invites Lacy over instead.

Lacy finds Sophie eating cereal in the kitchen and extends an invitation to her.

"You want me to come on your date with you?" Sophie snorts, raising a brow.

"It's not a date."

Sophie looks at her older sister skeptically. "He invited *you* over. Not *us*."

"He was supposed to come over to watch a movie. I would've asked you to join anyway."

"And I would've said no."

"Why?"

"Because it's a *date*."

"It's not."

Sophie lets her spoon fall into her bowl with a loud clash, eyes narrowing. "Mina and I saw you two holding hands last night."

Lacy exhales sharply, pulls out her phone, types something, and flips the screen toward Sophie.

Sophie stares at Sam's reply: Of course, she can come

"Why did you do that?"

"I want you to come."

"Why?" Sophie studies her. "Do you not like him back?" she says, knowing the words aren't true as they leave her mouth.

Lacy hesitates. "I... I don't know. I'm scared."

"Of what?"

"Of what his expectations are. Of being alone with him, at his place. And... I don't think he'd try anything if you were there."

Understanding settles in Sophie's expression as she takes in her sister's words. She nods. "Okay. Let's go."

As impossible as it seems for more threads to bind them together, Lacy is stunned to learn that Sam has been renting their old condo from their mother. Sophie spends the entire subway ride railing against their mother for being a landlord, how she's financially exploiting their friend, declaring it's their moral obligation to do something about it.

When they step into the familiar building and ride the elevator to their old floor, a wave of nostalgia crashes over Lacy, slowing her steps. Memories surge forward, vivid and untamed, like a dormant current breaking through the surface. Sophie notices her hesitation, hooks her arm through Lacy's, and steadies her as they approach their old door and knock.

Inside, the condo is nearly unrecognizable. The rooms have been repurposed, the furniture rearranged into configurations they would never have imagined. The space they had inhabited is gone, rewritten by Sam's presence. And yet, instead of loss, Lacy feels something like relief, proof that spaces, like people, are not fixed in time. The past does not dictate the present. A home, like a self, can be reimagined.

Lacy falls instantly in love with Sam's cat. The fluffy creature watches them warily, copper eyes flickering between caution and curiosity, hesitant to approach these strangers in her domain.

"She's not feeling well today, so she's extra shy," Sam says, gazing down at the cat with unguarded affection.

"What's her name?" Lacy asks.

Sam scratches the back of his head, half-laughing. "Uh... I haven't named her..."

Sophie's tone is incredulous. "How long have you had her?"

"Like... a year?"

"Sam," Lacy laughs. "She needs a name."

"I can't do that!" He gestures helplessly. "She's her own person. I don't think I have that kind of authority over her."

"She's *your* cat," Sophie says pointedly.

"She's *my* cat, the same way she's my roommate. I don't own her. I just found her," he says, lifting the cat into his arms. She rubs against his neck, melting into the crook of his shoulder. Something about the sight pulls at Lacy's heartstrings, this hesitant, frightened thing pressing into Sam, finding safety in his presence. The unbearable tenderness in it makes her breath catch.

As they settle into the couch, Sophie picks out a psychological horror movie. Sam brings the duvet from his room, making a mental note to invest in a proper throw blanket if he's going to start having people over more often. If Lacy is going to be here more often.

As the movie unfolds, Sam savors the way Lacy leans into him whenever there's a sudden scare, her head tucking into his shoulder like it's the most natural thing in the world. He fights the overwhelming urge to wrap his arms around her, pull her closer, run his fingers through her hair, and reassure her when the tension peaks. Instead, he searches for her hand under the blanket. Their fingers brush under the sheets, and in the dim glow of the screen, Sophie notices—a knowing smile tugging at her lips.

After the movie, Sam and Lacy listen in awe as Sophie dissects its symbolism, the coming-of-age narrative, the raw portrayal of queerness and identity using the terrors of modern technology as a narrative device. The conversation unfolds naturally, leading them to discuss their personal relationships with queerness.

Lacy speaks about her attraction to women, a part of herself she's never fully explored in conversation before. She exhales, the words coming slower now, more deliberate.

"I never really thought about my sexuality as a concept, like the whole time I was with a woman, I was so swept up by *her* that I didn't think about what it meant for *me*. Now looking back, I have had a lot of queer experiences, I just never framed them that way." She pauses, shaking her head slightly, a small, wry smile forming. "Maybe I didn't have the language for it. Had no exposure to queer people growing up in that small town."

She talks about high school, how she always preferred kissing girls over boys at parties, how a lingering touch or a shared glance with another girl sent a thrill through her that she couldn't quite explain. She wrote it off as *just the way girls are*, because no one had ever given her another framework to understand it.

She hesitates before speaking, the weight of her words settling over her. "For a long time, I don't think I cared to explore what it all meant. Life was just... happening *at* me. School. Relationships. Expectations. Responsibilities. I never really stopped to think about myself. I was just trying to keep up." She pauses, a quiet thought rising in her. "Life was always too loud for me to hear myself."

But now, in this moment, with Sam and Sophie, something shifts. For the first time, Lacy gives herself the space to look back, take ownership of her own story, not just as a series of things that happened to her, but as something she can name.

Sophie listens intently, seeing a new facet of her sister she's never been privy to. She asks about her friendship with Mina, how she had always sensed something different about their bond compared to Lacy's other friendships. Lacy admits that she and Mina have never talked about it. Maybe there was something more brewing between them when they were young, something neither of them fully understood at the time. Something they had played out subconsciously.

Sam absorbs each revelation like layering brush strokes onto a canvas, the picture taking shape with every added detail.

Lacy is struck by how effortless it feels to talk about this with Sam, how natural it is to be seen in this way. David never brought up her sexuality except to twist it into something for his amusement, always sexualizing the picture he'd seen of her and Josie, his interest never extending beyond what he could take from it. Here, though, she feels no discomfort, no need to perform or suppress.

Sam opens up about his aunts, about how their deep connection to each other and their place in the queer community made them some of the most empathetic people he's ever known. How they helped shape the way he sees the world, in ways he's still coming to understand.

As he speaks, he realizes how much he misses them. The thought of visiting them crosses his mind, but something about them coming here feels more enticing. And he realizes it's because he wants them to meet Lacy. And Sophie. And the rest of their friends. He imagines the lively, impassioned conversations they would have, dissecting movies like this one, exchanging ideas, perspectives, and stories.

When he exhales at the thought, his breath comes out easy.

Lacy and Sam start talking every day, spending more time together, hanging out with his cat, watching movies, and going to restaurants. There are lingering glances and subtle touches—hands brushing as they walk, the way she reaches over to touch his knee when he makes her laugh, how he tucks her hair behind her ear, fingers lingering just a second too long.

Slowly, their friend groups begin to merge. Sophie and Lacy grow closer to Paul and Celeste, becoming regulars at their movie nights. Over time, their friends blend into a little group of their own.

Tonight, they sit together, Sam's arm draped along the back of the couch, their knees touching. Lacy leans into his shoulder, and his hand slides around her.

Earlier, she and Ben shared a joint outside, their laughter drifting in through the window. Sam rolled his eyes at the sound. Now, he watches as the weed works its soporific enchantment upon her heavy eyelids, her body warm and slack against him.

By the end of the night, Lacy is fast asleep beside him. Sophie and Paul are deep in conversation, hands gesturing wildly as they storyboard a horror animation idea based on Filipino folklore. Sam listens absently, studying the chiaroscuro and luster of the TV's cool-toned glow against Lacy's warm skin.

When Paul and Sophie finally stop bouncing ideas back and forth, it's late. Paul offers Sophie and Lacy a room. Sam's stay is a given; they still act like he lives here.

Sophie hesitates before heading to the guest room. She glances at Sam. She trusts him, but cannot shake the small knot in her chest at the thought of leaving her sleeping sister alone with a man.

"You good?" Sophie asks.

"Yeah." His answer is steady, unquestioning.

Sophie's soft footsteps disappear up the stairs.

Lacy stirs after a while, blinking sleepily at the empty living room.

Sam is watching another movie with the sound off when she suddenly startles awake. "Where's my sister?"

"In the guest room," he tells her.

From the storage closet, he grabs bedding, a small towel, and a toothbrush for her.

"Where's yours?" she asks, standing in the doorway of the powder room.

He reaches around her to open the vanity drawer, pulling out his toothbrush, one of those skinny electric ones, bristles slightly frayed from use.

"You come here a lot?" she asks, watching as he rips open the frosted packaging of her toothbrush and tiny tube of toothpaste from some fancy hotel, handing them to her along with the towel. Lacy takes them, her finger-tips brushing the back of his hand.

Sam laughs. "I used to live here."

She hums, then asks, "So… would you happen to know if there are any security cameras in the house?"

"No, just the doorbell camera. Why?"

She shrugs. "Just curious."

Understanding dawns on him.

"There aren't any," he reassures her. "Paul would've told me."

"You guys are close?" she asks, squeezing toothpaste onto her toothbrush, then offering up the tube to him.

"Yeah. He's my brother," Sam says, extending his toothbrush to her.

Sam shifts in the recliner, its boucle texture a sensory night-mare against his skin. The chair whines under his weight.

Into the charged darkness, Lacy asks, "Do you want to sleep on the sofa bed with me?"

Sam hesitates, twisting to look at her. "Do you want me to?"

"If you want to."

Neither of them moves, both trying to gauge the other.

"Okay," Sam finally says, the gears in the recliner squeaking as he pushes himself up. He slides into bed beside her, the air between them taut.

Barely above a whisper, Lacy blurts, "This isn't an invitation to have sex, by the way."

Sam stiffens. "Yeah. I didn't think it was."

"Okay. Sorry."

"Don't be sorry."

Silence stretches, heavy but not uncomfortable. The streetlamp outside casts soft, golden lines across the ceiling.

After a moment, Lacy blurts, "You know Casey likes you, right?" The first thing that comes to mind to fill the quiet. She's been wondering if Sam has noticed Casey's lingering glances, the way she laughs a little harder when he's around, her subtle iciness toward Lacy.

He shrugs. "I don't care about that stuff." Then, after a beat, "Except with you."

She's grateful the dark hides her stupid grin, the burn in her cheeks.

"Ben obviously has a crush on you," Sam volleys.

"He does?" she says, feigning ignorance.

He bumps his shoulder against hers. "Don't pretend."

She lets out a small laugh.

"So..." she teases. "You think I should give him a chance?"

She doesn't have to see him to know he's rolling his eyes. "I'll fire him if you do."

Lacy laughs, the sound is like magic to him.

Silence settles again, softer this time. Her knuckles brush his, and without hesitation, he takes her hand, threading his fingers through hers. His thumb grazing over the soft web between her thumb and forefinger.

"My ex would've been mad at me for that joke," Lacy says quietly. "He was really jealous."

"Mine too."

"Are you?"

Sam exhales. "Sometimes." He remembers the flicker of heat in his chest when he saw Ben pass her the joint, the way the tip passed from his lips to hers. "You?"

"I don't know. I've only felt jealous once, when I watched my girlfriend cheat on me."

He squeezes her hand. "I'm sorry."

She turns toward him, their faces close in the dark, her eyes sleepy. "It's okay. It was my first relationship. Maybe we weren't even technically in one. Maybe we were open the whole time, and I didn't know."

Sam gives her a dubious look. "I don't think that's how it works."

She just shrugs.

"My ex always accused me of cheating," he says after a moment. "I was scared to even look at other women. She'd pick fights over nothing. I'd reassure her constantly, but she always assumed the worst."

Lacy's brows knit. "Why?"

"I don't know." He exhales. "Maybe something happened before she met me. Something that scared her too much to let her trust me."

Lacy nods. She understands.

"Something like that happened to me, too."

He squeezes her hand again, then brings it to rest against his chest, his heartbeat steady beneath her fingers.

"It scares me, too," she whispers.

"What does?"

"How much I like you."

The next morning, Sophie and Lacy walk home. It's too nice a day to miss the sun's warmth. They stop at the Chinese bakery for some buns, picking up a few for their housemates. Then, they cut through the park, making their way to the looping art structure. They sit inside its curvy forms, large, alien, almost otherworldly, their smooth, sensual lines creating a quiet space to eat and talk.

Sophie wobbles in her seat, settling into the crevice of the sculpture's curves. "Look, I get why you're worried this could blow up in your face, but I don't think it will this time, Lace."

Lacy pulls her gaze away from the dogs playing in the park, turning her attention back to her sister.

"I think this is the real thing," Sophie says, taking a big bite of her sausage bun. "I've never seen you like this."

"Like what?"

"Like... happy."

"I have been happy this whole time. Living with you guys." And she means it.

"I know. That's why I think this is real. You weren't looking for it, but it found you anyway." Sophie studies her sister for a beat. "I've never seen you the way you are around him. And I like how you are with him. I like how he is with you."

Lacy lets the words settle, the truth of them sinking in.

And as she thinks of Sam, the time spent with him, the way he looks at her, the way he makes her feel, the way she knows she makes him feel, she realizes that learning to trust him, in some quiet, certain way, is teaching her to trust herself.

*T*hey start seeing each other every day. Lacy makes a habit of visiting the studio during lunch, bringing meals for Sophie and Sam, who tend to forget to eat when they get caught up in their projects. Their conversations are easy and fun, the kind that stretch longer than they mean to, full of quick banter and inside jokes.

Sometimes, Paul, Ben, Casey, or whoever else is around the studio joins. Ben has toned down his flirting, wary of his boss's mordacious looks. Casey has grown closer to Sophie as they work together. She's even warmed up to Lacy, her attraction to Sam waning in the face of his clear devotion directed elsewhere.

After work, Sam usually likes to come over. They retreat to the basement to watch movies, talk, and cuddle. Hanging out in her room feels too intimate right now.

Tonight, their hands are entwined, her head resting on his shoulder. Tears gather in Lacy's eyes, threatening to spill as she watches another one of Sam's childhood favourites, a Japanese animation about a cursed boy and a wolf girl.

Edward's voice suddenly calls down from upstairs, breaking the moment. "Remember the couch rule!"

Sam blinks. "What's the couch rule?"

Lacy shakes her head, laughing sheepishly. "No sex on the couch."

Sam nods. "Got it."

Weeks have passed since they started spending time together, and they haven't even kissed yet.

"Sorry," Lacy murmurs, uncertain.

"No, I agree—no sex on the movie couch is a solid rule."

"No..." Lacy hesitates, voice soft. "That we haven't... done anything physical yet."

Sam's eyes widen, his face softening with concern. "Please don't ever apologize for that," he says firmly, bringing their clasped hands to his lips and kissing her fingers. "I don't care about that."

"You don't?"

"No—I mean—yes, of course, I care. But it's not..." He stumbles, struggling to articulate his thoughts. "Just— don't say sorry. You have nothing to be sorry for."

They settle back into the movie. A moment later, Lacy shifts, her gaze locking onto his.

"I want to, you know," she admits, her eyes flicking between his and his lips. She leans in just enough for him to feel the warmth of her breath.

His eyes glaze over. "Me too." His voice is thick with longing, making her pulse quicken.

"I'm just... scared," she finishes softly.

"Me too," Sam says again, brushing his finger over her lips. "Don't worry."

Lacy studies him. "What are you scared of?"

Sam exhales. His gaze drops to his hands, fingers curling slightly as if trying to suppress a tremor. "I don't know. Sex is... complicated for me."

"Why?" Lacy's touch is gentle as she covers his hand with both of hers.

Sam swallows, throat tight. He takes a deep breath, gathering his courage, then begins to tell her about Anna. The manipulation. The threats of suicide. How her insecurities controlled them both. How she destroyed his office. And then, the night he woke to find her performing oral sex on his unconscious body. The tangled mess of fear, disgust, pleasure, and shame that roiled through him, still lingering, warping his feelings around intimacy.

"I'm sorry that happened," Lacy whispers, eyes glistening. She cups his face, thumb brushing his cheek as a tear escapes.

"Don't worry about me, angel," he murmurs, leaning into her touch.

As the credits roll, a quiet settles between them, heavy with the weight of the film and everything they've shared. And yet, somehow, Sam feels lighter.

"Will you tell me about your dad?" he asks softly.

Lacy's heart tightens. The last person she told was Josie, and that ended badly. And when David found out, his disappointment in her was unbearable.

"There's a lot," she says quietly.

"I know a little," Sam confesses. "I looked you up. I tried to find you after your store was gone. I saw some stuff online."

Lacy exhales, bracing herself. She hates that this is part of her story, but if Sam is ever going to understand her fully, he has to know.

She begins, voice trembling.

Her father never touched her, but as she grew up, she began to notice a change in his gaze. The way he eyed her outfits. The wording of his compliments. The language he used when talking about the teenage girls on the shows she watched. The way she wasn't sure if his gaze followed girls at her school, or her. Or worse, her little sister.

Then, the day she came home and found the camera in her room. She knew, instantly, it was him. She couldn't explain how she knew, only that fear gripped her the moment she saw it. She brought it to Sophie, and together, they found another in the bathroom they shared.

Terrified, they didn't know how to tell their mother, unable to process the implications of what they were discovering. When they did, Dawna took charge. She found more cameras. Their first instinct was to call the police, but Dawna wasn't sure they could trust them.

Lacy describes how her mother tried to access her father's computer but couldn't. How Sophie, in a moment of fearless desperation, ripped apart the computer to remove the hard drive. They searched his office, barricading the door to buy time. Lacy remembers the sound of her father pounding on it, each slam reverberating through her body. She remembers how badly her hands shook as she rifled through his drawers. How Sophie took a hammer to the locked cabinets and found the external hard drives, handing them to Dawna.

Her mother finally called the police. The door was almost off its hinges.

Not knowing if they would come.

Not knowing if they would arrest him, their boss.

The sheer, bone-deep aloneness of that moment still haunts Lacy. As she recounts, her hands begin to shake, and Sam pulls her into his lap, her body trembling against his. He holds her tight, his warmth and steadiness grounding her. She reminds herself that she's not alone anymore. She can trust him.

She continues.

The police arrived. Some of them, she could tell, were his conspirators. Others looked confused, uncertain why their chief was so panicked, why his family was barring him from entering his own office.

"Do you think they found it?" one officer muttered.

"It might not be that," another whispered back.

"Stop freaking out. Let's get in there and see what they have," someone else said, trying to calm things down.

The rest is a blur.

She remembers the courtroom. The photos. The more graphic ones were kept hidden from her, but still, she saw enough. She'd asked to see everything, needing to know how much had been exposed. She hadn't seen it all, and still, it was more than she could've prepared for.

Mostly photos of her. Some of her sister. A few of her friends.

Guilt still gnaws at her. She should have spoken up about the lascivious looks, the unease in her gut. Maybe they could have stopped him earlier, spared her sister and friends before the images spread.

"I was scared of being photographed after that. Scared of men. Their desire toward me. It all felt perverse."

Sam's heart aches for her. For everything she's endured. And yet, she remains kind. Funny. Compassionate. He marvels at her strength.

"I think it still scares me," she confesses. "Sex with men. David made it worse."

Sam stiffens at the mention of her ex. Lacy rarely talks about him. All he knows is that he hurt her, that her friends despise him with a unified intensity, and that he's rich, obscenely so.

She doesn't go into detail but shares enough for him to understand the nature of their relationship. The coercion. The feeling of being reduced to an object by him, and eventually by herself. How, sometimes, she said no, and he didn't listen.

Rage burns in Sam's chest, seething like nothing he's ever felt before. He pulls her closer, stroking her hair, his touch impossibly gentle. "Thank you for telling me," he murmurs into her hair, his voice thick with emotion.

"Don't use it against me," she whispers.

"I would never," Sam promises, his voice steady and sincere. "I promise, angel."

She looks up at him, the weight of everything they've shared pressing between them. And then, unexpectedly, a small smile tugs at her lips.

"What?" Sam asks, mirroring her expression.

"Is it so inappropriate that after all that, the only thing I am thinking about right now is how much I want to kiss you?"

"Fuck no," Sam breathes, tilting her chin up and pressing his lips to hers.

The weekend finds Sam and Lacy at an outdoor vintage market, wandering hand in hand through rows of eclectic stalls. She tugs him along toward whatever catches her eye, and he follows without hesitation, content just to watch her light up with each new discovery.

Lacy pauses at a stall lined with vintage watches, her gaze drifting to the jewelry beside them. She picks up a pair of scarab beetle earrings, turning them over in her hand, inspecting them curiously.

"Those are pretty," Sam says, draping an arm around her waist.

Lacy nods and sets them back down. She moves on to another table, where she spots a small, mislabeled pot.

"This isn't a powder jar," she says to the shopkeeper. "It's a hair receiver. You could probably sell it for more online. It's pretty sought after by collectors."

Sam watches as the shopkeeper quickly checks something on his phone before tucking the item away.

"What's a hair receiver?" Sam asks as they move on, lowering his voice near her ear.

"Women used to collect their hair in them," Lacy explains.

"For what?"

"To make hair pieces, I think. Sometimes people embroidered their clothes with the hair of their loved ones to remember them."

"That's... sentimental."

Lacy smiles at him. "What? If I died, wouldn't you want my hair to remember me by?"

"Please don't joke about that," Sam says, his voice serious.

Lacy squeezes his hand gently. "Okay."

"Do you miss it?" Sam asks after a pause, his voice thoughtful. "Having your own store? Being surrounded by this stuff?"

Lacy considers his question for a moment. "Yeah. I do."

"Why did you close it?" he asks.

"I didn't," Lacy says with a hollow laugh. "David closed it. He gave me the store as an engagement gift, and when we broke up, he took it back."

"Bastard," Sam spits, tongue bitter.

They walk in silence for a moment before Sam speaks again. "What do you miss about it?"

Lacy takes a deep breath, her eyes scanning the market around them. "I miss finding cool old things, thinking about how many memories they've absorbed. How much someone has to care for an item for it to outlive them, stay pristine and unchanged, even after all that time. And I loved watching people find things they've been searching for a long time, or discover some old, beautiful thing they never knew they wanted. Seeing them fall in love with it, consecrating it with it with new memories."

Sam watches her as she speaks, completely captivated. "I get it," he says. For the first time, he understands the appeal of antiques beyond their aesthetics. "Like, even though it's from the past, it's not stuck there. Someone always comes along to love it again. Its essence reaching through time, infuses the present with its utter unyielding."

"Wow," she says softly, her lips curling into a small smile. In this moment, she feels completely seen in a way that catches her off guard. Warmth blooms in her chest. She rises onto her toes and kisses him.

They stand in the middle of the bustling market, wrapped in each other's arms, hearts racing, the rest of the world fading away. A sudden flash from a nearby camera interrupts their moment. They pull apart, blinking, and spot a man nearby in a full Victorian getup, holding a vintage Polaroid camera like it's a prop from a play.

He holds out his hand. "Twenty dollars for the photo."

Sam's brows knit together. "What? You took it without asking."

The man just shrugs, casually shaking the film.

"We didn't agree to the photo."

"That's fine," the man says. "I'll keep it."

Before Sam can argue, Lacy hands the money to him. "It's fine," she says, voice unreadable.

She snatches the photo from the man and tucks it into her bag without looking at it.

Over lunch, their conversation circles back to her old store.

"He could've just let you keep it," Sam says, frowning. "It's not like it would've made a dent in his bank account."

Lacy lets out a dry laugh. "Especially considering I'm still paying him for it."

Sam's face darkens. "Wait, what do you mean?"

"He backcharged me for rent."

His blood boils. "How much?"

She leans in, whispering the number in his ear. His eyes go wide.

"You're kidding."

Lacy shrugs, her expression resigned.

*S*ummer arrives with backyard barbecues, patio dinners, and loveliest of all: more kisses.

One evening, Lacy walks into Sam's apartment to find him holding a bouquet. The room is dimly lit, candles flickering on the dining table where a meal is set.

"Hope you haven't eaten," Sam says, leaning down to kiss her.

Lacy is momentarily dazed by the flowers in her hand, the beautiful meal, and the soft glow of the candles. A part of her wonders, half hopeful, half nervous, if this is Sam's way of signalling that tonight might be *the* night. Her heart flutters at the thought. Not like her matching underwear was a coincidence.

As they finish up their meal, she thanks him, her emotions in knots. She's grateful for his effort, but her mind races about where the night might lead them.

"It is truly my pleasure, angel," Sam says with a smile. "I made this a lot for my aunts."

"You perfected it," Lacy replies, lifting the last bite of spaghetti con le cozze to her mouth.

"Speaking of my aunts," Sam continues, his voice slightly nervous. "They're visiting soon. I'd like you to meet them."

Lacy's heart leaps, both thrilled and a little nervous.

"And," Sam leans in closer, taking her hand, "I've been wondering how you'd feel about me introducing you as my girlfriend?"

Lacy's breath catches in her throat. She blushes, her heart racing as she bites her lip.

Sam continues, a touch of shyness in his voice. "Because... I'd really like to be your boyfriend."

Before she can process it all, she nods, lifting their joined hands to her lips, pressing a kiss onto his skin.

He pulls her into a deep kiss, holding her like he never wants to let go, his fingers grazing her waist as the hem of her shirt lifts.

Later, they wash dishes elbow to elbow, the domesticity of the ritual feels sacred in its simplicity, soft and unspoken between them. When they change into their pyjamas, Sam shows her the drawers he's cleared out for her. "I also cleared out a nightstand for you," he says, smiling nervously.

Lacy doesn't speak, just stares at him.

"Is it too much?" Sam asks, his smile faltering slightly.

"No!" Lacy says quickly. Her heart is beating fast, overwhelmed by the certainty that he's beginning to feel like home. "I'm just really happy."

"Me too, Lacy."

"And a little scared," she admits.

"Me too." His gaze is full of affection and vulnerability. "But the way I feel about you is stronger than any fear."

They end the night curled up under a fuzzy blanket, watching a movie as they settle into the peaceful luxury of each other's presence.

The next morning, Lacy wakes up in bed, her head resting on Sam's chest. His steady breath rises and falls beneath her. She watches him sleep for a while before he stirs, his eyes meeting hers.

"Morning," he smiles, reaching up to gently touch her head.

"Sorry, I fell asleep last night," Lacy murmurs, still a little dazed.

"Should I also apologize for sleeping last night?" Sam asks with a teasing grin.

"I mean, I fell asleep on the couch... so early."

"That's okay. We were in our comfy clothes. It was bedtime."

"I know, but I thought maybe you wanted to..." She trails off.

"Wanted to... what?"

"You know..." Lacy mouths the words, too shy to say them aloud: *have sex.*

Sam laughs softly. "Lacy, I wasn't planning for it."

"But the candles and dinner..."

"I just wanted to do something nice for you." He pulls her closer and wraps his arms around her, his voice soft. "Especially since I was asking you to be mine."

"I'm yours?" Lacy teases.

"Yes," Sam says, grinning as he tilts her head toward him for a morning kiss. "Like I'm yours."

In July, his aunts come to visit, and Sam spends a week road-tripping with them, visiting small towns and camping in provincial parks. The final stop: a big lakeside cottage in Muskoka that he's booked with his friends.

The car ride over is filled with chatter and laughter. Sam updates his aunts on Paul and Celeste, whom they've met before, and tells them about his new friends.

"Sophie works with us. She's incredibly real and so funny. Our resident movie dilettante. Has incredible taste in everything. She's always pulling these niche references that fit exactly what we need. Always has a hundred ideas on the go and is good at explaining them to people, which I didn't realize was a skill until I met her. We hired her as an editor, but she contributes so much more than that at this point. She cares a lot about telling meaningful stories, really believes art can make a difference in the world. I can tell Lacy is so proud of her. She's protective of her little sister, but she also looks up to her in a really sweet way.

"There's also Edward. He says he was Lacy's best friend in high school, but Lacy maintains she was too much of a hermit to have any friends. He's an architect. One of the most caring people I've ever met. The type of guy who brings extra blankets to movie nights, tops up the hot water in your tea before you even notice it's low.

"And Jacob is his boyfriend. Just the coolest guy. It's like his confidence is contagious. It fills the room and makes everyone feel at ease. He's loud, but never obnoxious. I think it's because he's so secure, so himself all the time, it sort of forces you to let your guard down. Kind of like you guys.

"Then there's Mina. She actually was Lacy's best friend in school before Lacy moved to the city. They reconnected a few years ago. I'm not that close with her, but she's nice. She reads a lot, so we talk about books sometimes. She's always up to date on what's going on in the world. You'd get along with her. She's quiet around new people, but I've seen her with her friends. She can get passionate talking about things she cares about."

Aunt Sam glances at him. "And who's this Lacy?"

"Lacy is... Lacy." Sam can't help the grin that spreads across his face.

Until now, it had always been, "Lacy would love this," or "I'm taking a picture to send to Lacy." Everything reminded him of her. He'd struggled to stop bringing her up. Yet now that he has the chance, he feels suddenly shy, like no words could fully encompass her, what she means to him.

Aunt Sam studies him. "You seem happy, Sammy."

Auntie Jackie shifts forward, resting her chin on her wife's shoulder.

Sam smiles, eyes focused on the road. "I am."

"I've never seen you smile like that." Aunt Sam nudges his arm playfully. "What's got you smiling?"

Auntie Jackie grins. "It's not what. It's *who*."

Aunt Sam reaches over to ruffle his hair. "What have you been hiding from us, Sammy?"

Auntie Jackie wraps her arms around his shoulders from behind, giving him a playful shake. "Who have you been hiding?"

When they pull up to the cabin, Edward, Jacob, and Mina are outside, unloading bags from Jacob's truck. Sam steps out and stretches, rolling his shoulders before shutting the car door behind him.

Jacob grins, arms spread out to receive him. "She's in the kitchen putting the groceries away," he says before Sam even has the chance to ask.

Inside, Sophie catches sight of him and beams. She's holding his cat. The housemates had been watching her for him while he's been away. "Sammy's here!" She bounds over and drops his cat into his arms, where it immediately nestles against him. Sophie pulls him into a quick, tight hug before turning to greet his aunts.

Then, Lacy steps into view.

As soon as their eyes meet, Lacy's face lights up. The next second, she's moving toward him, and he's moving toward her, a week apart feeling far too long.

Sam pulls her into his arms as soon as he reaches her. She wraps her arms around his neck as he lifts her off the ground, spinning her once, savoring her laughter before pressing his lips to hers.

When he sets her down, she glances at his aunts, cheeks flushed.

"Aunt Sam, Auntie Jackie, this is Lacy," Sam says, his hand on the small of her back. "My girlfriend."

Lacy beams, warmth spreading across her face at the pride in his voice. "I've been looking forward to meeting you both."

Aunt Sam's handshake is firm and warm. "It's nice to meet you," she says, eyes flicking briefly to Sam before meeting her wife's gaze.

Auntie Jackie pulls Lacy into a quick hug.

The cat weaves between Sam and Lacy's legs as they help carry his aunts' bags to their room. Lacy asks them about their trip, listening intently, nodding along, genuinely interested.

"Jackie made us stop at every bakery in every small town to try their butter tarts," Aunt Sam tells her, shaking her head.

"It made the drive so much longer," Sam grumbles in jest, duffel bag hoisted over his shoulder.

"And so much yummier," Auntie Jackie counters with a wink.

Lacy excuses herself when she hears the sound of Paul and Celeste's car pulling up. Sam notices the way his aunts exchange a look as Lacy walks off to help her friends unload. Their expressions are unreadable at first, but then their gazes turn to him, full of something warm and knowing.

"What?" he asks, bracing himself.

Aunt Jackie starts, "She's..." and for a moment, old panic grips his chest, years of their disapproval making his stomach tighten.

"She seems lovely, Sammy," Aunt Sam finishes, and relief floods him, glowing warm in his chest.

That evening, Paul and Celeste prepare a beautiful dinner for everyone. The others pitch in, chopping vegetables, mixing sangria, setting the table. The cottage hums with laughter and conversation, an effortless rhythm of voices and movement, the air thick with the scent of roasted garlic and fresh herbs.

At the table, conversations intertwine, branch off, then blend again. Sam watches his aunts settle seamlessly into the group. They're used to being the only queer people in the group when they visit him, but here, surrounded by community, they belong.

After dinner, Jacob and Sophie handle the dishes while Lacy and Mina tidy the kitchen. Outside, Sam and Edward start a fire as his aunts prepare s'mores and hot chocolate.

They bring out blankets and settle around the fire. There aren't enough chairs, and Sam pulls Lacy into his lap, draping a blanket over her legs. She leans back against his chest, tracing absent-minded patterns along his forearm.

Jacob, Edward, and Mina squeeze onto the loveseat, Jacob and Mina's legs tangled over Edward's.

They play campfire games, laugh through a round of Two Truths and A Lie, and slip into conversations that ebb and flow. Sophie, Paul, and Aunt Sam debate the cliffhanger ending of a show, while Mina, Celeste, Jacob, and Jackie passionately discuss a newly passed bathroom bill affecting students in Ohio. Edward is peacefully sleeping on Jacob's shoulder.

As the night stretches on, words fade into the background, replaced by the orchestra of the forest: the soft breeze strumming through the trees, the rhythmic crash of the lake's waves, the symphony of crickets and night birds, the occasional contralto hoot of an owl. One by one, everyone drifts off to bed, lulled by the drowsy spell of the nighttime chorus. But Sam and Lacy aren't ready to sleep yet. They grab a blanket and walk down to the lake.

The moon hangs opulent and large in the night sky, her bright glow reflected in the lake's deep darkness. Sam sits first, spreading his legs so Lacy can settle between them, her back against his chest. He wraps his arms around her, resting his chin on her shoulder.

"Your aunts are the coolest people I've ever met," Lacy murmurs, lacing their fingers together, the backs of her hands captured in his palms.

Sam smiles against her hair. "Yeah, they're extremely cool." He presses a kiss to her temple. "They think you're lovely, by the way."

"They told you?"

He nods, squeezing her gently.

A beat of quiet. Then, she asks, "Is Aunt Sam your mom's sister or your dad's?"

"My mom's."

"Have you always been close to her?"

Sam lets out a quiet, hollow laugh. "No. We weren't in each other's lives until I was an adult. My parents didn't approve of her. Didn't let her see me."

Lacy tilts her head, looking up at him. "Why?"

So, he tells her.

He tells her about how his mother severed ties with Aunt Sam because his father disapproved of her lifestyle.

How, after his father moved to Italy, his mother softened, rekindling her bond with her sister. How after his mother killed herself, Aunt Sam stepped in without hesitation, and Auntie Jackie, basically a stranger at the time, had done the same. He exhales, his breath warm against her skin. "They saved me," he says, voice firm in his deference.

Lacy sits in silence for a moment, her fingers gently tracing the calluses on his hand, rough from the way he grips his pencils. Her voice is soft, almost fragile, as she murmurs, "I didn't know your mom killed herself."

"Yeah," he exhales, a hollow sound that seems to come from the very core of him. "She died the night we were supposed to meet at our beach. Weird, right? I lost two important women in one night." His shoulders sag slightly, the weight of the words settling over him.

Lacy's heart shatters for him, and she shifts in his arms, turning toward him to hold him close.

"At least you came back to me," he says softly, meeting her gaze, the intensity in his eyes almost overwhelming.

Lacy presses her lips to his in a soft, tender kiss before pulling away just enough to ask, "Tell me about her. What was she like?"

Sam's expression softens as he begins, his voice quiet, reflective. Mia had to play both roles, mother and father, always busy working, taking care of the house, and him. Despite her efforts, there was never enough of her left to be fully present. She was always too burdened by her exhaustion and depression to be there for him. His father's volatility pushed them both to their limits, leaving little room for him to fit into their dynamic. When his father would leave, things would get better between him and his mom, but it never lasted. He remembers the fleeting hope that would build up each time his father left, only for it to crumble when Leo inevitably came back, dragging them back into that same painful cycle.

"He eventually moved to Italy, as you know. He started dating someone new. It seemed like he was getting his shit together, but then, like always, he couldn't keep it up. After my mom died, I went through her phone, desperate for some answers. I saw that she would text him every few months, and he'd barely reply, but she was pretty consistent with checking in. He called her the morning he died; they talked for over two hours. I don't know what he said to her. That shit haunts me."

Lacy remains silent, her eyes locked on his. She doesn't know the right words, but she's here, she's listening, and she wants to understand.

"My dad had packed up all his stuff that day," Sam continues. "So, I'm guessing he was planning to come back to her, like he always did. Just when she started getting her life together again... healing things with her sister." His eyes glisten with unshed tears as he glances up at the midnight sky.

"You know he died in a jet ski accident? They found alcohol in his system," he scoffs, shaking his head as a bitter laugh escapes him. "A fucking jet ski accident. Right after I was born, my dad got into a drunk driving accident. He hit a minivan, a single mom with a baby in the back. If the baby's car seat had been on the other side... that kid would've been gone."

Lacy reaches up to wipe away the tears now streaming down his face. He leans into her hand, his breath shaky as he continues. "He was just so fucking dumb. Had no concern for his life. Or anyone else's. A walking wrecking ball. Cheating on my mom, hitting on my teachers, always fucking drunk. Just for it all to come down to a jet ski accident— if it even was one." He laughs again, his voice raw. "What a fucking waste, to kill yourself over a man like that."

Lacy moves to hold him, wrapping her arms and legs around him in a tight, desperate embrace. He rests his head on her shoulder, catching his breath as she rubs his back in rhythm with the waves, soothing his nerves.

"Sorry," he chuckles softly, the sound is wet. "I just keep thinking about how great Aunt Sam is... how much love, how much care, how much healing she missed out on because she picked my dad, over and over again. She barely got to know Auntie Jackie, and... she'll never get to meet you." His voice trails off as his emotions press down on him.

"I wish I could have met her too," Lacy says, kissing his cheek, the salty taste of his despair on her lips.

Sam cups her face, searching her eyes, desperate for something he's not sure he deserves. "Lacy, I..." he starts, voice wavering, "I love you." His voice is so fragile, yet so resolute in its truth. She smiles at his words, an electric warmth spreading from her chest out to every inch of her body. She pulls him into a deep, lingering kiss, her hands sliding into his hair. His hands wrap around her waist, moving to caress her nape, diving into her hair.

Their hands roam, tender and desperate, their lips part, then meet again.

And again.
And again.

The next day is warm and unhurried, filled with the kind of sun-drenched fun that is reminiscent of childhood summers. Sophie, Jacob, Edward, and Paul are in a heated game of tossing around a yellow ball, the wind carrying their laughter and playful taunts through the leaves. Mina and Celeste sway lazily in a hammock, talking softly as they stare up at the canopy of leaves. Sam's aunts lounge on a picnic blanket, reading side by side. Lacy sits in the grass nearby, the narrow leaves tickling her bare feet. Sam naps with his head in her lap as she absently strokes his hair.

Pareidolic clouds are painted across the endless canvas of the perfect blue sky. The trees rustle like wind chimes in the soft summer breeze. Everything feels light and easy here, surrounded by peace and safety.

A sudden flash catches Lacy off guard. Auntie Jackie snapped a picture with her disposable camera.

Sam cracks one eye open, crooks his finger to beckon Lacy closer, planting a quick kiss on her lips when she leans down. "I'll tell her to ask next time," he murmurs.

Lacy just smiles. "It's okay. I don't mind." She turns to Auntie Jackie and asks her to take another one.

Before she can react, Sam sits up and pulls her into a tight hug, making her squeal, the sound bright and unguarded. The camera clicks, capturing the sunshine on their faces, limbs tangled, genuine laughter—a vignette of joy on a perfect summer day.

In the evening, Mina, Edward, and Jacob make dinner for everyone. They end the night gathered around the fire pit again, talking, laughing, and enjoying each other's company. When the group finally drifts off to bed, Sam slips inside to grab his sketchbook before meeting Lacy by the lake.

She reclines on a blanket, watching him sketch the view, the water shimmering under the full moon's opalescent glow, her silver light spilling over them. A quiet magic hums in the night, thick with the scent of charred wood and damp earth.

When he finishes, he turns the sketch toward her. Her breath catches. How could pencil strokes capture the delicate dance of moonlight on the waves, the white of the paper luminescent against a sea of shadows?

"Can I draw you?" Sam asks, his voice low, full of yearning.

She nods, warmth blooming in her chest. She feels he doesn't need to ask anymore, yet that he does makes her happy.

As his pencil glides across the paper, his gaze lingers on her, charged with the same electricity as that night he drew her lying on their beach. With each glance, the space between them tightens, thick with something unspoken. Finally, he sets the pencil aside, his eyes never leaving hers.

"What?" she murmurs, her voice barely above a whisper.

"You," he replies, the word carrying the weight of a thousand unspoken thoughts.

"What about me?"

His thumb brushes a stray hair from her cheek, his touch featherlight. "You're breathtaking," he exhales, drinking in the way the moonlight caresses her skin, shines against her dark hair spilling across the blanket like silk. "I was thinking about the first time you asked me to draw you. How much I wanted to kiss you then." He can't help the slow smile curving his lips as pink dusts her cheeks. "How much I want to kiss you now."

Lacy's pulse leaps, wildly beating beneath her skin. With a coy smile, she pushes up onto her elbows, closing the space between them. "Then kiss me."

Sam doesn't hesitate. His lips meet hers, soft at first, a whisper of a touch, then deeper, hungrier, as if he's starved for the taste of her. She melts into him, her fingers tangling in his hair, pulling him closer. His hands roam her back, pressing her against him with a possessiveness that steals her breath.

Weeks of restraint unravel in an instant. Her tongue slides against his, igniting a fire that races through her veins. A breathy sigh escapes her lips, and Sam feels the sound shoot straight to his heart, straight to his cock.

She arches against him, and the hard press of his arousal sends a thrill skittering down her spine. A low groan rumbles from him as she presses her body to him, the friction drawing another ragged sound from his throat. Her hands slip beneath his sweater, fingertips tracing the planes of his abdomen, branding him with her touch.

But when her hand brushes against his erection, a flicker of self-awareness cuts through his haze, a fleeting embarrassment at the intensity of his desire.

Lacy stills, sensing the shift. "Want to stop?"

He swallows, feeling vulnerable, exposed, unsure.

"Let's slow down," she murmurs, her voice a soothing balm against the fever of the moment.

He exhales, resting his forehead against hers. "Yeah," he agrees, though every fiber of him protests.

They share the bed that night, limbs entwined beneath the sheets. Every touch lingering, every kiss deepening, unable, unwilling to stop now that they've begun.

He drifts into dreams of her, her taste, her touch. He wakes with her in his arms, her back flush against his chest, his body curved around hers in possessive warmth. The evidence of his desire pressing insistently against her bottom.

She stirs, turning in his embrace, her sleepy smile meeting his. Softly, she brushes her lips against his, once, twice, a languid greeting in the quiet dawn.

"Morning, my angel," he murmurs, voice thick with sleep and wonder. "How did you sleep?" There's still a hint of disbelief behind his gaze, like he still can't believe he's waking up beside her.

"Good," she hums, stretching beneath his touch. The hem of her top rides up, his fingers skimming the bare dip of her waist, sending a shiver through her. "I had a dream about you," she confesses, eyes sparkling with mischief and delight.

"Yeah?" His thumb traces idle circles on her skin. "So did I."

"What kind of dream?"

"You first," he says, voice dropping to a husky whisper.

"I asked first."

"This kind," he purrs, capturing her mouth in a slow, searing kiss, pulling her tighter against him. His hand slips beneath her shirt, palm warm against her ribs. "Is this okay?"

She nods, shifting until she's straddling him, her weight settling directly over the hard length of him. A gasp catches in her throat as his thumb brushes the swell of her breast, hands on her ribs.

"My dream was kind of the same," she moans into his mouth, arching into his touch.

"Yeah?" His breath hitches, the word barely audible between their lips. "Did you like it?"

"Mm-hmm." She rolls her hips against him, and a rough curse escapes him. "You're killing me, angel."

She laughs, the sound breathless and sinful, stoking the fire between them. His fingers tug at the waistband of her shorts, grazing the soft skin beneath her stomach, hungry, yet hesitant. "Can I touch you?"

Please. The word burns in her throat, a silent scream. *Please touch me.* But her voice betrays her, smothered by the overwhelming heat swelling inside her.

He withdraws his hand, a cruel irony. All the times she'd said yes when she meant no, and now, when every nerve in her body is singing *yes yes yes*, her voice fails her. And he won't take what she doesn't offer, won't claim what hasn't been given. And *god*, she wants to give herself to him, not as surrender, but as a promise.

The afternoon sun bathes the lake in liquid amber. Their laughter echoes through the trees as they splash in the water. Aunt Sam, Paul, Sophie, and Jacob race each other in their kayaks, their paddles slicing through the water in frantic, competitive strokes. Mina and Auntie Jackie lounge on the dock, their skin glistening with sunscreen, trading dog-eared books and easy gossip.

Edward, Mina, Sam, and Lacy take turns on the paddleboards, their balance precarious, their movements uncoordinated. One by one, they tumble into the lake with graceless splashes, emerging breathless and laughing. Sophie and Jacob paddle back from their triumphant race, grins like trouble, splashing them mercilessly as they try to clamber back on the boards. Their shrieks carry on the breeze, light and carefree.

Lacy rises from the lake, sun kissing gold across her skin, silver droplets trailing down the curve of her thighs, the wet fabric of her swimsuit clinging to her. The sight does something unbearable to Sam. A tight ache coils deep within him. Touching her last night had cracked something open in him, and now, every glance, every touch, her mere nearness only deepens the ache. The current of his desire relentless, undeniable. He can't keep his eyes off her, can barely keep his hands to himself. Reaching out whenever she's close, fingers brushing her thighs, moving wet hair away from her eyes, pulling her close under the guise of steadying her.

She catches him staring, again, head tilting playfully as she grins. "What?" she asks, voice teasing, eyes knowing.

He doesn't answer, his gaze lingering.

She splashes him, sudden and playful, and he gasps, then retaliates, shooting a stream of water at her with a laugh. As they play, something brews beneath the surface. Something hot and hungry in the way his gaze drops to her mouth, the way her breath hitches when his hand finds her waist in the water.

That evening, Sam takes charge in the kitchen with his aunts, gently steering Lacy out each time she tries to help, a playful smile and kiss on the cheek softening the push. She retreats, assuming they want some quality time together, and settles into the easy rhythm of chatter with her friends, laughter blending with the soft clinking of cooking sounds from the kitchen.

As the meal winds down, everyone abruptly stands and leaves the table. Lacy blinks, confused, left alone in the sudden quiet, until the lights flicker out. Moments later, Sophie and Mina emerge from the dark, their faces lit by the warm glow of candles atop a cake. The rest of the group trails behind them, voices rising in an off-key but heartfelt "Happy Birthday." Lacy blinks in surprise. Her birthday isn't for another week, but they've planned this surprise for her anyway. As the cake is set before her, she's at a loss for what to wish for, gazing around at the sea of loving faces. Her eyes find Sam's, and the realization settles in: there's nothing left to wish for.

With cake plates in hand, the group gathers around the fire pit for their last night at the cottage. Sam settles into a chair, making space for Lacy in his lap again. He feeds her a bite of cake, and her cheeks turn a soft shade of red as she shyly glances at the others around them, caught between warmth and bashfulness.

Aunt Sam's voice cut through the crackle of the fire. "So," she asks, grinning, "how was your twenty-eighth year?"

Lacy sits up, her gaze sweeping over the group gathered around her, and a wave of gratitude washes over her. For each person in her life, for the deep sense of belonging she's found with them. Sam's presence is a steady weight around her, his unwavering thoughtfulness and softness surrounding her like the warmth of the ocean on a calm day. In him, she's found a comfort she never thought possible, how safe he makes her feel, how effortless it feels to be with him.

"It's been the best year of my life," she admits, the truth settling into her bones.

As the fire burns low and the others begin to drift off to bed, Sam and Lacy remain, wrapped in their blanket. His fingers trace idle patterns on her thigh, unaware of the tension stirring between her legs. Goosebumps rise as his touch lingers.

"Are you cold?" Sam murmurs, his breath warm against her ear.

She shakes her head, though she lets him tug the blanket tighter around them. She touches his cheek, her hand moving into his hair, as he tilts her face towards him to kiss her. His hand moves from her waist, into her sweater, over her camisole.

"Is this okay?" he asks, cupping her breast in his palm, knowing the answer from the way her nipple peaks beneath his thumb, but needing to hear it anyway.

She nods, arching into his touch. A whimper escapes her as his thumb rubs over her nipple, the thin fabric of her undershirt doing little to dull the sensation. She clasps a hand over her mouth, embarrassed by the noises she's making.

"Should we stop?" His voice is rough, but his hands are patient.

"No," she barely breathes out, biting her lip to stifle a moan.

Sam's lips find hers, swallowing her whimpers as his fingers tease her. "How do you want me to touch you?"

"I don't know," she admits, her eyes lifting to meet his, cloudy with lust, but her voice betrays hesitation.

He stills, searching her face. "Is everything okay?"

"It feels..." Her words falter, her cheeks flushing. "Embarrassing to ask for what I want out loud. Especially when I don't even know what I like."

Sam's thumb strokes her cheek, his touch tender. "How about I touch you, slowly, and you tell me what feels good. If anything doesn't, tell me to stop. You're in control."

She exhales, leaning into him. "I trust you. Just... touch me how you want."

His response comes in a kiss, deep and devouring, and then, his hands are everywhere, mapping her body with desperate reverence. Fingers tangling in her hair, skimming down the delicate curve of her waist, slipping beneath her sweater, under the flimsy silk of her camisole.

His palm cups the weight of her breast, his thumb circling her peaked nipple through the fabric, and she arches into his touch with a whimper. Restraint non-existent, he ducks his head to her chest, capturing the hardened bud between his lips through her clothes, drawing a shuddering gasp from her lips.

She writhes in his lap, thighs clenching reflexively as pleasure coils tight in her core. Sam notices—how could he not, when every tremor of her body speaks to him in a language more intimate than words. "Want me to touch you there?"

She manages the barest nod, her world narrowing to the exquisite friction of his touch.

His hand finally dips lower. The first brush of his fingers against the damp cotton of her underwear draws a ragged curse from him.

His fingertip traces the seam of her over her thin underwear, so lightly it's torture. A sharp, breathless moan escapes her as his palm presses firmly between her thighs, the heat of his touch searing even through the fabric. His other arm anchors around her, pulling her flush against him while his other fingers tease her nipples. Her gasps grow louder, unsteady, unfiltered.

He silences her with a kiss, swallowing her whimpers, her pleas, the way her breath hitches when he presses his thumb on her clit, finds just the right rhythm.

Then—his name.

Not just spoken, but wrenched from her, ragged and wanting. It unravels something primal in him, a possessive hunger low in his gut.

"Yes, angel?" His voice is rough, thick with desire.

"It feels... I can't..." Her words dissolve into breathless whimpers as his thumb traces slow, maddening circles before shifting to urgent strokes, each movement spurring her closer to the edge.

"Do you want me to stop?" A thread of strain beneath his words.

"God, no," she gasps, her pupils dark and pleading. Her desire laid bare before him sends a surge of heat pooling low in his gut.

"In that case, I'd really like to make you come now," he murmurs against her lips, the command in his voice like velvet. "I want to watch you ride my hand."

His fingers dip beneath the fabric, slick with her arousal. His fingers find her soft spot, the heel of his palm grinding delicious friction against her.

"Oh my god, that..." Her voice splinters as her pleasure crests, her hips canting against his touch. "Feels so good."

Her praise is gasoline to the fire inside him. His fingers glide between her folds, teasing, coaxing, until her breath hitches and her body bows taut beneath him. With a cry, he feels her shatter around his fingers, her back arched, his name a broken hymn on her lips. He kisses her through it, his breath ragged against her mouth as he savors the taste of every gasp, moan, and shudder, sweet and desperate against his tongue.

When she finally stills, legs weak, she nuzzles into the hollow of his throat, her lips brushing the sensitive skin. "My turn?" Her fingers trail down his chest, dipping teasingly beneath his waistband.

He catches her wrist gently, presses a kiss to her palm, his lips lingering there. "Next time," he murmurs, his voice thick with a longing that feels almost holy in its ache. He won't risk it, not tonight, not when his own pleasure is a fickle, messy thing that might break the perfection of this moment. Tonight is hers, as much as it is his. The way her cheeks flushed with heat, her lashes fluttering close, the soft, breathless gasps, the way she came undone in his arms, every moment etched into his soul.

"Let's go to bed," he whispers, and she nods, her gaze soft and adoring, like he'd hung the moon just for her.

The sun wakes Sam, light spilling gold across his eyes and chest. Its warmth pales against the radiance of waking with Lacy curled in his arms.

She stirs too, as if some unseen thread ties her consciousness to his, a delicate pull in the hazy realm where dreams linger, tethered by something deeper than waking life.

"Morning angel," he says into her hair, breathing her in, a scent that makes him nostalgic for something he's never known.

She mumbles an incoherent good morning, twisting into his arms, her head resting in the nook of his neck and bicep, her sleepy breaths tickling his skin. His cat hops up on the bed from somewhere silent and unknown, curling between their legs to sleep.

Sam looks out at the glory of the morning, heavenly rays streaming through veils of dawn clouds, and makes a silent pact with the sun. *Let me keep this—this peace, this warmth, this boundless beauty—and I will never ask for more. Not for all the days of my life.*

When it's time to say goodbye, Sam feels almost foolish for how much he'll miss her. They won't be apart for long, yet even the smallest distance feels unbearable, the quiet ache of his restless soul pulling helplessly toward hers. He wonders if this is how Anna had once felt about him, a longing unreciprocated. The thought unsettles him. The idea of Lacy not returning the depth of his feelings sends a pang of sympathy through him. He had never been drawn to Anna the way he is to Lacy, as if his heart had always been waiting for her, had known all along it belonged to her. How could he have known? How could he ever have believed in a love like this? Surely, no one has ever felt this before. Not like this. Like every lovesick fool before him, he believes his love is too vast and too singular to ever be replicated. Not since the first heartbeat of the universe, when love, raw and infinite, shaped the world itself. And in this love, he feels infinite. Unbound by what was or what should be, only what he dares to reach for, what he dares to create, a life with her by his side.

"I'll miss you," Sam tells Lacy as he loads her bags into Jacob's car. "I'll be thinking about you the whole drive back."

"No, you won't," she teases, nudging him with her hip. "You'll be too busy having fun with your aunts."

"I'm good at multitasking." He grins. "So... will you be thinking about me in the car?"

Lacy laughs. "As if I have a choice."

His eyes glint with playful delight. "And what will you be thinking about me?"

"The truth."

"Which is?"

She smiles sheepishly, cheeks flushing. "That I really like you."

"You do?" Sam feigns shock. In one swift motion, he lifts her, pinning her against the car as his mouth crashes into hers. Her arms loop around his neck, fingers tangling in his hair as he pulls her closer, one hand slipping beneath the hem of her top, palm searing against the bare skin on the small of her back.

Her lips part, tongue meeting his. Her fingers hook into his belt, tugging him flush against her. The groan he lets out sends a thrill through her, the world around them fading into a distant hum. Time stretches, infinite, until—

"What are you guys waiting for?"

Sophie's voice shatters the moment. Lacy jerks back, blinking as if surfacing from a dream, and finds her friends lingering nearby, pretending to be occupied, waiting to load up the car.

"Oh." Heat floods her face. "Sorry." She offers Sam a shy smile, avoiding his gaze. "Thanks for carrying my bags." Before he can respond, she darts off to bid hasty goodbyes to his aunts, then Paul and Celeste, before slipping into the car without another glance his way.

Sam helps with the remaining bags, hoping to catch her eye, but Lacy doesn't look up, eyes glued to her phone. He hesitates for a moment, sensing the shift in her, but says nothing.

The entire ride home, Sam agonizes. Had he gotten too carried away with that kiss? Had he been too much this weekend?

When he arrives home, he texts her: Home safe

An hour later, she replies: Glad you guys made it okay.

You back yet? He asks.

Sophie:

Almost.

Let me know when you're home.

Sam picks up two overpriced pizzas for dinner. As they settle in front of the TV, his aunts rave about the green curry pizza, their enthusiasm almost making the price tag worth it. But Sam can't focus. His eyes keep drifting to his phone. Lacy hadn't replied since the afternoon, and now it was well into the night. He knows she's home. Sophie was active in the group chat, and Sophie never texts in the car because of her motion sickness.

Auntie Jackie notices first. Not just the restless fidgeting but the shadow behind his eyes, the same telltale worry she's seen before when his thoughts spiral.

"Something on your mind?" she asks gently.

"It's nothing," he says too quickly.

"You sure?" She pats his knee, stilling its nervous bounce. "Whatever it is, we're here."

Aunt Sam reaches for the remote, pauses the movie. "Tell us what's weighing on you."

He hesitates. It feels selfish, pointless. These are their last days together, and the last thing he wants is to pull them into his relationship anxiety.

"You do know," Aunt Sam says with a teasing smirk, "my wife is a tenured professor of psychology. People pay good money for her advice."

Sam exhales a half-laugh, but it doesn't reach his eyes. He'd shut his aunts out in his last relationship, convinced he could handle it all on his own. And look where that got him.

He hesitates, then lets it spill, the words tumbling out like a confession he didn't know he'd been holding in. His fear that he'd been too much with Lacy. Too intense, too fast. Too physical. That maybe he'd overwhelmed her. That saying *I love you* might've been a mistake, too soon. He'd crossed some invisible line without realizing it.

His aunts listen the way they always have, the way they did when he was in denial about his mother's death, when his grief had nearly swallowed him whole, when his last relationship had decimated his self-worth. They don't tell him how to feel. They ask questions, guiding him toward his own answers.

"Did she say it was too much?" Auntie Jackie asks.

"No."

"So, you don't actually know if that's true?" she clarifies.

"No. But something feels... off. I can feel it."

Aunt Sam leans forward. "How did the weekend feel for you?"

Sam exhales, remembering. "Like... magical. The best weekend of my life."

"Don't let fear rewrite your memories," Auntie Jackie says gently. "You can't read her mind. Just ask her."

Days pass before Sam sees Lacy. Her texts, when they come, are slow and stilted, short bursts of conversation that leave him more anxious than reassured. When she finally visits, it's quiet in the apartment. His aunts are out for the evening.

Sam watches her, searching for signs of discomfort as she plays with his cat. "Good job, kitty," she coos when the cat pounces on the feather toy she's brought over.

Sam clears his throat. "Hey Lacy," he starts, voice unsure. "Can I ask you about something?"

At his tone, she sets the toy aside and joins him on the couch.

"At the cottage, when we said goodbye... You seemed distant. And your texts have been a bit dry. Is that just me?"

Lacy folds her hands. "No, it's not you. It's not really anything."

"But it *is* something?"

She exhales, as if releasing held breath. "I guess I felt weird after we kissed."

His stomach drops. "You didn't want to?"

"No! The opposite. I was embarrassed because..." She flushes. "I was so lost in you, I didn't even notice everyone was watching us. That I was keeping everyone waiting."

Sam's shoulders relax. "They didn't seem to mind. If they had, they'd have said something."

"I know. But I hate that feeling." She tells him about a high school game of spin the bottle, how it had left her feeling dirty and scrutinized, all those eyes on her.

He listens, absorbing every flicker of emotion in her voice. When she finishes, he squeezes her hand, his touch warm and steady. "Thank you for telling me," he says softly. "I'll keep the PDA to a minimum."

"I like a little PDA," she amends, lips quirking.

"Ah." His grin turns wicked. "So just don't kiss you so good that you can't think of anything besides jumping my bones? Got it."

She laughs, rolling her eyes as she bumps him with her shoulder. "You wish."

He grins, leaning in just enough to make her breath hitch. "Oh, I *absolutely* wish."

"I'm sorry I pulled away," she murmurs. "I felt... off, and I didn't want to burden you with my weird headspace. Make you feel like you'd done something wrong."

He pulls her close, resting his chin on her head as he says, "I get it. But when you disappear, it makes me feel like I *did* do something wrong. Next time, just tell me. You are never a burden to me. I want all of you, the good, the messy, everything in between."

The raw sincerity in his voice makes her throat tight. She answers with a kiss, soft and lingering, a silent promise.

Later, as they chop vegetables side by side, Sam suddenly pauses, knife hovering mid-air. "Wait, so you've made out with Edward *and* Jacob?" His delayed focus on this detail makes her burst into laughter.

"Yup," she says, popping the *p*.

Sam resumes chopping with exaggerated precision, lips pursed in mock contemplation. "So, you've kissed all your roommates... except your sister."

"Huh." Lacy blinks. "I never realized that." Noticing his suddenly glum expression, she nudges him. "What? Jealous?"

"Please," he scoffs, planting a dramatic kiss on the cat's furry head as she lounges on the counter. "For the record, I've kissed all my roommates too."

Lacy giggles, planting an equally theatrical kiss between the cat's ears. "Me too." Then, in one smooth motion, she loops her arms around Sam's neck and pulls him into a kiss that's anything but performative, slow, deep, and unmistakably possessive, erasing every trace of doubt in him. When she pulls back, his dazed expression says everything. "Still jealous?" she teases.

The morning of Lacy's birthday dawns bright and cloudless, perfect for the beach day Sam had planned. He'd taken work off, loading the car while she slept in, waking her with a gentle forehead kiss. Three hours later, they arrive at a sunny beach, surprisingly crowded for a Tuesday morning.

They trek down the shoreline until the crowds thin, Sam carrying nearly everything: the chairs, umbrella, coolers, and an overstuffed beach bag. Lacy trails behind, holding only their towels. The winds play with his chestnut curls as he walks, his singlet revealing the effortless strength in his arms and shoulders. Lacy notices the appreciative glances he draws from other beachgoers, the subtle double-takes, the lingering looks, and feels a swell of pride. *Is this gorgeous, thoughtful man really mine?*

"You're staring," Sam remarks as he screws the umbrella pole into the sand, his voice teasing. The corners of his mouth twitch when she doesn't deny it. "What's that smile for?"

"Nothing," she demurs, but her grin only widens.

He adjusts the umbrella, waiting.

"Fine," she relents, smoothing their blanket over the warm sand. "You're just... really fucking hot."

Lacy rarely curses, and the bluntness of her admission sparks a laugh out of him. When he looks up, the sight of her nearly steals his breath, sunlight filtering through her white dress, loose braids framing her face, that elusive dimple appearing in her left cheek whenever she's truly happy. "*You* are really fucking hot," he counters, shaking sand from his hands.

"I'm serious," she insists, unpacking their books and snacks. "Do you have any idea how many people have been checking you out?"

The question gives him pause. Years with Anna had conditioned him to deliberately not notice such things, every glance twisted into some perceived betrayal. But Lacy's observation comes without jealousy, only amusement. He settles beside her, close enough their shoulders brush. "I don't really notice other people when you're around."

The blush that blooms across her cheeks is immediate and devastating. Sam can't resist. His thumb traces gently across the warm pink, as if he's memorizing its hue. He kisses each flushed cheekbone, then the tip of her nose for good measure. "You're too distracting."

Hours melt away in a sun-drunk haze of reading and stolen kisses. When the heat becomes unbearable, Sam piggybacks her into the lake, her laughter vibrating against his spine as waves lap at their waists. She slips down when the water reaches her chest, realizes she can't touch the bottom, and clings to him. He turns to her as her legs wrap around his hips, arms draped around his neck. His arms wrap around her waist, protective and unwavering. Together, they steady themselves, swaying gently as the waves wash over them.

In the lazy warmth of mid-afternoon, they picnic on his meticulously prepared arancini balls and frozen grapes beneath the umbrella, feeding each other chips between passages of their books.

By the time they return home, exhaustion has settled into their bones. They cancel their dinner reservation, instead ordering Lacy's favorite cold noodles to share with her friends. They sing, blow out candles, and cut another cake for Lacy. Later, Sam drives her home to spend the night at his apartment, his cat purring contentedly on the couch beside them as he presents a small velvet box to her: the scarab earrings from the antique market. The ones she'd admired weeks prior but deemed too extravagant.

Lacy's gasp is halfway to a sob as she lifts them to the light. "When did you—?"

"I found the vendor on Instagram and asked her to hold them for me," he admits, grinning as she bolts to the mirror to put them on. From the couch, he watches her head turn from side to side, the abalone-shell casting an opalescent glow where her cheek meets her ear meets her jaw, where he always likes to kiss her. It's a rare gift, seeing her admire her reflection.

"Look, they match." She shrugs her cardigan down to bare her shoulders and sweeps her hair aside. The display is bewitching, the elegant line of her neck, the delicate hollows above her collarbones, the ethereal luminescence of her skin, kissed by blue hour light. Sam has his thumb between his teeth, his gaze turning hazy with the urge to touch her, with his hands, with his pencils.

"Let me draw you," he rasps, propping his chin on one hand, wanting to capture her in her pearlescent jewels.

"So cliché," she laughs, but her eyes shine. "Want me to only wear the jewelry?" she mocks lightly.

"Christ, yes." The hunger in his voice thrills her, not just because she can inspire it, but because she wants to stoke it, to bask in the certainty of being so thoroughly wanted.

The cardigan slips off her, pooling at her feet. With deliberate slowness, she undoes her jeans, the zipper's metallic hiss loud in the quiet room. She shimmies out of them with an awkward grace, not used to taking control of her body this way. Sam watches, transfixed, his thumb dragging absently across his bottom lip, imagining the taste of her.

The straps of her camisole slip from her shoulders, the fabric whispering down her skin before sinking into the soft heap at her feet. She steps free, silently thanking her earlier self for choosing this black lace—half hope, half dare. Goosebumps decorate her arms, not from cold but from the courage that trembles through her bones. Her joints lock tight, instincts flaring: cover up, turn away, dis-appear into shadow. But she doesn't. She meets his gaze and is held there. And in that steady look, she finds her shelter, not in hiding, but in being seen.

His breath catches audibly as she closes the distance between them. The ardent yearning in his eyes sends electricity skittering down her spine. His hands flex at his sides, knuckles cracking with the effort of restraint, every muscle screaming to reach out and claim her.

"How do you want me?" Her voice wavers only slightly as she stands before him, vulnerable yet powerful in her offering.

Sam's hands find her waist, his touch branding her even through the lace. His gaze travels down her body with deliberate slowness, a starving man standing before a feast, then back up to meet her eyes, dark with want. Wordlessly, he rises, guiding her to the couch.

"Are you cold?" His voice is wrapped in velvet, eyes drinking in the way her nipples pebble in the cool air.

She shrugs. The sheepish smile that follows makes his stomach flip.

He drapes the throw over her as she arranges herself in a sinuous curve, one leg bent to highlight the swell of her butt, the other extended in a graceful line. When she rests her cheek on her arm, looking up at him through her lashes, it takes everything in him not to pounce on her.

The pencil becomes an extension of his desire as it glides across the page. He captures the dip of her waist, the way the lace cups the underside of her breast, the tantalizing shadow of cleavage. Each stroke is a caress he longs to make in flesh, the sketchbook on his lap the only barrier hiding his arousal. When he finally turns the page to show her, the graphite has transformed her into something mythic, rendered in smoke and silver.

You made me look so..." she breathes, walking over to take a closer look.

"You are *so*." His hands find her waist again, pulling her close. The kiss he presses to her navel sends sparks across her skin. Her fingers tangle in his curls as his mouth trails lower, each kiss a searing brand. His lips brush the lace at her hips. "Can I taste you?" His voice is gravel and fire, the words rough with the effort of holding back, an arrow shooting straight to her core.

She nods and he carries her back to the couch, laying her out like a sacrament. His descent is worshipful, kisses peppered along her inner thighs, each one closer to where she burns for him. He slides her underwear off and when his tongue finally presses against her slit, licking up to the pearl between her folds, the cry it tears from her throat is pure, unfiltered pleasure.

He feasts like a man possessed, urged ravenously by her desperate moaning as she comes undone by his doing. Just as her aftershocks subside, he adds a finger, then another, crooking them as his tongue continues its devilish work. Drenched in blissful ecstasy and desperate need, she tugs his hair. "Do you have any condoms?"

"Yeah...somewhere..." he whispers against her thighs, catching his breath.

"Can you grab one?"

At the realization of what she's asking for, his head resurfaces. His hands grip her tighter as he lifts her into his arms, their lips never breaking contact, desperate for each other as if they'd drown in the space between.

He carries her into the room, the weight of her against him igniting something wild. He sets her gently on the bed. A condom wrapper tears between his teeth.

"Let me put it on for you," she murmurs. The sight of her delicate fingers rolling it down his length sets him on fire.

"Is there anything you want me to know before we…"

Lacy considers, her eyes locking with his as she pulls him down for a kiss. She pulls back slightly, her voice a quiet command: "Don't trap me under you. I want to be able to move."

Sam nods, lowering his body to hers as they kiss, and she can feel his tip rest against her opening. The pleasure of anticipation roils within her, settling right below her stomach, making her toes curl.

"Would you rather be on top?" he whispers against her lips.

A stitch of worry zips through her. It has been a while since she's had sex. Sex with David had required little from her, just stillness, patience, and endurance, as she waited for it to be over most of the time. She's never been on top before, and the idea of trying it with Sam excites her. But when she positions herself above him, hesitation flickers across her face. "I've never… I don't know what to do."

"You don't have to do a thing," he breathes against her lips. "I just want to make you feel as good as you make me feel."

His words unravel her as surely as his touch. Slowly, reverently, he guides her down. The stretch burns, a sweet agony, a fullness that makes her gasp. He draws his knees up just enough for her to settle flush against him, taking in every inch.

When she fully envelopes him, the groan that tears from his chest is primal. His head falls back, the tight sensation almost too much to bear. "Lacy..." Her name falls from his lips like a benediction, a surrender.

No thought exists, only sensation. Her body moves against his instinctively, arching to meet the rhythm of his hips, melding to the contours of his embrace like waves against the shore. Every touch ignites something electric in her, the trailing fingers along the curve of her waist, the flare of her hips, the delicate ridges of her ribcage. Nails graze down his chest as his palms cup the weight of her breasts, her thigh hitching higher around his waist to pull him deeper.

Their pace quickens, the pressure building between them.

"Am I doing something wrong?" she asks, feeling his grip tighten on her hips, halting her movement.

"No," he grits out, his voice thick with restraint. "The opposite. You feel too fucking good. I don't know how much longer I can last."

Her answering smile is wicked as she leans down, her lips brushing his. "Give in," she whispers, like an incantation. "I want to see you lose control."

His hands lock around her waist, fingers pressing into her soft flesh as he drives up into her with reckless abandon. Each thrust wringing desperate gasps and moans from them both. She arches above him, fingers scrambling against the headboard for purchase. The sight of her, flushed and wanton, breasts swaying with every roll of her hips, sends another bolt of want through him. He can't resist capturing a peaked nipple between his lips, laving it with his tongue before sucking hard, reveling in her sharp cry. Needing more—always more with her—his hand snakes up to cradle the back of her neck, dragging her down until their mouths collide, desperate for a taste of her lips, her tongue, her soul. His hands roam her back, her sides, anywhere he can reach, as if beneath the soft glow of the moon, he's trying to memorize her through touch alone.

"Fuck," he growls against her mouth. "You feel—" The words die in his throat as she clenches around him. He swallows her screams as she shatters, like communion, sacred and consuming. The feel of her pulsing around him drags him over the edge, his own release crashing through him like a tidal wave.

He eventually pulls out of her, his cock so sensitive that he has to go slow. They lie tangled in the wreckage of sheets, hearts pounding in sync. Sam drapes an arm across his eyes, utterly ruined. "That was..." He can't find the words. No language for something he's never known until now, something that didn't exist before her.

"Yeah," she agrees on a breathy laugh, her entire body limp, mind lost to an effusive stupor.

*T*he rest of the summer slips by in a halcyon haze, each day bathed in golden sunlight, each evening stretching into an endless horizon. As the weather starts to cool, Sam and Lacy find themselves daydreaming about the cozy pleasures of fall: hot drinks, soft blankets, and warm hands as the world outside darkens and chills. One evening, they're tucked in her bed, laughing at the silly videos Sam had saved to watch with her on his phone, when a knock interrupts them.

"Hey, I need to talk to you," Sophie's voice drifts through the door.

Lacy exchanges a glance with Sam before sitting up, creating space between them. "Come in."

Sophie enters, offering Sam a quick greeting before turning her gaze to Lacy. "There's something I need to discuss with you, privately."

A flicker of worry. "Okay. Of course." Sam is already slipping out of bed, clearly sensing the seriousness in the atmosphere. He pauses at the door, looking over his shoulder at Lacy, but she offers him a reassuring smile.

"Actually... maybe it's better if Sam stays," Sophie asks, turning the question to her sister. "What do you think?"

Lacy, unsure of what's coming but willing to go along with it, looks at Sam, who gives her a shrug. "Yeah, it's fine," she says.

Sam shuts the door, leans against it, and slides his hands into his pockets. Sophie sighs and takes a seat at the edge of the bed, her energy suddenly shifting. "Okay, so... I've been thinking about our business."

They had put a pause on their online VHS rental business after Sophie was hired to Sam's studio.

"What about it?" Lacy asks.

"I want to start it up again. Reopen your store. But this time, with me running it along with you, if you're interested."

Lacy and Sam exchange a look of surprise. "You want to reopen the store? Why?"

Sophie's voice grows more animated as she explains. "Streaming platforms are getting greedy, prices keep going up, ads are sneaking in. What happened to the whole point of avoiding cable? And I've noticed more and more people are talking about how they miss physical media, want to own their movies again. I've been checking the business's email and socials. There's been a huge increase in inquiries. People are asking for rentals, even offering to come to us directly."

"Okay..." Lacy raises an eyebrow. "Would we quit our jobs to do this? How can we afford this?"

"I've worked out a business plan with a friend, and he's offered to back it," Sophie says, her enthusiasm building. "This time, we'd make it something more, like a café and a community space. A place where people can come together over movies. We can offer movie sales and rentals, host screenings, make it somewhere people come to hang out, make it affordable. Just enough to cover our expenses, to keep the store alive without it feeling like we're chasing profit."

She pauses to gauge Lacy's reaction, then adds, "And Lace, you could work remotely from there. I could be there most days. My boss is chill," she says, flicking a furtive glance at Sam. "I think we could balance it, the store and our jobs."

Lacy turns to Sam, who is listening thoughtfully. "Where you work isn't a concern. Most of our meetings happen over calls. Although..." He hesitates, brows knitting. "You know, what you're describing sounds a bit like what libraries already offer, and they do it for free."

Sophie doesn't skip a beat. "Yeah, you can borrow movies from the library, but we'd have obscure indie titles, and a café, a place for people to sit and enjoy. People online are always moaning about the loss of third spaces. God forbid, the internet becomes our only one. We'd have a movie room, like a space where people can come watch a movie on a fancy projector. Not everyone has big living rooms and basements to host movie nights like we do. For people who love movies and want to share them, this could be their place. We could make it rentable." She lets the idea linger in the air before adding, "I'm also thinking of creating a movie club. We could have weekly themed events, like Saturday Morning Cartoons, Spooky Sunday Scares, Wednesday Weepies, Thirsty Thursdays."

Sam looks intrigued, his voice playful. "Thirsty Thursdays are for romantic films, I'm guessing?"

Sophie nods with a mischievous grin. "Thursday just feels like the most romantic day of the week, don't you think?"

Lacy can't help but smile. "It's a nice idea. Sounds like a lot of work."

"I think Paul would be all in for this," Sam adds. "He'd definitely want to be involved. Probably start his own Film Bro Fridays or something."

Sophie laughs, but then her tone softens. "Lace? What do you think?"

Lacy hesitates. The idea of running a store again, especially one that feels so laborious, makes her wary. "I loved having the store... but it was a lot of work for not a lot of money, especially if you're trying to make it accessible for people. Back then, I didn't have to worry about money because David—" She stops herself. Sam's subtle eye roll does not go unnoticed.

"You said your friend wanted to fund this for you?" Sam asks, steering the conversation away from David.

"For *us*," Sophie corrects quickly. "And yes. It's a real offer. He wants this to be worker-owned. Whoever works there gets a cut of the business. We wouldn't be getting taken advantage of."

Lacy raises an eyebrow. "Which friend? Have I met them?"

Sophie's expression shifts, guarded, cautious. "Actually... you have," she exhales slowly, bracing herself. "It's Oliver."

"Who's Oliver?" Sam asks.

"Oliver," Sophie repeats, her voice quiet. "As in... David's brother."

Lacy freezes, shock overtaking her as the realization sinks in. "David's brother?" she repeats, stunned. A flood of questions rises, choking her. "How are you even friends with him?"

Sophie shifts uneasily. "I met him at your engagement party, remember?" She doesn't meet Lacy's eyes, but continues. "We exchanged numbers and... well, we've kept in touch since."

Lacy's mind whirls. "You've been talking to him this whole time?" Her voice cracks with disbelief. "Why didn't you tell me?"

Sophie sighs. "I didn't want you to feel like I was betraying you. When you broke up with his brother, I should've cut him off, but I didn't. I just... I didn't want you to be mad at me."

Lacy swallows, the weight of the past heavy in her chest. "You trust him enough to go into business with him? Do you realize how much money I owe that family?"

Sophie nods, her face unwavering in its earnestness. "Yeah, I do. He's using his own money to buy the store back from David, and all the debt you owe would be rolled into your ownership." She reaches out for Lacy's hand, her eyes pleading for understanding. "I know what you went through, Lace. Believe me when I tell you Oliver isn't like his brother. I trust him. I just need you to trust me."

Lacy stays quiet for a long moment, chewing on the offer. "I don't know, Sophie. I'm just not sure I want to be involved with that family again. And if you've been hiding your friendship with him this whole time—"

"I get it," Sophie interrupts. "But Oliver cares about this, about building something real, something meaningful for the community. Unlike his family, he wants to do something good. It's more than just the store—he's offering a chance to be part of something bigger."

Lacy sighs, conflicted but moved by her sister's fervour. "I need time to think. This is a lot to take in."

"I'll show you all the paperwork, I swear it's legit." Sophie's eyes gleam with determination. "I'm serious about this, Lace."

Lacy nods, watching the fire in her sister's gaze, feeling the weight of her steady belief. She knows Sophie isn't one to rush into things blindly. For now, she'll trust that.

"Ask Mina to look over your business proposal. And Paul. And Sam, even. They know how to run a successful business."

Sam shrugs, a small, easy smile tugging at his lips. "I'm at your service."

"You should do this even if I'm not a part of it," Lacy says, offering her sister the only blessing she can for now, support for the idea, but not her involvement, not yet.

Sophie exhales, tension softening into a smile, relief flickering across her face even as she practically vibrates with anticipation. "Okay. Take your time. I know you'll come around."

Several months slip by, every piece settling into place with quiet precision. The paperwork comes through as promised, no shady fine print, no last-minute surprises. Fastidiously handled under Mina's watchful eye, reviewed by the business advisors at her bank, polished to perfection by Paul's trusted lawyer, the same one who helped him navigate the legalities of establishing two successful animation studios. The documents lay out the details of their vision: a legitimate worker cooperative, with Sophie and Oliver as equal partners, while Lacy retains a minority share, her financial ties to David now severed without obligation to participate beyond investment. Paul's involvement comes as no surprise. His entrepreneurial instincts had been circling the project from the start, unable to resist the allure of creative collaboration with Sophie, not to mention the chance to curate his own retrospectives.

As for Edward and Jacob, they both enthusiastically join in on the fun, commandeering the Sunday morning slot, their plans for queer cinema programming evolving by the minute.

"The retrospective will be called Pride and Popcorn... No, wait, Reel Screen Queens... Or—wait—*The Lavender Lens*," Edward declares, his hand slicing through the air with theatrical flair.

Jacob's eyes light up as he builds on the vision. "We could host Drag Race viewing parties! And a queer literary series where we discuss both the books and their film adaptations."

"Yes, yes, yes!" Edward cheers, practically dancing with the idea.

Lacy watches, a mixture of admiration and skepticism gnawing at her. She can't help but feel a flicker of hope at the sight of her friends all pitching in, working together with an energy that fills the room, but she remains wary. She had learned to protect her heart from the sharp edges of uncertainty.

Against her expectations, the venture takes shape with remarkable cohesion. Lacy handles the inventory transfer from the storage unit, while Edward, Jacob, Sophie, and Oliver take the lead on designing the store. Edward's architectural background, paired with Jacob's contractor expertise, helps cut costs significantly. Sophie and Oliver occasionally chime in with design preferences, rolling up their sleeves for manual work when needed. It feels like a true fresh start—a labour of love in every sense.

Sophie, Paul, and Jacob, each with a sharp eye for social media, get to work capturing candid behind-the-scenes moments of their process. Their posts quickly go viral, fueled by their effortless charm, authenticity, and the palpable passion they're pouring into the project. The buzz around the space grows rapidly, drawing people in. Soon, everyone wants a piece of this cool spot that promises to be affordable, something the community has been craving for ages.

Lacy can't help but be struck by how easily Oliver seems to move through life. Unlike David, who was constantly driven by the need to accumulate more wealth, elevate his status, and prove himself to everyone, Oliver treats his wealth like the absurdity it is—limitless, almost comical. He shares it freely, without concern for who or where it goes. Buying meals for everyone without a second thought, especially on nights they're working late, exhausted after their day jobs. The difference between the two brothers is sharp, almost painful for Lacy to witness, especially considering how much of her life had been shaped by David's relentless, self-serving pursuits. Where David's ego ruled every moment, Oliver's lack of one is disarming. There's a raw authenticity to him that draws people in. He's grounded, present, a steady, uncomplaining worker who stays late without being asked, organizing inventory, assembling furniture, scrubbing toilets. Never once does he expect recognition or praise.

When the space finally comes together, the result is nothing short of dazzling. Everyone's aesthetic sensibilities blend into something stylish yet inviting—the kind of place that feels instantly familiar but full of discovery. Lacy's curated antiques add warmth and character: vintage film posters evoke nostalgia and spark conversation among cinephiles drawn to the rare, iconic titles. A restored projector lends both function and flair. The café, which doubles as a screening room, features a giant screen that plays original animated, mixed-media, and experimental visuals during regular hours—enhancing the atmosphere while spotlighting work by local artists. The space itself glows with soft, warm lighting, and the seating is thoughtfully arranged. Plush armchairs beckon solitary patrons, while clustered sofas welcome lively groups. Every corner feels intentional, a perfect blend of comfort and creativity.

As the store prepares for its soft opening, excitement hums through the air. They reach out to everyone they know, sharing on social media and sending personal invites to followers most invested in their journey.

When the night finally arrives, it exceeds every expectation. Sam's aunts fly in for the event, though their journey is nearly derailed by passport issues. Aunt Sam, whose gender marker on her new passport no longer matches, faces complications with TSA agents who refuse to accept her identification. She's forced to provide additional documentation, including an expired passport that still displays the *F* marker, before she's allowed to board. It's more than just an inconvenience. It's a constant, painful reminder of how her rights are being stripped. Each time she's asked to show her new passport, she's forced to disclose a part of herself that she hasn't chosen to share with strangers who have no right to judge her, invalidate her, or make her feel less than. All she wants is to see her nephew, so she endures these humiliations with quiet strength, but the weight of it all is undeniable. It's not just frustration. It's a soul-crushing sense of helplessness, watching the world grow more hostile, erasing her autonomy with every encounter. Despite the emotional toll, Aunt Sam refuses to let it overshadow the excitement of the night, her resilience always shining through.

When Lacy sees Sam's aunts posing for a selfie with him, she offers to take the photo. Sam hands her his phone, and she catches a glimpse of his wallpaper: the intimate candid of them kissing at the cottage. Her heartstrings tighten, and when she returns his phone, she subtly changes the wallpaper on her device, replacing the default image with the Polaroid of their kiss at the antique market. It's a quiet reminder of how safe she feels with him, kissing him in public, her guard utterly down.

Dawna arrives with Gerald at her side and her dog tucked into her purse. Her presence is composed, self-assured, slicing through the frenetic buzz of the room. Lacy introduces Sam as her boyfriend, casually, effortlessly, and Sam blinks. It's the first time he's heard her call him that. A word so small, yet it lands like a holy rite. He smiles like the lovesick fool he is, dazed. A little stunned. A little undone.

Naturally, Dawna is surprised. When did her daughter start dating her tenant? How? But the shock quickly settles into placid approval. Maybe she's not quite as dazzled as she was with David. David, with his polished charm and diamond-studded promises. But she knows Sam. Knows his salary. Has seen his credit score. He's responsible. Always pays his rent on time. A perfectly stable, dependable man for her daughter to build a life with.

Throughout the evening, she watches them. How he moves around her, attentive without show, steadily present. How he brings her food before she even asks. How his hands find her like it's second nature, holding her, caressing her face, touching her like she's something precious. She catches softness in his eyes when they land on her, the way he watches her like she's the only person in the room. The glances he steals when he thinks no one is looking, lingering, reverent, as if he knows exactly what he has, and will never take it for granted.

To Dawna, love like this had only ever existed at the edges of fairy tales, in adolescent dreams she once let herself believe, before life taught her better. And yet, impossibly, she sees it now in her daughter's face. Lacy glows under his gaze, lit from within. She gravitates toward him unconsciously, like a flower tracking the sun. Dawna hadn't realized how long it had been since she'd seen her daughter like this, unburdened, soft, joyfully alive. Maybe not since she was a child.

Later, she meets Sam's aunts, professors, both of them. Sharp, witty, warm. They treat her daughters like family, and it startles Dawna, how easily they fit into their lives, so effortless, it almost stings. Watching her daughters laugh with them, she hears Lacy say "Aunt Sam" like she's done it all her life, and a strange, bittersweet ache unfurls in her chest. Envy maybe. These women know her daughters in a way she doesn't. And maybe never has. She wonders, quietly, painfully, what else she's missed. What parts of them she never saw, never asked about. For the first time in years, Dawna feels the sharp, unfamiliar pull of regret.

By the end of the night, the place is packed to capacity. The atmosphere buzzes with excitement. The newly hired baristas keep up impressively despite it being their first shift, while Sophie's locally sourced baked goods become an unexpected hit, selling out faster than anyone had anticipated. Patrons eagerly share snapshots of the movie night and the delicious food offerings on their own social media accounts, spreading the word. Messages flood in from people eager to visit, their enthusiasm practically leaping off the screen. The place has struck a chord, offering exactly what people have been desperately longing for.

In the days leading up to the grand opening, Lacy spends most of her time there, quietly working on her own projects while helping to clean and organize. Oliver is there every day, sorting, wiping, testing equipment, making sure everything runs smoothly before the big day. She can no longer deny that Sophie's right—Oliver is completely different from his brother. Watching him with her sister, she begins to trust him more, drawn to their natural dynamic. She can't help but listen in on their spirited conversations—nothing is off-limits: movies, gossip, politics, philosophy, life. They weave and jump between topics without a script, both following the same invisible map. Oliver is the only person she's met who matches her sister's rapid-fire rhythm, finishing each other's sentences, voices overlapping. There's a depth to their connection, a rare understanding that Lacy has come to admire.

One afternoon, as the sisters work side by side, Lacy's curiosity gets the best of her. She glances up from her screen and teases, "So... You and Oliver. Just friends?"

Sophie gives her sister a little kick under the table. "Ew. Yes. Don't make it weird."

"Okay," Lacy says, hands raised in mock surrender. "I was just curious. You guys just get along so well."

"Yes, friends tend to get along," Sophie quips. "Believe it or not, people can be friends without kissing."

Lacy laughs. "Okay, okay, I was just curious. You never talk about this stuff. I don't even know if you like boys."

Sophie shrugs, her attention drifting back to her laptop. "I like what I like."

"Which is what?" Lacy asks, pressing further.

Sophie shrugs again, her nonchalance annoying. "Whatever I like."

Lacy squints at her, wondering how to push the conversation forward. "Tell me more. I don't know anything about you when it comes to this stuff. Who was your first kiss?"

Sophie raises an eyebrow. "Who was yours?"

"Sebastian Yang," Lacy answers without hesitation, hoping the disclosure might inspire Sophie to open up.

"What? The super loud kid who was into dinosaurs all through high school?"

"Yes. And he wasn't just into *dinosaurs*," Lacy defends with a grin. "He was into *paleontology*."

"Right, right," Sophie laughs. "He was pretty cute."

"*I know*. That's why I kissed him." Lacy nudges her sister's foot under the table. "Your turn."

Sophie scratches her hair, then rolls her eyes. "I don't know. Some pretentious nerd from my first-year film studies class."

"Is that your type?" Lacy teases.

"Ew. No way."

"Then what's your type?"

Sophie gives a half-hearted shrug. "I don't have one. Do you?"

Lacy thinks for a moment and comes up short. Her attractions have always varied, and she's been with people she wasn't entirely sure about. She finally answers, "Sam."

Sophie rolls her eyes at her sister's answer. "Exactly. People rarely actually have types. If they do, they probably have some biases they need to unlearn. Most of us figure out what we like when we're presented with it."

Lacy nods at her sister's clarity, admiring how easily Sophie sees things, her understanding of people and situations so grounded. "So, have you been presented with anything you like lately?"

Lacy doesn't miss as Sophie's gaze shifts quickly toward Oliver, stacking glasses behind the counter. Her eyes flicker for a moment before she looks back to her screen, her voice a little too casual. "Nope."

Lacy grins. "What about Oliver?"

Sophie's tone goes defensive immediately. "You millennials can never conceive the idea of men and women just being friends, can you?"

Lacy rolls her eyes, laughing. "I have a lot of male friends."

"Really?" Sophie retorts, leaning back dramatically in her chair. "The ones in a gay relationship, both of whom you've kissed? Or did you mean Paul, who's married to his high school sweetheart? Or Ben? Whose eyes turn into hearts whenever you're around?"

Lacy bursts out laughing, giving her sister's chair a playful kick.

"Exactly," Sophie says, making a show of adjusting her chair, her attention snapping back to her laptop.

Lacy takes a deep breath, her voice softening. "I wasn't suggesting you should date him. I wouldn't wish that family on you."

Sophie pauses, her fingers hovering over the keyboard. "Well, he has a girlfriend anyway. They've been together a long time."

The words hang between them, but Lacy can't shake the feeling that Sophie isn't as sure about it as she lets on.

$\mathcal{W}$inter settles over the city, and for the first time, Sam understands the quiet romance of the season. He watches as the sky darkens to a deep navy before it's even five, delicate snow falling outside the café, snowflakes catching the amber glow of the streetlights. The heat from the mug seeps into his skin as he makes a hot chocolate for the woman he loves, the simple warmth of it transforming the cold into something intimate, something worth lingering in. He thinks about their walk home later, boots crunching through fresh snow, the hush of the world beneath its heavy white blanket. Their breath meeting in the space between them, warmth curling and caressing in the crisp night air.

Lacy waits beneath their makeshift blanket, their coats knotted together by the sleeves. She looks up at him with sleepy contentment as he hands her the mug. When he settles beside her, her hand finds his thigh, her fingers tracing lazy circles through the denim. She rests her head against his shoulder, her thumb rubbing slow, hypnotic strokes along his inner thigh. The scrape of her nails sends shivers along his skin.

After a few minutes, Sam clears his throat, and Lacy looks over to find his eyes shut tight. Feeling her gaze on him, he opens his eyes and turns to her.

You okay? she mouths.

He offers a small, strained smile before turning back to the screen where an animated Christmas film plays, their friends gathered for one last private night before opening day.

Lacy laughs at a particularly charming scene, her body shifting closer to his, her arm brushing against the unmistakable hardness straining against his jeans. Sam releases a choked sound, a groan he covers up with a cough, and Lacy can't suppress her smile, biting her lip in that particular way he's come to recognize as a sign of her own arousal. Noticing his attention, she fights back a giggle.

He leans close, his breath warm against her ear. "You don't get to laugh at me." She can hear his smile in his voice. "You've been fondling dangerously close to my dick this entire time. I'm just a man."

"*Fondling* is a crazy word choice," she whispers back in mock outrage, her laughter barely contained. Her hand unceasing in its hypnotic rhythm, her arm now resting deliberately against his erection, amplifying each movement with tantalizing pressure.

"Oh my god," Sam groans, dragging his sweater collar up to cover his flaming face as his head falls back against the couch. Jacob, seated in front of them, turns at the sound and places a concerned hand on Sam's knee.

"You okay, bud?" he whispers in the dim.

Sam lowers the sweater just enough to reveal his eyes and gives a thumbs up.

"He burned his tongue on the hot chocolate." Lacy covers for him, and Jacob gives him a sympathetic frown, patting his knee before turning back to the screen.

As the movie nears its end, Sam exhales deeply, straightening up with sudden focus, as if willing himself to pay attention. He takes her hand, interlacing their fingers, bringing them out from under the coats.

"You could've told me to stop," she murmurs against his ear.

"Like I said, I'm just a man," he whispers back. "I lack the restraint."

"So, you restrain *me*?" Lacy laughs, lifting their clasped hands to her lips, pressing a kiss to his knuckles. "Typical."

He shrugs, letting go of her hand just long enough to wrap his arm around her shoulders before taking it back.

Sam stays seated as the credits roll, acutely aware of the strain against his zipper. Around him, their friends stretch and gather their things. Lacy offers to close up, an easy out that spares him the awkward ordeal of standing, and them the undeniable evidence of his adoration for her. He murmurs casual goodbyes from his chair, scrolling his phone in a convincing pantomime of distraction. The screen glows against his focused expression, as if he's deep in some urgent email. The lights dim as Lacy closes up. The quiet click of the lock echoes his relief.

When she returns, he's undoing the knot of their coat sleeves, ready to head out. His long coat would cover any lingering evidence of his arousal. But before he can rise, Lacy steps between his legs. She sinks to her knees elegantly, and whatever progress he'd made in his pants vanishes in an instant.

"What do you think you're doing, angel?" His voice is a low, velvety rumble.

"Looking at you," she murmurs, resting her cheek against his thigh, her breath ghosting over the fabric of his jeans.

He exhales a deep, unsteady breath, fingers threading into her hair, sweeping it gently out of her face. "Must you insist on torturing me?"

"Torture?" Lacy's palm glides up his other thigh. "I'm trying to do the exact opposite, if you haven't noticed."

His brow creases with familiar hesitation, but his hand doesn't stop stroking through her hair, fingers relishing the silk of it. "I don't know, Lacy."

"What are you afraid of?"

The irony isn't lost on her, how she had endured giving David head, an obligatory performance that followed all their make-out sessions, his hand heavy on the back of her head, steering her downward. How she often followed through just to get it over with, his oppressive grip an unspoken demand. And now, by her own will and want, she's refused. Out of gallantry, she suspects.

"I can already feel the spell you're putting me under," he says, cupping her face in his hands, his thumbs brushing over her cheeks. "I don't want to lose control and accidentally hurt you."

Accidentally hurt me? "We've done things way past this, and you've never hurt me. Why do you think you would?" she asks, leaning into his touch, a quiet testament to her trust in him.

Sam exhales, heavy with the weight of a memory he rarely allows himself to touch. The confession spills out of him. His last time, how he'd jerked awake from sleep and kneed Anna in the face, the sudden rush of blood from her nose staining her face, his pants.

As abusive as his father had been, he had never hit his mother. And yet, Sam can't shake the early memory of his parents fighting, his father threatening to leave again. His mother oscillating between anger, dissociation, and desperation—yelling, crying, clinging to him. His father was nearly at the door, bags in hand, his mother's arms locked around his waist, dragged along the floor, her legs dangling helplessly beside her. Finally fed up, he'd shoved her off. The force of it swung the edge of his luggage straight into her face.

Sam remembers sitting at the kitchen table, a book propped open in front of him, something far too mature for him to be reading, the words blurring before him as he stared at his mother, blood around her nose and mouth. The look of stunned horror on his father's face quickly curdling into anger, directed at *him*.

"What are you doing just sitting there? Help your mother!"

Then, the door slammed shut.

Lacy is sitting up now, listening intently as he tells her how he tiptoed on a box stacked on a dining chair, reaching for the first aid kit in some high cabinet. How, at six years old, he barely knew how to clean his own face, let alone his mother's bloody one.

"Sam," Lacy says, sitting back on her heels to take his hands in hers. "What happened was an accident." Her voice is gentle and resolute.

"What if this violence runs in my blood?" The words come out raw, stripped bare.

"I don't believe that." She presses a kiss to his knuckles. "Besides," she adds with a sly smile, "all the blood in your body seems to be violently rushing somewhere else right now."

His startled laugh breaks the tension.

"Do you trust me?" she asks.

He nods.

"Do you want this?"

A smaller nod.

"Then trust the trust I have in you."

"Okay," he breathes, the sound like a tight fist slowly unclenching.

With careful hands, she unfastens his zipper, her gaze locked on his face, his features darkening with undisguised lust. His breath hitches as she eases his jeans down, his arousal straining against the thin cotton of his boxer briefs. She runs her palms over the outline of him, watching his face contort with pleasure before leaning down to press a kiss to the damp fabric covering his tip.

The eye contact when she looks up nearly undoes him, her dark eyes full of warmth and wicked promise. She trails kisses down his length before freeing him from his underwear, his cock jerking free. Her hand wraps around him, pumping slowly, and his head falls back with a groan.

His eyelids droop as he watches her, each breath coming thick and uneven. He inhales a sharp breath, watching as she lowers her head, her lips closing around him.

"Fuck me," he gasps.

"I'm trying to," she teases before taking him deeper.

The sensation overwhelms him. The perfect pressure of her fingers, the wet heat of her mouth as his shaft disappears into her. He cannot suppress the whimpering breath that escapes him as her head bobs between his thighs, her hands working in flawless tandem.

"Fuck," he moans when his tip hits the back of her throat. His hands fist in her hair, not to guide, simply to touch her, to anchor himself as the mounting pleasure threatens to obliterate his senses. She works him with both hands now, her tongue circling his tip as she watches him through lowered lashes.

He is cursing god's name, or maybe hers, he can't tell anymore. His free hand seizes the armrest, knuckles blanched, as she takes him fully into her mouth. Every nerve in his body ignites as his being spills into her, release wracking through him like revelation. His cock twitches, the last of him given over. She wipes her lips with a delicate flick of her thumb, eyes gleaming as she looks up at him, grinning, triumphant.

"God, I love you," he breathes, still dazed, his voice raw with devotion.

$\mathcal{S}$ am is awoken by the incessant buzzing of his phone. He gropes for it in the dark, careful not to disturb Lacy beside him, her breathing slow and even.

The screen floods his vision with a barrage of notifications. For one disorienting moment, he has a psychosomatic flashback to that terrible afternoon on the plane, the same cold dread pooling in his stomach before he'd even read a word. His pulse kicks up now as his thumb scrolls through the messages, each new line sending a wave of panic through him.

Sophie:
SAM!!! CALL ME BACK!!!

Sophie:
SAM WAKE UP

Edward:

hey is lacy with you?

you gotta getto the store now

please call sophie back !!

Paul:

Have you talked to Sophie yet???

Jacob:

bro. Are u good? Is Lacy?

Paul:

Did Lacy see????

Sophie:

figuring it out with oliver!! please make sure my sister is ok.

Lacy stirs awake as he's listening to the voice messages Sophie has left him, mostly frantic, panicked pleas for him to call her back.

"Is everything okay?" Lacy murmurs, sitting up.

Sam can only shrug and shake his head, placing a hand on her thigh, too overstimulated to form words as he skims through the messages, trying to piece together what's happened. "Do not let her go on her phone. We are trying to take it down. I'm fucking locked out of the account right now," Sophie's voice crackles from one of the later recordings.

He's midway through Paul's next message, something about counter-hacking the account, when he notices Lacy has gone statue-still beside him, her hand pressed over her nose and mouth, eyes glued to her phone screen.

Peering over her shoulder, the phone looks obscenely large in her trembling hands, its glow harsh against the predawn dimness. A video, shot from behind the café counter, catches in the corner of the frame: Lacy on her knees, head between his thighs, moving in a rhythm too unmistakable to misinterpret, his own face just cropped out of view—now plastered on the café's official social media page.

His body moves before his mind catches up. He takes the phone from her grip, clicks the screen dark. She doesn't react, still locked in that same horrified posture, the video playing on a loop behind her unblinking eyes.

He drops the phone into a dresser drawer, closing it out of reach, then pulls up the café's page on his own phone. He scrolls past the video, his stomach churning at the thumbnail alone, reads the caption beneath: *Don't forget today is our Grand Opening! A taste of the customer service that will top you off at this establishment!*

A storm of emotions crashes over him. Panic, dread, the sickening sense of violation. Above it all, white-hot and absolute, a protective fury for Lacy.

She saw it, he texts Sophie.

Sophie:
fuckkkkk
she okay?

u okay?

IDK. I'm ok. Handle it

Sophie:
on it boss.
btw
he also printed pictures and pasted it all over the store
we are ripping them down

"Who the fuck is *he*?" Sam spits, the words sharper than he intended. Lacy flinches, and he immediately regrets his tone. He drags a hand through his hair, trying to rein in the storm inside him.

"Who?" Lacy asks, her voice small, dazed.

"Nothing," Sam says too quickly, already moving to her side. He doesn't know what to do, so he just pulls her into his arms. "I don't know."

"Sam." Her voice hardens, the fragility giving way to steel. "Tell me." She points to her phone on the dresser. "If there's something worse than that, I need to know."

He shows her Sophie's text.

"Who is *he*?" she asks again.

Sam fires off the question to Sophie, and they both watch with horror as her reply pings instantly: oliver thinks its his brother...

"What the fuck." The words curl with venom, rasping with a hatred so raw it burns the back of his throat.

Lacy is already moving, her body operating robotically. She snatches one of his sweaters from the floor, yanks it over her head, and is halfway to the door before he can process what's happening. She's shoving her arms into her coat, pulling on her boots with frantic urgency.

"Lacy, what are you doing?" Sam asks, his voice cracking.

"I have to get to the café. Those pictures. I have to take them down." Her tone is flat, mechanical.

"Okay." He mirrors her numbness, stumbling into clothes blindly. When he emerges, he finds her methodically pouring kibble into the cat's bowl. Lacy looks up, her eyes hollow. "Ready?"

The car ride is a blur of streetlights and silence. Sam grips the wheel, but his gaze keeps flickering to her. Her face is eerily blank, unreadable in a way that terrifies him.

She scrolls through notifications, reads them, doesn't reply.

"Angel, are you okay?"

She doesn't answer. *What kind of question is that right now?*

"A lot of people have seen it," she says finally. "All our friends. All the followers. People who will come to the store."

"It doesn't really show your face. No one will know it's you."

"It doesn't show your face either. But I'm still sorry, Sam." The hitch in her voice almost breaking through her monotony.

"Sorry for what?"

"That you're with me. That I'm a curse." The words land like a verdict, devoid of inflection, as if she's stating an immutable fact.

"You're not a fucking curse," he says, desperation clawing at his throat.

"How many people does this happen to? Much less multiple times?"

"This is not your fault, Lacy."

She doesn't reply, just stares at her phone, the screen flooding with notifications.

When they arrive, the scene is chaos. The café windows are plastered with blown-up printouts of the CCTV footage, a crowd already forming, some gawking, some snapping pictures. Edward and Jacob are ripping down sheets with their bare hands, Mina dousing the windows with a bucket of water, the colours on the paper melting, Celeste scraping furiously at the wet residue with some flat tool.

Lacy is out of the car before he can stop her. She stands frozen, taking in the spectacle, her friends' panic, the onlookers' morbid curiosity, the whispers slithering through the crowd.

Sophie bursts from the store, spots her sister, and sprints to her, crushing her in a hug that Lacy does not return. Sophie all but drags her inside.

Inside the store, Lacy watches through the glass as her friends scrub away the last remnants of the posters. The crowd outside seems to pulse—so many eyes, so many phones raised. She turns to Sophie, the question loud in her mind: *What the hell is happening?* But her voice is lodged somewhere deep inside her, unreachable.

"The post is down," Sophie replies, as if hearing her. Her fingers fly across her phone. "Enough reports got it removed."

"How long was it up?" Sam asks.

"About six hours."

Lacy loses feeling in her fingers. How many people saw it?

"We got locked out of the account. He changed the password and the email somehow. We can't see analytics."

Lacy nods, her eyes glassy and vacant.

"I'm emailing with support to regain access," Sophie adds quickly.

Oliver materializes from the back room, and Lacy's breath catches. She hadn't expected him to be here. "I'm so so so sorry, Lacy," he begins, his usually steady voice cracking.

"How did this happen?" Sam asks, reaching for her limp hand.

"David must've kept backdoor access to the security feeds."

"I didn't even know there were cameras here. Why did no one tell us?"

Sophie's mouth hangs open slightly like she's about to say something, but words fail her. Sam is right, of course, her sister should have known where the cameras were.

"What a fucking creep," Celeste snaps, slamming the front door, carrying in bags of sopping paper. "Was he getting off watching us this whole time?"

Ice floods Lacy's veins. Her hands start to tremble. Her nails dig half-moons into her palm. He had been watching her last night. Watching them. Colour drains from her face as she's yanked back into the bleakest corner of herself, where the curse waits, pulsing red, unrelenting. How could she have forgotten? Believed, even for a moment, that its grip had loosened? That she could be free. Her violent lust so sinful, so consuming, not hers to indulge in. How dare she try to seek pleasure in others? All she brings is ruin.

Then, Sophie explodes, tears streaming down her reddening face. "What the actual fuck is wrong with your brother?" Her voice shatters around Oliver like sharp glass. "He's a fucking pervert. A rapist." The words linger, rancid in the air.

Oliver takes the verbal blows without flinching, his expression carved from grief.

"Does he keep a hacker on retainer?" Sophie's voice frays at the edges. "All it takes is fucking hours to hijack our account? In the dead of night?"

Oliver's face transforms, some horrific understanding dawning.

Sam steps closer. "What?"

"It..." Oliver swallows hard. "It was my phone."

Sophie's tears dry in an instant, scorched away by the fury rising in their place.

"David accessed the account through my phone," Oliver confesses, realization hitting him. "Last night. At my parents'." Each word seems to cost him. "He borrowed it, said his died. Took it to the bathroom to make a call."

Sophie goes still. Her anger souring the air around them, the kind that quiets a room, sharp, focused, and terrifying in its clarity. "You were with David last night?"

"Sophie," he sighs, grasping for her faith. "I didn't know he was going to be there."

"You didn't come to the movie last night because you were with your brother?" Sophie whispers, then her voice erupts: "To let him into our account? Violate my sister? Sam?"

"I know, Soph. I know I should've left."

"Well, you didn't. Because at the end of the day, you're just like *them*. You come from a family that profits off the exploitation of the human soul. Your sensitive film bro act? That's all it is—an act. A performance. Just like your politics. You call yourself a communist, but you have property investments, for God's sake. You could buy an entire building and let people live there for free, and still never have to work a day in your life. You live in a fucking penthouse with your influencer girlfriend, who makes videos about how she spends *your* money every week. What will it be? Some European music festival? A new designer bag? All the tools for a new hobby she'll give up in a week?"

"Soph," Sam says, his voice low with warning.

But Sophie doesn't stop, can't. The words pour out of her like poison, caustic and unrelenting. It feels like she might choke if she doesn't let it all out, everything that's been festering inside her, everything she's bitten back, every word a bullet aimed straight at Oliver.

"You're fucking fake," she spits. "You're not my friend. I'm just an accessory in your poverty cosplay. *Look at me, I'm so down-to-earth, my best friend's poor. Her dad's in jail. I'm such a noble guy because I throw her some pocket change and call it community work. I'm not like those other rich people. I love to talk shit about my evil capitalist family, dis-*

tance myself from their wealth, but at the end of the day, I have no problem spending their blood money."

She catches a glimpse of Lacy's face, and guilt strikes her hard. How could she have forgotten to tell Lacy about cameras. Sophie's guilt starts to creep in, and she can't stop herself from redirecting the shame. "Why didn't you think to get a new security system?"

Oliver's eyes are bloodshot. "I'm sorry, Sophie. I made a mistake."

"Your mistake cost everything," she snaps. "Your mistake allowed David to digitally *rape* my sister."

At her sister's words, Lacy feels bile rise in her throat. She stumbles past them, rushing into the nearby storage closet, slamming the door behind her. She retches into a stack of takeout containers. Bitter yellow foam. *Proof of the poison inside me.*

The walls pulse. Her lungs burn from the lack of air. Sam's knocks bleed into the ringing in her ears. His voice, frantic and concerned, filters through the door, but she can't make sense of it.

Her knees give out, falling back against the shelves. VHS tapes tumble around her. One bounces off her head, but she doesn't feel it. Her mind so far away from her body, so far from this room.

The door bursts open.

"Oh, my baby," Sam breathes, gathering her into his arms. His hands frame her face, and she looks into his kaleidoscope eyes, brimming with love. *Like sunlight through leaves*, she thinks, dazed.

"Are you okay?" His voice cracks with raw concern.

Another casualty of my curse.

She closes her eyes for a long moment, willing her voice to return. "Are the pictures still out there?" she croaks.

"No, they got all of them."

"Where?"

"In the trash, I assume."

"Inside or outside?"

"I don't know," he says. "Where do you want them?"

"Inside," she says urgently. "I don't want anyone to find them."

"Okay, we'll burn them." He pulls her into him, holding her gently. She is limp in his arms. "Is this okay? Or do you not want to be touched right now?"

The sensation of her body against his grounds her, but her mind keeps racing, the video endlessly looping.

The video's not online anymore, but it still exists. People could have recorded it. People outside took photos. More posters could be plastered somewhere else. Hidden in corners of the internet she doesn't even know about.

The walls close in on her. The edges of her vision darken. She can't breathe. There's not enough air in this room.

She tries to push past him. "I need to make this go away."

"You don't have to figure it out right now. Sophie's got it. Trust her."

As if on cue, she hears Sophie's voice, muffled but clear. She's talking to someone on the phone. "I need to get into the account right away." Assertive, confident even in this chaos.

Lacy's reminded of her sister's competency. Sophie's the smartest person she knows, and she knows what she's doing. She loves her. They love each other.

"I'm dealing with an emergency. A literal crime, actually," Sophie asserts to the person on the other end.

This is a crime, Lacy realizes. She doesn't want to be a victim again. Her throat tightens, and her vision blurs. Suddenly, the world feels so vast and overwhelming. The internet feels too liminal, untraceable. The world is so big. She feels too small, her legs too weak.

"Would you like the door closed?"

She nods. He kicks it shut with his foot.

"Locked?"

Nod.

He locks it, then pulls her into his lap as he sits on the floor, letting her curl up against him, her head resting on his chest.

She can't see his face through the blur of her tears, and that's when she realizes she's crying.

"I don't want to cry," she says, wiping fiercely at her tears, but it feels like she's in another body. Her voice sounding far away. "I'm fine. I'm okay."

"None of this is okay."

"I don't want to feel like this," she chokes, tears and snot flooding her face. "I don't want to feel like this again."

"I don't either." He pulls her closer, her body curled into him like a ball. "But you are safe now. You're safe to be sad, scared, angry. You're safe with me."

"You're not safe with me," she says coldly.

"I am. I am safe with you. So are you."

I'm safe. I'm safe. I'm safe, she tries to chant to herself but can't be convinced. *I want to die. I want to die. I want to die,* her brain repeats instead.

Sam can hear her mumbling it, and his heart drops. He remembers all the times his mother said it. "Please don't say that."

"I can't believe I actually let myself believe I could be happy," Lacy says, her quiet voice hoarse. Her words breaking his heart.

"We *are* happy. We aren't right now, but we will be again." Sam's voice is urgent, his arms tightening around her as if he can transfer this truth into her. "I love you. I love you so much."

And then she wails. Her sobs shake her whole body. She can hardly breathe. She's overwhelmed with sadness, anger, and fear. She feels violated, thrown back into a darkness she thought she had escaped. The worst day of her life, happening again. The rage inside her is suffocating, yet she's freezing cold. The only relief comes from being held in Sam's warmth. She loves him so much. She's never told him that. Afraid her love will curse him more. Knows she doesn't deserve him, nor his warmth.

Sam strokes her hair, rocking her as she sobs into his chest, his shirt soaked with her tears, mucus, and saliva. He feels the stain of his own tears and tastes the salt on his lips. He feels the rage in his chest, the deep sadness tightening his throat, the worry swirling in his stomach. But he reminds himself that they'll get through this. They will. He trusts himself. He trusts her. This pain will pass.

He holds her close, letting his soul break at the sound of her gasping sobs. He imagines his body absorbing her pain, breathing it out with each exhale, counts the seconds of his breath like Auntie Jackie had once taught him.

He doesn't know how long they sit there. Her sobs slowly turn into shallow breaths, and her breathing begins to match his. He feels the heaviness in his chest lighten. Maybe she's absorbing and releasing his pain too.

Finally, she pulls away from his shirt and pauses for a moment. She exhales a small, sniffling chuckle, and the sound is like sunshine breaking through a typhoon. She points to his shirt, and he sees the vague shape of a face in the tear stains. He laughs too, almost deliriously, and for a moment, he's reminded of the first time they met, laughing together in the middle of their beach, in the midst of their mess.

*L*acy had wanted the store to make headlines, just not like this.

The incident spreads like a virus, dominating local online spaces. What begins as a handful of shocked posts turns into full-blown discourse. Strangers regurgitate and dissect the details with grotesque fascination, spinning out imagined embellishments for dramatic effect. Some frame it as a tragic violation, a cautionary tale about digital safety, while others reduce it to lurid gossip, gleefully recounting their own interpretations of what really happened.

Earnest discussions are being had, buried under the noise. Thoughtful comments condemning revenge porn, calling for stronger laws, lamenting the cruelty of an internet that turns someone's nightmare into public property. And just as many voices wield their outrage against the store itself. Self-appointed moral arbiters swarm the comments, branding the business reckless, unprofessional, unhygienic. Why didn't they have better security? What kind of place lets something like this happen? Maybe they deserved to fail. The store, once envisioned as a sanctuary, now a spectacle.

Local news outlets seize the story, reporters wait at the storefront like vultures, cameras rolling, waiting for a soundbite. The opening is postponed indefinitely. The dream put on hold before it ever had a chance to breathe. Lacy barely registers the logistical fallout, Sophie handling the calls, Oliver intercepting journalists. In her mind, it all distills into one singular, deafening truth: *I ruin everything.*

The thought loops in her head like a broken transmission. *It's my fault.* She alone had caused the store's downfall. The weight of it crushes her, pressing down on her ribs like she's shrinking inside her own body. She's furious at David, of course, but she's just as furious at herself. After all these years. After all that practice, all that hypervigilance, all those rules she set for herself to never let this happen again, and here she is. Paralyzed. Just like before. Maybe worse. The last time it happened, at least it was contained to the suffocating fishbowl of high school, their small town—neighbouring towns at most. Now, this city feels too vast, the internet too endless, the damage too irreversible.

Then, the journalists make the connection that Oliver owns the store. And suddenly—silence. Coverage slows, news channels lose interest. Some news outlets drop the story entirely. Not exactly a coincidence, considering his father owns half of them.

But what the mainstream media abandons, the internet devours. To her utter horror, the bored and miserable corners of the web uncover her identity. They follow the trail from Oliver to David, discover he was the store's original owner, and match his ex-fiancée to the video with disturbing ease. It doesn't take much, not when the court of public opinion requires no evidence to hand down a sentence. Some get close to the truth, pinning the video leak on David. But the story quickly mutates. It becomes a parable of class warfare: a worker-owned community space sabotaged by the reckless son of a media dynasty. Others use it to evangelize, pinning the sins of the world on a deleted video—lust, the gravest among them. Her story is folded, bent, and twisted to fit the perfect narrative for every forum passerby. They chew on her life, spit it out, stir it into something louder, crueller, farther from the truth.

And Lacy? She can't look away.

She tells herself she won't check the comments, but the temptation is a razor's edge, slicing through her resolve. Each hateful word embeds itself in her skin like shrapnel.

She should of seen this coming. Shes dumb for letting herself be recorded in the first place.

So disgusting. I'll never set foot in that place if this is what they do behind closed doors.

So nasty to do that in a public space. Hope your ashamed.

It doesn't matter that most of them barely skimmed the details before spewing their opinions like venom. It doesn't matter that they don't know her—that their words are tossed carelessly into the void, more kindling for the internet's endless pyre, its appetite for spectacle insatiable.

There's an eerie intimacy to the way strangers on the internet speak about her. They don't know her, but they know of her, and that's enough. Their words feel personal, not because they are, but because her life is personal, and that's what they're tearing apart. The story of her life told by strangers with more authority than she feels living it. She starts to internalize their voices. Her screen becomes a black hole, dragging her into the world's pity and vitriol, settling into her like smoke in her lungs. The whole world has seen her shame.

Sam takes her phone away, recognizing it for what it is—an instrument of self-harm, a blade disguised as a screen. He locks it away like a loaded gun, out of reach, out of sight. He watches her with mounting dread, the way she moves through the days like a ghost, present but untethered, her eyes vacant as if staring into a place only she can see. She drifts in and out of conversations, her responses delayed, automatic, a tide pulling in and out, caught in the moon's indifferent cycle. The resemblance is unbearable, mirroring his mother's unraveling too closely—the slow, silent descent of someone slipping further and further from the world.

His own melancholy stirs, rattling its cage, rises like a tide against the seawall, relentless and unyielding. He braces himself against it, refusing to let it spill over, not now, not when she needs him anchored. Turmoil fractures his own life in ways he hasn't even begun to process, but he swallows it down, locks it up, focusing on the only thing that matters: keeping Lacy from vanishing into herself completely.

Sophie thanks him for taking such gentle care of her sister while she's been tied up with the studio, damage control for the store, and building the legal case against David. She sees his world fraying at the edges but admires how patient and steady he remains. He brings Lacy food when she doesn't eat, wraps her in blankets she never thinks to ask for, reads to her. He doesn't push, doesn't pry, and doesn't involve her in the lawsuit—even though she's a key part of it. He stays close, unshaken ground beneath her feet.

Every evening, Sam sits hunched over his laptop, eyes red with exhaustion, combing through legal documents. One set tackles the charges against David, a case he shares with Sophie and Oliver, complicated by the fact that the two parties aren't speaking. At the same time, he's trying to carve out a path to bring his aunts here. His aunts, who were supposed to visit, were turned away by agents over new complications with Aunt Sam's passport, raising terrifying questions about her safety and rights. They're stranded, watching the situation escalate, their fear mounting with every headline. With each new restriction, every closed door, their options shrink. The storm closes in, but he doesn't falter. He shows up, again and again, steady and unyielding—for them, for her, for himself.

After consulting her roommates, he suggests taking her to visit his aunts in Ohio. "A change of scenery," he offers. They agree it's worth trying. But when Sam asks her if she wants to go, Lacy assumes it's pity. He wants to leave. This is his polite way of unburdening himself of her.

"It's okay," she says, voice calm and quiet. She should let him go. She should be selfless. She hasn't been. He has been here every day, holding her together while his own life comes apart. "You should go spend time with them."

"Yeah, I want to." He nods. "I want you with me. You know they'd love to see you."

Since the video leaked, Lacy's body has become a vessel of grief. A pit lives in her stomach, another is lodged in her throat. Her eyes sting constantly, but the tears never fall, leaving her head congested, heavy with an invisible illness.

At Sam's words, the dam breaks. At the first drop of tears, Sam is beside her. "Oh, my Lacy." His voice fractures, trembling, and she hates that she's the cause.

"What's wrong?"

She shakes her head, face buried in tear-soaked sleeves. How many times will he watch her fall apart before he realizes she's someone unworthy of his love?

"Please talk to me," he pleads. "Let me in."

She looks up at him, bleary-eyed, and says, "I love you."

The words land like an echo in an empty room. It's been months since he first said it, months of her dancing around it, almost saying it. But now that he's finally heard the words, they feel... hollow.

405

"Really?" he asks, immediately hating his response. Not how he'd imagined himself responding when she finally says it back.

She nods. "Like, so much." But her voice is flat, colorless.

Sam feels shame for fixating on her tone instead of her words.

"I've felt it for a long time," she continues. "Probably before you said it to me."

He doubts that. He's felt love for her from the moment they met. Existing long before it was named, before it was spoken aloud. Like a seed waiting to push through the dirt, reaching for the light.

The words hang between them, luminous and weightless, like the first snowfall of winter. Sam's heart cracks open, raw and aching at her revelation. She is offering a piece of herself to him, and he wants to cradle it in his palms, keep it close. But just as he begins to unearth the warmth in her words, she says, "That's why I think we should break up."

Somewhere in his mind, he hears glass shattering, the sound slicing through time. He's frozen, suspended in the fog of her words. Incomprehensible, completely at odds with everything she just said.

"What?" His voice is rough, jagged. "Did you really just tell me you love me, just to break up with me?"

Sam has never been broken up with before, but he never imagined it would feel like this, like holding tightly to something he hadn't realized had already slipped through his fingers.

"That's not happening," he declares.

"Sam," she begs, his name trembling on her lips, packed with meaning, with grief.

"I don't want to hurt you."

"You were doing a great job of it until this exact moment."

"Being with me will hurt you more in the long run."

"Says who? We've been together almost a year. Do I look like I'm hurting? I'm the happiest I've ever been, if you haven't noticed. Other people certainly have."

"I'm a curse. Everyone I love gets hurt eventually. I'm doing this for your own good."

"No, you're not," he snaps. "You're being selfish."

Selfish? This is amputation. This is bleeding out. This is the opposite of selfish. She stares at him, wide-eyed, wounded.

He takes a breath, tries to soften. "Yes. You are being selfish," he says, his voice gentle but unwavering. "I know you're hurting. I know you think I can't handle it, but you don't get to decide that for me. I want to be here, and for that to happen, you have to let me in. You have to let me carry some of this with you, not the weight you think you are, but the burden of the pain, grief, and fear that are all natural responses to everything that has happened.

"And I know that scares you. I know it's hard to trust me. And that's okay. I'm not going to pressure you to talk. I want us to get out of this place, be with my family, and breathe in a new space. And I will keep being patient. What I won't do," he says, voice low and resolute, "is let you quit on me. On yourself. On us. I'm in this too. I get a say."

She shakes her head, tears slipping free. "Something will happen, and you'll regret staying with me. And by then, I'll have fallen even more in love with you, and when you leave, it will end me."

He knows what she's doing. The way she's pulling away. The distance she's placing between them triggers something deep inside him. Every moment she shuts down feels like he's losing her bit by bit. It terrifies him, the thought of being left behind. It would end him, too. Sam cups her face in his hands, thumbs brushing away the dampness on her cheeks. "Lacy, don't you get it? I am never leaving. Not even death could tear me from you."

She swallows hard.

"I would just come back and haunt you," he adds. "Not in a scary way. In a romantic way. Like, I'd make books fall off your shelves and open to some love poem."

A laugh breaks through her tears, the sound brittle and beautiful. Relief floods him like a tide pulling back, leaving behind solid ground.

He presses his forehead to hers, closes his eyes. Breathes her in.

"So, unless you've stopped loving me, nothing will stop me from being with you. Nothing will stop me from loving you. Not even you."

*E*dward and Jacob help pack her bags, their quiet efficiency eerily familiar. It reminds her of the night they pulled her out of David's apartment, their movements steady and careful, while she stood motionless, hollowed out. She never thought she would relive this.

She looks forward to getting out of the city, seeing Sam's aunts, and being in a new place. As grateful as she is for her friends, she feels like a burden to them. She's let her responsibilities fall to the wayside, her friends picking up the slack, carrying her through her pain. Always making sure she's eaten, bringing her water, washing her dishes, folding her laundry. Small, quiet acts of care she hasn't had the energy to properly thank them for.

She knows she isn't the only one struggling. Sophie has been quieter lately, something on her mind she isn't sharing. Ever since her fight with Oliver, her energy has dimmed, her usual sharp wit replaced with a weary sort of focus. Lacy barely sees her anymore; her life is consumed by work, the animation studio, shifts at the store, sched-uled in a way that keeps her and Oliver apart. Ships passing in the night.

Jacob was laid off. No new construction projects in this economy. He pours his energy into the café, trying to make ends meet. Mina and Edward take on extra work to help cover the bills. Sam chips in with rent, and Lacy feels the sting of it—the shame of not working, financial depend-ence. The machine of lovelessness grinds on, indifferent to the breaking hearts it relies on to run.

On the way to Ohio, Sam carries all their bags, leading the way through security with that calm, steady presence that always grounds her. He picks up snacks and drinks without asking, already knowing what she likes. He's always like this, seeing her, anticipating her needs, caring for her in these small and seamless ways that feel so natural to him. Lacy watches as he helps a woman juggling her coffee and stroller, lifting her suitcase with ease, carrying her drink to the table without a second thought. He chats with her cas-ually, warm and unhurried. Something soft and certain settles in Lacy's chest. Her Sam—so solid, so loving, so end-lessly kind. The way his very being is constant proof that goodness exists, a defiant light against the dark powers tirelessly working to erode our faith in the world.

His aunts pick them up from the airport, warmth radi-ating from them before a single word is even spoken. Sam hands Auntie Jackie a small cooler of frozen butter tarts, saying they're from both of them. Lacy hadn't even thought to bring anything, no small gesture, no token of gratitude for their generosity. The guilt sits heavy in her chest.

Their house is charming. Knick-knacks from their travels line the shelves, books are stacked in every corner, and soft light spills through lace curtains. An antique grandfather clock ticks steadily in the corner of the living room. It feels lived in, welcoming in a way that immediately puts her at ease.

She spends her days with Aunt Sam and Auntie Jackie while Sam works in their office. They watch movies, read in the backyard, and exist together in an easy, companionable quiet. It reminds her of how Sam must have healed in this space after losing his parents. The same stable presence, the same quiet care. They never ask about what happened, and that, more than anything, allows her to breathe.

Her friends had done this for her, too, back home. Sitting with her, curling up in bed with her, reading or watching their own thing next to her without needing to speak. But something about being here makes it easier. Maybe because the aunts weren't there when it happened. They don't know the shape of the wreckage, don't see straight through her in the way her friends do. Instead, they are still getting to know her. And in getting to know them, their stories, their quirks, the way they move through the world with so much gentle resilience, she's learning more about herself, too. That she is more than what has happened to her. That there are still new things to discover, about herself, about others. And she clings to that, the idea that she is still unfolding, still growing, still becoming.

A few weeks in, Sam takes time off work, and they explore Ohio together, visiting galleries, museums, and antique stores tucked away in small towns. He shows Lacy all his favorite places, and she imagines a younger Sam wandering bookstores and art supply stores, sketching at the park. With each passing day, the knot in her stomach loosens. She thinks less about the video, about the store, about David, about her father. And eventually, like all wounds, this one stops bleeding. It scabs over. Fades into a faint pink scar.

One afternoon, as Lacy helps the aunts declutter their basement, she spots a photo frame she hadn't noticed before. She picks it up, smiling at the image of a man holding a baby Sam, unmistakable even as an infant.

"Who's this?" she asks.

"That's me," Sam says.

"I know," she replies, heart squeezing at the sight of that familiar crinkle in his nose when he laughs, something he's carried with him his whole life. It's endearing, seeing him like this, unchanged in the small ways that make him who he is. "Who's holding you?"

"That's me," Aunt Sam says.

Lacy blinks, surprise flickering across her face, not in judgment, just gentle curiosity. And just like that, Aunt Sam begins to share her story. Sam has introduced his aunt to many people close to him, but even Anna had never known her story. And he's never heard it told like this before. He'd lived it, of course, had pieced together his own understanding over the years. But hearing her speak it aloud, sharing it with Lacy, feels like something sacred.

An offering. A kind of trust that binds her to his family in a way he hadn't realized he needed.

Sam watches Lacy as she listens, the quiet attentiveness in her, the way she absorbs the story, how deeply she cares. He thinks about his aunts, about the way they've shaped him. Their convictions in facing the world with their steadfast values, their unwavering choice to lead with love, uphold it in everything they do. Love and strength, intertwined, coloring every part of their lives. And now, he sees that love stretching to envelope Lacy, wrapping around her like it has always been waiting for her to arrive. The thought settles deep in his chest, warm and steady, some final piece clicking into place.

Lacy video calls her sister one evening, the conversation light, revolving around her time in Ohio. They avoid the elephant in the room, skirting around it until, for the first time in two months, Lacy breaks.

"How's business?" Lacy asks, her gaze drifting to the cat in Sophie's lap, the little creature purring contentedly with its eyes closed.

Sophie looks up, surprised by the question. She pauses, her hand halting mid-scratch on kitty's head. "Good," she finally says, giving a small shrug. "Business has been steady."

Lacy swallows. She imagines the shadowy hand of her curse stretching over everything she loves, suffocating it. "How much did what happened affect the store?" she asks, ripping off the bandage.

"A little at the beginning," Sophie admits. "But a lot of people came out to support us because of what happened. We've built a good community here."

Lacy exhales, a tightness in her chest loosening. Maybe she hadn't ruined everything after all.

Sophie tells her about the shawarma truck across the street, how they've started selling knafeh made by the owner's wife. Their businesses naturally complement each other—customers grab a meal from the truck, then come to the café for a place to sit, a drink, and something sweet. "We're like business besties," she says with a grin. "They send people our way, we send people theirs."

"Cute."

"And we had to get rid of the BJ couch."

Lacy groans. "Please don't call it that."

"It's in our basement now," Sophie reassures her. "Fits perfectly."

"I'm so sorry I did that, Soph. I don't know what came over me."

"Well, I know what *came inside you*," Sophie says with a smirk, before disgust curdles her expression at her own joke.

"Ew..." Lacy groans, but this time, she's laughing too. It feels good to laugh about it, like the weight of it isn't pressing down so hard anymore.

"I'm sorry I forgot to tell you about the cameras, Lace. Oliver replaced them all. There aren't any inside anymore. Just at the entrance and exit."

Lacy blinks, unsure what to make of that. "Is that a good idea?"

Sophie shrugs. "If a shoplifter is good enough, they deserve to get away with it."

"Fair enough," Lacy laughs. "How's Oliver?"

Sophie's expression dims, the lightness in her voice gone. "How would I know?"

"It wasn't his fault, Soph," Lacy says, only recently finding that forgiveness herself.

"Can we not?" Sophie sighs. "We're taking space. That's it."

"Don't you miss him?"

Sophie rolls her eyes. "The only people I miss are you and Sam. When are you coming back?"

A few days later, while Sam takes his aunt to a doctor's appointment, Lacy sits alone with Auntie Jackie, both of them fumbling with crochet hooks as they try to follow a tutorial on her laptop. Lacy's stitches are a mess, loops slipping off, knots forming where they shouldn't.

Jackie hums, amused, and for a moment, they fall into a comfortable silence, the sound of the video playing softly between them. Maybe it's Auntie Jackie's therapist aura, the confident calmness she carries, or maybe it's just the right moment, because, for the first time since coming here, Lacy feels the urge to talk.

"I miss my sister. And our friends. And our cat," she says, eyes still on the tangled yarn in her hands. "But I'm scared to go home. I don't know if I'm ready to face it all."

Jackie nods, looking up from her half-finished piece. "What do you think being ready will feel like?"

Lacy shrugs.

"What has it felt like in the past?"

Lacy exhales slowly, thinking. "I don't think I've ever felt ready for anything. Not for facing what my father was. Not for moving across the country. Not for everything that's happened with my ex."

Jackie tilts her head slightly, considering. "I think that's quite sage. I don't know how many of us truly recognize when we're ready. I didn't think I was ready Sam told me she was transitioning. I didn't know if I was ready to face what our relationship would look like after that. And I definitely wasn't ready for her to have cancer. But I faced it anyway, with both Sams at my side." She glances at Lacy with a knowing smile. "Life doesn't wait for us to be ready. We just... are."

Lacy looks down at her hands, her fingers brushing over the soft yarn. "I don't remember ever feeling ready for love," she admits. "But I still chose Sam. Chose to trust him. Chose to love him."

Jackie's smile widens, warm and understanding. "You're right. You've been healing all along, Lacy. This urge to go home didn't come from nowhere. Trust yourself. You wouldn't want to go back if you weren't ready."

Lacy nods, one knot in her chest loosening, while another tightens. The one that doesn't want to leave her newfound family.

Lacy asks Sam how he feels about going home and Sam agrees that it's time. He misses his life there, his friends, his cat.

They book their flights back, spending their last days soaking in every moment with their aunts. They linger over breakfast, extend their evening walks, stretch conversations late into the night, unwilling to let go just yet. Sam tries to push past the worry gnawing at him. Leaving them feels different this time, heavier. The weight of the world presses down around them.

Every day, his phone churns out another headline more insane than the last—book bans, teachers punished for promoting inclusivity, ICE agents acting like the fucking Gestapo, a daily drumbeat of dread. Just last night, over dinner with his aunts' professor friends, the conversation turned to research grants being denied for including "DEI" language, as if these words are as dangerous as bullets. The sheer absurdity of it all makes his stomach twist. He can't stop worrying about when he'll see them next. How long will they be safe in this world? How to escape it. How to change it.

The night before their flight, they curl together in bed, limbs tangled, arms locked around each other like they could fuse their bodies into one. Lacy turns to face him.

"Thank you for this trip. Thank you for sharing your aunts with me. I love them so much. I love you so much," Lacy says, her breath warm against his lips.

Sam's heart stutters. He'll never tire of hearing those words from her mouth, never grow immune to the way they unravel him.

"Thank you for loving them and loving me," he murmurs. "I love you." He pulls her close, kissing her deeply, feeling the heat of her body as her hands find his hair, her knees pushing between his. It ignites something inside him, a hunger he's kept leashed while he's been focused on caring for his family.

Their hands move urgently, grasping at each other's clothes in their desperation to close the distance between them. Lacy yanks his top off, hands roaming over his chest as they kiss feverishly, teeth clashing, tongues tangling. He pulls her top off, the limp piece of fabric hitting the wall as it falls to the ground. He stares, breathless. Even after all this time, taking in the sight of her feels like winning the lottery.

He covers her, mouth descending to her chest, lips circling a nipple. She gasps, nails scraping his scalp as he grinds against her, his hardness pressed to her pulsing core. She begs to feel him inside her.

"Fuck." His groan is frustration, not arousal. "I didn't bring any condoms."

"Why not?" Her whine is pure, petulant need.

"This—" he gestures between them, "—wasn't exactly on my mind."

They kiss again, slower now, teasing. He pushes her underwear aside, fingers tracing her folds, dipping into her slickness, circling her clit until her hips jerk. He claps a hand over her mouth to stifle her moan.

"Bite me if I press too hard, okay?"

She nods, laughing, doesn't mention that she sort of likes the pressure of him, the restraint. Her hand slips into his boxers, gripping him, stroking—fast, then slow, tight, then teasing. Her thumb swirls over his tip, smearing the liquid evidence of his pleasure over himself, and the sensation is too much. He rolls away before he ruins this. He cannot let their first time in weeks end in him making a mess in her hands.

"I'm going to see if my aunts have any condoms," he grits out.

"You're going to ask your aunts for a condom?" Lacy asks, incredulous. "They're going to know we're having sex!"

"They probably already heard you," he teases, laughing as her cheeks flush. "I'm kidding. I'm going to check the bathroom."

He vanishes. Lacy pulls the covers up around her, aching at the thought of him. Her own need mirroring his, a desperate throbbing between her legs.

She hears the sound of his footsteps. Sam bursts back in, triumphant, waving a pink wrapper.

"You found one?"

"No. They woke up as I was rummaging and asked what I needed.

"And you told them?"

He shrugs. "Yeah?"

Lacy buries her face in her hands. "So, they know we're having sex in here?"

"Lacy, I'm their adult nephew who's obsessed with his girlfriend. They've probably assumed we've been doing it this whole time and don't give a fuck."

She collapses back, pillow smothering her shriek of embarrassment. Sam sits beside her. "Want to call it off?"

Lacy shoots back up in bed. "Hell no."

He laughs and pounces.

"Want to be on top?"

She shakes her head. "I want you to cover my mouth."

He peels her underwear down. Kneeling over her, he teases—fingers pinching her nipples, palm skimming down her stomach, dipping into her wetness before dragging back up to her clit. She writhes as he positions her legs over his shoulders, easing into her with deliberate, almost agonizing languor.

Her eyes slam shut when he's fully inside her, fingers clawing the sheets. The stretch of him leaves her limp, muscles too weak to grind. He grips her hips, steadying her as he thrusts. Her hands drift to her breasts, squeezing and playing, and the sight of her pleasuring herself nearly shatters him. He pumps harder, her moans climbing in volume until his hand muffles them again. She grabs his wrist, pressing his palm tighter over her lips. Then, suddenly pulls his fingers into her mouth, sucking.

"Fuck—" His hips stutter. Two fingers slide deeper between her lips as he drives into her, her tongue working him in time with her body. The feeling of his cock and fingers smothered by her warm and wet wrecks him. He comes with a groan, accidentally pushing his fingers too deep. Tears beading in her eyes.

He pulls her close, wiping her cheeks, kissing her softly. His fingers glide between her legs, coaxing her toward the edge, his limp cock twitching at the slickness coming off his fingers. Her whimpers turn to louder moans as she begins to ride his hand, her hips gyrating. Her hand reaches out to wrap around his cock, stroking him back to hardness. Her moans getting louder, he kisses her to smother the sounds, savoring her pleasure on his tongue. Eventually, she gets a bit too loud again, and he covers her mouth with his hand. She maneuvers his hand, bringing his fingers into her mouth again, mirroring the motions of her mouth with her hand, swirling her tongue around his fingers as her thumb does around his cock.

"Fuck... Lacy..." he moans. "You've got to stop," he says, pulling his fingers out of her mouth. "You'll make me come before you do again." He's so fucking hard, the shortest refractory period of his life.

"I'm so close," she sighs into his mouth. "I want to try something..."

He watches as she turns, pressing her back to him. His arms encircle her as she kisses him over her shoulder. Though facing away, she's utterly open to him. His hands claim her breasts as his hardness presses between her cheeks.

She spreads her legs and he guides himself in slowly, clamping a hand over her mouth when she nearly screams. Her hips roll against his deliberate thrusts.

"Faster," she begs.

"I'll have to hold you kind of tight," he warns.

"I want that."

He pins her down with his hips, palm pressed to her mouth, the other spreading her thigh wide. She arches into each thrust, her moans vibrating against his palm.

"Harder?" He thinks he hears her say under his palm.

She nods.

He obliges, grip tightening, hips slamming into her.

"Faster," she whimpers.

He obeys, losing rhythm, fucking her with abandon. When her walls clench around him, he releases her mouth, capturing her lips instead as she comes with a cry. He follows, shuddering, collapsing over her.

Breathless. Tangled. Alive.

*L*acy returns to a house abundant in love, held for her even while she was away. Her friends embrace her, their joy at her homecoming unmistakable. She believes them when they say the house felt emptier without her, that her absence left a hole in their lives. And for once, she doesn't question it, knows her weight in their lives is not a burden but a grounding force, just as they are for her. She belongs here. As much as they need her, she needs them.

That night, they pile onto the couch bed, the movie forgotten as conversation takes over. Lacy's presence lifts the house, laughter bouncing off the walls, the kind of effortless joy that can't be scheduled or replicated. Even as sleep tugs at their eyes, no one wants to end the night. They wash up, drag their blankets and pillows back to the couch, and collapse in a cozy heap, the glow of the TV flickering against their closed eyelids. This place is warm. This place is safe.

After picking up his cat from Lacy's place, Sam heads home. She purrs in his lap as he drives, and a smile tugs at his lips as he remembers the moment he walked through the door. How his usually quiet kitty had meowed non-stop, pressing against his legs, pawing at him as if to make sure he was real. She hadn't stopped until he scooped her into his arms, her purring deepening as she nestled against his chest.

His condo feels untouched, like a space frozen in time, waiting for him to return. He moves through the quiet, feeding his cat, unpacking his bags, washing dirty laundry. The city hums faintly outside, but inside, it's just him and his cat, her soft purring, the low tumble of the dryer, the quotidian rhythm of a life settling back into place.

Later, he falls into bed, and kitty curls up against his chest, her small body rising and falling with each of his breaths. He knows, with a peaceful contentment, that he won't be able to leave without waking her. And he doesn't mind.

It takes Lacy a few days to visit the café. When she finally does, it's anticlimactic. She had pictured the worst. Crowds whispering about her, patrons pointing her out, the ghost of the leaked video clinging to her like a scarlet letter. But no one even recognizes her. The baristas barely glance her way when she comes in, too busy taking orders.

Sophie, sitting at a table with her laptop open, looks up and grins. "Hi! You're here!" She's on a serious video call, and Lacy gestures that she can wait. But Sophie waves her over. "No, it's fine."

Lacy recognizes the man on the screen as the baker who supplies their pastries, Dean.

"We're talking business. Want to join?"

Lacy hesitates. She knows her sister is trying to pull her in, trying to get her engaged in the business they share, the one she's put so little effort into but still benefits from. She pulls up a chair. Mostly listens.

"We run out by mid-afternoon. We need to at least double the supply," Sophie says.

Dean nods. "I might have to start coming in to bake on-site. Probably need to hire some helpers."

"Let's do that. Jacob will probably want to learn. He's tried his hand in every role at this point."

She watches her sister lead the meeting, pride swelling in her chest at the sight. And then—guilt. For letting Sophie shoulder so much. For staying quiet. For the business's lawsuit still looming, still unresolved, still largely ignored by her.

Lacy nods along as Dean describes the savoury pastries he's planning to add to the menu. She offers to design the new menu print, eager to contribute, to feel useful in some small way. The café was never meant to be a profit machine, and that freedom trickles down into every decision. Watching Dean get the same creative liberty in his baking makes Lacy feel unexpectedly at ease, excited to return to her work here.

She realizes, then, that the world has moved on. No one cares about the video anymore. The catastrophe she had braced for never came. The business wasn't ruined. Her friends weren't ostracized. The local community isn't scandalized. In the grand scheme of everything happening in the world, it was just another story, already faded.

When she finally logs onto her computer, she finds old emails from journalists asking for her comments. She ignores them. She won't be the one to stir it back up.

Except—one recent email catches her attention.

She recognizes the sender's name: a staff writer for a feminist cultural site. She's read some of her work. The email links to an essay the writer published about the female casualties of powerful men in politics, blending historical context with present-day testimonies. The essay gives names to women usually forgotten in the headlines, their stories drowned out by the men who harmed them.

Lacy reads it, moved. She feels seen, understood. Less alone. She replies to the email, thanking the writer for sharing her work, deliberately avoiding the part where she asks for an interview. The writer responds quickly, thanking her for taking the time to read. Asks again if she'd be willing to be interviewed. Mentions that the piece includes an interview with the ex-wife of the richest man in the world, as if that could sway her.

As they email back and forth, Lacy feels herself waver. A part of her sees the value in sharing her story. Another part recoils at the thought of opening herself up, of letting the world take another piece of her.

She turns to Sophie for advice, knowing her social media-savvy sister has no hesitation about putting herself out there.

"How are you not scared?" Lacy asks.

Sophie shrugs. "I'm not scared of what people will think or say, because anything they come up with, I've probably already thought about myself, but funnier."

Lacy doesn't know if that's healthy. But she doesn't argue.

"Do you think sharing my experience will actually help people?"

Sophie considers. "I don't know. It feels like there are so many stories of men hurting women now that people have gone numb. But maybe if David's new girlfriend reads it, it'll help her."

Lacy hadn't even considered that. "He has a new girl-friend?"

"I don't know. I'm just saying, if someone wrote about my boyfriend, exposed him as a rapist, revenge porn guy, I'd read it. Maybe it'd help me snap out of being with him."

Lacy wonders if she had read a warning from an ex before getting involved, would it have changed anything? She thinks maybe it would have. And if she could help just one person... maybe that would be enough.

She replies to the writer. Agrees to the interview.

"Hi, I'm Gigi," the writer says, finding Lacy in the café. She had requested the interview take place here. She sets her bags down, moves through the space, taking pictures, and asking questions about the business.

Sophie closes the store for an hour to give her sister some privacy.

Lacy watches as Gigi lifts her phone, snapping a photo from high above, mimicking the angle of the leaked video.

"Ready?" She settles across from Lacy, places her phone on the table between them. Presses start on her voice memo recording. "How did you meet David?"

"In university."

"How did you start dating?"

"We spent time together. Eventually, it just... happened."

"So, he never asked? It was just assumed?"

"I suppose so."

The conversation unspools from there—how she and her family came to rely on him financially, how he filled her life with extravagance, encouraging her to maintain a certain status, a certain look. It became easier to go along with what he wanted, but she can't deny that, in the end, she chose to play the part, chose to rely on him.

"What about sex?" Gigi asks. "Had he ever violated you before the video?"

There's a part of Lacy that craves revenge, wants to expose David's darkness, drag it into the light, shame him, cancel him. She wants every woman he dates to know exactly what they're stepping into. To warn them about the pressure he applies, the slow erosion of self. But there's fear, too. A deep fear of his powerful family, the control they wield over so many lives. How could she possibly stand against that? And then there's another part of her—one that recoils at the idea of offering something so personal, so painful, to someone like Gigi. Someone with no real place in her life. She twists the napkin in her hands, words tangled somewhere between her throat and her heart, unsure how to answer.

"I take your body language as yes?" Gigi presses.

"Do you think reading about this actually helps women? Actually motivates them to leave bad situations?"

Gigi gives her a bright smile. "That's the hope, right? Or at least it gets people thinking about whether or not this behavior is okay. They might not even realize they're in abusive relationships."

Lacy hadn't thought she was in one. She thought David was better than her father, and that seemed enough at the time.

"Do you think people who do this—hurt women—know their behaviour isn't okay?" Lacy asks.

"Did David?"

The question makes Lacy shrink back into her chair. She doesn't know for sure, but "I think he didn't care to think about it. He just wanted to do it."

"That's usually the case. We're so obsessed with intention over impact. Who cares if these men were conscious of the hurt they were causing? The point is they did bad things, and they should be called out for it, held accountable, rot in jail for it."

Like her father is right now, Lacy thinks. But, "Do you think these men will actually be held accountable?"

"It's rare," Gigi sighs dejectedly. "All the more reason for us to roast them at the stake, publicize their wrongdoings."

"I don't know if it matters to them. These little op-eds." The word *little* slips out before she can stop it, and Gigi's wince makes Lacy wish she could take it back.

"Who cares about them? I intend to share stories about survivors, show women that they don't have to be victims forever, that they can move on, thrive. Like you."

"I don't know if I'm the picture of thriving."

"You have this thriving business. You didn't let what happened stop you from chasing your dreams," Gigi says cheerily, gesturing to the space around them.

"I haven't exactly contributed to the success of this place. I hindered it." The admission tastes bitter.

"You don't think your story attracted people to the business? People love to align themselves with the underdog. My piece will drive even more traffic here."

The room suddenly feels suffocating. The thought of people coming here because of *her story* coils around her throat like a noose.

"I rescind my consent to this interview," Lacy says abruptly.

"What?" Gigi's perfect smile cracks, a lightning flash of anger crossing her face before she schools it back into neutrality. "What do you mean?"

"I don't want to do the interview anymore. I don't want you to share my story."

"Why not?" Gigi's blinks, her smile not reaching her eyes. "I flew here for this interview."

"I'm sorry. I just don't feel comfortable about this. I'll reimburse you for the flight."

"Lacy. I've interviewed a lot of women. You've read my work. I won't paint you in a bad light if that's what you're worried about. I will represent you accurately."

Lacy believes ger. Believes that she will try her best anyway. "I'm sorry. I just think so much of my privacy has been publicized without my consent. I don't want to give up more if I can help it. I hope you can understand."

"Of course," Gigi says, nodding. Her pen taps impatiently against her notebook. "What if I kept you anonymous in my piece? Just write about how your abusive, wealthy ex-fiancé ruined the opening day of your community-centered business. Posted revenge porn on your social media. I won't name you—or your business."

"That sounds like it could still be easily traced back to me."

"Okay..." Gigi sighs, packing up her bags. "I didn't want to have to pull this, but I do have your written consent to do this interview. You sent an email agreeing. And I also have our interview recorded." Lacy's eyes shift to Gigi's phone, the red square blinking like a warning. "Toronto and New York, where I'm based, are one-party consent states, so I technically have the right to use this story."

Lacy almost laughs at the irony: a woman who profits off stories about stolen consent, threatening to steal hers. "Okay," she relents, too exhausted to fight. She pulls out her phone and hits record. "I agree to the release of this story under the condition that I remain anonymous. No names. Not mine, not the business, not the city, not the street." Not even *his*.

A hollow ache spreads through her chest. Part of her wishes she could reclaim this narrative, take control of it, but a larger part of her just wants to bury it all. She wonders what she owes to other women. She thinks of all the survivor stories she's read, how they made her feel less alone in her pain, sometimes even empowered. But they didn't make her any less sad. They didn't ease the anger. If anything, knowing how many other women have lived through this same kind of sorrow makes her feel even more desolate. As if the trauma that's defined so much of her life is just another story in a sea of them. Because horrible people are all too common.

"Can I at least allude to his family's media empire? Most people won't even bother to look this up. But the ones who know will know."

"Sure," Lacy sighs. "Whatever."

A week later, Gigi sends her the published essay and only a fraction of the promised payment. Lacy doesn't argue, she hadn't held up her end either. She reads the piece.

Gigi had landed interviews with two of the billionaire's ex-wives, their stories echoing each other in an unsettling pattern—quick marriages, strict expectations around their appearance, demands to dye their hair a certain colour. One account features a model Lacy recognizes, once paraded as arm candy by an aging actor now revealed to be as monstrous as he is mediocre. Then, her own story. A few lines in a tide of similar tragedies. *Rich husband buys wife a business. Pressures her for sex. She leaves. He destroys everything. Was surveilling her all along. Posted the revenge porn of her, threatening her financial independence.*

And then, the final paragraph:

And so the cycle repeats, an inevitable machinery grinding through the bodies of women who, for a time, mistake survival for love. They enter these men's lives with a hopeful pragmatism. Who among us hasn't, at least once, made peace with a bad situation because it promised stability? And they leave bruised, poorer in ways that can't always be calculated. The men, of course, move on, the damage they cause absorbed frictionlessly into their net worth. They grow older, their options younger. The women they've hurt recalibrate, lick their wounds, tell themselves they will be smarter next time. And maybe they will be. But smartness was never the problem. The problem is that in a world organized around the whims of powerful men, some women will always have to choose between being used and being discarded, a choice that isn't a choice at all.

Lacy stares at the screen, numb. It's a good essay, she admits. Polished. Impactful. But despite Gigi's lofty promises of empowerment and reclamation, Lacy just feels reduced. Just another woman duped by a man. The irony stings. She hadn't even loved David.

"You okay?" Sam asks, walking into the room.

She shows him, and he reads.

"What do you think?" she asks, hearing him exhale after reading.

"I think if you didn't want to do it, she should've listened." He pauses. "But she did keep your part short. Anonymous. How do *you* feel?"

"I feel weird," Lacy admits. "I thought reading it would... I don't know, give me some sort of catharsis. But I just feel the same."

Sam nods, giving her the space to say more.

"It all feels pointless," she murmurs. "What was it all for? To become a few sentences in an essay about shitty rich men? To make some money?" Her voice cracks. "What's the point of my trauma if it only poisons me? Hurts people I love? If I don't want to package it, sell it, brand it on my skin, what do I do with it?"

Sam takes her hands, thumb tracing circles on her wrist. "I guess we just hold it." He shrugs. "That's all we can do. What else do we do with the things we aren't ready to let go of? Carry it, let others carry it for us sometimes."

"Is that how it is for you?"

He nods, considering thoughtfully. "I miss my mom every day. I think about my dad sometimes. I worry I'll become like them, the worst parts of them, so I fight not to. Work harder. Love harder." He smiles ruefully at her. "I know I got good things from Mom, too. I work hard. I'm good at cooking. In that way... my grief helps me hold on to her." His voice drops. "When you're sad and distant, I worry I'll fail you like I failed her. Then I try to remind myself, it wasn't my fault. And I try to be better. Do better. Hope it's enough."

Lacy watches the lamplight catch his eyelashes. Gold on gold.

We all feel it," he continues. "Why else would we tell so many stories about it? The *ache* of existing in a world that feels like it's always on the edge of collapse. Our wounds leak out, seep into everything. Maybe that's what they're meant to do—spread, connect, transform, become art. In the end, it all comes out in the wash.

He pulls her onto the bed, holds her close, her body slotting against his like they were made to fit this way. "We'll just keep holding on to each other," he murmurs, breath warm against her temple, "until the weight doesn't feel so heavy. Until we forget it's even there."

Acknowledgements

If you've found this book, resonated with it, heard my song somehow, thank you. The magic of your hands on these pages ripples back to me in numinous waves. Thank you for spending these hours with these characters. It's still unbelievable to me that they can exist in anyone's head but mine, and I am endlessly grateful to everyone who helped bring this dream to life.

To my sister, on this journey with me from the very start, from listening to my rapid-fire word-vomit one random midnight when the story first spilled onto your couch, to catching every typo and inconsistency in the first messy draft. Thank you for showing me what sisterhood means. It has shaped my whole being.

To my creative allies, my cover artists who sat through hours of indecisions, helping me find the vision I couldn't yet see. Being creative with you has been so fulfilling. To my early readers, your enthusiasm, encouragement, and honesty shaped not just this book but my relationship to writing itself. Your words continue to echo through me, inspiring and motivating. To my wonderful editor, who understood the heart of this story, who gave me new confidence as a writer, and who knew exactly what was needed to take the book further. To my patient book formatter, for answering my unending questions and crafting an interior that perfectly encapsulates the atmosphere I wanted for readers.

To my parents, inheriting your work ethic is the reason I could finish a novel while working full-time. Your belief in me carried me through the hardest days.

To my beautiful friends, thank you for the gift of community. The only reason I can write about good, loving people is because I know you.

And to my love, thank you for being a constant reminder that storybook romances can be real. Your love inspires my will, my writing, and my belief in the stories I tell.